The Hedgewitch Queen

Books by Lilith Saintcrow

DANTE VALENTINE

Dante Valentine (omnibus):
Working for the Devil
Dead Man Rising
The Devil's Right Hand
Saint City Sinners
To Hell and Back

JILL KISMET NOVELS

Night Shift
Hunter's Prayer
Redemption Alley
Flesh Circus
Heaven's Spite
Angel Town

ROMANCES OF ARQUITAINE

The Hedgewitch Queen
The Bandit King

As Lili St. Crow

THE STRANGE ANGELS SERIES

The Hedgewitch Queen

A Romance of Arquitaine

LILITH SAINTCROW

www.orbitbooks.net

Orbit
Hachette Book Group
237 Park Avenue
New York, NY 10017
www.orbitbooks.net

Originally published as an e-book by Orbit Books
First print on demand edition: January 2013

Orbit is an imprint of Hachette Book Group. The Orbit name and logo are trademarks of Little, Brown Book Group Limited.

The publisher is not responsible for websites (or their content) that are not owned by the publisher.

ISBN: 978-0-316-25161-7

Printed in the United States of America

For Mel Sanders, with saddles and waterclosets

acknowledgments

Thanks are due to the usual suspects: Maddy and Nicky for keeping me sane; Miriam Kriss for believing, once again, in the story; Devi Pillai, who was the person I wanted to have it; the long-suffering Jennifer Flax, who is on to bigger and better things; and N.D., for teaching me what a good man will do. Last but not least, as always, thank you, dear Reader. Come, once more, and let me tell you a story.

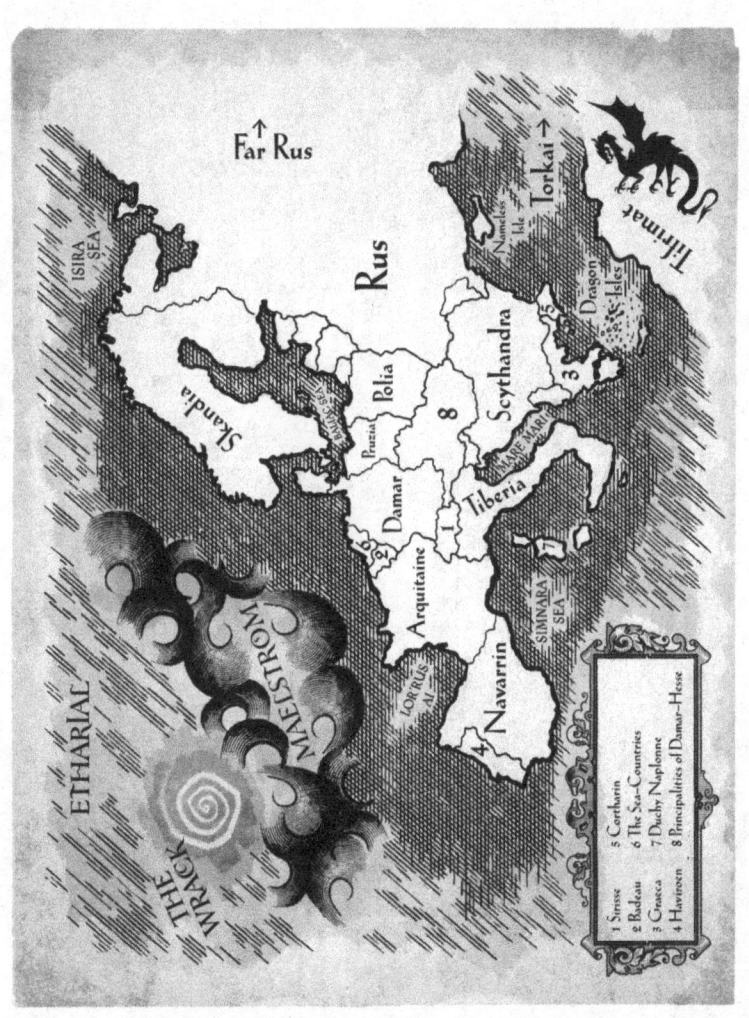

Contents

THE LADY

Chapter One

If not for a muddy skirt, I would have been dead like all the rest. Dead—or worse, perhaps.

The green overskirt was attached to one of Lisele's bodices—an old one, to be sure, but I had remade it prettily enough—and I returned late from the herb gardens that day. There had been a hard rain the previous night; mud daubed my hem and my perfume was hedgewitchery, sweat, and crushed green things. I could not attend Lisele in this state, so I ducked into the kitchen for a slice of bread and a wet rag to work some of the mud off the green velvet before I ran through the corridors to change quickly into a primrose silk. The primrose would set off Lisele's new pale-green gown, just arrived from the royal dressmakers yesterday, to perfection. She had been absolutely mad with impatience and anticipation.

The kitchen was a-chaos with preparations for the night's feast, so Head Cook Amys gave me a slice of bread thick with eldrin jam and shooed me away. Fowl chattered in the cages attached to the wall, and a wooden tub full of dazed and writhing eels in well water sat by the cellar stairs.

I allowed myself one nose-wrinkle and a shudder. "*Those things?*"

Amys, a stout red-cheeked woman in a plain gown and a cap of starched white, laughed. "I know. Yet the King requested, so eels it is." Her voice belled merrily through the din of the kitchens, and she turned away to scold a hopping scullery boy as Jirisa ducked close to me, setting down her basketful of *baguetton* on the step.

I smiled a greeting, and Jirisa's fair round face blushed scarlet. She wiped her hand on her rough woolen skirt and thrust it at me. A soiled bandage flapped against her palm, its ears coming loose.

"*D-d-d'mselle—*" She was all but speechless with fright. Poor Jirisa was painfully shy, and the distance between her station and mine simply made it worse. In the four years she had been at the Palais I had never heard a complete sentence from her.

"Tis no matter, Jirisa. Let me see." I set the bread aside, the growling in my stomach protesting, and carefully unwrapped stained cloth from her moist, tender paw. "You should wash the bandages. It may take the rot if you do not."

"Not with you charming it, *d'mselle*." Amys had caught me out, and stood with her fists on her broad hips. Her sleeves, pushed up, showed forearms thick with muscle. "And she should not be disturbing a great lady so. The Duchesse has other things to do with her time, Jirisa."

"It will make me no earlier nor later to bind this up, Amys." The slash along Jirisa's palm was healing nicely, the careful charm I had laid against her skin still pulsing and tingling reassuringly. Instead of a deep muscle-slicing cut, it was now a fragile pink scar.

Satisfied, I dug in my pocket for some antiseptic balm-lemon leaf and crushed it between my fingers, binding the resultant pungent mass against the slice and tying off the bandage. Jirisa snatched her hand back as soon as I finished and bobbed a courtesy, then scooped up her basket and was on her way, her blonde head down as if she were walking against a heavy wind.

"You should not encourage such familiarity." Amys quite enjoyed sounding scandalized.

You are far more worried with my reputation than is quite proper yourself, m'dama. I rescued my slice of bread and smiled up at her, dabbing at my hem with the damp rag. My emerald eardrops bobbed, swung heavily against my cheeks. "There is some chivin coming in that should flavor the eels nicely."

She was not to be dissuaded. "Indeed there is, and what is a lady like you doing in the herb garden? Why, you're all over mud!" She was working up to a fine scolding, those being her way of easing feastday tensions, but she had not the time because one of the undercooks set a butter sauce on fire and I escaped, almost catching my heels on my skirt in my hurry.

Amys had known me when I first came to Court, a provincial girl with a very noble name but no prospects save the income from a small estate in Vintmorecy my father received from the King as payment for me attending the Princesse—necessary, if I was to buy my own dresses. My father had been a gentleman in waiting to King Henri in the days of his youth, when he had been Prince Royal and, later, newly ascended to the throne. I had heard it whispered at home that Father had saved the King's life once in a Court intrigue, but I never knew the truth of that tale. For that matter, gossip also had it that the King's father dallied with my grand-dam; I did not know the truth of that, either. King's bastards swirl among nobility like loose leaves in cheap chai, especially in Arquitaine.

My noble mother died of an attack of fever and left it as her final wish that I be brought up properly at Court. How proper an upbringing one could find at the Court of Arquitaine I cannot guess, having seen my fair share of things that might have driven my poor mother to her grave twice had she known I witnessed them.

Yet Court my mother had wished me to attend, and my father—just before he took the fever himself and stepped into the arms of the Blessed to join my mother—had faithfully packed me off at my ninth birthday with an introduction and a new dress as well as a request for maintenance that the King, being in a gracious mood, granted. And so Duchesse Vianne di Rocancheil et Vintmorecy, at your service, became lady-in-waiting for Princesse Lisele di Tirecian-Trimestin, daughter of the King and heir to the throne of Arquitaine.

But that was so far off, we worried over it not a whit. Or at least, Lisele did not.

I climbed up the disused back stairs from the kitchen. As far as I knew, I was the only person of quality who used them, and I took care not to let anyone see me except the servants. They would discover me as a matter of course, so I did not bother. And Duchesse Vianne the hopelessly gawky and mud-splattered, Duchesse Vianne more interested in herbs and books and peasant hedgewitchery than the Court sorcery the rest of the nobles used, was of no account anyway. Nobody marked my comings and goings, and nobody with any sense grudged me my position as honored lady-in-waiting and confidante to the Princesse, quiet intrigue-hunter and scholarly counterweight to Lisele's frivolity.

Some days I did not envy myself that honor.

Lisele would be working herself into a fit of pique over the dress just about now, and I would have to hurry and leave my hair half braided. Luckily, artfully disheveled hair was the fashion now. If I had not been muttering in the garden seeking to save some of the dying priest's-ease in the south beds, I would not have been late. Still, I thought the plants would survive now that I had found a charm to keep greentip flies from eating the tender shoots. Twas a good morn's work, and one that satisfied me a great deal more than the prospect of tonight's banquet with its stultifying protocol, even if there was sure to be dancing afterward, and a wonder or two of illusion worked.

Court sorcery is all violence and air-and-light illusion, and my interest in the more practical peasant's magic was, while odd, not entirely *improper*. It was simply a mark of my provincial upbringing, or a childhood nurse versed in the rustic art.

Though a di Rocancheil has nothing to be shamed of when it comes to blood. My mother's family is of the oldest and finest nobility, that of the sword; my ancestors rode to war as boon companions of Edouard Angoulême the Merovian, first conquerer of Arquitaine. Twas no small thing to be a di Rocancheil, and my father's family of Vintmorecy was no less noble. If I chose to waste my time with herbs and healing, twas nobody's business but mine.

Besides, it was the only area of my life that decidedly pleased me. So much of life is what one can *stand*; it is a relief to have a small corner be otherwise. Or so I have found.

I let out a small sigh. Another long slow afternoon of reading aloud from romances or doing needlework in frames before the banquet, maybe broken by a maidendance or two. I would be called upon to give a lesson on Tiberian verbs or needled about my hedgewitchery, and Lisele would turn her sharp tongue on whoever needled me.

I often thought Lisele protected me because I was a pet without claws, an ugly girl with no prospects except a noble name and no chance of making a good marriage, since I seemed to have forgotten men existed. Or so twas said. I held my peace, though I longed at times to point out that men were troublesome creatures indeed, and a marriage sometimes worse confinement than the endless round of dresses and dancing. As an unmarried girl I could study Tiberian and hedgewitchery if I wished. As a woman with a Consort, who knew? Then there was the trouble of childrearing, though any hedgewitch can mix a draught to ease *that* burden before it begins.

Besides, nobles of the sword must seek the King's leave to marry. I had not yet met the man who might prove worth such an endeavor, noble or no. I had been at Court too long to trust any courtier's promises, no matter how I might bandy light words and glances.

What else is there, at Court? Empty words, light glances, and being on my guard not merely for myself but for Lisele as well. I loved her, but sometimes I had the utterly disloyal thought that she was not suited for a royal life.

I climbed the stairs and finished the last of the bread and jam, licking my lips and my fingers in a decidedly provincial fashion. I hummed a lately famous tune about the *Chivalier* Coeurre di Jaronne, skirts and eardrops both swinging merrily, and entered the gallery running alongside the armor hall. I could reach the women's rooms from there, and—

"And what are *you* about here?" someone snarled, and there was the sound of a blow.

I stopped dead, the wet rag clenched in my hand. Growing up at Court meant I needed but a single word to place a voice. Yet why would anyone be in this hall? Especially *him*?

"You cannot prevent it. Tis too late." A whining, breathless, triumphant sentence.

I recognized *that* voice, too, and I peered around the corner, the damp rag in my suddenly-hot fingers. I twitched my skirts back without thinking about it—Court had taught me one thing at least: skirts may be seen around a corner when a woman eavesdrops.

I had to peek past a tapestry, and could see two men in the hall.

Baron Simieri and the Captain of the Guard. I winced inwardly. I did not know the Baron well—he was the King's Minister Primus, born common for all he was granted a title, and he did not participate in much of the dances and fêtes that are the female side of Court life. I had danced with him once, a pavane at Lisele's Coming-of-Age. His hands had been wet and trembling, and he danced woodenly. None of the ladies-in-waiting liked him, but he was only the Minister Primus, not even a noble. Too busy to court a lady, so we did not have to bear his clumsiness for long if at all.

The other man was…something else. Tristan d'Arcenne. He was tall and serious, always in attendance on the King, overseeing the endless drills and training for the King's Guard. Quite a few of the Court ladies had left nosegays for him, but to my knowledge he had never shared a pillow with any of them. Court rumor had him painted as the King's Left Hand and assassin—but, of course, he could not be. If he were, there would be no rumors.

On the other hand, anyone chosen to be the King's Left Hand would be wise enough—and skilled enough with rumor and innuendo—to divert suspicion away from himself by dropping a choice word in the right quarters. So, there.

The Captain of the Guard had the Minister Primus by the throat, held against the dusty tapestried wall. The Primus, a soft, small man, had always reminded me of an oiled farrat.

D'mselle Maratine had a farrat she trained to beg for sweets. The poor thing did not live long, stuffed to its back teeth with chocolat pettites. A faint flash of nausea went through me. What was happening here?

"The details, Simieri. For my edification, you understand." Tristan's voice was low but not cultured at all just now—the accent of a nobleman had turned harsh, with an undercurrent of violence.

I had danced with him twice, once at Lisele's Coming-of-Age, and again two months ago at the Festival of Skyreturn. D'Arcenne did not dance, and the fact he had done so twice with me caused some comment.

The rumormongers were doomed to disappointment, since he said not a word to me beyond requesting the turn and afterward giving formulaic thanks. He was tall and moved well, his dark hair long as was a *chivalier*'s fashion now. He had held my hand and watched me oddly during the dance, only occasionally glancing over my shoulder to direct us through the whirling crowd. I was sure I had imagined his hand firmly on my waist but trembling slightly, and his flush when he thanked me afterward. He was a fine figure on horseback, even if rumor did paint him as a bit of a fop.

As well as the Left Hand. Two very contradictory things, indeed.

"Too…late," Simieri choked. I risked peering a little further around the corner. The tapestry here was red and green, a treatment of the last War of the Rose. A particularly ambitious and awful treatment, I might add. "No…time…"

"Why? Why *here*?" Tristan shook the Primus and shoved him back against the wall again, and I winced. The small man's head bounced against stone. "Tell me!"

"Tis…too…late," Simieri repeated, and a queer rattling noise rose from him.

My nostrils flared. There was a breath of sorcery in the dusty air, of rancid apples and matted fur. My hedgewitch training cataloged the scent, compared it to old treatises, and gave me an answer I did not believe. *Apples, and a wet dog. A poison killspell?*

But why? Poison killspells had not been used for over a hundred years; their onset was too delayed to fine-tune the effects.

I noticed the passageway I traveled almost every day was disarranged. A small end table of fragrant wood obediently growing thicker with dust now lay smashed on the floor; there was a spatter of something fresh, wet, and red on the bare stone floor. A Ch'min vase lay in pieces, and two of the tapestries were ripped to shreds.

What happened here?

Tristan d'Arcenne stepped back, and Simieri's body fell limply to the floor. From where I stood I could see the Minister's face, twisted into a grotesque, plum-colored mask. A thin thread of something dark trickled from his nose, and his eyes puffed shut with the killspell's swelling.

The Captain of the Guard swore viciously, and I was too shocked to remain silent. I do not know if my gasp was very loud, but it certainly had an effect.

He whirled, and the sound of a blade leaving its sheath stunned me further. He carried a sword by the grace of the King—the Guard was trusted implicitly, and the Captain even more so. The bright length of metal glittered in the hall's gloom.

It looked very sharp.

Tristan d'Arcenne regarded me over the length of his sword. He was breathing heavily, and so was I. The Minister Primus lay dead on the floor, smashed like the vase and the end table.

No few of the older ladies-in-waiting had succumbed to fever; I had even nursed Lady Atterlina di Herence a year ago until she died. One would have to be blind to avoid seeing death in the world. Yet I had never attended a hanging or a beheading, it being faintly improper for a young noblewoman to see such a thing with the common crowd, and besides I am possessed of a weak stomach. I felt faint each time I saw a duel begin, and usually watched no more than the first exchange of blows.

I could barely even watch a chicken being prepared for the feast. And now, this.

"Vianne di Rocancheil et Vintmorecy." D'Arcenne's tone had lost its violence but none of its quiet, as if he reminded himself who I was. And yet, there was something—an accent, perhaps, or simply the way his lips shaped the words—that seemed highly improper.

Heat rose up my neck, stained my cheeks. I dropped the wet rag. It made a small sound as it hit the floor.

"You—you—," I stammered. "You k-k-k—"

"Not I. The spell was laid on him by another." His blue eyes burned in a sharp face. I had never before noticed how much he *looked* like one would expect a d'Arcenne to. They are mountainfolk and have the faces to prove it, sharp and handsome. "Are you part of it, then, hedgewitch? *Are you?*"

My fingers curled around the corner, the sharp stone and the dusty tapestry. I smelled crushed green things from the garden, my own sweat, dust in the air, and a different horrible odor of violent death, the killspell's reek vanishing as the spell faded.

He moved toward me in a quick light shuffle, a swordsman's

move. I stayed where I was, staring woodenly at the Minister Primus.

The corpse who had *been* the Minister Primus.

"*Are* you?" D'Arcenne almost spat the words.

I tore my gaze away from the body and up to his blue eyes. He examined me for a moment. Slowly straightened, and sheathed his sword. "No, I do not think you are," he continued meditatively. "Unfortunate timing, tis all. Duchesse—"

That was all I heard, for I turned and bolted back the way I had come.

I gave him a good chase. I streaked down the stairs and passed through the kitchen like a shadow—a wild-eyed shadow in a mud-splattered green velvet dress, glittering ear-drops, and half-unbound hair. I doubt any of the kitchen staff even saw me, but perhaps they saw Tristan d'Arcenne, who was almost on my heels.

I was already tiring by the time I reached the rose garden, and the cloying of blooms remained for a long while after a smell of terror to me. I had a stitch in my side and flagging feet by the time I pounded up a crushed-shell walk, bursting past Baronesses di Clency and di Amoranet as they ended their early-afternoon promenade. I suppose I must have scandalized them dreadfully, as I am sure I looked frightful, but I never saw them again.

I knew the King would be taking chai in the Rose Room, and *that* room had a tall, broad casement that looked out on the garden. I skidded to a stop. The window was open—I wrenched at it, hearing the bootclatter of my pursuer right behind me. I ducked into the Rose Room, toppling another small table—this one thankfully did not break—and threw myself to my knees before the surprised King and two of the Guard, who had their blades half drawn.

"M-m-majesty—" I could not make my tongue work. "Tristan d'Arcenne—murder—the Minister—Majesty—Your Majesty, *please*—"

The King was a tall, graying Arquitaine noble with the stamp of the Tirecian-Trimestin family on him, dark eyes and a hawk nose. That day he wore blue velvet, and rings on every finger, his long, graying hair coiffed elaborately in ringlets. He glanced up from his chai-table, laid with dainties and a piping-hot sam'var, and waved a hand at the two Guards. "Wait outside the door, if you please," he said mildly.

The Guards paused for only a moment before obeying, closing the door behind them.

"M-m-majesty—," I stammered again. My knees throbbed, bruised from the floor. *Why* would my tongue not work? I was quick enough most times; I can only surmise the shock had temporarily unseated my words.

He looked down at me. "Well, Tristan."

I cast one terrified glance over my shoulder to see Tristan d'Arcenne step inside the casement and half-turn to shut it with a gentle *snick*. The uniform of the Guard—black doublet and white shirt, red sash and breeches—suited him very well. He turned back, folded his arms over his chest, and regarded both the King and me with his blue d'Arcenne eyes.

He would have looked entertained, had his jaw not been so set.

"It seems," the King continued, "you've been rather untidy."

"Simieri was part of it. Died of a poison killspell, the same work as one or two of the others. I suspect I shall have no luck at stalking this one to its source, either." The Captain said this lazily, as if he had not chased me through half the Palais. "Someone is covering their tracks very well, my liege."

"And this young *d'mselle*?" The King looked down at me. I must confess my jaw dropped. "The di Rocancheil girl. Vianne, is not it? I might have known. Your father was always too curious by half."

Curiosity did not kill him, sieur, *the fever did.* My heart started out through my ribs. "Y-your M-majesty," I said with all the dignity I could muster. Forced the unruly words to obey me. "I saw—"

"Forget what you think you just saw," the King said. He poured chai into a delicate Ch'min porcelain cup and saucer, picked up a pink-frosted pettite-cake. "Tristan, is she…?"

Am I what? There was no help for it—I was before the King and unable even to protest my innocence, since I had no idea what in the Seven Realms was afoot.

The Captain answered, saving me the trouble. "An innocent, my liege. She uses the back passage between the kitchens and the women's quarters to avoid being seen in a…disheveled state." Irony tinted d'Arcenne's voice, equal parts amusement and something darker.

I shot him another look over my shoulder. This one was pure venom. He wore a faint relieved smile almost as shocking as the King's utter calm.

"I have never had reason to distrust a di Rocancheil." The King sipped at his chai, and I began to feel light-headed. I had not taken much breakfast, worked in the herb garden all day, and had only bread and jam. The smell of food shocked me into faintness. "Shall I start?"

D'Arcenne made a movement, for I heard bootleather creak. There was a fire in the grate, and it popped, nearly driving me out of my skin.

The King put down his pettite-cake and regarded me again. "Still, you have given every appearance of being faithful, and loyal, and extremely discreet. A good influence on my Lisele. Who needs one, I might add. A few intrigues caught, her name neatly kept clean, and I have rested easier knowing you are at her side."

So you have noticed, Your Majesty. I thought I kept it all so very quiet. I did not drop my gaze. Twas insulting to stare at the King so, but I hoped he could read innocence upon my features. The edge of a red rug lay under my left knee, and I struggled to stay upright. Sinking into the floor could not be accomplished, no matter how devoutly I wished for it.

Finally, the King seemed to notice I still knelt on hardwood. "Well, Duchesse. It seems I must set you a task."

I realized my jaw was still hanging, closed my mouth with a snap. I bowed my head, dark hair falling forward over my shoulders. I was in complete disarray, and I had just burst in on the King of Arquitaine during his chai.

Dear gods. Perhaps I should play at draughts; I've used up all my day's worth of bad luck. Day? No, perhaps my whole month's worth.

The King continued, with the ponderousness of a man who knew his every word was well attended to. "Duchesse, you must remain silent. I ask this as your liege and King, and as your half-uncle, child. Tristan has been hunting a plot to murder me for some years now, and it appears Simieri was part of it. My most trusted Minister…" Here the King paused, and glanced past me to d'Arcenne. "If you speak of what you saw, Duchesse Vianne di Rocancheil, you will place me—and our Lisele—in grave danger. If you do not speak, the King of Arquitaine shall owe you a boon." He paused, and I realized he was waiting for my response.

Half-uncle? Plot? Murder the King? The world had fallen away underneath me. "Y-Your Majesty." I pulled scraps of my tattered dignity close about. "You owe me no boon to command my obedience. I shall be silent." My shoulders went back and my chin lifted, though I hoped my stained dress would not speak against me.

The King examined me again. Something very much like a smile tilted up the corners of his mouth. The tapestry on the wall, framing him, was the Tirecian-Trimestin family crest in gold and purple, swan necks and *fleurs-di-lisse* worked in gold thread. This was a beautiful room, and one I had only seen once or twice. "I half believe you will," he said meditatively. "Oh, get up, child. You need not address me from your knees. Tristan, help her."

I was only somewhat shocked to find d'Arcenne at my side, offering his hand. My heart gave one shuddering leap.

I now had to make one of those split-moment decisions one makes at Court. Did I ignore the King's words and d'Arcenne's hand to struggle to my feet under my own power, or did I take the Captain's hand—the hand of a man I had just seen murder the Minister Primus?

Although, to be strictly logical, a poison killspell did not seem like something d'Arcenne would use. Why bother with a spell that could possibly be tracked back to its source when he carried anonymous steel at his side?

The King decided for me. "Take his hand, child, do not simply stare at it." Now the King *definitely* sounded diverted.

I am overjoyed he finds my predicament so entertaining. But he was the King, and I decided obedience was the safest course. I took d'Arcenne's hand. It was warm, and callused from sword practice. He pulled me to my feet and a novel contest ensued—me, seeking to take my hand back from the Captain of the Guard, and the Captain equally determined to keep it. I gracefully twisted my fingers loose with one practiced movement called "freeing the swain," used after a dance when a man becomes too insistent.

"My thanks, Captain," I said formally. Then I turned to the King and practiced my very best courtesy. If there is one thing I have learned to satisfaction, it is not to fumble while performing *that* movement. My ear-drops swung heavily, my ears ached. So did the rest of me. "Your Majesty. My apologies. I thought only to warn you of a—"

"A murder. And of course, if you had caught the Captain of the King's Guard committing the violent murder of a Minister, I would be the only person who could possibly protect you." His dark eyes narrowed slightly. "I believe you have some sense, Duchesse. I may find a use for you. Would that please you?"

"I would be happy to be of service, Your Majesty." I rose from my courtesy. Shock added upon shock: Tristan d'Arcenne's hand closed around my elbow. I sought to pull away without the King noticing, but I failed on both counts, for His Majesty's mouth twitched again and the Captain kept his grip.

"Tristan, would you be so kind as to escort the Duchesse to her chambers? I believe she must dress for dinner. Make certain none see you, or more gossip will rise." The King picked up the pink-frosted pettite-cake again and regarded me. "I shall send for you tomorrow, Duchesse."

I would have courtesied again, as protocol demanded, but Tristan pulled me toward the second door—the one that led to the Painted Gallery. "Of course, Your Majesty. I would be honored to serve Arquitaine in any way."

The King most definitely smiled as I tried again, without success, to pull my elbow out of Tristan d'Arcenne's iron-hard grip. I could not for the life of me understand what was so amusing—I had just witnessed a murder. Nevermind that I was now fairly sure d'Arcenne had not used the killspell; its scent did not cover him at all.

Hedgewitches are sensitive to such things, and now that I had leave to *think*, I realized it must be so.

Don't I feel like a silly goose now.

At least the King had not ordered me clapped in irons. Or had he? Tristan would need no more than a word or a phrase to understand what the King wanted done with me—the Bastillion, perhaps, or summary execution in some dank cell.

The thought brought a cold bath of dread, but I stiffened my knees as best I could.

"Remember I require your discretion, Duchesse di Rocancheil," the King said. "Not a word."

I nodded. *In audience with the King personally for the second time in my life, and I am wearing a muddy dress and garden-boots. At least I have my ear-drops on.* "Your Majesty." I managed to sound tart and respectful at the same time. "I have already given my word."

The King outright laughed this time. I did not see what was so amusing, but I supposed then that kings had a different sense of humor than ordinary mortals, even nobles. We were almost to the door when His Majesty spoke again.

"Vianne?" He used my given name, and Tristan stopped, turning, so I could see the King, his fingers still playing with the pettite-cake.

"Your Majesty?" I did not moisten my dry, numb lips, though I ached to.

"Did you not have Tristan to vouch for you, I would be

forced to order you thoroughly…questioned. He must favour you, child." The King's dark eyes sparkled, and a mischievous smile played under his graying mustache. He leaned back in his chair, reaching for the small silver bell to summon the guards.

A thousand acid responses rose to my lips and were strangled, and what ended up coming out was almost as mortifying. "I doubt the Captain favours me overmuch, Your Majesty. I would be forced to take your word for it."

The King's laughter followed us out the door.

The Painted Gallery is a long hall, frescoed walls broken by slim *fleurs-di-lisse* columns, brilliant daubs showing the history and noble Houses of Arquitaine. Red velvet curtains hung over slim leaded-glass windows with iron fretwork, and doors every so often pierced the walls, some locked, others merely unused. In the time of Queen Toriane, she had often paced the Gallery, and after her death her King was wont to roam here at night as well. Perhaps searching for the shade of the woman he had decided he could not live without.

Some said he roamed in search even into the present day, but never often enough to frighten the Court ladies. Still it was not an overused passageway, at least not during the day. At night, certain assignations were made. But I kept well clear of such things.

The Captain's grip on my elbow was firm, and he said nothing until we were a quarter of the way down the Gallery, his boots clicking on parqueted floor, my own making a more decorous tapping. He indicated a door half hidden under another red velvet curtain, this one artfully hung to frame a fresco of the Battle of Arjeunne.

"Here." He unlocked the door with a small iron key from

a ring hung on his belt. Of course, the Captain of the King's Guard would have keys.

The entire time, his hand was clasped around my elbow.

"You may set me loose." I sought to sound very decided about the notion. He had shortened his strides for me, but the stitch in my side and the burning in my lungs had hardly abated. "I shall not run again, Captain, now I know you acted with the King's blessing."

"Indeed." The creaking door revealed a dusty, small corridor, free of any ornamentation, and the rock in my throat turned dry. This was a secret of Palais D'Arquitaine to which I had never been privy.

He pulled me through and locked the door behind us, and I did my best to swallow the boulder lodging in my neck. "Am I to be arrested, then? Or sent to execution?"

"Stop chattering," he muttered in my ear, his breath touching my hair. "Someone will hear you. The King ordered me to make certain none saw you, Duchesse, and you are making it difficult. It will be challenging enough to keep the Guard silent, not to mention the Baronesses you flitted past. I am half-certain your name will be linked more closely to mine now. It may make you a target."

"A target?" *For what?* I am fashionably irreligious, of course, but a prayer to Jiserah the Gentle, queen of the hearth and protector of the foolhardy, would not have gone amiss at the moment.

"Hush." He set off down the corridor. A tingle in my nose at the dust in the air added to my miseries, and the idea of locking myself in a watercloset and succumbing to a fit of tears was extraordinarily inviting.

Soon, I promised myself. A nice, lovely sobbing fit and a cool washcloth to drape over my eyes was just what a hedgewitch physicker would prescribe. Twas common knowledge I suffered the half-head pain. If I pleaded a headache, I might even escape the banquet.

Of course, if I was locked in the Bastillion, dinner would be a moot point.

The corridor led to a set of rickety wooden stairs, and d'Arcenne pushed me before him, relinquishing my arm. Under the smell of dust, green garden simmering, and my own sweat was now the tang of leather and male, of sharpened steel, of a Guard.

A new thought occurred to me, and it escaped my mouth before I could stop myself. "Tis true, then. You are the Left Hand."

Too late I realized that even should I suspect such a thing, saying it aloud was extraordinarily dangerous.

"Up to the second level. I told you to stop chattering." He took a step up. That meant I had to climb the stairs, or have him crowd me most improperly.

I cursed under my breath, a term most unladylike. D'Arcenne made a small sound that might have been a smothered laugh, and I set myself to climbing the narrow stairs. They twisted crazily, and I was half afraid the entire edifice would come crumbling down at any moment. When we finally reached the second level, I breathed a sigh of relief, and d'Arcenne touched my shoulder. "To your right, Duchesse." His hand closed around my elbow again.

My sense of direction was completely bewildered, more by shock than by actual location, so I had no idea where in the Palais I was. "Captain," I began again, "please, have mercy on me. Tell me if I am to be arrested, or executed, or—"

"Cease." Quietly, again in my ear. My skin tingled with the warmth of his breath. "This particular corridor is hidden only from eyes, not ears. A chance eavesdropping will place you in even greater danger. I would not have that."

"But," I whispered frantically, "dear gods, please, can you not *tell* me?"

He half-turned, spinning, and pushed me. I retreated, nearly tripping on my skirts, and my back met the wooden wall. I could go no farther. Tristan d'Arcenne put his hands to either side of my shoulders and leaned in as if he were a courting swain, his nose less than an inch from mine. "You are not to be arrested *or* executed, *d'mselle*," he whispered fiercely in return. "The King told me to take you back to your chambers without anyone noticing, and that is what I intend to do. Do not force me to stopper your mouth, Duchesse. I might enjoy myself, but I doubt you would." His lips curled up into a half smile, and I noticed his eyelashes were charcoal, and thick enough to make any vain Court noblewoman envious.

My heart galloped along inside my rib cage, rattling me. Perhaps it was only the shocks to my nerves that made it behave so.

The King called himself my half-uncle. So it's true, Grand-dam dallied a bit. No wonder Father sent me to Court. Then I thought something even stranger. *Tristan d'Arcenne is the Left Hand of the King. The rumors are true. Did he start them himself?*

"No doubt the King will explain what he wishes from you tomorrow," d'Arcenne whispered, less forcefully now. "But for the present, Vianne di Rocancheil, I must ask that you trust me."

The King said you favoured me. A flush rose in my cheeks. It was not a proper thought for a lady to have—and it was an even more improper thought to have while the Captain of the Guard was leaning in close enough to kiss.

I bit my lip. D'Arcenne studied me, his blue eyes suddenly speculative. *It cannot be true.* I seized on disbelief as a drowning man seizes a rope. *I've only danced with him twice.*

Yet it seemed to me d'Arcenne had been quietly hanging in the background of Court functions, sometimes watching me, sometimes not, for a very long time now. And whatever part of the ballroom or Great Court chambers I wandered to, he was frequently in the same place. Twice was also precisely twice more than any *other* Court lady had danced with him.

You are being ridiculous, Vianne. Simply set yourself the task of repairing to your chamber, and repairing your attire. Lisele will be in a perfect fit *of impatience by now. Attend her dressing, plead a headache, and retreat to your bed with a cold washcloth over your eyes. Send for a glass or two of unwatered wine to steady your nerves, and by tomorrow this will simply be a past shock you may add to your collection of unpleasant experiences. You may set your wits then to whatever task the King gives you. It is bound to be even more unpleasant, whether you will or no.*

I do not know how long Tristan d'Arcenne stood waiting for my reply. Finally, I looked up at him, opened my mouth, remembered not to speak, bit my lip again, and nodded.

Yet whatever I would have said was drowned in the noise and clamor starting almost that very moment, the moment the world completed veering off its accepted course and descended into confusion.

He actually jerked, as if struck by a fist. His eyes widened, and he grabbed my shoulders. "Curse me for a fool," he said, conversationally. I was later to learn that very same soft impersonal tone was the voice he used while dueling. "Duchesse. *Vianne.*" His fingers bit my shoulders, slipping against green velvet. "Listen to me very carefully. Go down this hall to the third door on the left. It should be unlocked. Take care no one sees you exit it; we may have to use this passage later. You should find yourself in the Blue Hall near the women's quarters. Attend the Princesse *at once*, do you hear? You should be safe enough in her presence, and she may very well need—well, no matter. If she requires explanation tell her I will make amends, for I was sent to bring you to her royal father and you had not time to change. Take this." He thrust something into my hands. It was a small ring of keys—not the official ring from his belt, but a different set. "I shall expect its return later. Put it in your pocket, and do *not* lose it."

Did he think me some featherbrained ninny? I took the keys and put them in my skirt-pocket. Alarums now could only mean one thing—the conspiracy the Minister Primus had spoken of was now loose, and the Princesse was at risk even as the King was.

Lisele. I must protect her. I nodded.

Footsteps, shouting voices, and steel clashing now resounded through the deserted hall. I gasped, for d'Arcenne's hands tensed even more. I would be bruised both on knees and shoulders, come morning.

"Take care, Duchesse." His expression was very strange as he gazed down at me. "Take *exceeding* care. Promise me you will."

I was now beyond words. I nodded, my cheeks flaming. Even at that moment I did not think a conspiracy could matter. It was serious, of course—the conspirators would be locked in the Bastillion, then beheaded, their bodies buried turned away from the West and the home of the Blessed.

But a conspiracy could never *truly* affect the Court or the King, could it? The King was eternal. He was Arquitaine itself, the seal of the gods in flesh and blood, no matter that the Blessed left us largely to our own devices here on the imperfect earth.

"You." The word caught me by surprise; I found what I wished to say. "Take care yourself, d'Arcenne. My thanks." I managed to sound calm, and lifted my chin so I could gaze directly at him.

He swore again, and did another passing-strange thing. He shook me so hard my head spun, then leaned forward and pressed his lips to my forehead. The touch sent a scorching flush through my every limb, my dress suddenly rasping-tight against me.

He released me, turned, and ran lightly the way we had so recently come. I knew where he went—he was called to the King's side.

As I was called to Lisele's.

I stood there, dazed, for a few moments, hearing the clamor of alarum bells and shouting. Those moments I later cursed myself for, though I sorely needed them to quiet my racing heart and laboring lungs.

When I could think again, I shook myself and ran along the corridor. My skirts dragged, weighing me down.

I found the third door on the left—twas a narrow aperture with a slim wooden panel, hardly qualifying as a *door*—and slipped through it, finding myself indeed in the deserted Blue Hall, still hung with the traditional *cour bleu* tapestries; someone would have to take them down before the Fête of Sunreturn. The Blue Hall is little used in spring and summer, being stifling, but in winter it was where the Princesse's retinue gathered on long evenings to read aloud, or perform plays and songs. Now it was hot with late-afternoon spring sunshine, and I sweated even more as I ran, keeping to one side so I could duck into a window-*couvre* if anyone happened along.

I reached the hall that housed the Princesse's suite not long after, with a stitch gripping my side and bringing me tears.

There I had my first horrible intimation of utter doom.

The Guards on duty all afternon—*Chivalieri* di Tatancourt and di Belletron—both lay slain at the door to the Princesse's afternoon chamber. I gasped and clamped my hand over my mouth. Blood washed the floor where they had fallen—di Tatancourt, who had a splendid waxed blond mustache and who was courting Lady Arioste di Wintrefelle, had a horrible gaping grimace under his chin. A slit throat. Di Belletron was gashed and terribly torn; I supposed he had put up a stouter resistance.

Hot sourness rose under my breastbone. It was a lucky thing I had taken no chai, for the slice of bread and jam was demanding to be released from the confines of my stomach. I resisted, and heard myself give a dry barking sob instead.

Lisele. She will be terribly frightened. Where is she? "Lisele?"

I had to gather up my skirts to go over the fallen Guards. The door—a door I had passed through hundreds of times, I hardly noticed anymore its carved bunches of grapes and the royal crest worked in gold and blue—was hacked apart as if by axes, and spattered with dark fluids I dared not think on too closely. I ducked through, my garden-boots slipping in blood, and I am not too proud to say that just inside the door the long-resistant slice of bread escaped me at last. I vomited, having enough presence of mind to pull my skirts back so I did not foul them more.

There was Lady Arioste, sprawled in a corner, graceless in death as she never was in life. And beside her a stout headless body I recognized from her pink and gold as Baroness di Vonstadt. *Dama* Elaina di Cherefall and *D'mselle* Courceline di Maritine lay tangled together by the gilt fireplace grate—they must have been clutching each other as they died. *D'mselle*

Robertine, *Dama* Pirial, Baroness Iliana di Chantrour et Val, the Marquise di Valancourt, and the Comtesse di Cournburiene—

I lost count. I looked for one face, and did not find it.

I followed the trail of destruction. Not one of the Princesse's attendants remained alive.

Except me.

The door to Lisele's inner receiving-room was hacked open as well, and the Comtesse Rochburre lay across it, fearfully wounded and with her eagle eyes closed. I stepped over her, miserably determined to find Lisele. *Please*, I begged, not knowing which god I pleaded with, since I was fashionably irreligious like most of the Court. We laughed at the pious, but never too loudly. After all, Arquitaine bore the mark of the Blessed, just as other countries had their own gods…

I found my Princesse, my Lisele, lying across a half-couch of watered-blue silk we had been wont to sit giggling upon in our girlhoods, and later. Her harp lay cast aside, its strings cut. Had she tried to defend herself with it?

I cast myself to my knees, bruising them anew, and shook her. "Lisele—*Lisele!*" She was covered in blood, and there was an awful wound to her breast, dewing the pretty pale-green silk. She had been dressed without me.

I sobbed, repeating her name, and when her dark eyes opened and she drew in a terrible tortured breath I actually recoiled. Those eyes fastened on me, and I heard a horrible sucking sound. A punctured lung. I had read enough treatises to know, though I had never treated more than a fever or pneumonia, or a wound on a scullery maid's hand.

Treatises? Of course. A healing charm, anything to stem the flow of blood.

"Vianne," Lisele said, in a choked whisper.

"A healing charm. Oh, Lisele." *Cease, you ninny. Find a healing charm in that warehouse of oddities you call a brain.*

I did. It was the same simple bit of hedgewitchery I had used on Jirisa's hand, meant for binding a small wound and staving off infection, but I repeated it quickly, flattening my hand against the bloody hole. I repeated it again, heat draining through my palm—hedgewitchery draws its power from the witch when it cannot draw from a bit of free earth. A tree, the open sky, or even a clod of dirt, none of which were to hand.

I repeated it a third time, my vision blurring with exhaustion, before Lisele's fingers came up and gripped my wrist with surprising strength. "No...Stop, Vianne...too late."

"I can heal you, I *can.*" *Remember a charm, Vianne. A stronger one. A* better *one. Think!*

"Do not be a silly goose." She looked so *weary.* A smear of blood marred her pretty cheek, and her dark hair lay tangled over blue watered silk. *She must have been waiting for me to braid it.* Guilt twisted my heart. *Was she dying while Tristan d'Arcenne kissed my forehead?* "Listen to me, Vianne...carefully. I...command it."

So rarely did my Princesse command anything from me, I swallowed my tears. "Lisele..." I ceased to speak. The spell still worked through my palm, its power coming from my already weary body. Her grasp curled around my wrist, cold and waxen.

Lisele firmly pulled my hand away from her wound. I cried out, the charm breaking, and she pushed something hard, metallic, and warm into my fingers. A momentary flush of strength filled her, turned her cheeks crimson and brought her words without gasping. "Take this. Keep safe. I could not wake...If they have killed me, Father is dead too. Go to mountains...d'Arcenne. Go to Arcenne. Father said...*loyal*...please, Vianne...do as I..."

The mention of Arcenne caused a guilty start in me, but it was too late. Lisele sighed, a long, low sound, and slumped back into the blue silk. Something fled her, a spark I could see only with the small amount of magical Sight I possess.

"Lisele," I whispered. "Lisele, no, Lisele, no, no, no—"

I do not know how long I crouched there, sobbing, repeating the same small hedgewitch charm that availed naught since there was no life left in her body for it to foster, no spark for it to conserve. I wept and heaved dryly until I heard something. My head jerked up, as if I'd been stung.

Footsteps, coming this way. Booted feet, purposeful strides.

I fair leapt to my feet. Lisele's eyes were closed. She lay pale and perfect, her pretty sharp-chinned face smooth as if she merely slept.

I could not wake, she had gasped. What it meant would have to wait. I looked wildly about the room. There, beside the fireplace, a door that led to a half-stair, and from there I could...do what, precisely?

Where could I go? What place was safe?

Clutching whatever Lisele had given me in my sweating palm, I ducked through the door and locked it just as the bootsteps reached Lisele's receiving-room. Four or five men, I guessed, listening with Court-sharp ears.

I hesitated, my hand on the knob, the key in my fingers. If they were from the King I should make myself known, not hide like a thief.

If they are from the King they will take me to him, and d'Arcenne might be there. I struggled with temptation, caution and a small deep irresistible instinct nailing me in place, freezing the words in my throat and my hand on the dusty crystal knob.

It would be foolish not to see who they are, Vianne. Do not be a fool.

I slowly lowered myself to my knees again, peered through the keyhole. I could only see a small slice of Lisele's receiving-room, and thankfully none of the blood. I could, however, see the edge of Lisele's dress. If I tried hard enough, I could imagine she simply slumbered, perhaps given a draught of night's-ease and valeriol to quiet her dreaming.

I sought to calm my heaving sides. My own harsh gasps sounded loud as a trumpet in the quiet.

They thundered into the receiving-room. I saw plumes and blue sashes.

The Duc's Guard. The Duc Timrothe d'Orlaans, the king's brother, perhaps the finest Court sorcerer in Arquitaine. He dueled regularly, and rumor said he allowed his opponent to survive only if there were official witnesses present. For all that, he was blood royal, and had he killed a few, noble or common, nothing could be done. Still, his Guard was perhaps here to protect the Princesse.

I let out a relieved sigh and was about to rise and make myself known when yet another voice I recognized sounded deep and harsh.

"Check the bodies. Make absolutely certain none live." Garonne di Narborre, the Duc's servant, otherwise known as the Black Captain for the coal of his hair and eyes. I had danced with him several times, had even taken a rose from his hand at the last Fête of Flowers. He cut a fine figure, yet somehow few of the women cared for him. I had found his fingers too hard on my waist and my hand, but twas not politic to refuse him a dance.

Not politic at all, and while he was occupied with me he did not watch Lisele so closely. I simply did not like the way he gazed at her. He could not hope to win her hand, and there was no tenderness in his watching, and since the Duc was just after Lisele in the Line of Succession and she was just barely of age…well. I danced with him, and Lisele told me afterward she did not like him overmuch.

"Aye, *sieur*." A lieutenant—I think it may have been Gregoire di Champforte.

"Have they found the di Rocancheil girl yet?"

I started violently, tasted bitterness on the back of my tongue. Bit my lower lip, *hard*, to stop any betraying noise from my treacherous, dry throat.

"No, *sieur*. She was in the gardens this morn, has not been sighted since."

"Well, perhaps Simieri caught her; he was waiting in the passage. And d'Arcenne?"

Simieri was part of this, and meant to catch me in the passage? Why? My heart pounded in my ears, and I swayed.

Do not dare faint now, Vianne. Do not dare!

"Taken to the donjons, *sieur*. Executed come morning, the orders are being drawn up now." The men were stepping among the bodies. I heard a crunch, and a wet stabbing sound.

They were making certain no woman survived.

My gorge rose again, and I trembled. Whatever Lisele had closed in my nerveless hand was still there, pulsing.

"Look, *sieur*. On the Princesse."

"Hedgewitchery," someone breathed. "The di Rocancheil girl has been here."

A tense, indrawn breath. "Find her. Search the Palais and the gardens. She wanders about in the gardens and the kitchens.

Find her! Bring her to the Duc. He needs her."

What? I am of no account, and I have not done *anything!*

Yet I knew even an innocent could be caught in a net at Court. I hesitated. Should I announce myself, and be taken to the Duc? But they were making certain the women were *dead.*

They had not said aught of "rescue."

The Duc is next in line to the throne, with Lisele…gone. It was the only answer that made any sense at all. And yet…

My wit, weak and weary as it was under these successive shocks, began to work again. *I must hide. But where would they not find me?* I cast about frantically, taking care not to lean on the door—varnished wood, and suddenly thin as an eggshell. Such a fragile, flimsy shield.

The North Tower. Tis locked, and none have used it for a hundred years or more. My wits began to work, racing inside my head with little pattering feet, rather like a collection of cats chasing about in my skull. Stunned and witless, with my Princesse's blood on my fingers and something in my hand she had entrusted to me, I closed my eyes and forced myself to *think.*

You must find food, and clothing, and you must wait for night-fall.

Then what do I do? I wailed silently. My eyes squeezed themselves shut, and had I been more pious I might have begun praying again. Instead, something horrible occurred to me.

Tristan d'Arcenne is in the donjons, and they will take him to the Bastillion and behead him. The fingers of my free hand crept into my pocket, found the cold metal ring. Among them would be keys to a donjon door, perhaps?

But there will be many guards, and the whole length of the Palais between you and him.

It does not matter. He will know what to do.

Footsteps echoed. Boots, approaching my sanctuary.

Oh, dear gods. I rose, silently, and backed away from the door. My mouth gapped open so my breathing would not betray me, and tears trickled hot down my cheeks, dripping onto my collarbones.

"We must find the di Rocancheil girl." Di Narborre sounded very close, and the door rattled as he tested it. Had I left a trace of blood on the knob on the other side? "Let us go. Our lord the Duc will be crowned tonight."

I let out a soft, shapeless breath, dropped the key that had held the door closed between me and di Narborre, and fled.

Chapter Two

I could not return to my own rooms, but I did stop in Lady Arioste's tiny *closette* between the Princesse's bedchamber and mine. She and I were of a size, though thankfully not of matching temperaments; I dug in her wardrobe until I found a serviceable dark blue velvet-and-silk, frightfully old but still good. I took hair ribbons and a servant girl's bag I filled with fruit from the bowl on Arioste's night table; and a sewing kit, as well as extra stockings. For some reason I also took a comb, instead of a hundred other items which might have proved useful.

The table was not laid for chai, since Lisele would have ordered chai in one of her own reception rooms, and Arioste would have been in attendance.

Carrying the dress carefully so as not to foul it with mud or…other things, I made my way through dusty passages to a little-known door that gave into the North Tower. Several times I heard running feet. Once I even hid in a niche, lost behind dusty red-velvet curtains as a detachment of the Duc's Guard thundered past, no doubt searching for me or on some other unsavory business. Tears rolled unheeded down my cheeks and dripped onto my poor muddy gown.

One of the keys on the ring d'Arcenne had given me fit a neglected door at the end of a long, chilly passageway. I might have simply sunk to the floor and given up if it had not. I was famished, exhausted, and at what I thought then was the end of my strength.

I closed the door behind me and locked it carefully, took my first faltering steps into the gloomy dust of the North Tower. The narrow hallway of the servant's entrance hung thick with cobwebs, a sour exhalation from the masonry full of neglect and rot; the lower windows still sealed tight.

The Tower had been stopped up when the King's treacherous great-great-grandmother, the Dowager Elisaine, was bricked inside it to die. She conspired with the Damarsene, who would *always* like nothing better than to swallow our land—you would think they had enough and to spare, but no, they are greedy. The Dowager had plotted to kill her elder brother's son Archimvault the Tall, before he came of age to be crowned. That treachery had been averted just in time, the Damarsene ambassador sent home in disgrace, and the White Dowager starved to death in the North Tower. The sealing-bricks from the entrances had been taken away with her body, and used to line her tomb. It was said that when her body was found she was clutching a statue of Jiserah, and the goddess's face had turned away.

When Lisele and I were young, we had dared each other to spend a night before the great ironbound main door to the Tower, carved with Elisaine's device—the swan and the serpent over the crown of Arquitaine.

None would think to look for me here. At least, not for a while. And none would suspect I had a key, except Tristan d'Arcenne. Would they torture him to find what he knew? What would he say?

The sweat coating me was suddenly cold as a lemon-ice. *Still, they must have greater matters at hand than a hedgewitch lady-in-waiting, even a di Rocancheil.* The assurance was hollow, at least in my ears.

I penetrated the mysteries of the North Tower a short way and found nothing but decay. I climbed to the third level, where some of the windows had not been sealed, and found a room with wan sunlight coming from a high casement, piercing the gloom. Dust lay in great sheets over everything, and the furniture was covered in white drapes grown gray and moth-eaten with years. I took two more steps and sank to the floor, buried my face in my filthy, sweating hands, and proceeded to weep like an absolute fool.

The storm of tears did not last as long as I thought it would, since I was too hungry and exhausted to cry much more. So I did the only thing I could—gathered up the dress and the bag and carried them further up into the Tower until I found a half-hidden door behind a rotting tapestry of Elisaine's crest. This led into a sitting room, close and still and cold as all the Tower, even in the late-spring heat. I changed into Arioste's gown with shaking hands. I had no servant girl to help me, so it took two or three tries, but the lacings were relatively easy.

With that done, I tossed a dusty sheet back to reveal a frightfully old divan done in faded red and gold satin, chewed by gods alone knew how many tiny animals but sound enough. I sank down, dropping the bag of fruit and other things next to me, tucking the strap as if I were arranging an embroidery bag prettily on one of Lisele's wide sophas.

Another wave of faintness went through me at the thought. I shook it away, transferred the keys to my new skirt-pocket, and fished the thing Lisele had given me out of my old skirt as well.

I opened my fingers, found my palm full of a medallion that occupied my hand to the first joints in my fingers, with a thick antique silver chain. The medallion itself was three serpents twisted in a complex knot—copper, silver, and black gold, set with rubies and clear glittering diamonds for eyes.

The world slipped from beneath me again.

It was the Aryx, the Great Seal of Arquitaine. It lay cool and weighty in my hand, the source of all Court sorcery and the servant of the bloodline of Edouard Angoulême, however diluted in the house of Tirecian-Trimestin. It belonged in the possession of the King. Why had Lisele had it—and why had she given it to me?

If the Duc's men had found it, they would have taken it to the Duc, and he would be the king in truth. I touched the medallion with one trembling finger smudged with garden-dirt and blood. I had scrubbed my fingers on my green velvet, but it did very little to help. *Lisele is the Heir—of course she would hold it sometimes; the Festival of Skyfall is soon, and the reigning monarch and the Heir pass the Aryx between them at sundown. The whys and wherefores matter not a whit. It only matters that you do not let the Duc find it. Lisele charged you with keeping it safe.*

I found the clasp and fastened the chain about my own throat with trembling fingers, silently praying it would not take a notion to fry me for my insolence. The histories said the royal family of Arquitaine knew the secret to using the Aryx as a weapon, but it had not happened since the time of King Fairlaine's suicide, after the death of his beloved Queen Toriane. Since then, we had not needed the Aryx's power in battle or in the defense of the King's person. King Fairlaine's death had brought the Great King Tibirius to the throne, and he had been the architect of a lasting peace, even if that peace meant paying tribute to the Damarsene across our borders with their hungry army—and to the Damarsene alliance with the Pruzians, those mercenary masters of cold warfare.

If the King had carried the Aryx, the Duc could not have killed him, and Lisele would still be alive.

I had more pressing matters at hand. I dropped the Aryx down into my bodice, thanking the gods Arioste had been relatively modest—at least when it came to showing her twin charms. Heartless and fickle, with no more brain than a poisonous serpent, she still had not deserved...that. A cold shudder racked me.

The neckline concealed most of the medallion, leaving only a meaningless curve of copper that was a serpent's back but might have been anything.

Chill metal settled against my skin as if it belonged there. The Aryx began to throb, softly, taking on the quality of a heartbeat—my own heartbeat, rapid and thready as it was in my own ears. Strangely, it comforted me to have that warmth against my skin.

I ate an apple, and my hands ceased their trembling. The window set high in the wall let westering sunlight through, making golden motes of dust dance in the air. I thought of Tristan d'Arcenne locked in the donjons, and hoped they would not torture him. I thought of him because otherwise I would have to think of Lisele, and her blood on my hands.

I ate another apple, and wiped at my cheeks with a bit of my green velvet dress. Then I combed out my tangled hair and braided it back, weeping afresh because I had twisted Lisele's hair so many times. I had taught her to braid in the style of di Rocancheil too, and it had been quite the fashion when we were eleven together. By then we had been fast friends, and Lisele had come to trust me as much as a princesse could trust a confidante of noble blood. She was my Princesse and my lady, and I bound to serve her, but she was also my friend, and I tried to be discreet and trustworthy for her.

Yet I failed her when she needed me most. Had I not been standing uselessly, feeling d'Arcenne's lips on my forehead, I might have been able to…

Do not be ridiculous. They would have killed you as well, and found the Aryx to take to the Duc. You did what you should have, Vianne.

But oh, I did not believe it.

Chapter Three

I did sleep, a thin troubled slumber broken by restless starts whenever I thought I heard a footstep or a mouse scratching. It would not be long before the North Tower was searched as well.

And I dared not sleep too deeply lest I waste the night.

When darkness crept slowly through the windows, I wished I had brought a candle. Yet if I had one, or if I practiced my limited Court sorcery and used a witchlight, how would I wend my way to the donjons without being seen? And if I could reach the warren of prison cells without being remarked, what chance did I have of setting d'Arcenne free? Did the keys he'd given me include a donjon key among them?

I waited in the darkness for what seemed like ages, until the clock in my head—probably thrown off by shock, but the only measure of time I had—told me twas the hour of the planned banquet. Court dines late in summer, and only a touch earlier in late spring; besides, the Duc would be anxious to bring the Palais under his control. I wondered what tale would be given to the Ministers, and to the lords and pages and *chivalieri*. The women who had not seen the attack on Lisele, of course, would be dead or taken somewhere, whisked out of the way for their own safety. I wondered grimly who would be blamed for the afternoon's events, where the Duc would pin the conspiracy that had left him King.

He is not King without the Aryx. I left my green velvet dress on the divan and covered it with the dust cloth. The disturbed dust would not hide where I had spent the afternoon, but I felt compelled to conceal what I could.

I used a dry abandoned watercloset to relieve my aching bladder and crept through the North Tower to the servants' door, again. I listened, my ear pressed against cold wood, for a long, agonizing time, before I unlocked it and stepped out.

The hall was empty.

Now I had only to reach the donjons without being seen.

I had mulled the matter long and hard, and decided I would use the Sculpture Hall, since it ran almost the whole length of the Western Palais and was rarely guarded, being completely enclosed by the King's Pavilion. There were plenty of niches and passages to hide in. Lisele and I had explored the Palais as children, and I knew not all of it, for there were some places children and women did not go, and passages both secret and forgotten. Yet I knew enough to possibly pass unseen if I wished to devoutly enough.

The Sculpture Hall proved to be under heavy guard by the Duc's blue-sashed men, so I was forced to use a different route—a dusty garret over the north end of the Sculpture Hall leading to a jumbled, confusing patchwork of servant's passageways. I kept my ears tuned and had to hide once or twice, and was almost discovered by a fumbling pair of servants eager to find a place for their assignation. From them I learned the whole Palais was at sup in the Coronation Hall, the Court putting on a brave face over the tragedy of the King slain by his own Captain, Tristan d'Arcenne.

Who was scheduled to be executed tomorrow, beheaded after his tongue was torn out. My stomach turned over afresh when they dropped that choice morsel of news.

I held my breath while the lovers fumbled to their niche, and I passed by them silently as they were engaged in their congress. I was not innocent of the ways of lovers, but this brought a silly flush to my cheeks. I seemed to feel lips against my forehead, and to smell leather and steel.

I slipped unseen through the Palais, helped by a generous portion of luck, until I reached the entrance to the donjon in the west wing, tunneled into the rock of Mount di Cienne, which loomed over the Palais and the Citté. Its dark mouth yawned; there was only one entrance and a single Duc's Guard at it. Everyone else had perhaps been called to duty elsewhere—searching for me, and serving in the Coronation Hall.

Why are they seeking me? Will they blame me for Lisele's death, as they are blaming d'Arcenne for the King's? What could they want with me?

I tucked myself into a niche down the hall, wondering how I would get past the guard until I noticed him leaning back in his chair, almost certainly asleep. A leathern skin dangled from one limp hand. As I watched, the skin slipped from his fingers and thumped on the floor, but twas drained enough not to spill.

Wine. I sniffed quietly. D'Arcenne's Guard would never be caught sopped on duty. Then again, a new King was cause for celebration, even if the old King had been slain. D'Orlaans needed his Guard loyal and satisfied, too.

It took far more courage than I thought I possessed to step from my hiding place. I moved soundlessly as I could, halting and trembling like a rabbit whenever the guard snorted or muttered, slipping past him and through the half-open gate. I did not recognize the man, but he wore a blue sash. His feathered hat tipped down over his face and his chair leaned back precariously. I had a moment's mad desire to kick the chair and spill him onto the stone floor.

Trembling so hard my ear-drops swung, I found myself in the donjon.

Luck was with me again. Torchlight ran red over stone floor and bare iron bars, and Tristan had not been thrust into one of the deeper cells. No, he was in the third cell to the left, and he was alone. The other cells were empty.

Of course—the Duc's Guard might have killed everyone else, but they needed a public beheading for Tristan. I felt almost sick at the thought, and at the cold logical way my mind ran now. Had I ever been this calculating before?

They will tear out his tongue before they kill him. Cannot have him speaking, of course. And that is the traditional punishment for traitors, is it not?

I sank to my knees by the door of his cell. I could see him through the bars, flung down on the floor, his red sash half torn off, his dark hair lying on stone. He still had his boots, but his swordbelt was gone. "D'Arcenne," I whispered.

He did not stir. Had they killed him already?

"D'Arcenne." A little louder. I felt for the keys in my pocket and drew them out, as softly as I could. "Captain!" I nearly wept again, I was so distraught. "Captain, *please*!" I almost forgot to whisper.

He stirred, but he said nothing, made no noise. Relief scalded the inside of my throat. He was alive.

"'Tis Vianne," I whispered. "Vianne di Rocancheil. Please,

you must tell me which key will work, if any…*please*, Captain, for the love of the Blessed, wake *up*!"

He curled up to sit, suddenly; I gave an undignified little squeak, choked off halfway as I remembered to be quiet. I fell backward off my knees onto the floor, and my teeth clicked together painfully. *From bruised knees to a pratfall. Tis a good thing I am not known for my grace.*

He was at the bars, reaching through, his hand shot out and clasped around my wrist. "Is it you?" he demanded in a whisper. "Or have the gods driven me mad with hope?" He dragged me forward. Torchlight ran red over his face. He had taken a beating—one eye swollen shut, split lips, and half his face terribly bruised. His hand was bruised, too.

"You look awful," I murmured. *Of all the things to say, Vianne.*

Still, it brought a wisp of amusement to his blue eyes—or eye, since the other one was puffed nearly shut. "Thank you, *d'mselle.*" There was the shadow of a bow, his body inclining stiffly. "I did not even dare to hope—you brought the keys?"

I turned my wrist in his grasp, so he could see. "Tell me which one, and I shall unlock the door."

"None of these will work. My belt hangs near the door of the guardroom—my sword, my keys, everything else. You shall have to fetch it for me. How did you get past the guard?"

"He's sotted. I must fetch your belt?" I sounded blank and witless.

He nodded. "Quietly, Duchesse, and quick. We have not much time." He let go of me, finger by finger.

I made it shakily to my feet. Ghosted over the floor, and almost collapsed as I reached the entrance again. My knees wished to simply fold, and I fought the desire to sink to the floor, put my head in my arms, and let the world do whatever madness took its fancy next.

Move, Vianne. Do not stop now. The guard still slept, his breathing heavy and whistling, and I padded past him.

The guardroom was lit only by a single small lantern. I found Tristan's belt hanging on a row of pegs driven into the stone, took it down with trembling hands. Twas heavy and clumsy, so I cradled it in my arms as I peered down the hall again and set out past the guard for the third time. The sotted man mumbled once as I passed him, and I nearly fell headlong as my knees threatened fresh mutiny. The torchlit dimness of the donjon was almost a blessing.

I found the Captain's keyring and passed it through the bars. He selected a thick heavy iron key, and in a trice the door was unlocked. Why had they left his belt there? The Duc must have been confident—or extremely hurried, not to take it and lock it up. Then again, the plan had gone smoothly, and if there were none loyal to d'Arcenne still left alive there was no worry, was there?

The door squeaked slightly as Tristan eased out. He moved stiffly, but seemed otherwise hale. I offered his belt, but he caught me by my shoulders and examined me from top to toe. His gaze snagged on the copper peeking out under my neckline, then met mine with a question unasked.

"The Aryx," I whispered. "Lisele was dying, she gave it to me. They killed the women—and Lisele…" My voice refused to work further.

He whispered an oath that would have normally made me blanch, and pulled me forward into a rough embrace. I nearly cried out as my face crushed against his chest. He breathed another curse into my hair, as the hilt of his sword jabbed me in the shoulder and his belt made a clinking sound.

"Gods." His arms were bruising-tight. "*Gods.* I thought you dead, or worse. Where did you hide?"

Why does he hold me so? "The N-North T-T-Tower." The urge to weep returned, but I was mercifully out of tears.

He nodded and released me all at once, subtracting the belt from my numb fingers. What was clumsiness in my grasp turned into supple, well-behaved leather in his; he buckled it on deftly. "Come." His hand worked a knife free of its sheath with a whisper. "Stand by the door, Duchesse. You do not wish to see this."

He led me to the half-open gate, and I stayed where he placed me. He glided away. I stood, my fists clenched, trembling from head to foot.

A number of things passed pell-mell through my throbbing, too-full head. *He's betrayed me* was one, and: *Of course—he's gone to kill the guard* was another, overwhelmed by the ever-present song below all the others—*Lisele, oh Lisele,* a grief-stricken refrain like a myrmyra bird's call. Then, *Why did he embrace me?* And, *But he only danced with me twice.*

The most unsettling thought of all—*"Dead, or worse." What would be worse than dead?*

He returned with a cat's soft step. Something I did not care to examine too closely glittered in his one good eye. Something like rage, and satisfaction.

"Come." No need to whisper now, but he still spoke softly. "We must free you from this place, *d'mselle.*"

I was all too ready to leave. But he did not turn to lead me out through the gate. Instead he drew his sword and dropped to his knees, offering me the hilt.

"You have saved my life." His ruined face lifted to mine. "I owe you my service, *d'mselle*. I give you my oath."

I almost choked. At any other time it might have been a pretty picture, and very romantic, even if terribly embarrassing. But this moment I was tired and hungry, and the entire world had gone spinning merrily off its course. And Tristan d'Arcenne, Captain of the King's Guard, was acting like the hero of a silly courtsong.

"For the sake of all the gods," I hissed, "get up and let us *go*!"

Something dark crossed his marred face, but he stayed where he knelt. "Accept my oath. Please?"

I touched the hilt of his bare sword with two fingers. "Very well, then, I-accept-your-oath-*chivalier*-now-may-we-*please*-flee? They shall catch us, and if they do they shall kill us both."

He rose to his feet in one motion and sheathed his sword, his eyes—eye—gleaming balefully. "They shall try to kill me, but they will seek to take you alive."

"Why?" I still held the ring of keys, hastily offered them to him. He pushed them into a pouch depending from his belt, gazing so steadily over my shoulder I expected to hear someone behind me, and I sidled nervously.

His hand twitched, but he brought it back to his side. "Because your father was an illegitimate son of King Taristide." Slowly and softly, as if talking to an idiot. "The King is—*was*—your half-uncle, and so is the Duc. You are the last person alive who can challenge his hold to the throne since the Princesse is dead. But he will not kill you; he will marry you, and found his new dynasty."

For perhaps the hundredth time that day, my jaw dropped. I stared at the Captain, stunned and speechless, and he took my hand and started not out the half-open gate, but deeper into the donjons.

Marry the Duc? "But I do not wish to marry him," I finally managed, stupidly. "And where are we—"

"There is a passage that will take us from the Palais, and I will take us from the Citté as quickly as possible. It does not matter if you *wish* to marry him, Vianne. If it is a choice between marriage or death, I would counsel you to marry and live. There is no princesse of marriageable age from any other country, and any other noble domestic House will become dangerous if a daughter of theirs marries a King who attained the throne with bloodshed. *Bloodshed does remove a king so throned.*" He made no attempt to shorten his stride; I had to run to keep pace, my bag bouncing against my hip. "Perhaps the Duc thinks you are stupid and tractable. Though I cannot see how he can reach that conclusion." He glanced down at me and slowed abruptly. "Your pardon, Duchesse. I do not mean to run you to death."

"'Tis no matter." My voice sounded choked and thin, small in the gloom. *There must be other royal bastards, plenty of them female and more suited than I. Why would the Duc want* me?

We passed out of the reach of the torches, the ground sloping down and becoming rocky. I wondered if there were other prisoners locked down here and shuddered. Perhaps a moldering body or two—I did not think the King had ever ordered anyone held in the Palais donjon.

No, he had them sent to the Bastillion before execution. The Duc, perhaps, wanted Tristan kept close at hand. But why? Something to do with the conspiracy, no doubt.

"What do you have in your bag, Duchesse?" Tristan asked in the darkness. I stumbled but he righted me, and we continued to descend. I was now wholly at his mercy, in the dark and confused.

"F-fruit. I took it from Lady Arioste's rooms. And a d-d-ress, the one I wear now. I brought a comb, and a sewing kit, and some stockings…I could not bring anything useful, it seems. I wish I had *thought*."

"You did well." He slowed even further. I sensed him feeling along the wall with his other hand, but his fingers were warm in mine. I realized his hand was bruised, and he held mine so tightly it must have hurt, but he made no mention of it. "I would not have thought to bring a bag of apples. It was probably the only food you could find. No water, though—you must be thirsty."

His words reminded me, and of a sudden I was parched. "A little."

"'Tis been rather a trying day for you." It struck me that he spoke not out of need, but because he sensed my panic and sought to soothe me. Ridiculous. I was worse than useless to him now, and well I knew it.

*Go to Arcenne. Loyal…*Lisele's tortured voice echoed in my ears. "Lisele told me to go to Arcenne. She said you were loyal; she said to go to the mountains."

"Eventually we shall." He sounded grimly pleased. "First we must escape the Palais, and then the Citté, and learn if any of my Guard have survived. Then we traverse league upon league of hostile territory until we reach Arcenne. There the mountains will protect us. The difficult part is reaching safety and surviving the winter. Then we can set our thoughts to war in the spring."

"War?" I let out an undignified, thready squeak of alarm. He paused, made a quick movement, and there was a rusty screeching sound. I jumped nervously, though we were far out of the gate-guard's hearing, had he even been still alive.

"Do not think on it. Right now, follow me, and go carefully.

The door will close of its own weight. The passage is close, so hold my hand."

I squeezed his fingers, and he inhaled sharply. "I beg your pardon," I said immediately. "Captain—"

"Tis Tristan, and you are Vianne. Surely we have passed the point of formality." He drew me through the door—at least, I thought it was a door. I could only see very faintly, and of course neither of us would risk a witchlight to alert any trackers. "Hold my hand as tightly as is needful. I do not mind."

I remember very little of the nightmarish sqeeze through the narrow rock passage out of the donjons. The air was still and foul, and sometimes the Captain had to turn sideways to fit through the gaps, the hard length of his sword once sharply striking my knees. The passage twisted until I was lost, and I could see nothing. It was blacker than any night I have experienced before or since, and my breath came short. I could imagine all too well Mont di Cienne bearing down on us, squeezing the life out of our fragile human bodies. Even though the Mont, set in the middle of the rolling fertile land of Arquitaine, was little more than a hill compared to other mountains, it seemed still large enough to crush us.

I repeated to myself the first cadre of Tiberian verbs, starting with the irregular *esse*, but that did not help. I fell back on a teaching-rhyme about the Twelve Blessed.

I suppose anyone would have thought of the gods and prayed for help, down there in the dark.

These are the gods of our land, listen well. These are the Blessed of Arquitaine, six Old and six New, married by the Angoulême. Gentle Jiserah, hearth, hopeless, and home; Danshar her consort, warrior unknown. Kimyan the Huntress, maiden and bow; her twin is Torvar, of Sun, rain, and snow—

"Breathe, Vianne," the Captain said, kindly enough. It interrupted my inward recitation. "If you swoon I shall have to carry you."

How undignified that would be. Still… "Will the mountain crush us?" Childishly, the hot flush of embarassment rose to my cheeks again.

"Of course not." He paused. "Look, 'tis not so dark. Courage, we are almost through."

He was right—I could see the faint outline of my free hand as I lifted it before my face, and I further saw the Captain as a shadow cast by a pale glow. Starlight, or moonlight.

My chest unloosed. My arms and legs were made of lead, the relief was so intense.

We ducked out of a low cave scarcely big enough for a goat to pass through, and found ourselves on a long, rocky slope. Faint light struck my hot, aching eyes, sweeter than any candle or glowglobe lit in a nursery to comfort a dark-fearing child.

The Palais reclined, a white-glimmering bulk, in the distance. Below, the torches and lamps of Citté D'Arquitaine sprawled in glimmering patchwork; the river was a mellifluous gleam at its heart, a bright thread bridged with thin stonce arcs. I gasped, startled, and a flare of brilliance surprised me. It was a beam from a covered lanthorn, shone directly into my face. I heard steel drawn from the sheath before the Captain spoke.

"In the King's name," he said, calmly enough, and clearly, too.

I held my breath.

"For the King's honor," replied a tenor male voice. "Tristan? Gods above, is that you?"

"'Tis. I am even relatively hale. How many with you, Jierre?"

Jierre? Jierre di Yspres. Lieutenant. I placed the voice just as the lantern was hurriedly recovered and someone pushed roughly past me to catch Tristan in a bear hug.

My eyes recovered slowly. I saw a little over a dozen men. Horses, too, all standing quietly, a tail occasionally flicking. The men moved forward, some of them whispering, and surrounded us. Jierre di Yspres held the Captain at arm's length and hugged him again. "I saw you clapped in chains, my friend, and Adersahl had to hold me back. You are the *luckiest* bastard—"

"Not quite." Some of the tension had left the Captain. "I was rescued by a *d'mselle* with far more presence of mind than any of us. Jierre, you know Vianne di Rocancheil et Vintmorecy?"

"Aye, Tristan. Who does not, who knows you?" Now the lieutenant sounded suspicious. "How did she—"

"She witnessed me catching the Primus at a deadly game. Events moved rather quickly afterward. She stole down to the donjons to free me after hiding in the North Tower."

A collective indrawn breath. The North Tower was reputed to be cursed, and none of them believed it, of course...but still. Rumor said no statue of the Blessed, including Jiserah, would enter its walls since the Dowager had been carried out. Any who sought to bring one into the Tower's environs would be unable to enter, held back by an invisible hand.

Though nobody had tried such a feat since Archimvault's time. It was, like anything concerning the Aryx, a question better left unasked.

"As the only remaining scion of the King's blood she is the rightful heir to Arquitaine, now that the Duc d'Orlaans has committed regicide and fratricide in one fell swoop," Tristan continued implacably. "Mount up, Guard. We have leagues to travel before daylight."

Only remaining scion? There are bastards sown the length of

Arquitaine, Captain. Even I know that. Weariness swamped me. I held my peace, uncaring.

Jierre started to protest, interrupting my gasp. "A woman? A Court woman? Who knows where her loyalties lie? She may be *part* of the plot! And she will slow us. Speed is essential—"

"If she was part of the plot, would she have freed me? Come now, Jierre. You waited for me; you must have trusted I would not lead you astray. We have little time. Let us be gone."

"We have no spare mount." Jierre's tone bordered on anger, rough and dismissive.

I swayed on my feet, too exhausted to care. If they left me there on the mountainside, my only feeling would have been weary relief that I could finally sink down to rest. I cared little what the morn would bring. "Take the Aryx." I pitched my voice low enough none of others would hear, as the Captain leaned down to listen. "Leave me. You will go faster without."

"If the Duc seizes her, all hopes for holding him accountable for his crimes are gone," Tristan said sharply. "Do you challenge me, Jierre?"

"Of course not." Now di Yspres seemed shocked. "I simply…tis been a long day of unpleasant surprises, *sieur*. I spoke unthinking; pardon me." He did not sound repentant in the least. I shut my eyes and swayed again, Tristan's hand closed around my arm. "Bring the Captain's horse! Come, *chivalieri*, we ride!"

They moved. There was the creak of leather, and a huge horselike shape loomed out of the night.

"One more task," the Captain said in my ear. "Just one more, Vianne. The saddle has a low back; we shall do well enough. I will help you mount, then do you kick the stirrup free for me. Can you do as much?"

I nodded, though I sorely doubted I could. But Tristan helped lift me up, and my foot found the stirrup. I had only ever ridden sidesaddle before, and my skirts caught awfully, but I was finally on the broad back of a Guard warhorse, who stood blessedly still as Tristan shoved velvet out of his way and settled himself behind me. His arms came around me, and I held myself stiffly forward, afraid to relax.

There were orders, given softly, and the remainder of the King's Guard—little more than a dozen men out of more than four hundred—started down the slope of Mont di Cienne. Afterward it became a courtsong—the Dawning Ride, the minstrel called it, and had more than half of it wrong.

I would like to say I remember enough of it to correct the matter, but I do not. I fell asleep less than a dozen steps down the Mont.

Chapter Four

It took a moment to remember where I was, for I lay on a rough, dark wooden bed covered with homespun linen. There was a window, firmly shut, and no fire in the grate. There was a pitcher of water and a cup, which I seized with a will. Someone—probably the Captain—had taken off my garden-boots, put me in bed, and pulled the covers up over me. The large ease-chair by the fireplace had a blanket tossed over it, and a familiar torn red sash lay on the floor.

Had he slept there?

I finished a cup of water and poured another, looked for a watercloset door. I shuffled like an old woman. My knees hurt, and my shoulders—my entire body, for that matter. I had never been a-horseback for more than two hours at a time, for picnicking and easy riding when Lisele went hawking.

At the thought of Lisele a fresh pain arrowed my heart. I sank back down—was it a peasant's bed? Had I been left behind? I heard voices, but could not tell of what they spoke. I had a confused memory of riding, the Captain's voice in my ear, very soft but extremely important, and a hurried whispered conference while I leaned against something warm and hard, trying very hard to stay upright.

I finally went to the door that did not open to the water-closet and found it unlocked. I found myself in a low, pleasant hall that said "small house" instead of "inn," and followed the voices until I came to a flight of exceedingly rustic stairs.

"—cannot take the risk." Jierre di Yspres, I recognized his accent.

"I am with the Captain." This sounded like a young man—perhaps Pillipe di Garfour? I could not tell. "We cannot leave a *d'mselle* here. Tis not safe. The Duc will find her."

"Not if we leave her in the right place." Di Yspres, grimly determined to win the argument.

"I understand your concern." The Captain, now. "However, we will not leave her behind. If you cannot accept that, Jierre, you may strike out for whither you will. I will *not* leave her to be married to the Duc and deprive us of the chance to make him pay for his crimes."

"They slaughtered the rest of the Guard." An older male, one I did not know. I knew few of the King's Guard, except for those often set at Lisele's door and some of the officers. "Our fate's likely to be the same, rebellion or not. D'Arcenne's right. And what ails you, Jierre? What *chivalier* would leave a *d'mselle* here?"

"Tis trouble," di Yspres pointed out. "The Duc will pursue us if we have her—but if we simply flee we may escape with our lives."

"True," someone else said. "But again, what kind of a Guard would we be if we left the King's only remaining flesh and blood to a usurper?"

Only remaining? My heart beat dry and thick in my throat.

That cannot be true. If it is, how did it happen—and why did I never hear of it?

"We cannot afford to be blinded by sentiment, Tristan. What says she was not part of the plot?" Di Yspres, even more resolute. "And merely waiting for a chance to betray us to the Duc's henchmen? His spies are everywhere."

There was a hot, prickling silence, then the sound of a chair scraping back and metal leaving a sheath. "She came down into the donjon and risked her own life to set me free." The Captain, very softly. "She accepted my oath of service. Speak against her honor again, di Yspres, and I will have no choice but to hold you accountable."

A long pause, my nerves winding tighter and tighter. Nobody in their right mind would wish to duel Tristan d'Arcenne, even beaten and bruised as he was. I had not ever witnessed him duel, but I had heard.

There was a reason he was Captain of the Guard, and had held the position from such a young age.

"I go south," the Captain finally continued, "to Arcenne, to shelter in the mountains until we can gather an army and take the usurper from the throne. If the need grows dire, I will cross the border into Navarrin and petition their King for aid. And I am taking the Queen with me. You may accompany me if you like or go to the nine hells of Far Rus if you please, but if you come with me you travel as the Queen's Guard. With an oath of loyalty taken to Duchesse Vianne di Rocancheil, the true Heir to the throne of Arquitaine."

This must be a nightmare. I eased back along the hall. All the doors were locked except the one I had come through. That room had a window—but twas painted shut, for it did not budge when I tugged at it.

I turned back to the room, searching for anything that would help. I could not break the window, and I was on the second floor. And where exactly would I go?

Dear gods, anywhere but here. This is madness. There must be somewhere—

I heard footsteps and dropped down to sit on the bed, my hands clasped together, my braid disheveled and pushed forward over my shoulder, my skirts spread prettily as if I was on a divan at Court. The last bit was habitual, my busy fingers accomplishing it without any direction from the rest of me.

A courteous knock at the door. I had to try twice before I could say "Enter, an it please you" in anything resembling a normal voice.

The door opened and revealed Tristan d'Arcenne.

He had bathed, and his face looked both better—because he was relieved—and worse, because it was now apparent he had been very badly beaten. His hair was combed back damp, and he had no red sash. He wore a white linen shirt, a black leather doublet, and a pair of breeches. The *siang*-stone signet glinted on his left ring finger. He had not worn it yesterday—someone must have brought it to him. His sword was in its accustomed place, his boots freshly brushed, and his gloves thrust through his belt.

I felt even more rumpled. "Captain." I tilted my head just as I had seen Lisele often do.

Oh, but the thought of Lisele sent another arrow through my already-torn heart. My eyes prickled hotly.

"Duchesse." Equally formal. "You heard."

I shrugged. "I thought to come find you. Or to see if I had been left." I sounded wistful instead of polished, so I pulled my shoulders back, giving myself a sharp mental slap.

I was Duchesse di Rocancheil et Vintmorecy, and I had to act so.

"You did not leave me to the donjon, I would not repay your kindness by leaving you here." He examined me, and I saw he had a fall of cloth over one arm. I glanced at it, then up at him. He shrugged, blue eyes darkening. The swelling around his one eye had gone down quite a bit. "Well. One of the Guard—Tinan di Rocham. He is a slight boy, and we may belt in a pair of his breeches for you. You cannot ride in that dress. This will be more comfortable. And a group of men traveling will raise little suspicion, while a group of men traveling with a young noblewoman may cause comment." A high flag of color stood out along his cheekbones, a novel occurrence.

I glanced again at the clothes he carried. "'Tis true. I shall only be trouble to you."

He dismissed the notion with a single gesture, his signet glinting. "Your father and mother both have bloodlines tangling with the royal tree. Did you not ever wonder why you were brought to Court?"

"My father told me twas my mother's dying wish. I am a noblewoman of Arquitaine, and tis good enough for me. Lisele…" Grief rose again, and my eyes began to fill. I gazed at the floor, seeking to swallow the rock lodged in my throat.

The Captain swept the door shut behind him. "Gods," he said quietly, but with great force. He strode across the room, tossed the clothes on the bed beside me, and went to his knees, taking my cold hands in his. It was highly improper, but I could not move, I seemed nailed in place. "Vianne, you *must* listen. Whether you will or no, you have the last drop of untainted royal blood in Arquitaine. Lisele and Henri are both dead—*you are what is left*. It is your duty to free us from the Duc d'Orlaans." His eyes were burning now, and I found it increasingly difficult to breathe. "He killed your Princesse," the Captain continued, pitilessly. "Would you leave her death unavenged?"

It was a sharp pinch in a sensitive place. I started, and stared down at him. *What does this matter to you? I have nothing you want, Captain.* And I realized twas not true just as he spoke again. I did have something he wanted, and it rested on a chain around my throat.

"The Aryx has accepted you as its holder. And furthermore, I *need* you." A pause, while he struggled with the words. "An army will need a rallying point. If I am to somehow enlist the help of the King of Navarrin, he is a distant cousin of yours and your pretty face will put a debt on him. I ask you for duty, and for honor, Vianne. Please."

A horrible realization dawned. Tristan d'Arcenne, Captain of the King's Guard, had danced with me and followed me at Court to keep watch—to see if I was any danger to Lisele. If I had shown any sign that could be interpreted as ambition, I might have been spied upon more assiduously. He had been relieved to see me as he lay trapped in the donjon—not for myself, but because I was *useful*.

I was a way to serve the King, though the King was dead. As usual, I *myself* had very little value.

All my value lay in how I was to be used.

"Oh." Fresh tears filled my eyes. I had been a fool. Thank the gods I had never said, or done, anything *more* foolish.

He waited, examining my face. Anger washed through my whole body, a great hot spate of it. I had been shipped off to Court at nine years of age, needled and buffeted because I was not content to simply be an empty-headed featherbrain, watched constantly because I was Lisele's friend, and taunted because I chose to work with herbs and practical spells instead of gaudy, violent Court sorcery. Now, even a rash of death and conspiracy did not free me. I would be forced to marry a man who had murdered the King—the King my half-uncle, who had only addressed me directly twice in my life—or compelled to become a figurehead for a rebellion and a civil war that could devastate Arquitaine.

Yet in the midst of that anger was the vision of my Lisele, lying on her back on blue silk, her hair tangled and her chest full of blood. *Make certain.* I heard the terrible voice again. And the horrible crunching sounds as the Duc's Guard obeyed, making certain the witnesses to murder would forever hold their peace.

I licked my dry lips. "As you like, Captain d'Arcenne." *But do not think I will always be this easily manipulated.* I watched relief and fresh worry cross his face. He really was very handsome, though it would do me little good to mark it. *Fair face may hide a foul heart,* I heard the Comtesse Rochburre's voice intone piously from the mists of my childhood.

She had often glanced at Arioste di Wintrefelle while she did so; the Comtesse worried for Arioste.

I could have told her not to bother. Those with di Wintrefelle's wits and charm seldom fail to land afoot. It is the rest of us who should worry, for they tend to trample wherever they *do* land.

And now the vision of Arioste's crumpled body rose up in vivid, horrifying detail. Dear gods. Had the Blessed received her? They must—Jiserah welcomed all, she was the Merciful.

But still, I wondered, and the thought of her slumped, lifeless form—

"What's this?" His tone had taken an abrupt turn into something like concern. "Vianne?"

Do not use my name so freely, sieur. "I must dress myself." I sought to pull my hands from his. Much to my surprise, he allowed me. "There is little time. We may be tracked; the sooner we depart, the better."

"I cannot argue, but why are you suddenly so pliable? I distrust your meekness."

And well you should. He had sworn me service in the donjon of Palais D'Arquitaine, but I did not doubt he would just as easily kill me if it suited him—if I showed any sign of disloyalty. "I hate to be used, Captain. By Duc d'Orlaans or by Captain of the Guard, I hate to be *used.* I will accompany you and aid you however I may, because I owe it to Lisele." I felt my throat closing with tears and denied them, feeling my eyes burn. "But do not think for a *moment* you can force me into anything…dishonorable. I will act as the holder of the Aryx, but I am not a Queen. Surely someone else can be found. There are royal bastards everywhere."

He shrugged. His cheeks were pale and the bruises stood out in livid relief. "I do not seek to use you, *d'mselle.* I would never stoop so low."

"You have need of me to avenge the King's death, Captain." I scraped together every ounce of haughtiness I could muster. *And I half-believed the King when he said you favoured me. Silly me.* "For your duty. I have been doing *my* wretched duty all my life. I intend to continue in like manner. Now, I really must dress myself. I shall thank you to let me do so."

For some reason, his face suffused with anger and just as quickly smoothed. He made it to his feet and stalked away, his step almost soundless despite his boots. "There is hot water," he said over his shoulder. "Bathe quickly, tis no telling when we'll have another chance."

I stood shakily and gathered the garments. I have never been a clothier, but I thought they might fit me. Sometimes I had envied the freedom of breeches and men's clothing, and now I would take no joy in it.

He paused, his hand on the latch. "Duchesse?"

I glanced over my shoulder. His back was rigid, as if he was at parade-ground drill.

"Captain?" I answered cautiously.

"Why did you free me from the donjon? May I ask?"

Because I am a stupid, silly, thoughtless girl. Because I thought you would make this nightmare fade, as the nurse's voice makes a child's night-fears leave. "I could not bear the thought of your beheading, Captain. I am known to have a weak stomach."

He nodded, and the set of his shoulders eased. "I danced with you at the Fête of Flowers, did I not?"

My temper almost snapped. Why on earth did he ask *me*? He had never danced with anyone else; surely he should have remembered the occasions! "No. At Lisele's Coming-of-Age, and at the Festival of Skyreturn. Both times you caused quite a bit of comment. Though I wondered why, since neither were *memorable* occasions." The last was an unjustified cut, and I was briefly ashamed to hear myself utter an insult so far beneath me.

"You remembered." He swept the door open.

I wish I did not. "I hold grudges," I shot after him.

"Tis not what gossip says of you." With that parting sally, he closed himself out of the room.

I strangled the desire to run to the door, wrench it open, and scream something nasty after him. I looked about for something to throw, but there was nothing, and neither action was fit for a Duchesse. So I settled for hissing at the door in exasperation and carried the clothes into the watercloset.

Yet I must admit the annoyance was a tonic, and the anger made my fingers cease their trembling.

Chapter Five

I had a momentary difficulty with the doublet's laces. The doublet was of leather and far too large, but it hid the curve of breasts and hips. I plaited my hair and found a ribbon in the bag I had filched.

I wondered if I should cut my hair to pass for a boy. One of the men could lend me a kerchief or hat to hide it, perhaps.

I struggled back into my garden-boots and dropped the Aryx down my shirt, cursing to myself as my hand brushed my emerald ear-drops. I had forgotten them completely, and now I looked at them with fresh eyes, as the survivor of a shipwreck might gaze on something that had once been a ship's pride.

Scallops of silver, delicately whorled, filigreed around large emeralds burning dark green like hedgewitchery itself, smaller chiming bits of silver and similarly caged, tiny uncut emeralds depending from the larger gems. They were a prize, the finest work Amercio Tavanche of the royal jewelers did four years ago, and dedicated to me by the *artiste*. I usually preferred to patronize bookbinders and scholars, but Tavanche hailed from my home province and had presented himself—and been laughed almost into tears by no few of the ladies, since he'd tripped and landed face-first during his presentation.

Fortunately, I had some little weight with the royal jewelers, and had introduced Tavanche to the head artisan of their workshop. The ear-drops had excited no little marvel at their presentation at Court during the annual Salonne, and their gifting to me handled far more adroitly by Tavanche than his presentation had been. I wore them habitually—Arioste would say I had no other jewels, but this was not true. I merely liked these overmuch.

I weighed them in my palm for a moment, and slipped them into my pocket.

The dress I bundled up and decided to carry downstairs with my servant-girl's bag. I hoped Arioste's maid had survived the carnage in Lisele's rooms. I could not remember her body, and did not want to think too deeply lest I do so. My own maid, the shy but occasionally tart-tongued Meridia, had been granted a week's leave to visit her ailing mother, and right glad of it I was. At least away from the Palais she was safe enough, though at the time it had annoyed me to put up with the clumsy fingers of other ladyservants.

This time, I had to take a deep breath before leaving the safety of the room. I heard the murmur of voices again, and set off down the hall. Each step was more difficult than the last.

Panic beat under my ribs as I reached the stairs, and I stood irresolute atop the flight. Men's voices resounded below. Without the protection of a woman's skirts, what could I expect from them?

The problem was larger than that, though. Without Lisele's protection, how could I manage in the world? I had never been on my own, safely trammeled by childhood and later by the rules of Court protocol and etiquette. I knew what was expected each day of Court, when to sit and when to stand, who was of the sword and who was of the robe, who was of the lower order; and I knew each arcane bit of manners for the festivals, feasts, and fêtes.

I was not such a fool to think this was knowledge prized outside the Palais.

I could not depend on Tristan d'Arcenne, that much was certain. He wanted his revenge and a biddable Queen Pretender; I was only a hedgewitch with an accident of royal blood.

The Aryx warmed, hard metal against my skin. I lifted my chin. *Duchesse Vianne di Rocancheil et Vintmorecy. Walk so, and speak thusly, and never forget you are of noble birth.* I heard again Comtesse Rochburre's voice as she taught a gaggle of noble girls how to behave at Court, and imagined I was sweeping in procession down the stairs into the Great Ballroom at Lisele's side, the train of ladies behind us in their silk and velvet and jewels. After a moment's thought, I pulled the Aryx from its hiding and settled it against my chest. Let Jierre di Yspres feast his eyes on *that*, and we would have no more talk of leaving me to the Duc's mercy.

For by now, you see, I had decided I had little wish to be left so.

I came down the stairs slowly, one at a time, pausing between each as if waiting for the train of a dress to catch pace with me. By the time I was halfway, they noticed me; three steps after they were rising; when I reached the bottom of the stairs they had all removed their feathered hats. I stood on the last step and surveyed the room with the cool haughtiness of a Court lady. My gaze moved unhurried from one man to the next, and most dropped their eyes immediately. The ones that did not looked down after only a few moments.

My looks are nothing special, as the ladies of the Court reminded me so very often. But a good posture and the right expression can make any woman regal.

Of course, my Lisele had called me beautiful, but I always laughed. I knew my place. Had not I been taught it often enough?

"Good morn to you, *sieurs*." I addressed them clearly, as if I were administering the beginning of a dance. Tristan d'Arcenne stood by the fireplace, blue eyes bright with something I could not decipher. Relief that I was playing the rôle for his troupe? Perhaps. "I have you to thank for my escape from the Palais, and I hear I have you to thank for the relief of traveling to safety."

A few of them colored, and Jierre di Yspres, in his place next to Tristan, stiffened—a movement I caught easily at the corner of my gaze.

Good.

There was a slight cough, and one of them—a slight young lad barely past his first shave—stepped forward. He had dark hair and the angular features of a mountain noble. "Tinan di Rocham, Your Majesty." He clutched his red-feathered hat in both hands. He looked absolutely mortified, but proud at the same time. We were of a size—I am not too tall for a woman, and he was slight and young—and it was his clothes I wore.

"My thanks for the camouflage, *chivalier*." *Now let us see what comes of it.*

His cheeks turned crimson, his hand darted down. His sword whispered from its sheath.

The rest of them tensed to a man, and that was gratifying. But Tinan di Rocham simply reversed the blade and stepped forward until he could drop to one knee at the foot of the stairs. "I owe you my service. Accept my oath, *d'mselle*." He all but stuttered over the words. "I mean, Your Majesty. If I may be so bold."

My stomach turned on itself.

But their Captain expected somewhat of me, and were I to cut the young lad now his shame would be overwhelming. So I smiled and nodded gravely, reached down to touch two fingers of my free hand to the hilt. "I accept your oath, *Chivalier* Tinan di Rocham. My thanks." I sounded serious, though lunatic laughter had to be sternly repressed.

He rose, returned the weapon to its sheath, and bowed again, a Court bow that was a little jerky but surprisingly polished otherwise. "A pleasure to be in your service, Your Majesty."

Oh, gods. Do not let him address me as such. "Tis merely Vianne di Rocancheil, *chivalier*. I thank you." Faintly improper—had we been at Court, he would have addressed me as Duchesse. But I smiled prettily, giving him the compliment. It was surely not too soon to begin gathering allies.

I suspected I would need them, and shame filled me again. Cold calculation of this level was somewhat new, and I disliked it. I especially disliked that it seemed so natural.

He blushed even harder, and a murmur ran through them all.

A stocky, black-haired man with an amazing mustache—it drooped past his chin and was waxed in the Navarre style—came forward, and repeated the process. "Adersahl di Parmecy et Villeroche, Your Majesty." He had a clear carrying baritone of surprising profundity. "I owe you my service, *d'mselle*. Accept my oath."

I repeated my acceptance. When he was finished, another came forth, and another, until each of them had knelt before me. I thought some of them might even mean it. Jierre di Yspres was last of all but one, and he gazed at the Aryx as he knelt before me, his swordhilt proffered. "Forgive me, Your Majesty. I owe you my service. Accept my oath, an it please you."

I studied him for a long moment, watched color rise in his cheeks and die away. "Very well." I touched his swordhilt. "I accept your oath, *chivalier*."

He rose, slowly. Standing on the bottom step made us almost eye to eye, and I refused to look up at him, forcing him to stoop a little. My mouth had turned dry as summer road-dust. "I shall forgive you, if you forgive me the trouble I have no doubt caused you."

He mumbled something and looked stunned. The dress hanging over my other arm rustled a bit, and I wondered how ridiculous I looked carrying it.

But I had more to endure. Captain d'Arcenne was suddenly before me, and his sword rang free. He sank to one knee again, surprisingly fluid for one so battered. "I owe you my service, Vianne di Rocancheil. Accept my oath."

Gods, did not you already do this? I inclined my head gracefully, touched the hilt. My neck ached with tension, and I hoped my stomach would not start loudly demanding breakfast to embarrass me. "I accept your oath, Captain d'Arcenne. My thanks."

I did not ask him to call me simply Vianne.

He did not call me *Your Majesty*.

We were perhaps even.

He rose, swept me a bow, and took charge of the occasion. "Breakfast, *d'mselle*? You had no dinner last night, and you must be hungry." He also took the dress from me and handed it away, and I did not ask whether twas to be hidden or burned.

It mattered little, though the cloth could be sold. If they left me without protection, I would need rather more wits than I suspected I possessed, not to mention some money, to survive.

I set my chin stubbornly, though I was famished. "I will not be a burden, Captain. Are we pressed for time?"

"Not so pressed we cannot spare a few moments." Jierre di Yspres was thin and dark, having the lean saturnine face of the south of Arquitaine. Most of the surviving Guard were younger sons of noble families. It was sad to see only these had survived—or remained loyal.

I was soon seated at table with a bowl of porridge and a round red apple, as well as a steaming cup of chai. I concentrated on eating neatly and quickly, Court manners keeping my smallest finger crooked at the correct angle and my spine straight, my ears and eyes wide open to catch every nuance.

Our refuge was a small stone house. I heard the rumble of carts passing by, and the clip-clop of hooves. Sunlight fell in golden bars through wavering glass windows. There was no fire in the grate, and I wondered how all of them had slept. Later I learned each Guard had a bedroll rolled into a compact cylinder and attached to the back of his saddle.

I further wondered whose house this was and looked for any sign of the owner, but there was none.

Observe, Levontus of Tiberia had written in his most famous treatise, *and many questions will answer themselves. Always, observe.* 'Tis far more pithy in Tiberian, which is a language boiled down to its essence, but it is far from the worst advice for making one's way in a dangerous world.

Some of the Guard readied the horses, others sipped at cups of chai, a few went upstairs and I thought perhaps they stood watch. Jierre and Tristan spread out a map at the table and began to confer in low tones.

"'Tis a hard choice," Jierre began. "The garrisons or the forest."

The Captain studied the map, a vertical line between his charcoal eyebrows. I took a scalding gulp of chai.

At the Palais, judging by the fall of sunlight, Lisele would just be waking. Her morning chocolat would arrive on its little silver tray, and I would brush her hair. Lady Arioste would sing softly, plucking at her gittern, and Comtesse Rochburre would watch us all with her magisterial eye, ready to chastise for any impropriety. I would steal a scone from Lisele's tray and perch in the window seat to eat. There would be morning jokes and laughter, chatter from the younger girls, and of a while they would ask me to tell a riddle or a tale. *A wholesome tale,* Comtesse Rochburre would inevitably interject, and Lisele would laugh, tossing her dark hair. Arioste would make a sharp comment, and I would ignore it, though Lisele's eyes would flash…

I finished the porridge, but found I could not eat the apple. I set it upon the table and stared at the bloom of red and yellow on its firm skin as I sipped. I was still staring, smelling the dust of the North Tower, when I heard my name.

"—Vianne?"

The room had emptied without my notice; only d'Arcenne and I remained.

I blinked back hot swelling water. Swallowed, hard, and raised my face to his. Some explanation seemed necessary. I grasped for one. "I ate apples. Yesterday. In the North Tower."

He nodded, rolling up the map and tucking the mapweight in a small pouch at his belt. "I thought it likely, by your look. Do you need the privy before we start?"

"I should," I said thinly, and made it to my feet. It was passing strange to move without the weight of skirts around my legs. I had almost reached the stairs when he spoke again.

"Vianne?"

Do not use my name so freely. But I could not say it, could I. Not while depending on his good graces for my continued survival.

I half-turned, my hand on the stair's railing. "Leave me alone." I said it so quietly he may not have heard.

"You look…" He paused, searching for the word.

I supplied it for him, setting my foot firmly on the first stair. "The word you seek is *ridiculous, sieur.* I am wearing a Guard's uniform and my garden-boots, and I will mayhap be forced to shear myself to pass as a boy." I took another step. This one was not half so difficult, and I thought perchance they might grow easier if I simply focused solely on the one before me. Levontus of Tiberia had some very severe thoughts on the question of how far into the future one should plan. Diodoria Siclonus, of course, disagreed with him.

I brought myself back to the present with an effort. *Keep your wits, Vianne.* "I know very well I am only the silly, gawky, hedge-witch provincial that lucked into Court because her grand-dam was lightskirted. I know very *well* what I look like, Captain d'Arcenne. Please do not remind me."

With that, I swept up the stairs and left him standing. Twas satisfying to have the last word for once.

I emerged blinking into morning sunshine, wishing for a kerchief to hide my braided hair, and found myself in a small stone bailey. Jierre di Yspres and a tall blond Guard were already mounted, but Tristan was engaged in a last-minute conference with the young, slim Tinan, who broke away to present me with his hat. It had a magnificent feather, but was a touch too big for me. However, when I coiled my braid atop my head, it fit a little better.

"I suppose I look a fool." I glanced at the youthful *chivalier*, to gauge how idiotic I seemed. He grinned and ran his hand through his shoulder-length dark hair.

"Oh, no, *d'mselle*. You look, well. Very beautiful."

He uttered it in a tone of earnest reverence, and I was hard-pressed to swallow a laugh. I had tucked the Aryx inside my shirt, but I thought I could still see it reflected in his eyes.

"My thanks for the compliment, *chivalier*," I replied gracefully, offering my hand. He took it automatically and almost dropped it once he realized what he'd done. I covered for him as a lady could, moving forward, and we ended up ambling across the bailey as if on promenade. "I must say I disagree. In any case, it matters little. You are of Rocham?"

He nodded, his chest rising with pride. "My father's people are the riverfolk, but I favour my mother and she's mountain-folk. Our House is on the bank in Rocham, white colonnades and a red roof. My mother hates the roof, she says tis not well-mannered, and my father says tis well-mannered enough to keep the rain out and she should not complain. Then my mother remarks something, usually under her breath, and my father usually smiles, and—"

This time a thin, nervous laugh did escape me. It was not so amazing; he was very charming and I was exhausted, though I had slept so heavily. My laughter had the quality of a weary old cane being used for the last time. Hard on its heels the image of Lisele rose up, still and bloody while I was breathing, and I sobered.

Di Rocham saw this. "You look troubled, *d'mselle*."

And you are not, young man? We should all be troubled, the more the better. But while you think me distracted, let us gather some information. "Where are we?"

"We are on the outskirts of the Citté, a house di Yspres bought some time ago. The Captain believes in planning for every possible contingency."

"If it pleases you"—Captain d'Arcenne's tone cut through the morning hush—"we have wasted half the day, and must be setting out."

Tinan dropped my hand with a hurried bow and mounted his horse. He and Jierre trotted to the bailey entrance, and the tall blond Guard—his name was Jespre, I remembered, like the stone—followed, casting a sharp glance over his shoulder. I was left alone with Captain d'Arcenne.

I regarded him. There I stood in sunlight, foolishly dressed in a man's shirt and breeches and my garden-boots, which were good supple leather and waterproof but hardly dainty, and Tinan's hat perched firmly atop my braid, covering my hair. I sought the first cut of the conversation, since the scholarly Juen Servanties of Navarre's arid Erágon held it as a rule that to hold the offensive, in any verbal battle, was an advantage not to be thrown away. "Well. I suppose I am afoot, unless you have found me a horse."

"Buying a horse would attract attention, and stealing one would not be meet." He indicated his mount. Now I could see it was a large gray warhorse, and I felt my throat dry again. I was used to placid mares and occasionally a sprightly gelding, not the massive beasts the Guard bred and trained. "This is Arran. Come and meet him, Vianne; he is honored to bear the Queen."

I folded my arms. "Please, Captain. Do not name me something I am not, I pray."

His tone turned brusque and cool. "You are more our Queen than d'Orlaans is a king. What did I do to earn the sharp edge of your tongue today?"

The sharp edge is the only edge you shall receive, sieur. *To think I believed the King's jest.* "Time is wasting, Captain. Am I to walk, and the rest of you can trot along in front of me? A pretty sight that will make."

He moved forward, caught me by the waist, and lifted me as if I weighed nothing. My foot found the stirrup and I was in the low saddle in a trice, my entire body protesting. I had spent more time yesterday a-horseback than I had in the entire month previous, and my knees and shoulders were deeply bruised. But I would gift myself to the Duc wrapped in Festival silk before I showed Captain d'Arcenne any weakness.

I kicked free of the stirrups; the Captain swung up behind me. I held myself stiffly away from him as before. I did not know how long I could do so—but do so I would, for as long as was required. At least the saddle did not have a high back, which would force him to perch on the beast's rump. It had to be uncomfortable.

I found the thought of his discomfort pleased me.

"You will wear yourself out," he said in my ear as he twitched the reins.

Arran had a smooth gait, thank the Blessed, and I felt a little more secure when we trotted out of the bailey and joined the others, taking our place near the middle of a loose file down the cobbled street. The thunder of wagon wheels and voices rose in a wave, breaking over us. We were on the quays of the River Airenne, which explained the arrangement of the small stone house. It had in all likelihood been a boarding house for river-sailors at one time. Nobody took notice of us—we could have been any noble hunting party, bent on hawking or riding down prey in the copses and woods around the Citté.

The Captain was taut and alert, almost starting every time a barge driver shouted or a riversailor cursed. He remained tense as we went along the river, making for the King's woods, and a tide of beggars and human flotsam scattered in front of the Guard. They moved with an alacrity that bespoke familiarity with parties of noble-blooded hunters—for as the proverb says, *Whips sting when a noble hunter is hurried.*

Jierre di Yspres led the file, and he turned onto the road that pierced the wood. The sound of the quays faded slowly behind us. The horses picked up their pace to a steady trot.

I had thought I could lean away from the Captain all day, but I was simply too tired. By the time we reached the woods I had begun to sink. Besides, the saddle was too small, even if its back was low enough to perch on.

"Ease yourself, Vianne," he said in my ear. "We have a long way to go, and 'twill tire you. Best just to rest."

I did not believe he cared if I rested or not, but if I dropped dead of exhaustion it would slow him further and cost him his pretender to the throne. And there was little harm in it now, surely. The world had ended like a carriage overturning; we were merely wandering through the wreckage.

So I sank back ever so slightly and watched the countryside of Arquitaine pass on either side. We had been riding for perhaps an hour when a low whistle trilled from somewhere behind us.

As if by Court sorcery, the Guard faded back into the trees on either side of the road. The Captain took our horse to the side, behind a screen of sprawling lauryl bushes going wild. The horse stayed absolutely still, and I drew in a deep breath, held it until the world turned to a painted screen splotched with whirling colors.

"They will not see us." He sounded so sure, and I caught a

whiff of Court sorcery, blending with the hedges to screen us from view. The charm was so slight it would escape notice, unless our pursuers were going slowly and using a showing-spell.

I strained my ears, heard nothing.

Then, hoofbeats.

They came down the road at a gallop, and at their head rode thin, hungry Garonne di Narborre, angular and intent in a blue doublet. They wore the embroidered surcoats of King's Messengers though any fool could see they were not, for they wore swords. The surcoats held black braid meaning a King had died, and gold braid meaning a new King had been crowned.

But the Duc does not have the Aryx. At the coronation, he will have to produce it. Ah, that is why they gallop.

I touched the hard warm pulsing of the Aryx, pushed under my shirt as an afterthought. It gave a double beat, and I felt an odd shifting inside my head. I was only a hedgewitch, not a well-practiced Court sorcerer like di Narborre, who was rumored to have dueled more than one man with Court sorcery and killed him. The King had been angered after one particular duel, but had not done anything except put Garonne in the Duc's service instead of his own, since the Duc was such a Court sorcerer himself.

Now I wondered what more there was to the tale of di Narborre and murder, and what else the King might have done that rumor spoke not of.

The women of the Court were sometimes cutthroat ambitious, and the dancing for station never ceased. Some of the ladies even played Court men against each other, for privilege and position. I had been drawn into more than one game and usually acquitted myself well. Not only that, but twas my duty to catch intrigues meant to trip my Princesse, and I did a fair job of it.

There had been a particular affair involving my Princesse, the Lady Courceline Maritine, a batch of silly love letters, and a Duc's Guard named Arrebourne. The letters could have forced a scandal, and Lady Maritine was merely misled instead of over-ambitious, but it had still taken much thought and care to re-trieve the letters from Arrebourne's clutches. Of course, there had been an odd thing or two about that affair, and now I won-dered who Arrebourne had been reporting to. I had consigned that question to the realm of mystery and Kimyan's Riddles long ago, and been well rid of it. But now…had there been a deeper intrigue I had saved Lisele from, all unknowing?

I took in another deep, jagged breath, and the Captain's hand clapped over my mouth.

My temper snapped. How *dare* he? I forgot myself entirely, and I suppose only the shocks of the previous day could have made me do what I did next.

I bit the Captain of the King's Guard. I sank my teeth in and worried like a trained terrier.

His arms tightened, silently. He whispered, a breath of air brushing my cheek. "Do you truly wish to be dragged back to the Duc, wedded and bedded in less than a night? Being d'Orlaans's Consort might make you wish you had stayed in the North Tower, Duchesse."

I sank my teeth in harder, past caring. How *dare* he? I had gone straight to the King instead of planning to blackmail the Captain, though twould not have mattered an hour later what I had seen and whyfor. I had even rescued him from the *donjon*, by the Blessed. And he *accused* me?

How could I have thought he fancied me?

The Duc's Guard passed us by, and Captain d'Arcenne took his hand from my mouth. I had not broken the skin, but I had come close, and on his bruised hand besides. "Now, what was that, Vianne?" Very softly.

"What did you think I was about to do?" I whispered back fiercely, turning my head, suddenly very aware of his arm around my waist holding the reins. "Scream for rescue from the Duc's hired murderers? They killed my Princesse, Captain, and I am afraid they will do the same to me—or worse, if I can believe your warnings. And yet you think—you think I would—" I was almost too furious to speak, though I whisper-hissed. "You swear me obedience, you give me your oath, and then you act *thus*? Some Captain you are, no more loyal than—"

"Careful, *d'mselle*." The same quiet tone, even and without temper. "Be careful what you brand me as."

I subsided into silent seething, so furious tiny red speckles danced a pavane before my eyes, but long years of Court training made me loosen my limbs, seeking control. *A lady should be languid even in anger,* I heard the Comtesse Rochburre say in her low, adamant tone. *If you are angry, you cannot plan your revenge.*

I schooled my face and my trembling hands, and forced my shoulders down. A fine tremor ran all through me. "I should have left you in that donjon," I muttered, unwilling to let him have the final word.

"Your pardon, *d'mselle*." The low conversational tone was gone. Did he now sound *surprised*? I was past caring. "I have no doubt of your loyalty—I simply thought the sight of di Narborre would be a shock to you."

Speak softly, Vianne. You need this man's protection. "You thought aright. But if I cried out at every shock I would not have lasted long at Court."

"True. Forgive me."

"Perhaps." I fell into stiff silence. *Why would you crave my forgiveness? It will do you no good, and me even less.*

After a long while there was another low whistle, and we moved out onto the road again. Jierre di Yspres rode back, brought his horse next to Tristan's. "We could have slaughtered them, Captain." But there was no heat to it.

Nor was there in the Captain's reply. "And warned the Duc of our exact direction? We shall strike off the Road soon enough."

"How does she?" Jierre's dark eyes moved over me. "You look pale, *d'mselle*."

"I am extremely unhappy, *chivalier*. I wish I were home in my herb garden." It was impolitic, though, to anger them. So I let the corners of my mouth curl up into a bright Court smile. "But if I am to be pursued the length of Arquitaine, I cannot think of better company than the King's Guard."

Di Yspres blinked, and swept me a correct little half-bow over his pommel. "We are glad of your company, *d'mselle*." His eyes met the Captain's. Meaningless, Court-pretty words, and if they thought me a liar, well, they were half right.

I felt the Captain's shrug. "We have far to ride today, and we must be doubly careful now. We shall leave the road on the outskirts of Tierrce-di-Arbon."

Jierre nodded. "So be it." He wheeled his horse around and trotted for the head of the Guards, who were waiting patiently. They fell into line behind him, Tristan taking a place three-quarters of the way back. They were silent, the more-or-less half-dozen, now my only defense against…what?

A shiver jarred me when I thought of the Duc d'Orlaans's ring-laden, manicured hands on my flesh.

I would kill myself before I let that happen. And after yesterday, I might well consider it a mercy. Sometimes a noble-woman's only avenue was to take refuge in the Blessed…but that was a terrifyingly bleak thought.

Instead, I turned my mind to methods. I wondered if I would have the strength to use a knife—or a hatpin, like the Lady di Courcenne in the courtsongs. I was no Tiberian, and the idea of opening my veins turned me decidedly weak in the knees.

Yet a knife was not the only way. I could mix a poison draught; any hedgewitch worth the name could do so. And I was a fairly good hedgewitch, even if I was a very bad Court sorcerer. All I would need was a moment's freedom in a garden and a few moments more in a stillroom. Or, were I pressed even further, a window high enough and the open air, and a stone paving below. That would require no hedgewitchery. Nothing but enough momentary courage to fling myself to freedom.

If I had strength enough to wait in the North Tower for darkness and creep into the donjons to free a captive, of what else might I be capable? I had done so many impossible things in the past two days I was fast losing count.

Tristan waited until we were farther into the small woods before speaking again. "I misjudged you. Your pardon, *d'mselle*."

"Misjudged me?" I could hardly believe my own senses. When did Captain d'Arcenne misjudge *anything*? And then a hidden meaning to those words arose, and cold sweat suddenly bathed me. *Misjudged* me—and was I now superfluous?

If I was, what would be done to me?

But he perhaps took my sudden silence for anger, for he spoke again. "Twas wrong of me to think you would cry out to the Duc's men, even for a moment, for any reason. Forgive me."

The sound of Tristan d'Arcenne begging my pardon again was gratifying, but less gratifying than it would have been a week ago at Court. I sighed and took my hand away from the pommel to rub delicately at my aching eyes, even if it would ruin my looks. Relief threatened to unstring my nerves. "Forgiven, Captain. Do not trouble yourself further."

"Why so formal today, Vianne?" As if we were not fleeing for our lives, riding double on a Guard horse because a palfrey could not be bought or stolen. The absurdity of the situation rose up to choke me, and I had to wrestle down the pained sound seeking to escape my lips. Leaf-dappled sunlight made the line of horses and men a very pretty painting, one I would have passed without thought in a gallery or at the yearly Salonne.

How could I answer him? Formality was my refuge, and he would not cease using my name so freely I had all the more reason to use it. "You watched me at Court." I felt him tense again.

He reached up with one gloved hand as if he needed to scratch at his cheek, and I leaned away from him. He replaced his hand on the reins, and I relaxed slightly.

"I did," he admitted. Did I imagine him tensing again?

"To see if I showed any sign of ambition, to see if I was a danger to Lisele." *You do not know me. She was my only anchor. My Princesse.*

"Is that what you think?" Thoughtful, as if I had just posed him a riddle.

I watched the sunlight move fluidly between leaf-shadows. Twas a beautiful day, but Lisele's eyes would never see it. Had they laid her in the Royal Tombs under the Ladytemple, the Great Dama? She would have wanted black velvet sewn with pearls, and I had not even been able to braid her hair one final time. Instead, I had left for my early-morn digging in the garden with a jest, lightly and laughingly promising to return with an armful of stinkcabbage for a nosegay.

I brought myself back to the present with an effort. Even the small spots of sunlight jabbed at my tender head through my burning eyes. "I have no doubt it fits neatly into your plans for revenge to have a bastard royal with the Aryx at your side, no matter how unsatisfactory she may prove to be. I further have no doubt you would kill me, King's Captain, if I showed any sign of second thoughts."

He had no easy reply, and there the matter lay. Tears rose again, and I denied them. I would weep no more. I swore it to myself, as I rode in front of the Captain with my heart aching and my throat full of terror and grief. Court had held few friends, but I had Lisele's protection; the open friendship of the Heir not something to be derided. Now…

Now I was adrift, and who knew what I would be required to do in order to merely survive?

Chapter Six

We left the Road after a hurried lunch of bread and cheese near the blue-roofed town of Tierrce-di-Arbon, famous for the quality of its woven cotton cloth, and struck out across fields and rolling plains toward the great forest of Shirlstrienne. The small stands had begun to run together in larger groves, and there was one large enough to shelter us from sight.

I was too exhausted to care by the time the Captain lifted me down from the horse's back. My feet met solid ground and I stumbled, but he righted me gently and led me to the fire one of the younger Guards had started by flintstrike. I collapsed to my knees, then eased gratefully down to sit, biting back a small moan. Tinan appeared, wrapping a blanket around my shoulders. A cup of sweet red traveling wine was deposited in my hands by a whip-thin Guard with dark eyes and a neatly cut mop of light brown hair. I searched for his name—Jai di Montfort—to thank him, and he swept me a bow the envy of any courtier. I took off di Rocham's hat and let my braid down, sighing in relief.

I sipped at the wine and watched the Guard make camp,

thanking the Blessed I did not have to find a convenient tree to serve as a privy yet. The Captain would probably insist on setting a guard over me while I did so, and that potential embarrassment seemed a final, ultimate humiliation. Why having to relieve myself in the woods was such a horrifying prospect after all I had so recently endured I have no idea, but so it seemed at that moment.

I finally settled myself with my legs to the side, on dry leafmould with no skirts to worry about and the weight of them sorely missed. I drew the blanket about me, cupping my hands around the wine. Even though twas late spring, the night would be chill.

I wondered where I would sleep that night and gazed at the fire, just now taking its form as a merry blaze. One of the Guards set a tripod over it, and another brought a cauldron filled with water from the brook just to the south. I gazed into the flames and took a deep breath, finding my hands shaking again. Tears welled up.

Woodsmoke, horse and leather and males, spring greenery and the flat tang of mineral water from the brook—it was very pretty, and had we been a Court party out for a firefly fête or a night picnic, I would have no doubt enjoyed myself immensely.

I was occupied trying to swallow treacherous tears when Jierre di Yspres approached me carefully, and swept his hat off. He made a graceful movement and ended up sitting next to me, far more lightly than I had collapsed.

"*D'mselle*?" Cautious, he did not glance at me while he spoke. "May I have a word?"

I stared into the fire, kept a sob suppressed in my chest, and could only give him a nod.

It was not polite, but he accepted it. "I know I cannot be your favourite person right at the moment, Your Majesty."

I managed to speak. "Oh, for the sake of every god that ever was, address me as Duchesse, or even Vianne. Please." *Majesty* was Lisele's title, and I would not wear it. Not unless forced.

He paused. A tear trickled down my cheek, but I dashed it away and swallowed the rest with a gulp of wine. I would *not* cry. "Vianne, then. If I may." It was the first time I ever heard him sound anything other than disdainful of me. "I must beg your pardon, *d'mselle*. The world has turned upside down for all of us, and we know not whom to trust. I did not seek to make you my enemy, I merely wished to help Tristan. He is a fine Captain."

"No doubt." I stared at the blurring fire. The urge to weep retreated; I was simply too tired to sustain it. "I keep no grudges, *sieur chivalier*. I have had too many held against me." I offered my hand. "A truce between us, then?"

He nodded gravely and bent over my fingers. "As you say, *d'mselle*. Might I offer you counsel?"

I took my hand back, decidedly. *Ah, so he has a purpose. Caution, Vianne.* "If you like." Someone made a comment on the other side of the camp, and there was laughter—raucous but well-disciplined.

"The Captain seems harsh." Jierre seemed to search for proper words. "He has had a strict duty since he was a boy, and takes it seriously. He has sworn you his oath and means to keep it, *d'mselle* di Rochancheil. If his method of keeping it is not to your liking, I beg of you to remember that he has…well…"

I watched the flames twist as Jierre paused. I finally sighed, taking pity on him. I almost laughed at the turn events had taken. Truly the world had tipped sideways, like a smashed orrery.

"Lieutenant," I said, with all the gentleness I could scrape together, "tis not necessary to make apologies or excuses for the Captain. He is merely doing his duty to the King. Such loyalty is to be commended." *There.* I took a sip of the wine. Foul, too harsh, and unwatered, but what could one expect while fleeing? *Now will you leave me alone? That is my only wish.*

"Tis not his duty to the King now, *d'mselle* Vianne. Tis his duty to the Queen. Like it or not, you are the sole blood royal left not tainted by regicide. The rest have been assassinated."

The meaning of his words penetrated a fog of exhaustion. I stared at his lean dark face, my jaw suspiciously loose. "What?"

"For the last four years, the…ah, *hidden* branches of the King's line have been falling prey to unfortunate accidents." Jierre dropped his voice and leaned close to me. I felt my fingers grow even colder. "Simeon di Rothespelle fell from his horse—someone cut his saddlegirth. Trecie di Colbreux et Vantcienne and her brother were both poisoned; killspells were suspected. Marquisse di Faintroy fell from a casement to a stone bailey—and she had a visitor that day none can identify." Jierre nodded as I felt comprehension cross my weary face. "There were others, but that was enough to convince me—and convince the King, too. Tristan has been hunting this conspiracy for years now, and had a watch set over you at Court, lest an attempt be made on your life."

My jaw no longer threatened. It had dropped, but I closed my mouth hurriedly. It did not do for a lady to gape as a fish. *What else? The Moon will surely turn to cheese in the sky, and pigs begin to sing.* Yes, impossible things were coming thick and fast now. "But I never saw—," I whispered.

"Of course you never saw." Jierre's low voice turned dark. "Do you think the Captain that inept? And everyone knows he—"

I do not wish to know. "What more could everyone know, that I do not? No, do not tell me. Please, *sieur*. I can stand no more."

"I am sorry, *d'mselle*." I do believe he was. "I beg you, and it please you, to be kind to him."

Kind to him? "I loosed him from the Palais donjon. He requires more kindness from me?" I had not meant to say as much aloud. Attending Court does mean one is *required* to do much one would rather not; I knew my duty and had always performed it to exaction. What more could di Yspres want? What more did *any* of them want?

"True." Jierre shifted closer, his voice dropping still further. "Yet there is another donjon holding him, *d'mselle*. And you hold the key to that one."

What, the man is playing riddlesharp with me? I am not the opponent I once was at that game, sieur. But, miserably, I knew what he meant. Jierre sought to tell me d'Arcenne would kill himself avenging the King's death or seeking to put me on the throne—and his faithful lieutenant did not like the thought.

I did not blame him. The thought of d'Arcenne's death sent a strange panicked bolt through me. I had to find a way to loose the Captain from the chains of his own sworn oath. And not so incidentally, loose myself from this nightmarish conundrum.

Dear blessed gods, what am I to do now? But I am well used to planning; one cannot sponsor a fête or an entrance at the Salonne without overcoming some practical obstacles. One furthermore cannot hunt an intrigue, manage a small independence, or stock a stillroom without overcoming obstacles and stumbling-blocks, either. *Or* deal with a fractious Princesse.

I calculated swiftly and cast my dice. "Then I will need your help, Lieutenant," I whispered. "Can you make a horse ready for me, not tonight…Mayhap tomorrow night?"

Jierre gave me a strange look. His eyes narrowed.

"I do not seek d'Arcenne's death, either." I could swear his jaw dropped at my words. We were trading surprises, the lieutenant and I. "He will kill himself for what he thinks is duty. I think I can free him of it—but I need your help to do so. I can give you the Aryx and ride south for the ports, draw off pursuit and buy you time to take the Seal elsewhere."

He stared at me as if I were mad. "*D'mselle—*"

"Your Majesty?" It was Pillipe di Garfour, looming over me with a bowl in his hand. "'Tis stew, and hot, even if it is not Court fare. Tinan is not a very good cook, but he is better than some."

"Damn me with faint praise," Tinan called from the fire. "You had half the cooking of this, di Garfour, if 'tis gone wrong you share the blame."

Rudely recalled, I reached up. Di Garfour almost jerked his hand back, as if my touch singed him.

Jierre di Yspres made it to his feet. He stared down at me with something like astonishment. It struck me di Garfour and di Rocham sought to make me smile, so I dutifully gave them my bright, interested Court expression. "I am sure 'tis well enough. I am hungry, I did not have my chai yesterday."

My stomach flipped. I tasted the stew, and found it was hot and probably nutritious. That was all that could be said for it. But I took a few bites, and they all crowded around and began their sup, loosely grouped around the fire, some of them sitting on their saddles.

The Captain appeared at my side. "Blessed gods." A rare bit of humor lightened his beaten face. "You must be brave, *d'mselle* Vianne, to eat Tinan's cooking."

A general shout of laughter rose. The young Guard flushed, and I pitied him. "Well," I managed diplomatically, "tis not the worst I've had. Amys was preparing eels yesterday." I bit my lip, remembering the cook. I set my bowl aside, and tried to put a bright face on it. The art of conversation requires making one-self agreeable, amusing where possible, instructing gently other times. "I loathe eels, but I would always have to try them. She would always ask me how they were, if they needed more salt or chivin. Imagine my surprise when I found she thought I loved eels—someone mischievous had told her they were my favourite delicacy."

That caused more laughter, and di Rocham grinned at me gratefully. My heart lightened. The boy was charming, and he would have quite a career…if there was ever a Court he could return to.

The Captain settled next to me; I leaned away as subtly as I could. For some reason di Rocham hurriedly glanced away, his face falling as if he had seen something amiss.

I had done my duty and they did not look to me to amuse now. So I pulled my knees up and let their conversation drift around me. It was the closest to merriment I had heard from them, and with good reason. But they seemed easier now, and if I stayed silent and looked into the fire they might forget my presence a little.

"Tis not to your liking?" The Captain's hand fell to his side. Had he been about to touch my shoulder?

Startled, I did not flinch only with an effort. "What?"

"The stew. I will admit Tinan needs practice, but tis not so bad. Not like Jierre's cooking." His blue eyes were shadowed, and firelight made the sharp planes of his face softer. You could almost miss the marring from the beating he'd been gifted.

"Tis well enough." I touched the bowl with two fingers, decided I could not force myself to do more. "I simply have little appetite, Captain." My voice broke on the last syllable, and I cursed myself. This was no time to be a blithering idiot. "My life has taken a rather surprising turn, of late."

He nodded thoughtfully, looked down into his own bowl. "Try to eat, Vianne. You will need your strength."

I nodded. Hunger is the best sauce for any stew, but even hunger could not force me to swallow more than I already had. "I beg your pardon, Captain. I do not mean to be a burden."

Did he wince? It was impossible to be sure, dusk was gathering rapidly between the trees. "You are no burden, *d'mselle.* You've borne up with far more grace than any other Court dame would have." He raked his dark hair back from his face with stiff fingers, and I saw the shadow of stubble along his chin. Of course, he had not had time to shave. A few of the Guard sported mustaches in honor of the King, but Tristan was clean-shaven.

I wondered what that roughness would feel like under my fingertips. Surely it did no harm to wonder, as long as I remembered he would not, did not, care for me. "My thanks for the compliment. I feel a burden *and* a fool. If I had not been in that passage—"

Did the smoke sting his eyes as it stung mine? For he blinked, quickly. "Twas luck, Vianne. Or fate. Had you not happened along, you would have been with the Princesse, and taken or killed."

"If I had not been in that corridor, mayhap I could have saved Lisele." I touched the bowl again, running my fingers along the metal rim.

"One unarmed woman against men who slew two of my

Guard, then killed the Princesse and her ladies? You will drive yourself mad if you think such a thing." Shadows now leapt away from the firelight. Night falls swiftly with no candle or witchlight to hold it back, even in spring.

"I wonder if madness might not be a comfort," I said bitterly. My feet ached; the boots, however sturdy, were not made for this abuse. Nor was the rest of me. "I was not with Lisele when she needed me."

"You could not have saved her. You rescued the Aryx, and freed me from an iron cell."

Did he seek to ease my conscience? It was gallant of him, but I did not wish any comfort from his quarter. Still... *There is another donjon holding him,* d'mselle. *And you hold the key to that one.* "I would free you from your oath, and you could find service with another Court. Navarrin, perhaps, or even Badeau. They would be glad of you." *And their borders would keep you safer than most. The Damarsene would not take you, the Pruzians would kill you, and the Torkai, barbarians that they are, who knows what they would do?* The image of d'Arcenne in the turbaned Court of Torkai, spreading himself on the floor to bow to their King, would have been highly diverting once. Now it merely irritated me.

"A man accused of killing his own King?" His mouth drew into a firm line. "What folly are you speaking?"

It is not folly if it saves a life, Captain. I gathered myself. "Think practically, Captain. There is no hope of success. The Duc has been laying his plans for years, if what *sieur* di Yspres says is true—"

An almost-violent start bumped his shoulder against mine. "What *else* did Jierre tell you?" he broke in, rudely.

I pulled the blanket closer. The night would be cold, a coolness already touched my cheeks. "He told me those with royal blood, however begotten, have been dying for four years now. It does not take a bludgeon to make me see truth. If you arrive at a foreign Court, you can find a position for yourself and your men. If I may find a safe place to leave the Aryx I can perhaps trade on my smile and my knowledge of riddles and charming companionship to make my way in the world until I find a means to make the Duc pay. In any case, his rule will founder of its own weight without the Aryx. I am asking you to be released of your oath, and to cease your determination to throw your life away."

I had not realized my voice had risen dangerously until I finished, and heard the ringing silence around the campfire. All eyes were on us. "Look well upon me, *sieur* d'Arcenne," I continued. "Do I look anyone's idea of a Queen? Court protocol stifles me, games of politics and rumor disgust me even when I must play them for my Princesse's safety. I was *taught* to have no ambition. The lesson's held well enough everyone who conspired to teach it should be proud. An accident of blood—so my grandmother dallied with a King? What of it? Plenty of ladies have done both more and less; tis not my fault *or* failing. I do not want this—and I care not if you *do* kill me; it would be a blessing to die after what I've seen."

My voice broke, and I was perilously close to another fit of weeping. Instead, I rose blindly to my feet, dropping the blanket. "Look upon me!" I cried, and they did to a man. "Do I look a Queen? Nonsense. Am I dignified? Regal? I caught you at your game in that passageway because I was covered in *mud*, Tristan, is that a very queenly picture? And I crept down to the donjon to free you because I believed a King's idle jest. Very well, I am a fool, a provincial little *fool*, punish me for it! I have spent my life smoothing and covering the mistakes others have made and I am *sick to death of it!*"

Now I was weeping, after swearing not to. My eyes were blind with hot water, and I restrained the urge to stamp my feet with an effort that left me trembling yet more violently. "*I should have died in her place!*" I cried, aware only of the silence cloaking the firelit group of men. "My only friend—my *only* friend—and I was not there to save her! She gave me the Aryx by accident—and you call me a Queen. Queen of fools, perhaps. Queen of *idiots*." 'Twas as if all the words I had ever refrained from were rising up to betray me, a torrent of what should not be said. A breeze blew smoke from the fire, made the branches sough. "Now you ask me to be responsible for the death of you and your men. You could have left me to the Duc's tender mercies, and no doubt most of you wished to. But you did not, and I am most grateful, it would be poor indeed to repay you thus."

The effort not to scream left me gasping. I turned on my heel, stalked to the edge of the firelit circle and sought to master myself. My fingers clutched as if I still possessed skirts and could use them to hide my fists. I addressed the night beyond the circle of fireglow. Here was as good a place as any to cease this madness.

"I will not be the cause of your deaths. The Duc cannot rule without the Aryx. All I must do is keep the Great Seal from his hands for long enough and his rule will crumble, and there will be no need of any more death. I have seen far too much of death already." I shuddered at the thought. *Make certain.* The wet, crunching noises. The blood. The *smell*. "I will *not* be the cause of more."

"Vianne." Tristan's voice.

You presume great familiarity, chivalier. "Hold your tongue, Captain d'Arcenne," I snapped. "I will not be the cause of more death. I *refuse.*"

Silence, except for the crackling of the fire. I swallowed the lump in my throat and wiped at my streaming cheeks, wished I had a kerchief. I could have thought to bring one instead of a comb, twould have been more useful.

I took a step, another. A third.

"Where will you go, then?" It was not the Captain, it was Jierre di Yspres. "Tonight is no night for traveling, *d'mselle*. Stay with us, an it please you. Morning will make things look less bleak."

"Aye." Tinan di Rocham, grave and quiet. "We are all stunned at the death we've seen, *d'mselle* Vianne. We laugh and banter to keep from weeping. There is no shame in it."

Oddly enough, the words salved some of the aching in my chest. I dropped my head into my hands and stood, wishing the earth would open and swallow me, lightning would strike from the heavens and incinerate me. I should not have said even a quarter of what I had just flung at d'Arcenne. The black fit of sobbing threatened to drown me again, and I wondered if I would ever learn to be strong, and not such a sodden mess of weeping.

Like a heroine in a courtsong. Dark, unhealthy amusement rose at the thought. *I will dissolve in a puddle of salt, and there will be no more discussion of Queen this and Aryx that and the Fate of Arquitaine the other.*

"Then why do I feel so ashamed, Tinan di Rocham?" Muffled by my hands, I was amazed he heard me.

"Because you are breathing, and one you love is not." At least he was truthful. "Tis a common thing, to feel shame at surviving. I felt it when my brother died, and near it killed me. My mother pleaded with me…" He trailed off, uncomfortably. "Please, *d'mselle*. Do not do something rash now. There's time enough between here and Arcenne—if we reach the mountains whole, that is—to decide with clear heads what to do next. We are proud to have you with us. At least I am."

"And I." This from di Yspres. "It was no mean feat to rescue our Captain, *d'mselle*, or to hide in the Palais itself when you knew the Duc was searching for you. You are as brave as any Guard."

"Aye to that," Pillipe di Garfour echoed. There was a murmur of assent that fair threatened to break my heart in its well-meaning eagerness.

"Braver than any one of us," someone said—perhaps Luc di Chatillon.

I do not need empty words, sieur. *I need a hole in the earth wide enough to swallow me.* The strength ran out of my legs, and I dropped down again, put my head on my knees. It was no use. I had nowhere to go. I sat like that until someone brought the blanket, wrapped it around me, and sat near enough I could feel a friendly warmth.

There was not much talk after that. At least, I did not hear much before I fell asleep sitting up, leaning into someone's shoulder with my face buried in my knees.

I half-woke in darkness. Someone had removed my boots, and the ground was hard though I lay on something that sought to cushion it a trifle. There were two blankets over me. It felt very late, and the fire had burned down to a low glow.

"…garrisons," Jierre said softly.

"Or we risk bandits in the forest, yes," Tristan replied, and sighed. A faint rasping, as if he rubbed at his face. "Tis no pretty choice."

"The bandits will likely do us less harm. We are well armed, and can travel swiftly." This was Adersahl di Parmecy et Villeroche, the stocky one with the fine mustache.

"What of the *d'mselle*?" Jierre, now. "Her strength may not hold if we ride much harder."

"True," Adersahl said. "Have you ever seen such spirit, though?"

Mock me, I thought sleepily. *I have no means of stopping you. Do as you please. I care little.* A stone dug into my hip, but I did not chance moving.

"Aye to that." Jierre sounded anxious now. "Tristan?"

"The *question* is, the low route, or the road through the forest?" Tristan, oddly sharp. The fire crackled, banked and low. I longed for my own soft bed, a servant closing my door and taking away an empty glass of wine; I longed for the two leather-bound tomes on Tiberian history I had been reading and the small jeweled statue of Jiserah at my elbow as I dimmed the witchlight and settled back with a sigh, the door to Arioste's *closette* and the other door to Lisele's sleeping chamber wide open so my Princesse had only to call and I could attend. Most nights she would steal past Arioste's narrow bed—Lady Wintrefelle rarely woke, and for all her beauty she snored like a pig—and we would fall asleep in my bed, giggling or quiet with the silence that comes only after you have known someone since childhood.

I stirred uneasily. They were mute for a long while, and I had almost fallen back into sleep's black softness. The darkness behind my eyelids held shapes I did not care to examine too closely. Crumpled shapes in bloody dresses, lying so still.

So, so still.

"I would say through the forest." Jierre, finally. "Bandits are a lesser danger to us at the moment."

"I agree." Tristan sighed. "Did I go amiss, Jierre?"

There was another long, uncomfortable silence. "I would not presume, *sieur*," Jierre replied. "You acted honorably. I was wrong to doubt you."

"Tis not what I meant." Tristan sounded amused now, and bootleather creaked. "Gods above, this is a mess."

"Aye," Adersahl coughed, but it did not cover his laugh. "I never thought I would live to see this turn."

"Many thanks, Adersahl," Tristan said drily. "You are enjoying this courtsong?"

"Of course not," the older man returned. "I wish you luck, tis all."

Tristan cursed, but it was good-natured, and they all three laughed softly, so as not to wake the others. It was shared merriment, and I envied it.

Stealthy footsteps, going to different parts of the firelit clearing. Someone settled next to me, and I could not hold my peace. "Is something wrong?" Slow and sleepy, as if I dreamed.

"No," Tristan d'Arcenne said very softly. "Sleep, Vianne. We are standing watch."

"Captain?" I wished him to speak again. For when I heard him, the ugly visions faded somewhat.

"Try to rest," He did not sound angry.

Say something diplomatic, Vianne. My tongue was thick with fatigue. "Your pardon, Captain. I was not kind to you."

"Kind enough." He sounded amused. "You needed to lance that wound. I was beginning to worry."

"You never worry." I sought to wake myself. He laughed,

catching the sound back as if it pained him somewhat. "D'Arcenne?"

"Hm." An affirmative sound. I watched the fire's glow through my heavy, heavy lashes.

I wanted to ask him so many things, but I could not seem to make my mouth work. Instead, I fell back into the darkness of sleep. Before I did, someone's fingers smoothed back a loose strand of my hair. It was a gentle touch, and I welcomed it.

THE CAPTAIN

Chapter Seven

*T*he floor of the Sculpture Hall echoed underfoot as I hurried along, trying the doors. Each was locked, rattling like rusted chains, and I wept with frustration and fear. Behind me, they came—the Duc's Guard, with lean, black-eyed Garonne di Narborre at their head, coming for me to make certain, make certain, make certain.

"Vianne?"

Behind one of the doors was my Lisele, and she was bleeding. The blood washed under the doors, rising around my ankles, so much of it, and the walls between the doors were festooned with broken harpstrings. I knew the hedgewitch charm to save my Princess but I could not remember it, and I could not remember which door she was hidden behind, and all of them were bleeding. I tried them all, and my hands slipped on the doorknobs. My hands slipped because they were sweating, and covered with blood as well, Lisele's blood, for I was to blame—

"Vianne!" Someone had my shoulders, shook me. "Vianne, wake. Tis a dream, nothing more."

I woke fully in one terrified lunge, the scream dying on my

lips. Swallowed the last half of the cry and looked up at d'Arcenne while I clutched the blanket to my chest as if it could shield me.

It was early morn, and thick fog hung between the trees. One of the Guard doused the fire, but d'Arcenne gave me a cup of hot chai. "Here. Take this. Twas merely a dream. You are safe." He folded my hands around the cup, his warm callused skin against mine. My hands shook, but he held them steady for a few moments until I could draw a breath. My mouth tasted foul, and the sudden urge to tear my hands from his and examine them for traces of blood shook me.

He had shaved, and his face looked better too. The bruising and swelling was going down; perhaps one of the Guard had some skill at healing. Had I thought, I would have offered to charm the bruises for him myself, though it was faintly improper.

My breath came harsh and ragged. Was there blood on my hands? I could not tell. All I could feel was the warm metal of the cup, just on the edge of scorching.

The Guard moved about the camp, jostling each other, rolling up sleeping pads. I wondered whose I had occupied so thoughtlessly. I felt incredibly rumpled, and as the last vestiges of sleep fled I longed for morning chocolat and a hot bath. D'Arcenne still knelt at my side, his fingers warm and solid.

If my hands were bloody, he would not hold them so. The idea came and fled in less than a moment.

"Captain." I searched for something to speak of to push the dream away. *Anything.* "I never asked what happened to you, after you left me in the passageway."

He almost flinched, gave me a sharp look, his fingers tightening. Of course, who would wish to speak of something so awful?

His careful examination of my face made me blush, and when he finally spoke it was not in his usual calm tone. No, his words turned lame and halting, as if he chose them with care, blue eyes dark-shadowed and his mouth tight with distaste. "I found my way to the Rose Room. The King was dying. The pink petitte-cakes, they were poisoned. The Duc's Guard burst in, and I killed four of them before they took me down. And carried me to the donjons in chains, then beat me until the Duc paid the honor of a visit." His gaze had turned steely.

Now I was sorry I had asked. It could not have been pleasant to remember. "I beg your pardon. I do not mean to wound you." *Poison? I sensed no poison.* There were scentless poisons, though, even if a hedgewitch tended to be sensitive to the slightest breath of toxins. I had not been at my best in the Rose Room.

And yet…

He shrugged, loosed his fingers from mine. "I know, Vianne. Do not trouble yourself. The King asked if you were safe, and Lisele." D'Arcenne ducked his dark head, examining the ruin of the sleeping roll I had been tossing upon. "I lied. I told him I knew you and the Princesse were safe. I told him I would watch over you. That, at least, is true, and I shall see it remains so."

"Oh." Furious heat stained my cheeks, I wished I could stopper it. *It was merely the King's jest. You must be wary, this man may turn on you. You have no protection here.*

"I do not wish to wound you, either." Quietly, as he settled his knee more comfortably on the damp ground.

I gazed at the blankets and the rumpled sleeping pad. *Something else to speak of, Vianne. Quickly now.* "Whose are these?" The fog made the morning eerily quiet.

"Mine. Three stand watch at a time, so there are a few to spare."

Oh, dear gods. "My thanks, Captain." I found enough presence of mind to sip the chai. It was hot and sweet with stevya, and I was grateful. I felt queerly light and drained, as if the dream were still happening around me. The predawn hush was immense; even our voices seemed not to break it. "I feel I am dreaming still."

Why did he examine me so? "Break your fast, *d'mselle*. We have a few sweet rolls, and some cheese. We shall stop in Tierrce d'Estrienne for supplies before we enter the Shirlstrienne."

I shivered. The forest had a dark name as a haunt of bandits and thieves, and Lisele and I had thrilled to the dangers of the wood in the romances and songs. High adventure, lovers in disguise, honorable thievery and less-honorable menace. Rescues by *chivalieri* of fair ladies distressed by bandits, always in the very nick of time.

It did not seem so thrilling now. Then again, with some few of the King's Guard, I was perhaps safer than I had ever been at Court. I had not even known danger was stalking me, except for the familiar peril of rumor and politicking. "Through the forest." I sought to sound as if I considered it merely a maying-party.

"If we take the other way to Arcenne, we go through provinces with garrisons loyal to the Duc." Brisk now, he moved as if he would straighten, paused. "The forest only has bandits, and we may deal with them easily enough. Rest easy."

The chai's warmth and sweetness helped, though my skin held the damp chill of morn outside. I had never spent the night out-of-doors before. "Am I slowing your journey?"

He showed no further inclination to move. "I told you I would not leave you. Drink your chai, *d'mselle*. We will break our fast, and then another hard day's ride. I am sorry for it, but there is no other way." The small clearing did not seem a camp anymore; it was, instead, merely an anonymous dirtpatch with a ring of scorched stones in the middle. It took so little to erase the signs of our passing.

"I know." And I did. "I shall keep my mouth closed in the future, Captain." *If I can only remember what chaos ensues when I forget myself and open it. My reputation for discretion is suffering awfully.*

"That would be a shame. We would miss your voice."

It took every ounce of my self-control not to make a face. I settled for finishing the chai. It was still too hot, but they were in a hurry—and I had no desire to be caught by the Duc's men. Then I pushed back the blankets, and Tristan helped me to my feet, deftly subtracting the cup from me. "That way." He pointed, a swift gesture. "None of the Guard will bother you there."

He meant the privy. I nodded, hoping my cheeks were not scarlet.

I found a secluded spot and thanked the gods I was possessed of a small hedgewitch charm to keep me hidden while I attended to nature. Then I found the brook they had fetched water from yesterday. Fog pressed close, threading between the trees, etching every leaf with crystalline droplets. The brook murmured to itself, birds stirring in the distance. It was not like the songs, where a noble girl wakes in the forest and is brought berries by the grace of one of the Blessed—usually Kimyan, for the Huntress is particularly concerned with children and maidens. Once a girl is married or experienced, it is gentle Jiserah she turns to; my mother had been a devotee of the Bright Wife.

I washed my face and scrubbed at my hands. They held no trace of blood, for which I was grateful—but I still laved them more than twas perhaps necessary, wishing again for a hot bath, and some buttered scones, and morning chocolat. Oh—and a book, and a lazy divan to lie upon and read while Lisele played the harp.

As I am still dreaming, I might as well wish for a ride in the Moon's chariot. I shook myself. I was still alive, even if I was stiff, bruised, and aching from too much time spent in the saddle, and heartsick. Not to mention clammy under my borrowed clothes, and oddly light-headed.

I washed my hands, and washed them again. Rubbed between my fingers, dug under my fingernails to remove all trace of garden dirt and…anything else. Examined my water-wrinkled fingers, then scrubbed at my palms again. I never thought I would yearn for the Court, for well-known faces and voices, for a familiar day of complete boredom.

I was cupping water in my palm to drink when I heard movement on the other side of the brook.

I stood in a rush and would have fled back into the quiet fog-hung trees, having no woodscraft but still hoping to hide, but they were too quick, melting out of the brush on the other side of the water's thin chuckling. Two men, one with a brace of coneys dangling from a work-roughened fist, the other with two woodfowl.

Tis illegal to hunt in the King's forests. My eyes were round as platters; I stared as if they were sprites or *demieri di sorce*, those spirits of night and mischief.

They stared back, perhaps thinking the same. Ruddy-cheeked and dressed in rough homespun, they were obviously peasants or smallholders. One had a thatch of dark-blond hair, and the other was dark, with a winking milky eye under a scar. They both had seamed faces from time spent in the weather, and hard hands from hard work.

We regarded each other over the brook for a ridiculously long time, I having nothing to say, my heart hammering so hard it precluded rational thought, and they obviously suffering the same dilemma.

Finally, the blond elbowed the dark man, who coughed. That broke the spell, and I backed up a step. Two. A stick snapped under my garden-boot, very loud in the foggy quiet.

"Now, do not be going, *d'mselle*." The dark one stretched out his free hand, as if I were a stray dog he wished to coax. "We are honest folk, and we want no trouble." His hair was indifferently trimmed, and his accent almost too thick to be understood. Peasant, then, not smallholder. A small, dark-dripping bag slung by his side, full of something that looked heavy. More small animals?

I swallowed dryly. "Then we are alike, *sieurs*." I searched for good manners. Nothing in my Court training had prepared me for this. "For I wish no trouble either."

"Tha's good, then." The blond dropped the woodfowl with a thump that brought bile to my throat. They landed in a sodden, graceless heap, their slim necks terribly twisted. His hands were suddenly full of a bow, half drawn back. "Now, just you step lightly over the brook, *d'mselle*, and we'll have a fine morn of it."

I did not—quite—understand what he meant, but the snigger of his companion made it clear. I froze, indecisive. Should I run and risk an arrow in the back, or do as they said, and risk more?

"No." I had not come through the impossible events of the last two days to be accosted by a pair of *peasants*, by the Blessed. "Return to the woods, *sieurs*, and take your game with you. Forget you ever saw me."

Their eyes grew large. I doubt they had ever heard a woman speak so.

"Well, we would, noble *d'mselle*, but you see, we have the bow. And you're here, dressed like a lad. You must like a bit of rough—" The dark one was warming to his theme when there was a slight sound behind me.

I did not turn.

"Drop your weapon, peasant," Tristan d'Arcenne said. I was beginning to associate that calm, reasonable tone of his with danger. Something in it was a warning more effective than a shout.

The crude bow promptly dropped to the forest floor. The arrow bounced into the stream, floating and bobbing away on the water's chuckling surface. My sharp, surprised exhalation sounded almost like a word.

Four of the Guard advanced on the peasants, one with a bow, two with drawn rapiers, and one with leather thongs. In a matter of moments, both men had their hands tied behind their back. "We meant no—," the dark one started, and Pillipe di Garfour cuffed him so sharply blood flew from the man's mouth.

"Speak when you're spoken to." Di Garfour's pleasantness had turned to a dismissive snarl.

Wait. I found my voice. "And it please you, offer them no violence, *chivalier.*"

He shot me one amazed glance, but at least he did not strike again. The two were thrust to their knees, and I started to protest again, but a hand on my shoulder halted me.

"*D'mselle?*" Tristan's face was set and white under the fading bruises. I wondered why he did not use my name, then answered my own question.

He could not risk having me known to them.

"They simply startled me," I said quickly. "'Tis all. They meant no—"

"And the bow?" His blue eyes had turned cold. D'Arcenne, most probably, could guess at what two men would do to an unattended Court girl on a foggy morning far from the Citté.

My tongue ran away with me. "Would you not have a bow drawn, if you were he? Leave them be, Cap—ah, *chivalier*. I beg of you, leave it be." For I had an ugly intimation of where this situation could lead.

"They will speak of this." Tristan's chill expression did not alter.

I doubt it. "And admit to poaching in the King's forest, with all the penalties that implies? No. Let them go on their way. They simply startled me."

The blond peasant stared at me, perplexed. The dark one, his mouth half open, looked as if he had been struck with a sudden thought, and his gaze dropped to the stream.

"Your soft heart, *d'mselle*." Tristan's hand tightened on my shoulder. "Kill them."

He started to turn, to lead me away, but I found my voice again. "No!" I slipped from under his hand. "No," I repeated firmly. "I will have no more death on my account." The brook chuckled merrily, laughing at me. *Vianne, you idiot. Idiot Vianne.*

His shrug was a marvel of disdain. "'Tis not on your account, *d'mselle*. It is on mine. Now come."

"Do not presume to order me about, *chivalier*." I drew myself up, though my height was no match for his. "You were quick enough to promise me obedience when it served you. Now you must abide by it. I will have *no more death on my account*." The words rang against fog and a rising chorus of birdsong. There was no more silence. The wood was alive once more.

He folded his arms, cocking his head and staring through me. "They are beyond your mercy, *d'mselle*. Poaching in the King's woods is a treasonable offense. Even had they not threatened you, their lives would be forfeit."

"If I am what you say, even that point becomes academic. Release them."

He gave in suspiciously easily. "Very well; they will be released. Now, if you please, *d'mselle*, come with me." His hand closed around my elbow, and I let him pull me away. He cast one look over his shoulder, but I was too busy, my feet slipping on moss and rocks, to wonder at it.

We plunged into the trees, moving so quickly I had difficulty keeping up. I set my jaw and did my best. When he rounded on me, blue eyes flashing, I almost lost my footing. But he had my shoulders instead of my elbow, and he shook me, once, as he had in the passageway two days—or a lifetime—ago.

"You noble little *fool*. You will cost us all our lives. Do you think this is a game? It would take only one peasant in his cups to tell the Duc's spies we have gone this way, and the entire countryside will be roused against us. My men are few enough. I have no wish to lose more of them."

I merely let my gaze accuse him. His fingers bit into my shoulders and I winced—I was already bruised there, and would be again. He did not notice, or care. And why should he?

I was only a *thing* to him. A means to an end.

D'Arcenne shook me once again, so sharply I flinched. "Gods above and below, Blessed witness me, why is it *nothing* I do pleases you?"

"I could ask you the same question." I seemed to have been

possessed by a completely different person—a Vianne with no discretion and none of my usual quiet. A strand of my hair fell in my face, the mixture of being disheveled, aching all over, clammy-cold, terrified, and heart-wrung as volatile as the sylph-aether used to fuel burners for distilling hearth-binding charms.

He stared at me for a few moments, his jaw working. I had never seen him angered thus. He looked on the verge of murder.

I remembered Baron Simieri's plum-colored face with an internal shiver. But that had been a poison killspell. D'Arcenne would have used his dagger, or his sword.

But he has murdered, Vianne. The Guard in the donjon, do you think Tristan merely gave him a rose and a courtsong? And he is right, twould take only one peasant in his cups to rouse an entire province against us, if the Duc has laid his plans aright. Years this conspiracy was in the making; of course the Duc would plan for this. He has foresight enough.

Yet I could not brook it. Something in me rose up in rebellion, hot and brittle. The fog had begun to thin as birdsong exploded, every winged thing greeting the Sun's fiery chariot wheels. I heard—but no. I could not hear that, not with the bird noise.

It sounded like a choked cry.

As the Captain of the Guard needed nothing but a single glance from his King to understand an order, so those of d'Arcenne's Guard would need only a single glance—a nod over the shoulder, perhaps—to comprehend him.

And obey.

My body drew up against itself, every muscle tightening, yet my knees felt queerly loose. "Oh, no," I whispered, my lips numb. A thin trickle of sweat touched my back. "You did not. You *did not.*"

His face darkened with something I did not want to name, so I took a step back. He let me, his hands dropping.

He did not even have the grace to look shamed. "Tis not on your conscience; it is on mine. I cannot risk the lives of my men for the sake of your *gentle* feelings." His dark hair had fallen over his forehead, and the dew had been at him, too—either that, or there was a sheen of sweat on his sharp mountain face.

My throat was dry as the Days of Forgiveness. "They meant no harm." *They* did *mean harm, Vianne. You are lying even to yourself.* The voice of good sense was faint and lost. My entire body quivered with a feeling too unsteady to be anger and too hot to be sorrow.

"Of course they did. Had you been alone..." He did not complete the sentence. We both knew what could have happened. There were stories and songs of young noblewomen caught in the woods without the protection of chaperone or male relative, left for dead or dishonored and committing suicide afterward. *The mother's blood is all that counts*, the proverb ran—but dishonor tainted even that.

Tristan d'Arcenne and I stared at each other. What difference was there, between the peasants and the man who stood before me now? Either would seek to use me for their own ends; and what protection did I have? My wits, and the fact of the Aryx at my throat. Both such fragile protections.

"Blame me, Vianne," he said finally. "You did seek to save their lives; let that be enough."

I willed my hands to stop shaking, made myself as tall as possible. *I am Duchesse Vianne di Rocancheil et Vintmorecy, and I must act like it.* "You swore me your obedience."

"I did not order their deaths on your account, *d'mselle*." His voice turned taut and low. "I might have spared them for your asking it of me, had the lives of my men—*your Guard*—not been at risk."

"They are not *my* Guard." My throat ached with an unutterable scream. "They are *yours*—and the King's."

"The King is dead." His hands had curled to fists, and I wondered if he would be so base as to strike me. "You hold the Aryx, and have the last drop of royal blood in Arquitaine not tainted by regicide."

"I only hold the Aryx in trust." My hand slipped up, touched the warm curve of the Aryx under my shirt. The peasants had not seen it, thank the gods—but that did not matter now. "I shall return it to a true Heir when it is time." *Gods willing. Please.*

He tipped his head back, his jaw working again, and I took two nervous steps backward. My ankle turned on a rock, and I almost fell. By the time I had regained my balance, he had somewhat mastered himself. His blue eyes were incandescent, and a muscle ticked steadily in his cheek. "Under Arquitaine law, until the time the Aryx chooses another holder, you are the Queen, and you should act like it. You should not risk our lives, *d'mselle*. Tis not noble of you at all."

I could have screamed, yet again. But it was useless. I possessed enough knowledge of the Law of Succession to know he was right. I was the Queen while I held the Aryx. It mattered little why Lisele had it, or how she came to entrust it to me. Entrusted it was, and I was trapped. Lisele had made me promise to keep the Seal safe, and traveling with Tristan d'Arcenne and the Guard was the safest place for the Aryx—and for me.

But I had cost Lisele her life, perhaps. If I had been with her, mayhap I could have distracted the men long enough to buy her an escape. And the King—if Tristan had not been with me, perhaps he could have saved the King.

Now I was responsible for two more deaths. Peasants, to be sure—but still, two more awful murders.

So much death. We were wading in it, and it rose like the Airenne's infrequent floods.

A great chill settled over me, far deeper than my skin. It pushed all the way down to my bones. I cupped my elbows in my hands and hugged myself, shivering. I could find nothing more to say.

D'Arcenne said nothing, either, and we heard the footsteps of the Guards returning. Who had killed them? Perhaps di Garfour? No—he was too kind. Luc di Chatillon? No, his eyes were so merry, and he had offered his oath in a voice that shook just a little. Robierre d'Atyaint-Sierre? No, I could not imagine it.

You do not need to imagine, Vianne. It is done.

They filed into the tiny clearing. "Is the Queen harmed?" Pillipe di Garfour asked shyly, faith shining in his gaze.

He believed. The Captain had made them *all* believe they were the Queen's Guard, and the Queen's Guard they would be, to the last man. There would be no better defense for the Aryx.

I set my chin and raised my eyes. "Unharmed." My voice that sounded strange even to myself. "My thanks, *sieurs*. The Captain has informed me we are departing this place."

With that, I brushed past d'Arcenne. He gave a subtle push to my shoulder, telling me which way the camp lay. I was grateful for that, at least. I tried my best not to stumble, though my eyes were dry and felt full of sand. His fingers slipped, as if he had sought to catch me as I passed, but I did not let him.

At least I was not weeping. The tears had turned to stones, and settled behind my beating heart.

Chapter Eight

I did not break my fast, and d'Arcenne did not notice. He was too busy giving orders and planning. I simply sought to stay out of the way.

I alternated between silently reciting Tiberian verbs and hedgewitch charms. It was the only thing I could think to do. I leaned against a firgan tree and went through the first twenty Tiberian verbs, each declension a rough martial song, then recited a charm to salve a bruise. Now I could remember a dozen more—a charm to take infection from a wound, a charm to still bleeding, a charm to make a wounded person sleep and so, conserve their strength.

When it mattered most, I had been able to remember only a charm to mend a scullery maid's hand. A miserable hedgewitch, in truth. I was determined that should I witness another death, I would do all in my limited power to prevent it.

All, Vianne? That was another question, one which occupied me greatly.

We set out through the fog's eerie muffling, and I again kept myself leaning away from Tristan as long as I possibly could. The motion of the horse and my own numb hunger conspired to put me in a half-slumbrous state.

Moisture dropped from the slender trees, underbrush gemmed with crystal drops, the birds finishing their dawn chorus and settling into the day's gossip. Yet they were hushed, whispering—perhaps they, too, knew that the King was dead, and conspiracy stalked Arquitaine.

I thought on all the hedgewitch charms I knew, seeking to fix each of them more firmly into memory. At the Palais I would have my books—I wondered what had happened to my books, whether they were still in my bedchamber or if they had been taken. Surely the Duc must have known by now that I had escaped with Tristan. Or did he? Did he think I had left the Palais alone? Who else could have freed the Captain? Anyone loyal to him, certainly. Had there been anyone loyal to Tristan left in the Palais by the time the Duc was finished with his well-laid plans?

I missed odd things. My mother-of-salt comb, a keepsake from my mother. A bite of Cook Amys's honeycake. The scent of my pillows, the blue silk ribbon I had left carelessly draped across my mirror. The small silver gryphon statue Lisele had gifted me with on my naming-day last year, its eyes glowing rubies.

We rode all day, the copses blurring together and the clearings becoming more infrequent. I must have slept, barely waking when we stopped for luncheon and to rest the horses. Someone pushed a sweetroll and a thick slice of cheese into my hands, and a cup of chai, but my stomach turned to a roiling mass of snakes when I raised the sweetroll to my lips. I held the bread and cheese until I ascertained which way I should go to relieve myself, leaving the cup on the leaf-scattered ground.

I threw the sweetroll into the bushes, and followed it with

the cheese, sore tempted to send a muttered curse after both. A small charm to preserve my modesty, and another small charm to clean oneself afterward—at least I was hedgewitch enough for *that*. Here in the wilderness, it was easy. The charm took its power from the trees and earth, not from me. Thank the Blessed, for I was numb, and light. My forehead felt cold and wet to my hot, dry fingers when I pushed stray strands of hair back, seeking to repair my braid.

I did not go very far from the Guard, and when I reappeared, Tinan di Rocham handed me my cup again. "Drink it, and it please you, *d'mselle*. You are pale."

I raised the cup to my lips, but did not drink. The smell of chai made my stomach cramp, and I feared I would retch most unbecomingly. I lowered it gingerly, and he seemed satisfied.

"That will help you. Do you need aught?" His fair young face was concerned. I wondered what he would have made of d'Arcenne's commands to kill two helpless peasants.

What I need, young chivalier, *you cannot give. Leave me be.* I shook my head, and as soon as he was gone I tipped the chai unobtrusively into a thornbush. My stomach eased a little, but did not cease its boiling. My arms and legs ached, and my head split with pain. I longed for my bed, or for a certain window seat in the White Gallery. From that casement one could watch the gardens below, and bask in the Sun at any season. Lisele and I had often hidden there as children, pulling the pale draperies closed to hide from prying eyes, whispering and giggling as our dolls had adventures on the broad gold-figured satin of the seat.

We did not stop for long, and soon I was back atop the horse with Tristan d'Arcenne behind me. I tried again to avoid touching him—an impossible feat on horseback—and was again defeated by my third recitation of the second class of verbs. I fell into a dreamy haze, and was glad of it as the day wore on.

Nightfall came, and still we continued, skirting the fields of Vanstrienne to the east. The country grew thick with hills and stands of broader oak and vastvain trees; we passed many a country lane and small brook. I heard someone remark this was Adersahl's home province, and he knew it well. There was a manse, and some discussion of whether we could afford to rest there, sleep in real beds. But it was too dangerous—to Adersahl's family and to us. It was decided to simply push on through the night. In three days' time we should reach the place where a dark finger-dagger of the Shirlstrienne pointed into the heart of Arquitaine, and would be safe enough in that belt of forest—especially as it widened and became an ocean of trees, the Shirlstrienne proper.

Safe enough. Except for the bandits.

I found I did not care.

D'Arcenne occasionally made a remark into my captive ear, but I told myself I did not hear him and soon enough he did not speak to me. I occupied myself with reciting charms, and when I could no longer think of such things, simply staring at the horse's mane.

We stopped just before moonrise at a small brook, and I was led to a pad of two blankets that someone—perhaps Tinan—had put between the roots of a tall spreading chestnut tree in full leaf. I dropped down and pulled my knees up, resting my forehead atop them, stray strands of my hair falling forward to screen me. I had neither time nor energy to comb or braid; even the thought filled me with unutterable weariness. I shut my eyes and wished for sleep, but I seemed to have found an exhaustion too deep for slumber.

The men spoke in low voices and I ignored them, shutting

the sound out as much as I could, simply enduring. They offered me chai, again, and cold mince pie, but I did not answer, pulling more tightly into myself. There was some argument, then. Jierre di Yspres asking me to eat, Tinan di Rocham saying I looked fevered, Luc di Chatillon remarking we had no time for women's vapors, and Adersahl di Parmecy et Villeroche telling him sharply to hold his tongue. I found if I concentrated on the blood soughing in my ears I could ignore them much more effectively.

Finally, the food was taken away, there was more low but heated discussion, and d'Arcenne came and touched my shoulder. "Tis time to leave, *d'mselle*."

I rose to my feet slowly but obediently enough, my eyes fixed on the ground, and was placed atop d'Arcenne's horse. But he did not ride behind me—instead, he walked the horse, and I had to keep my balance. My entire body became a song of agony, and I noticed the other Guards walking their mounts, too.

I slumped in the saddle, struggling now to stay conscious as deeper darkness fell over the world.

At some point, in the middle of the night, the Guard remounted. I leaned into d'Arcenne's warmth with a traitorous feeling of relief. Now, instead of fighting to stay awake I tried to relax enough to slumber, yet I could not.

D'Arcenne began to speak. Quietly, his breath touching my ear or my cheek. I did not listen to his tale—something about Arcenne, or a castle in some high mountains, perhaps the impregnable Spire di Chivalier. Something about the trees in bloom, and the light on the white shoulders of snowy rock. It changed to something that vaguely alarmed me, a muttering as if Court sorcery were being cast—but I could not hear it through the sough of blood in my ears.

I cannot quite remember when I slipped into a twilight un-sleep. Eventually there was a cessation of motion, and someone's cold fingers on my forehead. The coolness felt wonderful, and I made a shapeless sound. "Feverish," someone said from very far away. "...did not eat."

"Shock." D'Arcenne, right next to my ear, though I could not tell if I was still a-horseback or on solid ground. "Give me your flask."

"Tis ansinthe," di Yspres said. "Bad for a hedgewitch. Only a little, now."

The flask was forced between my lips, and I took two swallows of something gag-sweet that burned all the way down. I coughed, and heard my own voice, slow and dreamy. "He told them to make certain none lived. To go among the women, and make *certain*."

"Who?" D'Arcenne asked, in the hush that followed.

The warmth from the ansinthe began to spread through my entire body. With the warmth came a little more strength. Why were they giving me green venom? It was a dangerous cordial; too much of it and a hedgewitch would hallucinate before her internal organs failed one by one. Court sorcery, on the other hand, protected one from its burning. "Di Narborre. You told me to attend Lisele...I was too late. She was bleeding, she died. But they came back, and I hid. He said to make certain."

Someone cursed. Someone else drew in a sharp breath. "The Princesse." Luc di Chatillon sounded shocked. "She saw?"

"I tried." I heard myself, slow and slurred as if I had drank too much unwatered wine at a fête. "I used a charm. The bleeding...I was so weak. I tried, Lisele. I tried."

"She is fevered." Jierre di Yspres, heavily. I heard wind in the treetops, or something else. The roaring was my blood pulsing in my ears, and a faint high whine. "Captain?"

"We ride on." D'Arcenne's tone held terrible fury. "We have no choice. We must halt in Tierrce d'Estrienne, and we will find supplies and a hedgewitch physicker there. Once we reach the forest we may tarry longer."

"We should halt overnight, mayhap," di Yspres offered. "She needs care, and rest. I did not know she was so ill."

"'Tis dangerous to tarry so long," Adersahl murmured.

"Do not worry for me," I heard myself say, in a queer, light, breathless rush. I sounded very young. My knees refused to work properly, I could not feel my hands. "Take the Aryx and leave me. I shall draw them away to the port. I can do that much."

"Tristan?" Jierre said. Someone felt at my forehead with chilly fingers.

There was a long pause. The touch on my forehead gentled, stroked my cheek, slid away. "We ride for Tierrce d'Estrienne," d'Arcenne said finally. "Keep the ansinthe handy, Jierre."

Movement again, but I could not tell if I was standing or lying down. I had only a hazy sense of movement, light and dark spinning around me. Every once in a while the motion would stop, and someone would feel at my damp forehead. I was given more ansinthe, and some hot chai. I felt the brush of Court sorcery and understood someone had boiled water with it, a prosaic and dangerous thing, for Court sorcery could be tracked if strong enough, as hedgewitchery could not. I was apologizing for the trouble, and asking to be left behind.

Strangeness enfolded me, full of the sound of beating wings. I carried a very large tray of fried eels in butter, as if I were a servant, except I wore the uniform of a Guard and had slippery leather gloves. I carried the tray into a hall, where strange masked faces gathered around. *Oh, good!* they cried. *The eels, the eels!*

I heard Lisele's laughter, bright and merry. I looked up to the dais, where my Princesse stood with the King, both of them in golden *cloth d'or*, glittering in red torchlight. *The eels,* Lisele said, tilting her pretty head. *Make certain the eels are dead.*

The bits of fried eels had begun to bleed, crimson overflowing the edges of the massive tray. The masked people grabbed at them with clawed hands, and I realized with a fainting horror they were not masks, they were monsters, the *demieri di sorce* old stories warned of. I had wandered into their halls and now had to serve them for a thousand years.

"Hush, Vianne," someone said. "I am here. Nothing can harm you."

The dream vanished. Something against my cheek—fingers? No. What was it? A raindrop?

The darkness deepened, a quality of starry sleep, deeper than the first. Tristan d'Arcenne's voice, from very far away, and only a whisper from myself in reply. What was he asking?

Then I heard, and saw, and felt nothing at all.

Chapter Nine

I do not remember reaching Tierrce d'Estrienne under cover of night. I do not remember the Guard entering the town, or the negotiation with the innkeeper. I do not remember being lifted down from the horse and carried, although I must have been, for I was awakened by morning sunlight falling across the foot of a bed.

I blinked in the flood of light, and the world spun. I smelled clean linen and lavender. Somewhere a fire crackled. Light-headed, I stared for quite some time at the ceiling, heavy beams and plaster, before darkness came. The darkness was my eyelids falling down.

I am home. It was all a dream. Yet the roof was not the fres-coed arch of my own room, and the bed was not mine, for all it was comfortable. I was too exhausted to care. Perhaps I was in the Palais infirmary, there having been some mischance—a hal-lucination, a fever from the damp in the garden? Lisele would be along shortly to bring me confits and order me to become well soon, for nobody braided her hair as well as I. And no lady or ladymaid laced her as well or as quickly as I did, either.

There was a short time of darkness. Finally, I heard voices, hushed as if they spoke in an invalid's room. A woman, and a man.

"Poor child. She is still very ill, *sieur*." Carefully accented, a merchant's wife, heavily lisping, or drawing out the vowels in imitation of noble speech. For all that, she sounded kind, and I wondered who she was. A nurse? A physicker brought into the Palais?

"Our other sister died recently, of a similar fever. Twas a great shock to her, and traveling perhaps overmatched her strength." Jierre di Yspres.

What is he doing here? I lay very still. Tried to open my eyes, could not, felt work-roughened fingers on my wrist, feeling for the pulse.

The covers were pulled up almost to my chin. The reason occurred to me slowly, as dripping water soaking through doubled flannel. Of course—the Aryx. Nobody could see the Aryx, because then…what?

It was not a dream. Lisele will not be along to bring you confits. I struggled to think through the haze.

"Broth and bread, and milk," the woman said. "And this tisane, a small cupful thrice daily. Her pulse is weak and thready. I'll charm her now, *sieur*, and return tomorrow." The woman's hand moved to my forehead, stroked my damp skin, and I smelled the peculiar heavy green of hedgewitchery.

Something very much like strength flooded me, a quiet warmth starting at my toes and rising through my body, warm and wonderfully cooling at the same time. I sighed.

A terrible thought struck me. "Tristan? Where are you?" *Why does it matter?* But I wanted to see d'Arcenne. I wanted to know he was alive. If this was no dream, was he still in the donjon?

"Seeing to the supplies, Vianne." Jierre, unwontedly gentle. He addressed me almost tenderly, and that was another mystery. "Rest easy, he's here."

"Her betrothed?" The hedgewitch. They had found a hedgewitch skilled in healing for me. Why? I was not ill.

The thought coalesced, slowly took shape. *Fever. They have stopped in a town, and are in terrible danger. Because of me.*

"Not yet." Jierre's tone was strange, as if he sought to hold back laughter.

"Clear to see he fancies her. And her such a pretty young *d'mselle*." The hedgewitch clucked her tongue. "Now, here's the tisane. And, *sieur*, not to be moving her for a good three days, that's my recommend. She is quite ill. If you move her, she may suffer more fever."

"My thanks, *m'dama*." There was the sound of cloth moving. The hedgewitch's fingers left my forehead, but the wonderful warmth remained. There was a clink—coin changing hands.

"Many thanks to you, *sieur*. Tis touching to see a brother caring for a sister so; and you two all alone in the world now." The woman sounded chatty as a Court *dama*, and I hoped he would let her stay. The sound of a woman's voice comforted me, reminded me of other voices. At Court, there was always chatter; it was a soothing sea-song behind even the quiet of the bedchamber.

But no, she left soon after, and my eyelids drifted open. I found Jierre di Yspres pulling a wooden chair up to the bedside. The angle of the sunlight had changed—late afternoon now, instead of morning. The white ceiling and thick beams were the same.

He saw I was conscious and smiled, his lean, dark face easing for a moment. Yet graven lines of worry bracketed his mouth, a single line between his dark eyebrows too. "Hello, *d'mselle*."

Softly and carefully. "We are in Tierrce d'Estrienne. The rest of the Guard has gone into the Shirlstrienne to wait for us. Tristan and I brought you to an inn, and contracted a hedgewitch physicker. How do you fare?"

I found I could speak, though still light-headed and dreamy. "Danger." I wet my lips with my oddly numb tongue. "For you."

He shook his head. "Not so much. The Duc's spies are seeking a noblewoman fleeing at haste with a group of men four dozen strong. There are *letres* and heralds in the marketplaces with the wrong description, enough to make one laugh. Garonne di Narborre is probably near to Marrseize by now—the rumor is those phantoms have gone further to the south, to take ship for Tiberia. We have some breathing room, *d'mselle*. Do not worry so."

I sighed. "The Captain?" It was the only question I could think to ask.

"Sore grieved you're ill, *d'mselle*, but otherwise himself. He would not hear of leaving anyone else with you." Jierre looked very serious now, but the lines had lessened. "He was very pale, when we found you had been struck by fever."

Pale? No doubt he thinks of the danger to his men, even if you are too kind to say so. "I beg your pardon," I whispered. "The trouble."

"No trouble, *d'mselle*. Little good it would do to have you die of fever. We can afford to halt a day or two." He was seeking to be comforting, I realized, and wondered at it. When had di Yspres turned into a tut-tutting nurse?

I blinked slowly again. "I feel strange." If he was a nurse, I sounded like a child. "My head feels light, and tis so cold."

"The hedgewitch left a tisane. Could you take some, do you think?"

I considered the question. The room was large and airy, probably the best the inn had to offer, and boasted a table topped with a pitcher and three cups, four wooden chairs, a large fireplace, a window seat, and a large clothespress made of dark wood. I wondered if the watercloset had a bathing tub. I longed for a bath. "I should," I finally whispered, when I remembered what he had asked me. "Thirsty."

"Say no more, then." He moved about, and poured me a small cupful of dark ruby syrup. I recognized the smell—hart's-fleet and fevrebit, the Feversbane. I wondered why she had thought to dose me with such a strong tisane. I could not be *that* ill.

But I was so *cold*. The warmth from the hedgewitch's charming had fled. My body was not my own, weak and numb. I hoped I had not soiled myself; the embarrassment—

He propped me up on the pillows and held the cup to my lips, then fetched me a cup of cool water. I began to wake my dozing wits.

"Did I do anything foolish?" I asked wistfully, and was surprised. I did not think Jierre di Yspres capable of giddy laughter. He tipped his head back, seeking to master himself, and his chuckles rang against the roof.

Eventually he calmed. "No, *d'mselle*." He lowered himself onto the chair by my bedside. "We were the fools, to think you an empty-headed Court dame. You did nothing foolish. In fact, you tried to insist we take the Aryx and leave you behind, until Tristan told you in no uncertain terms we could not think of leaving you and to stopper your mouth. Then you insisted we bypass the town and go into the forest, and you tried to prove you were well and hale by reciting Tiberian verbs. You showed great valor, *d'mselle* di Rocancheil."

His dark eyes gleamed with merriment, and the lines were gone completely. I bit my lower lip, thinking he was mocking me but unable to decide just how good-naturedly. "I beg your pardon. I do not mean to be any trouble, in such a dire situation."

"Your Majesty." Now he was dignified, drawing himself up, every inch the Guard. He would never be considered handsome, but later in life when his face settled on his bones he would be thought of as severe and dignified. His features would hold up well. "Tis an honor to serve you, and I mean every word of my oath. I spoke in haste once, out of anger and pain and grief. Please, do me the honor of forgetting that outburst and accepting my apology. I offer it in good faith."

My eyelids turned heavy, great weariness swamping me. "Really, *chivalier*. I am the least queenly person I have ever met."

"To yourself, mayhap." He folded his arms across his chest, his leather belt creaking slightly. "The Aryx would not accept your touch if you were not at least capable of becoming such. Why else did the Blessed gift it to us? Now rest, *d'mselle*, an it please you. Tristan should be returning soon, and he will wish to speak with you."

Oh, no. That thought made me sigh again. I had no desire to speak to the Captain. "What, to scold me?" I closed my eyes. "I am merely a silly Court girl with too-noble feelings."

That wrung another chuckle from di Yspres. He seemed very merry. Perhaps his wits were touched.

Then there were footsteps, and his laughter ceased as if cut by a knife.

Two knocks sounded on the door, a pause, then a third. The door was unbolted, and Jierre murmured something. The door closed again, and the bolt shot home.

"Well enough. How is she?" D'Arcenne, a heaviness to the words. Relief bloomed secretly in my chest, and I kept my lips pressed tight over it.

"The hedgewitch said we dare not move her for three days more, charmed her again, and left a different tisane. She will return tomorrow. The *d'mselle* was awake and seemed lucid, for a short time. Now I think she sleeps." There was a short pause as their footsteps crossed to the table. "She asked for you."

"Hm." It was the same noise I had heard before from the Captain, neither agreeing nor disagreeing, a noncommittal reply. Someone approached the bed.

I opened my eyes to see Tristan d'Arcenne gazing down at me, his blue eyes dark and thoughtful. His bruised face looked much better, but his mouth turned down at the corners, and his eyebrows drew together. He was pale. "*D'mselle.*" There was a strangeness in his tone. "How do you fare?" He lowered himself gingerly into the chair while Jierre busied himself with something at the table.

"I beg your pardon." My voice sounded thin and fretful, a thread in the room's quiet. "I will be better tonight—we must make haste to escape."

He shook his dark head. His voice was gentle, and I finally could think of the strangeness in it. I had never heard his tone so temperate. "I will not risk your death by traveling while you are feverstruck. Why did you not tell me you were so ill?"

I blinked at him, sinking into the bed—a real bed, such a luxury after the past few days. "I am not ill." I searched for words. "I was simply so tired."

"Unused to hard riding, and exhausted by grief," Tristan said. "I was thoughtless, Vianne. Forgive me."

The Captain himself, asking forgiveness? "What could I forgive you for?" I was honestly amazed. "Nobody craves *my* forgiveness, *chivalier*. It has been long since anyone asked it of me." It was not quite true—di Yspres had just asked my forgiveness, too. I knew of women who feigned illness to force such declarations, and it irked me to possibly be counted among them. There was *nothing* wrong with me, save exhaustion that could be staved off if I exercised will and wit enough.

A yawn took me captive. I covered my mouth, reflexively, surprised by how heavy my arm was, weighted with lead.

D'Arcenne said nothing for a few moments. He leaned forward. "Well enough. Will you promise to rest, so we may leave here as soon as possible? I need you to regain your strength, *d'mselle*, not waste it. Help me. I do not know how else to ask."

If he had leapt onto the table in a set of skirts and announced his desire to join the barbarian hordes of Tifrimat or Torkai, I would have been less amazed. As it was, I stared round-eyed at him for a long moment before remembering that he did ask me a question.

My wits were sorely blunted. *Come, Vianne. Sharpen yourself.* "You truly need my help?"

"Absolutely." He even looked serious, sharp mountainfolk face set. Then again, he always did. When he was older he would not look like di Yspres. No, d'Arcenne would retain his looks for a long time, the bones under the skin preserving a certain beauty. "Please. Promise me you will rest, and stop insisting on being taken from here so quickly. Let me worry about the Duc d'Orlaans. Let me believe I am still capable of performing my duty." Here he gave a bitter little laugh.

It was so unlike him, I thought perhaps I *did* have a fever, and it had strangled what wits I had left. "I will promise to rest, if…" *If you will not kill anyone on my account* was what I wished to say, but I could not make myself utter it. If I voiced the bargain, it would be admitting the murders had happened.

A noblewoman should not say such things. And I did not wish to. I hoped never to think on it again. I was so, so tired. If they *did* leave me in this room, I would be perfectly content. I would sleep, and the rest of the world could do what it would without my help at all.

D'Arcenne hovered, leaning close and watching me closely. "Anything you like. Set me your task, *d'mselle*."

As if this were a silly courtsong, tasks set and a lady to die for. I shook my head, my hair moving against the pillow. Fresh sheets, how luxurious; could I simply not stay here forever? "I shall rest." To prove it, I closed my eyes.

"Good." D'Arcenne did not move. He simply tarried in the chair, and I could feel his gaze upon me like sunlight.

There was a long silence, and my breathing evened out. I relaxed, but sleep would not come.

Finally di Yspres spoke, soft and respectful. "Eat something. She is safe enough now. What of the supplies?"

"We have more than enough," d'Arcenne replied heavily. There was no sound of movement. Did he still watch me? "I almost cost us everything."

"She'll need you strong, not starved. How much coin have we?"

Most interesting. They are planning. Listen well, Vianne. Keeping my ears open at Court had served me well; this was not eavesdropping, for I *was* seeking to sleep. I told my conscience to leave me be.

"Four or five purses. Enough to last through the next winter. Arcenne will shelter us, too, pay us through trade with Navarrin so d'Orlaans cannot trace it. I am more worried about the peasantry, and sorcery. The killspell on Simieri was well-laid, and powerful, d'Orlaans has been practicing. What might he cast at Arcenne?"

"Or at her? Do not borrow trouble just yet, we have enough."

"What did she say, Jierre? Tell me."

I heard a liquid sound. Wine, poured into a cup. "She thinks you mean to scold her, Captain."

"Does she." I heard them settle down, and smelled something heavy and rich. Mince pies. It made my stomach tighten into knots. I was not hungry.

I turned onto my side and burrowed under the covers, sighing. They were quiet. I curled around myself and hugged the pillow. The linens smelled of lavender.

"The hedgewitch thinks you her betrothed." Jierre sounded strained.

D'Arcenne said nothing.

"Twas easy enough to let her think so," Jierre continued. "Tristan, my Captain, you are hopeless."

"Indeed. A fine word for it."

From there the talk turned to the rest of the Guard, camped in the Shirlstrienne. They were worried but still in good spirits, and Tristan had delivered supplies to them. We would be ready to traverse the forest toward Arcenne in a few days' time.

If I could shake free of the fever, that was. I closed my eyes more tightly and resolved to do all I could.

Chapter Ten

The hedgewitch Magiere was a broad, red-faced woman, her graying hair caught in a snowy kerchief. She felt my pulse, peered into my eyes, and declared me much better. "But you must rest," she said firmly, her dark gaze skipping over my face, as if afraid to settle. I must have been a sight. "No riding for two more days, and mind you go slowly after that. Where are you bound, *d'mselle*?"

I knew not what lie to tell, but di Yspres smoothly intervened. "We are bound for Avignienne to visit distant family." He leaned against the mantel, a fine sight in his feathered hat with his sword at his side, slim and dark as the hero of any courtsong. "We have not much left, but we are lucky all the same to have each other."

Her back was turned, so she did not see the wink he tipped me. If I had not felt so slow and stupid I might have betrayed the game, but as it was I merely fixed my eyes on the hedgewitch and tried to look vapid.

It was no large feat. My wits simply would not answer me, and I sorely missed them.

She beamed, pouring another small cup of the syrupy tisane. "Such a devoted brother!" she clucked, and held the cup to my lips. I suffered it, drinking obediently, and accepted a draught of water while she rinsed the smaller cup from the pitcher. Her skirts whispered and rustled in the room's quiet. I heard footsteps in the halls outside my door and sounds from the street below, but it was surprisingly peaceful inside this room.

Pale pearly sunlight flooded through the windows. The sky had clouded, and it smelled of rain, a green odor filtering through doors and halls and windows to reach my own sensitive hedgewitch nose. I wondered about the Guard, sheltering in the forest, and bit my lip so I would remember not to ask di Yspres about them in *m'dama* Magiere's hearing.

"Excuse me, *m'dama*," I said politely, and she preened under my respectful tone. "I have some small knowledge of tisanes, and could not help but notice you've mixed me a strong draught. Am I truly that ill?"

She fussed over me, taking the empty cup and smoothing the blankets. "Oh, aye, *d'mselle*. Fever's a risk, especially for such a gentle lady as yourself. Why, two of the women in the town have died, and it not even summer yet. And a rumor of plague, too, but I do not believe it. You were fair taken when I saw you, *d'mselle*; and your betrothed white with fear."

Di Yspres made another smothered sound, and I glanced curiously at him. He examined a vase on the mantel with great interest, and I thought sourly that he had a very strange sense of humor indeed, calling the Captain my betrothed. But still, it explained why he rode with us, and it deflected suspicion. "He was?" I tried to sound pleased.

"Oh, aye. Tis clear to see how he fancies you. Now, you must have some broth and bread, and another cup of tisane before bed. I shall charm you now, *d'mselle*, an it please you." Magiere's apple-red cheeks crinkled as she smiled at me. I nodded.

"Many thanks for your trouble, *m'dama*." *You have made the same jest a King did. I hope it repays you more kindly.*

She preened again, and laid her work-roughened hand against my forehead. The charm she used was simple, but she had some power. I closed my eyes, feeling the same warmth stealing up from my toes to flush my entire body with its healing. When it was finished, I opened my eyes, smiling at her.

She gasped. *What did I do?* Puzzled, my sudden happiness drained away. "Your pardon. Is aught amiss?"

"No." She took her callused hand away, suddenly shy. "You're very pretty, *d'mselle*. And when you smile, 'tis a wonder."

She sought to flatter me, hoping Jierre would hear and add to her fee. I wished her joy of it, for she did her job well. "My thanks for the compliment," I answered with good grace. "And for your care, *m'dama*."

She fluttered away. Di Yspres paid her—I did not look to see how much—and she sternly reminded him that I must not be moved, and I should not ride hard for another week. The lieutenant agreed and accompanied her to the door. Their small talk held very little information, but I still noted everything in it, out of long habit.

It pays to remember such trifling conversation, and in good coin too. Once I had pieced together an intrigue from a single word, and moved to shield Lisele from it. It had only been a trivial one, involving dresses and jewels, but I was still rather proud of how neatly I outdid di Valancourt. Her face when Lisele appeared in a simple gown and put her beribboning to shame had been priceless, though I suspect I was the only person to see the flash of anger—and only because I had been watchful for it.

But you were not watching when it counted, Vianne.

I had other business now, so I did my best to ignore that thought. I slid my hand under the cover and found the pocket of my linen shift. The emerald ear-drops I had carried all the way from Palais D'Arquitaine bit into my palm as I brought my hand out.

I sighed as soon as the hedgewitch had quit the room. "Lieutenant? *Chivalier*? Here, I have summat to say."

He approached the bed cautiously. I had not asked where the Captain was—gone when I awakened; I told myself I did not feel the lack.

"*D'mselle*?" Di Yspres's tone was a great deal softer than his wont.

I opened my hand. The ear-drops, heavy silver and glittering green stones, lay obediently in my palm. "I was wearing these the day the Princesse…died." I heard the queer dullness in my tone; I was not sprightly in conversation today. "I know it costs coin to engage a hedgewitch. Perhaps you could…"

He gazed at the ear-drops, then at my face. Heat rose in my cheeks.

"Your pardon, *d'mselle* di Rocancheil, but if we sold them, it would cause comment. Maybe in the Citté we could do so without attracting notice, but here we cannot. And besides, we have enough coin for now. Keep those, an it please you."

I nodded, my cheeks hot. A well-bred lady would normally never discuss such a thing with anyone but a solicitor or a majorduomo. I bit the inside of my cheek and folded my fingers over the ear-drops.

"I beg your pardon." I gazed at the blue-and-white quilt. "I only thought to help."

"Much appreciated, *d'mselle*." He scratched his cheek. Twas a good thing we were both dark-haired and dark-eyed; still, I wondered if anyone truly mistook us for brother and sister. "Tristan went to see if he could buy a horse for you—a palfrey, perhaps, something with an easy gait."

"Oh. I must remember to thank him." Prim and unhelpful, giving him no purchase did he seek to embarrass me.

The lieutenant settled his hat on the table and dropped into the chair by the side of the bed. His lean face broke into a wide, unaffected smile. "I remember Tristan set a watch over you at Court. Once or twice I took a shift. He would always ask what you had done that day, if you seemed happy, who had spoken to you. We often discussed that you sought to minimize your lineage."

I sensed danger in this conversation, but could not tell what quarter it would arrive from. "You mean, I did not act like a bastard royal? I heard the rumors, but the rest of Arquitaine is—*was*—full of other nobles that could lay claim to a larger share. It mattered little to me."

"You had the benefit of blood from both sides of your family tree, and it may have mattered to the other ladies-in-waiting," Jierre noted, reasonably enough. "I think perhaps some of the...ah, the small troubles you had at Court were a result of this. It was known you were the King's ward, and under Princesse Lisele's protection. Who would have dared to slight you openly? But you could be snubbed in countless little ways—and the fact you seemed not to care only added fuel to the flames."

"Oh." I watched the squares on the quilt rise and fall as I breathed. Yet I did not say more. *And you are not simply making conversation to ease me. You have some purpose in mind.* Until I knew what that purpose was, best I keep my lips sealed.

"Tristan watched over you," Jierre prompted.

I gathered myself. Now was as good a time as any for me to chance a throw. "He was commanded to by the King. *Chivalier*, I know you do not wish Captain d'Arcenne to throw his life away for what he thinks is his duty any more than I do. I thought if I could give him the Aryx and ride south, I might draw some attention and leave you time and space to reach Arcenne safely." *And I may hide myself quite handily as a hedge-witch, or starve to death in Marrseize.* "The Captain seems determined to do himself some harm," I added delicately.

Di Yspres shrugged. His face had shut itself most firmly, all amusement fled. "You hold the Aryx, and are of royal blood. You cannot relinquish it, Your Majesty, as much as you may wish to. Arquitaine law says the Aryx chooses its holder."

I shifted uncomfortably. "But it did not *choose* me. I was late reaching Lisele's side, and she pressed it on me. Tis not mine." *What of this do you not understand, Lieutenant? I am seeking to save you* and *d'Arcenne some trouble; I will not go very far on this course without your help.*

"But it is." He was just as merciless as his Captain. "The Aryx is what all Court sorcery flows from. It is the heart of Arquitaine, and tis more than powerful enough to have chosen you instead of d'Orlaans."

It was perilously close to blasphemy, but I had to say it. "If tis so powerful, why did it not save Lisele? And the King?"

Jierre stopped, pushing his hair back with his fingers. His boots creaked slightly as he shifted, and his rapier tapped the chair. "Who knows, *d'mselle*? Yet for good or ill, we have sworn our service to you as the Queen."

"What if I released you from your service, *chivalier*?" My hand was a fist, wrapped around the ear-drops, but I lifted it and touched the hard lump of the Aryx under the linen shift. I had been able to wash myself that morn, though it had cost me far more effort than such a simple operation should entail, and Tinan di Rocham's clothes were away to be laundered.

I was grateful for that. The weight of the lump of metal at my throat, however, did no good. My chest could barely rise and fall under such a burden.

A single shrug. My protest was of little account to this man. "If you released us all tomorrow, we would simply take our oaths again. We are bound to this course."

"You could go over the mountains to Navarrin and take service there." *And you would live. I would not have your deaths on my burdened conscience. I have enough, by the Blessed.*

"We are d'Arquitaine." His chin lifted proudly, shoulders back. "And we are in the right. The Duc killed his brother and his niece. Such a monster is not fit for the throne."

I could not argue with that. "I wish you could find someone else." I dropped my eyes back to the quilt.

"So does Tristan. He could court the Duchesse di Rocancheil, but the Queen of Arquitaine is an entirely different tale."

You jest too much. I stared at Jierre, who leaned forward earnestly. My heart thundered as if I would faint, like any well-bred *d'mselle* in a silly courtsong. *Or is he mocking me? Both are equally likely.* I searched for a response that would not lead the conversation into even more dangerous waters. Now that I knew he would not help me, I would be forced to find what I could in another direction. The di Rocham boy. Or di Parmecy et Villeroche—he seemed, perhaps, easily led? I did not know enough about them to begin setting my snares. "Captain d'Arcenne does not seem the courting type." *What would Comtesse Rochburre say?* A bright pain pierced my chest. The numbness, my friend, was wearing away, and the truth of the horrors I had seen sinking in. I half-wished we were still riding through Arquitaine, so I could have something other than these memories to torment me.

"Do you not care for him, then?" Di Yspres leaned even further forward, intent. Was it cruelty in his bright dark gaze? "Because, *d'mselle*—"

"Please. Do not mock me, *Chivalier* di Yspres, I beg of you. If you will not aid me, leave me be." My voice broke on the last syllable, and a knock sounded at the door. *Rescued, and not a moment too soon.* I closed my eyes, sinking into the pillows.

There was a pause, and three more knocks. Di Yspres unlocked the door, and booted feet tramped. Sudden fear turned the taste of the Feversbane on my tongue to copper.

"Good morn to you, Jierre." Twas Luc di Chatillon's light, merry voice, and I slumped into the pillows, wishing mightily for anodyne sleep. "How does the Queen?"

"Well enough. How does the Guard?" There was the sound of men greeting one another—the slaps on the shoulder, the creaking of leather.

"Well enough as well." Di Chatillon gave forth another merry laugh. "Much easier, now that we know she'll live. We were fair worried."

"No less than d'Arcenne," Adersahl di Parmecy et Villeroche said. "May we speak to her?"

It was no use. I could not feign stupor at this point, and it would be unconscionable to waste such an opportunity for setting my wits to discovering which of them would aid me. The three of them clustered near the door, and I pulled my hand back under the covers, slipping the ear-drops back into the small pocket sewn into my shift.

"Take care not to tire her. The physicker says she will be fit to travel soon if we do not ride too hard."

Luc di Chatillon's blond head dipped. He approached the bed, Adersahl trailing him. The older man smoothed his fine mustache nervously.

"Good morn to you, Your Majesty." Di Chatillon's hazel eyes danced. They did not wear the red sash of the Guard here, but Court was evident in the bow he swept me, his hat's feather almost brushing the floor. "And a bright Blessed dawning. Glad to see you hale."

"My thanks for your concern." I felt real gratefulness, so I smiled as prettily as possible.

He grinned in return. For a first sally, it held promise.

"*D'mselle.*" Adersahl di Parmecy took my hand, which I had freed from the quilt. He bent over it, his black mustache tickling as it brushed my knuckles. "We feared for you."

"No need for fear." I took my hand back after he straightened. "But I thank you for it." *And I will see if you or your partner are easily led. A horse and some time is all I need. That, and to take this metal from my throat.*

"What news is there?" the lieutenant asked di Chatillon, drawing him away.

"None. Town is quiet, forest is quiet, and di Narborre is hunting to the south. We have some time." The blond man's grin faded a little. "Is the…is *d'mselle* di Rocancheil truly well?"

We shall not be accusing me of vapors now. "I am well enough." I tried to sound as firm as Countess Rocheburre. "I could ride today, were it required." All three men halted and gazed at me, perhaps astonished. I felt a completely reprehensible desire to laugh, suppressed it. "Truly. I do not wish the Guard in any deeper danger. The sooner you reach Arcenne, the safer you are."

Luc di Chatillon glanced at Jierre, one sandy eyebrow raised. Had Court not taught him to veil such speaking glances? He most patently did not believe me.

Di Parmecy smoothed his magnificent mustache. It seemed a nervous movement, as if he stroked a small furry animal to calm himself. "*D'mselle*…the fever was very dire. Very dire indeed."

I could have said that if I died, they could have taken the Aryx and been free of the burden of caring for me. They must have read such a thought in my expression, for di Chatillon looked grave and the eldest man kept at his mustache. An uncomfortable silence ruled the room, and my Court training rose up inside me, demanding something graceful and witty.

I had little left of grace or wit about me. Still, I should put them at their ease; twas never too early to cultivate an acquaintance for a plan, or to frustrate intrigue. Yet I searched for aught to say that did not sound ungrateful or transparent.

Luc di Chatillon finally broke the quiet. "You look very sad, *d'mselle*."

"I feel a little wan," I admitted diplomatically. My wits were not what they could be. "Your pardon."

"Oh, no. You were ill, *d'mselle*, and still you thought only of our safety. We are glad to serve you."

"Do not tire her," di Yspres interrupted. "*D'mselle*, they wished to see you well. Tristan should return soon."

"We caught him in the square, watching the people. He looked grim," di Parmecy offered, his mustache twitching.

"When does he not?" Luc laughed again, the rafters ringing. "He is your staunchest *chivalier*, *d'mselle*. He would not hear of another Guard taking a turn at watching over you."

My voice sounded strange even to myself. "D'Arcenne does his duty, tis well known."

The three men exchanged looks I had little trouble deciphering, much about them made plain in just that moment. To separate them and work them against the Captain's will would not be easy.

I doubt I am up to the challenge at this moment. I cursed my weakness and closed my eyes, sinking again into the pillows. "Your pardon, *sieurs*. I am not myself. Mayhap I am more ill than I thought."

"You seem to be." The lieutenant, kindly enough, but with a shadow of mistrust. Could he see what I planned? Of course, I had all but given him a map of my intentions. "We shall withdraw, to give you lee to rest."

Someone—I peeked through my lashes to see Luc di Chatillon—touched my hand where it lay against the coverlet. "Aye, Your Majesty. If we tire you, the Captain might flog us. He worries like an old woman for you."

"Leave the Captain to his business," Adersahl snapped. "You talk too much, Luc."

The first glimmers of a plan became evident. *So, di Chatillon laughs and does not think before he speaks, and di Parmecy et Villeroche is not so easily led as I thought. Perhaps the boy, di Rocham. Wait, Vianne. Your moment will come.*

"Aye to that." The lieutenant ushered them away. "Now we shall leave you to rest, *d'mselle*, but I will return soon." He swept the other two out, giving me a significant stare as they all swept their hats and gave me Court-fair bows. I waved a hand gracefully, and when the door closed behind them, I sighed.

Now. Test your strength.

I pushed myself up on my hands, looking about with interest. There was a pile of gear in one corner—I thought I recognized a pair of saddlebags belonging to the Captain. There was also a set of clothes laid over the back of a chair—a smaller linen shirt, a pair of breeches, and the leather vest I had worn from the riverside boardinghouse.

So they had brought me fresh clothes. Thank the Blessed. Which *would* one thank for laundry? Perhaps Jiserah; all things of the home were her purview. Certainly not Alisaar the Lovely—she was concerned only with love and artifice. The Huntress most emphatically would not care either.

Thinking on the gods led me to the Aryx. Why had it not moved to save Lisele's life? There were stories—old ones, aye, but still considered good—of the will of the gods striking through their serpents to protect their vessel. But that was in the times when the gods took an active interest, which they had not for a long while. Not in overt ways, though there was no drought or crop failure in Arquitaine. Those who served the Twelve Blessed often murmured that the gods had larger concerns than petty personal problems.

This is not personal, it is the fate of the land the Blessed call their own. Why did the Aryx not strike down the traitors?

I thought on this. It took some time to dress, since my fingers shook and I had to sit upon the bed and rest until I could attempt the lacing on the vest. I had never thought of the help a ladyservant was in such matters; would I ever have a girl to lace me up or attend to my hair again? Or would I end myself in a Marrseize slum? By starvation, or summat else?

Would I even sell some things I held very dear indeed, if I became hungry enough? For I did not think I was a fine enough hedgewitch to earn a mountain of coin. Still, I could give lessons on Tiberian, I supposed—but that might require a letter of introduction, did I wish to governess in a noble house. A merchant would perhaps not care.

I shuddered at the turn my thoughts were taking. Perhaps I could retreat to a cloister? Kimyan's Elect sometimes took those such as me, but I did not have a dowry.

That is a worry for another day, Vianne. Your concern is to free the Guard of your weight.

The watercloset was a relief; I washed fever-film from my face and immediately felt much more cheerful. Then I sat upon the bed and attempted to braid my hair.

Like most Court women, my hair has never been cut, only trimmed a bit now and again. As a result, it is always a task to braid when it has been loose for two days of fever-tossing abed. I had no comb—I did not know where my servant's bag was—so I had to untangle the knots with my fingers, and it took what little energy remained to me. I mulled on the nature of the gods, and the more pressing problem of how I would seek employment in Marrseize, and the still-more-pressing problem of how to escape the Guard so they did not injure themselves on my account.

When I finished braiding, I held the end of the rope. The thought of cutting the whole mass free and seeking to escape through the window like the Princesse Ducarne in the old courtsong was *highly* appealing.

I finally spotted a bit of green ribbon on the table next to the small cordial bottle that held the Feversbane. That worked to tie off my braid, and I stood by the table for a moment, swaying, ir-resolute.

What are you thinking? I scolded myself, and reached up to touch the Aryx's hard warmth under my shirt. *You are almost too weak to walk. You will not go far. Now is the time for planning in-stead of flight.*

Nevertheless, I pulled at the heavy silver chain, and discov-ered something disconcerting.

The Great Seal of Arquitaine would not budge. It seemed to have grown into my skin.

I opened my shirt and made my way into the watercloset, where there was a generous sliver of mirror over the washstand. I watched as I pulled on the chain, and the Aryx would not move. I saw the chain sliding through the aperture made by two snake-coils, but the Aryx itself fused to me. I felt no tugging sensation against my skin when I pulled on the chain, but the chain itself bit my fingers. A warning nip, like a small hunting dog.

I let out a soft, breathless sound, half a sob. I tugged on the chain again—the Seal would not move. The chain jerked free of my fingers, and I let it.

The Aryx chooses its holder. Could it read my mind, discerning I wished no part of it? If it was fused to my skin now, why had it not performed a more useful feat and safeguarded Lisele—or even *warned* her? I twisted frantically at the chain, disregarding a second, sharper nip against my fingers. I had lost all my breath, and I think that is perhaps why I heard the soft, sliding noise.

My entire body chilled, as if I had been doused with cold water.

I turned, my fingers curling around the edge of the washstand. It was heavy frigid porcelain, and I clutched at it with all my waning strength.

I did not hear the door open. Sharp fingers of unease touched my back.

The footsteps paced to the window, back to the main door. I could have peered out through the small space between the watercloset door and the jamb—I had left the door slightly open, in my haste.

Faint scuffing, and a deep silence.

The tingle of Court sorcery began to edge along my skin.

Sight blurred, my gaze weakly piercing the veil of the visible. Any type of sorcery is difficult when the physical body is ill, even the passive use of Sight. I swayed against the washstand, my hip bumping its unforgiving edge.

The Aryx pulsed against my chest, a second heartbeat. I put my free hand up blindly and felt warm metal move under my fingers. Now that I was not seeking to remove it, the Aryx slid freely against my skin.

The sorcery in the other room stilled. Someone was waiting…and I smelled something I had once before, something quite distinct. An odor like acid, magic, and rust; apples and wet dog.

A killspell. Not a poisonous one, but one that reeked of steel and iron-spill blood.

Tis not the Captain or di Yspres. My legs turned weak as water. The fever was returning, sick unsteady heat mounting in my cheeks, turning my fingers to slick heavy sausages. *Who? And why?*

I could not simply stay in the watercloset and let a Court sorcerer use a killspell on whoever entered the room. Di Yspres had said he would return—and Tristan d'Arcenne. They would be walking blindly into danger.

Why cannot he sense me, if he has enough sorcery for Sight? Of course, I am a practicing hedgewitch, I sink into the scenery. But still…

I cast about for something, anything, to use as a possible weapon, my fingers still clutching at the Aryx.

I was near frantic when inspiration struck. There was a hedgewitch charm that would turn a killspell back on itself. If I could only *remember* it.

My heart leapt against the cage of my ribs. D'Arcenne. A killspell would hurt him even if he had the presence of mind to shunt it aside; it could kill him if it took him unawares. He was a Court sorcerer too, but if he was caught off his guard there was precious little hope.

With a type of swooning terror, I realized I could hear other footsteps. Light feet in heavy boots, a gait I knew.

Stupid, silly fool that I was, I was still listening for him.

I cast about again. I could not for the life of me remember the thrice-damned charm. I wished frantically I had spent time training my memory instead of reading romances or dancing, frittering away time in the Princesse's chambers.

No, not hedgewitchery. Try something else, Vianne. Think!

I was an abysmal Court sorcerer, with only some tiny skill at rough illusion and enough power to light a candle despite all my sword-noble blood.

A killspell must be triggered. If tis thrown at someone in haste instead of laid with careful preparation, you must be able to see them. I remember that much.

There. I had my answer.

There was a brief courteous tap at the door, such as a *chivalier* might use to warn an invalid but not wake her if she slept. I dropped my hand from the Aryx and took two steps forward, reaching for the watercloset's door. Court sorcery took shape on my fingertips, a quick, growing shimmer.

The door from the hall pushed open, hinges squeaking slightly.

I jerked the watercloset door open and flung my own small magic in the general direction I guessed the intruder was hiding, just before the killspell roared free. Light burst free, a white-hot globe of witchlight, so intense it hurt to look at. I whispered the last syllable of my sorcery, heard a cry and the dry rasp of steel leaving the sheath before my head struck the floor.

Court sorcery is not as draining as hedgewitchery, but it still takes a toll on the body—a toll I was ill prepared to pay.

"—light—"

"—truly chills the blood."

"—Tristan—"

Confused motion. A group of men all speaking at once, yet seeking to keep the noise down. For all that, they would be lucky to escape notice.

Why must we escape notice? What is happening?

"No." Tristan d'Arcenne sounded ragged, and furious, as if he had been weeping. His voice broke. "No. Vianne—*Vianne.*"

"I will kill you—I will *kill* you!" A man, Court-accented, but not one of the Guard.

What are they doing in my room? For a mad moment, I once again thought I was safe at Court. Had I swooned? I was not given to fainting fits, that was Lady di Wintrefelle's trick—

"Keep him quiet. Gag him, if you must," Jierre di Yspres hissed. "For the love of the gods, Tristan, *calm* yourself!"

"I am still alive?" I asked wonderingly, high and breathless. Nobody could be more surprised than I at the thought.

Breathless silence. Someone smoothed my forehead, picked up my hands. I found myself reclining, the sheets still smelled of lavender. Warm, callused fingers traced the back of my hand, touched my cheek. "Vianne." Tristan d'Arcenne, husky and ragged. "You saved my life yet again, *d'mselle.*"

Hazy shapes played as my eyelids fluttered. "Twas a killspell, I knew you would be returning." I blinked, finding my gaze could focus now.

"You blinded him with a witchlight, *m'chri*." D'Arcenne's blue eyes blazed, and he had pushed his dark hair from his forehead. There was a fresh cut on his cheek, and a trickle of blood had found its way down to his chin. "And a fair one, too. When did you become such a Court sorcerer?"

"I never was," I protested weakly, and he stroked my cheek again. It was a strangely intimate, *highly* improper touch, and I would have blushed had I had not been looking wildly about for the source of the killspell. Sense was flooding me, and *uneasy* was too pale a word for the terror returning as I gathered myself. "Where—what did you—"

"Safely bound and awaiting questioning." D'Arcenne's gaze turned dark, and he ceased touching my face. "I think I will take particular pleasure in interrogating him. How do you feel, Vianne?"

"Tired," I breathed. "Dear gods. I thought he would kill you. Who is he?"

"I believe he is Yveris di Palanton. Do you remember him?" D'Arcenne recommenced touching my cheek. Oddly, the touch made me feel better. Comforted.

The name meant nothing. "Do not hurt him," I whispered. He seemed fearfully angry, for all his tenderness. *Why does he touch me so? It is improper.* "Please."

"When death comes for him, it will be merciful." Low and conversational again, and I knew enough of him now to guess at the danger such softness held. I shivered to hear it, and he touched my eyebrow, ran his fingers over my cheek, touched my lips.

Comtesse Rochburre would have been scandalized. "Why was he trying to kill you? None of this makes *sense*."

"I shall solve the mystery, Vianne. Rest." He held a small cupful of the tisane to my lips, and I took it gratefully. It tasted foul and medicinal against the copper fear coating my tongue. I almost gagged, but I knew it would help me. "What were you seeking to do?"

"I wished to be dressed." My eyelids were so heavy. A great lassitude stole over me. The Aryx pulsed against my chest. Now was not the time to admit I had wanted to leave him the Aryx and flee. *Or* that I had been planning to intrigue among the Guard to do so. "And the watercloset."

"Rest, *m'chri*," he urged quietly, and I wondered if I had misheard him. Why did he name me thus? It was such an intimate term I would have flushed if I had not been so sick and weak. "We shall speak of this when you wake."

"Be…careful." I sighed. My eyes closed, and I sank into the bed. The tisane formed a hard lump in my stomach, spread out in waves of warmth.

When next the Captain spoke, it was that soft considering tone of leashed violence far more frightening than screams or shouts. "Adersahl. Stay here, stand guard. If even a mouse moves in this room, kill it."

"Aye, Captain." I had never heard the elder man sound so grave.

"Jierre, Luc, bring our guest. I have a few questions I would ask of him." He sounded so calm, so reassuringly ordinary, that I sighed again. All was well. D'Arcenne would make it well.

"And if he tries…?" A di Yspres I had never heard before as well—a crisp, almost peremptory lieutenant. No, he would not intrigue against his Captain, even for his Captain's own good.

"Stick him in the kidneys. It will not matter much later."

I curled on my side among the pillows. Something pressed against my forehead. It was a kiss, a gentle one, and the smell of Tristan d'Arcenne, leather and steel and male musk, enfolded me for a brief moment.

It was the second kiss he had given me. "My thanks, *m'chri*." His breath warmed my ear, as if we were a-horseback and fleeing again.

They dragged the man out, and I wondered even in my daze that they were all alive. The man had a Court accent. How had he found us?

And could di Narborre be far behind?

Chapter Eleven

The angle of sunlight falling into the room said twas morning. I was also hungry—famished, in fact. I was about to reach for the bell on my night table to summon a servant when I remembered, yet again, that I was no longer at Court.

I pushed myself upright and saw the room lying quiet under its gilding of gray, muffled sunglow, and I blinked. I felt lucid, clear-headed, and very weak.

D'Arcenne was at the table, his head on his arms, asleep. His face turned toward me, his eyes closed, and the deep regularity of his breathing was…comforting. He looked as if he had been studying, and merely put his head down for a moment to rest.

The marks of the beating they had gifted him with were only shadows now. His eyelashes lay against his cheeks in two perfect arcs, charcoal-black, and his mouth was slightly open, relaxed. His cheeks were faintly brushed with stubble.

Jierre di Yspres slept on a bedroll by the door. I swallowed hard, and returned to myself in a rush. What had happened to the man last night?

Had he survived until morning? Somehow I doubted it.

Yveris di Palanton. I did not know the name. I thought I knew everyone at Court, at least by sight. I slid my feet out of the bed, inch by inch. The floor was cold, especially after the warm nest of blankets. I felt as one does after prolonged bedrest—weak, itching to move, but not quite sure how far one's strength will hold.

I tried to stand, my knees shaking, and a floorboard squeaked.

D'Arcenne bolted upright, his sword leaving the scabbard with a whisper. I let out a gasp and sat down so hard my teeth clicked together.

D'Arcenne blinked, examined every corner of the room with a swift glance. The sword vanished. His blue eyes met mine. "Good morn, *d'mselle.*"

"Captain." My throat dried like a drought-parched field. It seemed a bloodless way to greet him. So did *d'Arcenne.* Perhaps I had earned the right to address him otherwise. "Tristan."

"Vianne." A slight bow. "You saved my life again." His gazed locked itself to mine, and his shoulders were stiff. He stood straight as his own rapier, as if he were at drill in a courtyard. "I am beginning to think you a *demiange* sent from the gods to watch over me, *m'chri.*"

There it was again. Tristan d'Arcenne was calling me beloved.

A slip of the tongue, nothing more. He was close to death yesterday, that may make a man charitable. "Captain…" I chewed at my bottom lip, searching for something light and diplomatic to say. Nothing arose.

Jierre di Yspres yawned from his bedroll. "And a bright good morn to everyone," he grumbled, sleep's gravel evident in his tone. "What time is it, anyway?"

"Time for you to get our fair *d'mselle* some breakfast." Tristan's gaze had not moved from my face. I felt rumpled—I had slept in Tinan di Rocham's shirt and trousers. Someone had taken the leather vest—perhaps d'Arcenne. That thought sent a hot flare of not-entirely-unpleasant embarrassment through me.

Jierre grumbled a bit more, but he hauled himself upright and made a very pretty Court bow to me, sweeping a nonexistent hat. "Good morn, *d'mselle* Your Majesty, and lovely to see your fair face."

I gathered myself. "And better to see your smiling face, *sieur chivalier*." I found my accustomed tone, light and accented sharply, as all the Princesse's women spoke. "What happened?" *Is there yet another death lingering in this room?*

"Breakfast, Jierre." D'Arcenne's tone brooked no discussion.

The lieutenant rolled up his bedroll and stumped cheerfully out the door, scratching at his face and yawning. But he wore two daggers at his belt that he had not before, and I caught a dangerous glint in his dark eyes. I have not seen that look often, except before a duel at Court—a duel I would not witness, being weak of stomach.

It was the look of a man prepared for violence.

I was left with Tristan d'Arcenne and pearly, rainy light filling a room that did not seem to have enough air for me. I sought to breathe deeply, and had little luck. He stood rapier-straight, as if he had not been sleeping in a chair all night.

There, Vianne. Speak of that. It is a safer subject than most. "You slept in a chair, *sieur*?"

He shrugged. "Jierre and I took turns at the door."

So little was he disposed to keep to safe subjects. I supposed there was small use for such grace between us, then. "Who was he?" All my attempt at humor dropped away.

He shrugged. Even unshaven and after a night that could not

have been comfortable, he was still sharp as a fresh-honed blade. "A nasty little boy who played assassin for the Duc d'Orlaans. I think he is probably the one who killed Simeon di Rothespelle. Cut and spelled his saddlegirth, at least."

What little breath I had left escaped me. "To kill me?" I had difficulty making myself heard, though the room was quiet and I heard faint marketsong from the other side of the window—chanted songs of wares for sale, cart wheels, horse hooves, murmurs of conversation.

"I doubt he even knew you were here, and I doubt it was more than chance. He often visits his aunt at the manse less than two leagues from here, and he may have recognized me. I was his target, *m'chri*, and you stopped him." The Captain took one step, two, away from the table. He did not look at me, now, but at some fixed point above my head. "I owe you my life yet again. And more."

My hands trembled, so I clasped them firmly together. "I could smell the killspell. I—"

"I know." He took another two steps. Then another.

He stopped next to the bed, a bare step and a half away. He looked down at me with his blue d'Arcenne eyes, and I had to remind myself to breathe. The fever returned, beating in my wrists and throat and chest.

No—perhaps twas only my heart.

"Would you have killed him, Vianne?" Then he dropped to one knee, a quick, graceful movement, and took my hands in his, almost roughly. "Would you?"

Either the shock of his tone, or the question itself, or the feel of his skin on mine robbed me of sense. "K-k-killed him?" I stammered, and my fingers closed in a convulsive movement, remembering the witchlight pooled in my palm, the glow against my fingers.

I had been so afraid the attacker would harm someone.

Do not be ridiculous, the calm, rational voice of my conscience told me. *You do not have a killspell when you intend merely to frighten. A killspell is to kill. Tis why they call it what they do. It is not a peck on the cheek spell, or a goosefeather tickle spell.*

I looked down at d'Arcenne, whose face turned up to mine. His dark hair fell away from his forehead, and I freed one hand. The back of my fingers brushed his forehead, his cheek. My fingers moved of their own accord, without any direction from propriety or even good sense.

His face changed between one moment and the next. Wondering, as if seeing me for the first time, his eyes wide and guileless as a child's. "No," he breathed. "I do not think you would have, had you thought of it. You did not think, did you."

Had I done wrong? Stray strands of my hair fell free, touched his face. The ribbon must have come free during the night. I leaned forward, again without any volition of my own, as if drawn to him by sorcery, or as the needle is drawn to north's invisible realm. "I...no, I did not think. There was not *time*—"

"I see." He reached up with one hand, his fingers twining in a strand of my hair. "You were..." The hesitation pained me. He was not meant to sound so...unsure.

"I was afraid he might hurt you," I whispered, as if someone else might hear.

"So you blinded him with a witchlight that could have torn the roof from this inn. When did you become such a Court sorcerer?"

He is touching me. Had the fever come back? Or was it *him*? "I am not." My voice refused to work properly. "The Aryx."

His face hardened, and he nodded. My hair was tangled between his fingers, but he did not pull. Merely held it loosely, as he might a docile horse's reins. "The Aryx." He whispered as well, or something was caught in his throat. "Vianne."

"Tristan." My heart beat thinly in my wrists, in my throat. "What happened to him?"

"Di Palanton? He will never trouble another soul. Still, tis unsafe. He recognized me enough to attempt to kill me, and who knows what message he may have sent to his lord and master beforehand?" Tristan's accustomed tone came back, sharp and logical, and his fingers slid free. "We must leave this place. The forest is our only friend now, and a false friend at best. Can you ride?"

He spoke as if I was one of the Guard. My chin lifted, automatically. I could see why they followed him. It was impossible not to, when he was so quiet, with such steely purpose.

A man who spoke thus could make other men do wondrous things.

"I can ride." I sought to sound strong. "I am much better than I was. Have you a horse for me?" It would mean I would no longer ride with him. My good sense was returning, and it whispered that such an event might be safer. At least, to my weak, traitor-throbbing heart.

"I could not find a horse that can keep up with the Guard, nor even one that can stand hard riding. Do you mind?"

I could not decipher his expression. Was he pleased by this? Uncaring? Did he mind at all? "I shall manage," I said around the obstruction in my throat. The furious heat in my cheeks would *not* abate. It was akin to being embarrassed at a fête, only at Court there are ways to hide such embarrassment. Here there was no embrasure to hide behind, and no powder to dull my cheeks, no richly hung ladies' room to retreat to.

He stood, gracefully, his fingers tangled in mine. "Jierre

should return soon. Do you require aid to stand, *m'chri*?" Why did he not free his hand from my grasp? I did not seek to keep him.

Or did I?

He said it again. "No, I am steady enough." I forced my legs to straighten and carry the burden of the rest of me. D'Arcenne steadied me as I almost overbalanced. The floorboard squeaked again, and I found myself right next to Tristan, holding his hand, near enough for a dance.

Closer, actually. So near I could feel the heat of his body. "I think I had best visit the watercloset." Why was I still breathless?

"I think you'd best." He made no move. I did not try to take my hand back, either.

Tristan turned my palm up, lifted it. My knees threatened to fail and he caught me, sliding his arm around my waist.

Dear gods.

I almost laughed. The long series of impossible events seemed to find its madly logical culmination in Tristan d'Arcenne holding me close enough to pavane in an inn room close to the Shirlstrienne, and then—impossible of impossibles—lifting my palm to his mouth. He pressed a kiss into the soft part of my hand, and my heart gave a leap so hard it was as if the drums of the maying festival beat in my chest. "There. For safekeeping. My thanks, Vianne."

I nodded, unable to find anything even remotely sensible to think or do. I said the first thing that leapt into my silly head. "I can ride."

I winced at my own stupidity.

"Good." He folded my fingers over the still-burning kiss. Warm skin, callused from daily practice with sword and knife.

"Do you require any aid? Any at all?"

"I think I am well enough." I fought for air, tried not to gasp. The sudden need to explain something, *anything*, rose. "He would have killed you. I could not—"

"You still did not wish him dead." He shook his head, gravely. "I understand. Truly. For now, an it please you, we shall break our fast and leave this place."

I nodded. Tristan's hand still enclosed mine, and the kiss scorched against my palm. How long would it take for the burning to fade? "Very well."

He stepped back, reluctant, still holding my hand. I swayed, but stayed upright. New strength stole through his flesh into mine.

This man is dangerous, Vianne. What would you not do, for his asking? Especially if he turned this face to you more frequently.

"I watched over you at Court. Not because I feared your ambition, but because I feared for your very life. Once I began, I could not stop." His fingers slid free of mine, and if he was not reluctant to let go he was certainly feigning it well enough to earn a prize.

Why does he say this now? I stood, my fist clenched around the feel of his mouth, in Tinan di Rocham's shirt and breeches, barefoot and rumpled. The Aryx pulsed in time to my heartbeat. "I thought you watched me to make sure I did not—"

Boots in the hallway, thundering in the quiet though whoever owned them was simply striding normally.

I bolted for the safety of the watercloset, my legs threatening to shiver out from under me. I gained my sanctuary and pulled the door shut, just as I heard Jierre di Yspres open the door. "Breakfast, Captain, *d'mselle.*"

I let out a long, shaking sigh and leaned against the door. The sliver of mirror over the washstand revealed my face, flushed cheeks and dark eyes, my hair mussed and tangled, the copper serpent of the Aryx glinting above the collar of my shirt. There was nothing in the mirror to warrant attention.

Just the provincial hedgewitch, Lisele's strange pet lady-in-waiting. That was all. Nothing to catch Tristan's eye.

Yet it seemed I had.

Not just a King's jest, perhaps? I could not even speak my hope to myself.

Find something else to fret at, idiot. You are at the edge of the Shirlstrienne, pursued by di Narborre, and entrusted to the care of a bare half-dozen men who may turn on you in an instant if their Captain decides you are not queenly enough.

Or not tractable enough.

The Aryx, much as I wished to hand it over to the Captain and be shed of the burden, was my best defense. I touched the copper edge above my shirt, fascinated by the play of light on supple metallic scales. Pulling down the material a bit revealed the rest of the Great Seal of Arquitaine.

"Why do you stay with me?" I asked quietly, aware I was speaking to a magical object. If I was exceedingly lucky, it would not answer. "I am not the one you want."

But you may have to play at being so, like one of a Comedie-Trajique troupe. Imagine, Comtesse di Rocheburre used to say. Imagine, and you will do. She was speaking of being a noble-woman and moving gracefully, but I would hazard it applies here.

I may have to hazard it will apply here.

The Aryx only glinted, throbbing against my skin like a second heartbeat. I shook my head, my legs trembling with the aftermath of fever, and decided to set about making myself presentable.

But before I did, I studied myself for a long moment, one thought filling me until I thought I would cry out from the immensity of it.

Tristan d'Arcenne kissed my hand. I watched in the mirror as bright scarlet rose in my cheeks. When I could set the thought quietly down without blushing, I began to move again.

Chapter Twelve

Breakfast for me was broth and new bread, and I was finally hungry. I set to with a will, and the lieutenant peeled an apple for me, quartered it. They ate morning pies, full of egg and salted pork, and there was hot chai and fresh milk to wash them down. There were also slices of the Shirlstrienne cheese, soft and flavored with piniel, studded with nuts.

Afterward, di Yspres set to carrying saddlebags and gear downstairs. D'Arcenne gave me the leather doublet, and I retreated to the watercloset to make myself at least a little more ready to endure another day of horseback. I was combing my hair—Tristan had given me the servant's bag back—when I heard di Yspres.

"We must make haste," he said quietly. My fingers moved of themselves, braiding. "'Tis an uneasy air in the town this morn. I think we should take the back way out."

"Of course." D'Arcenne was manifestly unsurprised.

"I thought she was not a Court sorcerer." Leather creaked as di Yspres hefted gear around. He could catfoot when he chose to, but there seemed no call for it at the moment, so he was loud as a Navarrin metalsmith.

"She is not. The Aryx." A slight, embarrassed cough.

"The Aryx?"

I finished my braid and tied it off with a blue hair ribbon brought from the Palais. *Why could not I have brought something practical?* Chiding myself for it comforted me. *Something other than hair ribbons.*

"It seems to have awakened." The Captain's tone did not alter. Still, di Yspres inhaled sharply, as if he had been pinched.

Awakened? I wrapped the braid around my head, threading another ribbon through it. No servant girl to help with this, either, though I did not feel this lack as much as I could have. It was not quite an affectation to braid my own hair in the style of di Rocancheil at Court, but twas close. *It is the Great Seal, it never slumbers.*

How long had the King had it? Easily thirty years of his reign, since his crowning. I attended Lisele's dressing and had never remarked it in her possession. As far as anyone knew, the Seal lay in the treasure house of the Raven Tower, safely locked away until needed for a fête or particular ceremony.

I could not wake, Lisele had whispered. Had she been seeking to do so?

Why lock it away, unless it was dormant? The old books and tapestries spoke of the ruler of Arquitaine wearing the Aryx by the grace of the Blessed. Yet it had not been worn openly for many a year, many a reign. No war or invasion to make it necessary—Tiberius had not needed it; he made his diplomatic coup with the Damarsene by dint of sheer cunning alone.

Or so the histories said. Now I wondered, and my head hurt with the implications. Had Tiberius's cunning been exercised in keeping the Damarsene from guessing that the Seal of the Blessed slumbered, instead of in other directions? Had they known, very little would have stopped their fine army—and the hateful Pruzians, always at the back of Damar to make mischief or pick at the leavings—from trampling our borders. Arquitaine is a rich prize, and our gods are not as bloodthirsty as the Pruzian's black bird-god, or the Damarsene's jealous, bull-headed blasphemy.

The Aryx did help me with the witchlight. A chill touched my back. *But why? If it could do so, and yet not aid Lisele…*

I bit my lip, looking at the washstand. Porcelain shone white, as I worked the problem inside my skull and found my wits thankfully less dull. At least, there was not the maddening sensation of seeking to think through porridge. I felt much more my usual sharp-eared, intrigue-catching self.

If the Aryx fed Court sorcery, would it do the same for hedgewitchery?

I pulled the medallion from under my shirt easily. It glowed mellow in the skylight's shaft of gleaming sunlight. Three serpents—copper, silver, black gold, twisting around each other, two with ruby eyes, the black serpent with eyes of diamond. I cupped it in my palm, listening to its pulse.

It will not let you remove it, some deep part of me whispered suddenly, both awed and frightened. *It will never willingly let you remove it.*

I knew better than to doubt—it was the same voice that had told me once to comfort my Princesse while she sobbed, when she had sent all her other ladies-in-waiting away. The King had not come to celebrate her birthday, being delayed by a diplomatic crisis—something about the Navarrin ambassador's sudden about-face during trade treaty discussions, I thought, although I had only been twelve and had only the foggiest notion of politics. Their Prince was now a King, and his greed was likewise kinglike in size. Thank the Blessed the mountains made him an ally, by dint of Arquitaine being too difficult to attack. Of course, the fact that our naval power kept Tiberia in check as well had summat to do with Navarrin's good graces.

In any event, I had crept into Lisele's chamber and held her during that long-ago storm of tears, and afterward my place as her favourite was assured. Particularly since I never told a soul. The better I kept my Princesse's secrets, the more assured my place became. The voice of warning had risen since then, during difficult intrigues, when I had to navigate not merely myself but Lisele through treacherous waters and to safe harbor, with her pride intact and my own reputation kept small and eccentric.

The deep voice had never led me astray.

Coils moved against my palm, metal sliding as supple as living tissue, the serpents writhing, straining. Gemmed eyes watched me, unblinking. Beautifully carved scales rasped against each other, a faint whispering in the silence of the tiled washroom.

My mouth went dry as a Tifrimat sand dune. Even Court sorcery could not prepare me for this. If I tried to remove it from my throat, would it stick to my fingers, fusing to my flesh again? Bile rose to the back of my tongue, the breakfast I had been so hungry for craving escape.

My flesh shuddered on my bones at the thought of dropping the Aryx down my shirt again and feeling those delicately carved metal serpents slither-rasp against my chest.

The serpents slowed and ceased, but now the black gold was the uppermost and would show over my shirt. Trembling returned, settling into my marrow. *I cannot hide this. I cannot brook the feel of this against my skin.*

Then, I must. Tristan would wish it.

I braced myself against the wall, a most unladylike sheen of sweat on my forehead. I forced myself to consider this as if it were a riddle, or an intrigue. I had studied the Graeca philosophers' Rules of Logic—one could not study Tiberian and not hear of the Rules—and they would tell me to cease my thrashing and begin in a particular place.

First, what could I state with any certainty?

The Aryx will not harm me—or at least, it has not yet. And it does not slumber. I had used it to power the witchlight. Whatever it had been before, it was most definitely *awake* now.

What if the Aryx remembered I was not the royal it wanted—merely a hedgewitch pressed into service to hold it until someone else could be found? "Do not strike me down, I beg of you," I whispered to the Seal. "I mean no harm."

The snakes stirred again, slightly. I managed to restrain a flinch, but only just.

There was a courteous tap on the door that nearly sent me out of my skin. "*D'mselle?* Are you well?"

I had to try twice before my dry throat would give out a word or two. "Well enough." It took another effort to make my clutching fingers loosen and let the Seal nestle against my shirt over my breastbone.

I flinched. Heavy sluggish warmth spread from the contact, and the sensation was at once terrifying and queerly comforting.

I exited the watercloset to find the lieutenant alone, leaning at the mantel with his feathered hat clasped in one brown hand. His lean face changed at he gazed upon me. "*D'mselle?* Your Majesty?"

I swallowed again, drily. "*Chivalier* di Yspres." It took yet more courage I did not know I possessed to lift the Seal with damp fingertips. "Might I have you examine this?"

He took two steps away from the mantel, and paled, stopping dead. "Gods," he breathed. "The serpents...they have *moved.*"

"So I am not crazed." I should have felt relieved, but fresh unsteadiness welled through me. "I..."

His dark eyes widened until I saw an echo of the child he must have been. "You *are* the Queen. I thought...but you..."

To hear him flounder snapped me back to some manner of sense. "I seek only to be the Duchesse di Rocancheil et Vintmorecy, *sieur*. I *must* stop Tris—ah, the Captain from pursuing a ridiculous course of action and finding himself murdered for it." *You are not ideal, but I have you off balance now. You may even help me.* "Will you help me?"

His throat-apple bobbed as he swallowed, his gaze moving from the Seal to my face. "The Aryx has not awakened since the time of King Fairlaine."

"I thought..." There were indeed stories of the power of the Aryx before Queen Toriane's death—but none after. It was not spoken of, for the wonders of Court sorcery practiced by the nobles still held at festivals and fêtes. Hedgewitches practiced only among the peasants, and physicked their betters for coin.

Yet had not the nobles been using less and less Court sorcery? After all, it had become more difficult, even for those of noble birth. Some said the illusions wrought now were more wondrous and complex, yet...

I did not wish to travel further down that road. I had Jierre di Yspres in a state most conducive to intrigue now—or as conducive as he would ever be. I decided to return us to a more promising line of conversation. "I do not wish the Captain to kill himself seeking to field an army and put me on a blood-soaked throne. I do not *want* this, *sieur chivialier*." I used his given name, then, judging the time right. "Jierre. Please, aid me. *Help* me."

He looked about to reply, but just then Tristan d'Arcenne opened the door after a token knock. "Is she—ah. *D'mselle*. Are you ready?"

I dropped the Aryx back down my shirt, despite the crawling in my flesh at its warm living pulse. *Distract his attention, or di Yspres's face will tell all. The man is almost useless.* Irritation boiled under my breastbone. I had been so *close*.

"Ready enough." I tried a bright smile as if for a dress fitting. The Captain paced into the room to take my arm. The touch of his hand on my elbow sent a firebolt through me.

"You still look pale, Vianne. I wish there were some other way." A faint, vertical worry line between his charcoal eyebrows gave the words some truth.

"I shall be well enough," I lied, and let him lead me from the room.

Chapter Thirteen

Tierrce d'Estrienne huddled under red tiled roofs, narrow cobbled streets Tristan guided us through like thread through needle-eye. The market sounds came from a street away from the inn, which was a scrubbed-white building I would never be able to find again, did you return me to the town and ask me to do so at daggerpoint. Twas eerie to hear the life of a town echoing all about us, and yet every street d'Arcenne chose was well-nigh deserted.

Di Yspres rode silent behind us. I looked a boy too young to ride a destrier, perhaps—my braided hair safely hidden under Tinan's hat—and the peasants would not question obvious nobles.

But they could be questioned later, and they might remember. We could only hope our pursuers would not know the correct questions to ask. Much now depended on whether yesterday's visitor had sent a missive to his master.

Once we left the town's edgings, we found ourselves on a cart track slipping into the shadows of the forest.

The Shirlstrienne's fringes were lovely as a courtsong, trees arching up over the cart track, dappling the grass and dusty wheelruts with shade. They provided a measure of relief from the heat, though dust danced and swirled fair to choke one.

The sky remained clouded, yet the day was close and oppressive. Dark clouds stacked themselves in the northern sky, glimpsed once or twice before the trees closed us away. I shivered, the unpleasant sensation of approaching storm weighting my arms and legs. I was sensitive to such things even without the help of hedgewitchery; sometimes at Court the looming of a storm would send me to bed with half my head knotting itself tight with pain. Lisele fretted, and Comtesse di Rocheburre and Lady di Chvreil also suffered storm-pains and the half-head after, so I knew I was neither imagining the agony nor likely to die of it.

Though dying might have been preferable, once or twice. The half-head is distinctly unpleasant, and those who do not suffer it rarely understand.

D'Arcenne's arms tightened. "What is it?"

I prayed the Blessed would spare me the half-head. "Merely a storm. I am well enough."

Di Yspres was before us, gloomy light gathering between the trees. His horse paced, sprightly for such a large creature, and dappled leaf shadow ran wetly over beast and rider. The feather in his hat bobbed, a lazy counterpoint.

I searched for aught to say. "How far to the others?"

"Another hour." His breath touched my ear once more, and a hot flush went through me. "Perhaps a little less. They know we are approaching."

I nodded. Uneasiness prickled at my nape. But was it danger, or because his arms were around me? He could not help it; we had to ride double, and were I to perch on the back of the saddle and hold him I might well shatter any illusion I ever had of being graceful by falling and breaking my neck.

That would solve the present quandary nicely, would it not? I straightened, seeking to lean away from him, but his arms tightened again, pulling me back. The horse's hooves clopped on the dusty track.

"The trees become very thick. If the storm breaks we shall be dry for a short while at least while we unpack the cloaks. But you are still uneasy, no?"

I nodded. "Still uneasy." I gave up trying to lean away from him, and he sighed.

"You are safe, Vianne. I swear it." Was something caught in his throat? And why would he address me so familiarly? I was not dreaming.

Of course, I was important to him—if only because I was the means of his revenge. As long as he still thought me capable of serving that end, I was reasonably safe. And yet, I could not allow him to harm himself. Perhaps he would listen to reason. He *was* reasonable.

Sometimes.

I rested my head against his shoulder. It was easier to speak without his gaze on me. "I do not wish you to die pursuing this ridiculous course, Captain."

"I survived Court, and the Duc d'Orlaans's tender attentions. I *think* I have the skill to survive reaching Arcenne." Was he bridling? I could not tell.

"Afterward," I persisted, felt him tense. "After Arcenne. You plan to field an army, do you not? I wish no such thing. We may find another to hold the Aryx, one more suited, and all will be well."

"*You* are the holder of the Aryx." Tristan's tone was soft,

174

inflexible, gentle. "*You* are the rightful Queen of Arquitaine. Whence comes this uncertainty of yours?"

"I am an illegitimate royal at best. That does not make me a Queen. There must be someone else." *Someone who could direct this warmongering spirit of yours more fruitfully. And less dangerously.*

"There is the Duc." A humorless jest, delivered through clenched teeth. "He killed his brother to gain the throne, and would force you into a wedding and bedding within a day were he to capture you."

I blew out a long sigh, forgetting that such a thing was not pretty manners. My frustration was not mannerly at all. "But certainly there are others. There *must* be others!"

"There *are* no others. Did you not listen, Vianne? The royal bloodline has been exterminated, even its most diluted branches. Every royal scion the Aryx might find *remotely* acceptable is dead. Except for you and the Duc."

And that is exceeding suspicious. "Why was I not killed? Poison in a cup, knife in the dark?" *Or a poison killspell? I am no Court sorcerer, and no fair hedgewitch either, apparently. Since I could not scent poison on a pettite-cake.*

And yet I wondered about that. Something about the King's chai before his death disturbed me greatly. I could not lay my finger on it, and had not time to think, for d'Arcenne now chose to speak further.

"Do you think me incompetent? I watched too closely at Court. There was not an opportunity to strike at you. And the Duc watched too. You were at Court, a presence, he could not afford to move on you and warn the King the conspiracy reached even into the Palais. We kept the whole affair quiet, not wishing panic. So he waited. You fit neatly into the plan—a noblewoman with Court connections to smooth his way, legitimize his reign." Tristan's laugh was bitter, and his arms held me closer than was proper at *all*. "You fit so well into the plan I doubted you at times. Yet I kept watch, instead of taking you to the Bastillion for questioning."

"You doubted me?" *Did Lisele? Did she know aught of this? I would have thought there few secrets between us, my Princesse and I.* Tears pricked my eyes, I denied them.

"Only for a week or so. Then I heard you taking a hedgewitch lesson from that peasant woman, the one everyone at Court bought love-philtres or swellfree from. You scolded her for not taking better care of herself and brought her a cup of chai, and you spoke—not much, just a touch—of your loneliness. She did not know enough to listen, but I did. I realized—to my great relief, I might add—you were innocent of both conspiracy and counterplot."

I cast back in memory, at first unsuccessfully, to remember such a time. There *was* a hedgewitch lesson, before Drumiera died. She had been old, and ill, and I had brought her a cup of chai. We spent the day speaking of Court and hedgewitchery—carefully, for Drumiera was discreet and I was cautious. I had not even dreamed I was overheard.

Where could he have hidden to hear such things? Drumiera's quarters had been tiny, and just on the edge of mean. I struggled to remember that conversation now. It had been the only time I even hinted my life at Court was…unsatisfactory. Hooves clopped on the dusty track as I thought this over. "You were listening? How?"

"Do not you understand? I have watched over you for years, *m'chri*."

My blush was most improper, and I was glad there were no

eyes to see it. "Why name me thus? I am only of use to you, d'Arcenne, and dependent on your kindness. There is no need to sweeten me." I closed my eyes.

"Is it possible to sweeten your temper? But I ask your pardon. It must slip out. I did not think you would notice." Now, all the Blessed damn the man, he sounded *amused*. "Rest, then."

I saw nothing amusing, but much that was dangerous, in this turn of conversation. "How could I not notice when you call me *that*?"

"You have been oblivious of other suitors."

Which other suitors? I have had my share of attentions, but none I cared enough to jeopardize my position for. I wished to pursue the line of questioning further, but there were more pressing concerns. My mind seemed finally to be working again, and he seemed disposed to answer questions. I sorted through the many I had, chose the most important at the moment. "What did you do to him? The…assassin?"

"Nobody will find him." His tone now was calm and chill. "Do not trouble yourself over such refuse."

"Did he suffer?" *And why do I think there is something else, something you are not telling me?*

He was the Left Hand, was he not? He probably knew more than I had ever *dreamed*. And now, stealing a glance at that knowledge, just as a curious child might lift a blanket and peep underneath, had convinced me I wished to see no more.

"He did," he admitted without any discernable emotion. "He would have killed me, and brought harm to you. I had to know if the dog had sent word to his master."

"Did he?"

"It is very likely."

Very likely, but you do not know. So was the suffering useless?

Do you care? Silence again. My heart lodged in my throat, above the Aryx's pulse. "I wish this had never happened."

"I would give much for…" Yet he would not say what he would give much for. In any case, I could guess. He would wish for the King's survival, so he was not forced to these measures, depending on, of all people, *me*. And his sudden silence warned me.

Fever rose hot and weakening in my wrists and forehead once more, yet I felt safe. Other questions fell away. What use was asking more at the moment? "I wish I were home in my own bed. I could sleep for a week."

He whispered into my hair. "Sleep if you can. We've a long way to go."

I did not sleep, but I leaned against Tristan d'Arcenne and watched the forest from under my lashes. The light was failing, though it was morn, the clouds from the north cloaking the Sun's wheel-eye. My skull ached with the pressure, but perhaps I would escape a half-head. I could hope to be granted such luck, at least, and since I had been so unlucky of late perhaps the Blessed would take pity on me.

There was a slow ominous roll of thunder, but the storm did not break. Not yet.

Chapter Fourteen

Deeper in the Shirlstrienne, the trees drew together and grew much greater in girth, while the underbrush turned spindly and hunched like whipped dogs. I knew some of the plants from treatises, and cataloging them inside my head provided me with some relief from the growing pressure inside my skull.

Soon enough, a cannonade sounded and water crashed onto the forest's canopy. I roused myself when the thunder sounded, and we halted. Oiled cloaks were pulled from saddlebags, and Tristan wrapped a large one around both of us. The cloak trapped his warmth, closed it around me. Oddly enough, the heat soothed my aching head.

We joined the Guard an hour or so into the forest, and I only dimly remember the event, for I was half conscious, the relief of an averted half-head conspiring with the exhaustion of fever to make me a loose-jointed doll. I sank deep into my thoughts as if through a weight of cold water. We resembled nothing so much as cloth-swathed turtles atop horse legs moving through misty darkness though twas near nooning, each with a crested-feather hat, like an illustration in a bestiary from the Angoulême's time.

The day turned aqueous, and troubling thoughts lurked under the surface of my consciousness. I heard Tristan murmur once or twice, and I felt a tingling in my fingers and toes. The feeling melded into damp heat sticking my hair to my temples and collecting under my arms, at the back of my throat, and at the small of my back. Fever-heat, kept only slightly at bay by the soft prickling that crested every time Tristan whispered. Twas a long, weary day, and one I heartily wished over by the time we halted, early because of the swimming darkness.

I found myself half-falling from the broad back of the horse into Tristan's hands. He wrapped me in a smaller cloak, and I was set under the sheltering boughs of a giant tam tree. The tree made a half-cave that was actually quite dry and fairly level, and the abrupt ceasing of the tingling in my limbs made it somewhat easier to think. Someone had set down a pad of blankets for me, and I dropped gratefully onto them, pulling the cloak tight around my shoulders.

Tinan di Rocham brought me a cup of hot, sweet-spiced chai. Someone had started a fire—the tingle of Court sorcery warned me and I looked up in time to see flame bloom through the infrequent drips from the Shirlstrienne's roof. The wood hissed, and smoke billowed up. The fire would burn as long as the sorcery held. Dangerous—we could be tracked by it—but necessary.

"Drink, an it please you, *d'mselle*." Tinan's young face was grave and drawn. "I think we've more of the tisane. And meatpies for dinner."

"Not all at once, I hope." I sought for levity. He gave me a quick smile, unlike his usual easy merriment. That shook away some of my lethargy. "Why so worried? What it amiss?"

He was young to look so grave. "We have seen no bandits,

but they may be about. We shall set a heavy watch tonight." He closed his hands over mine, around the battered metal cup. "No worries, *d'mselle*!" he added hastily. "You are safe enough with us."

Safe enough? I seem to have lost the luxury of safety. Still... "After the past week, nothing could terrify me," I said slowly, to calm him. He was the most impressionable of them...and my plan tickled the back of my brain. *Tis never too early to prepare your ground, Vianne. Intrigue and gardening have both taught you as much.* "Certainly not bandits."

"Oh, aye." Tinan took heart, and his dark eyes shone. "I must help with the horses, *d'mselle*. Call if you need aught."

I shall call upon you soon enough, young one. I gave a small sound of assent and sipped at my chai, watching them work. I felt useless, a burden easily cast aside. All that held me to them was the Seal.

I closed my eyes, the Aryx thrumming under my heartbeat, against my skin. The comforting darkness behind my eyelids ran with ghostlights, as if I had pressed my fingers too hard against the tender flesh.

What could I do? My hand uncurled, unwillingly, from the chai-cup to touch the lump of the Great Seal under fabric. *If I knew enough Court sorcery to keep them hidden from trackers, I might be less of a uselessness.*

The Aryx pulsed.

Hedgewitchery could hide them, if I had the power for such a charm. The magic of the peasants and healers was opposed to Court sorcery, difficult and slippery to track even for a bell-hound; since it took its power from the land itself it tended to be well camouflaged. Yet I sighed. I was only a fairly good hedgewitch with the aid of my books and treatises, not good enough to hide a half-dozen men seamlessly from Court sorcery and sensitive bellhound noses, not to mention tracking-spells.

The Aryx pulsed again, insistently.

A silent shockwave blurred through me as wine pours into a cup, filling empty spaces, setting me alight. A perfect circle—I saw it from above, a wall of magic large enough to enclose the Guard, protecting them. It was not quite hedgewitchery or Court sorcery, but a seamless blend of both, doors inside my head thrown open, showing me.

You could do thus, it whispered. The touch was light and slow, scouring along the inside of my head, a hall of doors receding into infinity. One blew open, golden light spilling forth, and the glow scorched along my skin, filled the channels of my blood, and *pushed* through me, leaving a scalding wave of weakness in its wake.

I returned to myself with a jolt like a cart's axle breaking, my entire body trembling, chai slopping in the cup. The fever drained away, as did the power. Yet part of the knowledge remained, as if the doors had been closed…but not locked. Corridors of a magic I did not know how to use.

Yet.

You could do thus, beloved, the voice whispered again. I pushed it away, chai spilling, burning my fingers. I slumped, trembling afresh, and shook my head to clear it.

An idea rose slowly. My own thought, not an alien voice whispering inside my head: *The Aryx is indeed awake. It seeks to teach me.*

Why does it stir itself now?

Shouting, confusion. I sought to steady myself, the world whirling most distressingly underneath me. My heart beat a thin tattoo in my wrists and temples. My pulse now matched the silent beat of the Seal against my skin, its metal scorching and the serpents writhing. Their scales rasped pleasantly, not quite rough as a cat's tongue.

"Vianne?" Tristan's hands closed around mine. "Vianne!"

I found myself wide-eyed, meeting his gaze. "The Aryx," I whispered. Rain misted down, each drop a separate colorless jewel with its own name.

"You nearly flattened us all with that sorcery." Was he pale? Perhaps it was merely the chill in the air. His eyes were darker than usual, and worried. Behind the worry was something else, an expression I could not decipher since my head was aswim. "Drink your chai."

"Captain!" someone called.

He looked over his shoulder, his dark hair disarranged as he had shed his dripping hat. "Bring her something to eat, now. Pilippe, Adersahl is to set the watch. Tell him double. Find di Chatillon, send him to me." Tristan's fingers were hard and warm, and clasped too tightly in mine. "Vianne, *m'chri*, speak to me."

I managed another drink of chai, Tristan letting go of my hands for that brief moment. Then he caught my hands again, my fingers burning between his and the chai-cup. "Speak to me, Vianne." It was a command.

"Captain?" Was that me, the uncertain wonderment? *For the love of every god that ever was,* I thought, desperately, *stop whining, Vianne!*

"Here, and hale enough, though we've received rather a shock." He freed one hand to push Tinan di Rocham's hat back, peering under it to see me. "Can you tell me aught, *m'chri*? What does it feel like?"

I found a word for the expression under his worry.

It was *awe*. Of course, I had just performed a feat I should not have been able to even think of attempting. Any noble with even a touch of sorcerous Sight would have seen the moment the Aryx plucked the reins from my hands and pushed the spell through me, a wall of magic protecting them from tracking-sorcery.

"The Aryx." My voice came from very far away. "'Tis awake."

He nodded. "It is. I do not know why it has awakened now."

Strangely enough, that Tristan would admit to not knowing something made a thin curl of fear rise up from my belly. "'Tis…" I struggled to find words. *There are doors in my head, and they are so easy to open. What lies behind them? Do I wish to know?* "I am frightened." I finally whispered.

For the doors are easy to unlock, but what comes through them drowns me.

"I know," he murmured, as if he did. "I would not have had this happen. I tried to prevent it."

You do not know, sieur. None can know what this is. Tinan di Rocham's hat had been knocked aside, and my braid had suffered. Stray hair fell in my face. I blinked, and could finally see him clearly, blue eyes, his mouth drawn into a thin line. "I cannot do this. It will eat me whole." I managed to sound a little less stunned. "The Seal…it is hungry." My wits returned, slowly. *Do not admit weakness. What will he do, if he judges you unfit?*

But it was too late. I had just said what I should not. Again.

"Do not cast any sorcery without me," he said quietly, still holding my hands. "I would add my strength to yours. That may keep the Aryx from swallowing you. It is dangerous to attempt such things while fevered, *m'chri.*"

I nodded. *Say something else. Make him speak to you.* For the sound of his voice was an anchor, and if he turned silent I was afraid I would not stay here in this misty glade. I felt as if I might slip out of my flesh and into the long hall of the Aryx's sorcery, passing through those doors in a dream of golden light. "I never saw you duel."

His mouth twitched slightly, whether with anger or amusement I could not tell. "There was once or twice. I suppose you never noticed."

"I suppose I never did." The pulsing subsided below the surface of my conscious mind. I shuddered, my ribs heaving. The sensation of drifting outside my skin receded, bit by bit.

"Always with your nose in a book, or in a garden plot." His tone was light, but he examined my face intently. "Vianne, if I told you…" Maddeningly, he stopped short.

I dropped my gaze, studied the cup. It was of blue metal, with a curved handle, full of rapidly cooling, sweetened chai. "Told me what?"

But someone came with a meatpie, and Tristan told me to eat. I did, suddenly ravenous, the sorcery burning a hole in my stomach. Luc di Chatillon appeared, and felt my pulse while his fair blond face turned serious. He lacked hedgewitchery but had some physicker's skill, and pronounced me well enough, if still suffering the aftereffects of fever. He measured out the tisane and scolded me into taking it, and refilled my chai-cup.

The Guard seemed much easier now, laughing quietly, bantering back and forth. "Cook us something new, Tinan!" Jai di Montfort called from one end of the fire, and Tinan replied with an oath that would have made me blush at Court. As it was, I produced a wan smile, licking my fingers free of crumbs.

Jierre di Yspres brought me his flask of ansinthe. "Only a mouthful," he said quietly, sinking down into an easy crouch next to me.

I coughed as the green venom burned all the way down. "My thanks, *chivalier*." *And what do you wish from me, to bear me such a gift?*

"Think nothing of it, *d'mselle*." He shifted slightly, accepted the flask's return, and capped it with a quick efficient movement. "We seem never to finish our conversations."

On the other side of the fire, Tinan di Rocham and Jai di Montfort bantered back and forth. "You come and cook, then!" Tinan said.

"I am no woman." Jai's lip curled.

"You certainly complain like one," Tinan shot back, and there was a general shout of laughter. Tristan stood close to Adersahl di Parmecy et Villeroche, conferring, but his gaze rarely left me.

I found I did not mind as much as I should. "Then tell me what you wish to tell me, and have done with it." I had lost all desire to be decorous. "More to the point, Lieutenant, will you help me?"

I had chanced a throw, and his answer told me I had lost. "You ask me to act against my Captain. I cannot do that, *d'mselle*. Wait out the harvest and winter in Arcenne, then we may decide what course is best."

My heart plummeted. The weakness in my hands taunted me. Were they not clasped around the cup, they would shake, showing my feebleness even more plainly. "My thanks for your honesty, *chivalier*," I murmured. I even meant it. The fire's leaping light filled my vision.

His tone turned low and urgent. "You are a scholar, and a practical woman. You must set that sharp wit of yours to leading us aright. We have wagered our lives on this cast of the dice, *d'mselle*."

"Do you think I do not know? Why do you think I am asking your aid in such a manner?" My shoulders sagged. "If I had not seen the Captain in that passageway—"

"—we would all be dead. We would have waited for Tristan until d'Orlaans closed his jaws on us. You saved us all. Please, be kind to Tristan. He…he prizes you, *d'mselle*." His eyes were level, dark, and intent.

Oh, for the love of the Blessed. I almost choked on a sip of chai. "*Will* you cease with that?" My voice hit a decidedly indecorous pitch.

Silence fell. Di Yspres's cheeks flushed, and his gaze cut away from mine.

I searched for a bit of Court wit to use. A laugh rose out of me, a thin unhealthy sound but well enough to bear up appearances, as if di Yspres had jested, perhaps a riddle with an end not meant for a lady's ears. I leaned forward, touching his shoulder with my free hand, and the laugh quickly became natural.

The absurdity of the situation quickly made my merriment real—the Duchesse di Rocancheil in the Shirlstrienne with a group of King's Guard, sick with fever and the plaything of the Great Seal. It sounded like a courtsong, and not a very good one at that.

"Vianne?" The Captain, using my name as if it belonged to him, stood taut and inquiring on the other side of the fire.

"*Sieur* di Yspres and I were trading riddles." The lie rose so naturally I was almost afraid of it, my cheeks flushing as well. "Some are decidedly *not* fit for a lady's ears."

I do not know if Tristan believed me, but the other Guards laughed. Tristan's eyebrows drew together, a faint line between them. His blue eyes were shadowed in the failing light, fixed on my hand on Jierre's shoulder.

Di Yspres stood hurriedly, brushing his knees with a quick, habitual movement. "I gave her more ansinthe, Captain. She was shivering."

That brought the Captain to my side. He knelt, pressing his fingers to my forehead.

"I am well enough," I told him. "*Sieur* di Yspres merely worries."

"He should." Tristan's jaw was set. "How much did he give you?"

"Merely a swallow." I submitted to his touching my cheek, smoothing my hair down. "Truly, I am hale. He sought to ease my mood, for I confess I was most—"

"Ansinthe. What were you thinking?" He did not even look at me. His gaze had turned up to Jierre, who stood aside, pocketing his flask.

"I was cold, and I asked him for a swallow of summat to warm." I sought to calm him. "It does no harm."

He snapped me a glance that could have broken stone. I almost gasped at the violence in his expression.

Tristan straightened and glared at di Yspres. "Do not give her more. Ansinthe is dangerous."

"I *asked* him," I lied. "He was merely being kind." The Aryx fluttered against my chest. I pushed the sensation away with an effort. *No. I will not.*

It subsided.

"'Tis not a fit drink for hedgewitches," Luc di Chatillon said in the ensuing silence. "Truly, *d'mselle*. Hedgewitchery makes one most vulnerable to the green venom. And you must not risk the fever's return."

I thought he perhaps tried to soothe troubled waters, so I did not answer. Instead, I looked at the tips of the Captain's boots, muddy from the forest. I stared at that clinging mud for a long moment, until di Yspres made some movement—a shrug, perhaps, I could not see—and moved away.

I pulled the cloak closer about my shoulders, setting the cup aside. Rain dripped hissing into the fire. My fingers tensed, curling into fists in the harsh material.

I could use the Seal. It has chosen me, for now. I could use it—and do what? If I escape them, this will merely follow me, as crows follow the gibbets. Or I will let this thing at my throat use me, and become merely a vessel for it. Loneliness rose, fair threatened to choke me. Next was panic, a deep well of it. The Seal had worked that spell *through* me, as if I were only a door for *it*, and I was not certain I liked the feeling.

Not certain at all.

Silence stretched.

"Dinner." Tinan's voice was unnaturally bright. "Who hungers? They shall be fed!"

"And lo! Said the maid in the cow byre," di Chatillon gave the next line of the old maying-song, and a ripple of amusement went through the men. "For the want of a sausage, I'm dead!"

The Captain said nothing. I could not tell if he watched me or not. I kept my head bowed, staring at his boot-toes, reciting a string of Tiberian verbs in my head. Eventually the laughter and banter returned to normal as they ate.

I remained closed in my bubble of silence. The Aryx pulsed.

What can I do? I wailed into the darkness of myself. *I am far more helpless than before.*

Stop being a ridiculous little twit. Come now, think. Use that practical brain of yours, and reason through this tangle.

Without me, they would not be in danger. If the Captain reached Arcenne safely there would be some hope of his crossing the border into Navarrin. Despite his protests, any Court would be glad of his skill. And I thought it passing likely the Left Hand would have agents in foreign lands to shelter him.

He would *live*.

The Duc will pursue us if we have her—but if we simply flee, we may escape with our lives. Jierre di Yspres, speaking truth, for all he apologized for it later.

It was one thing to think of leaving them, quite another to think of being left and any possible step I might take afterward. I shivered, pulling the cloak even tighter. The Captain stood, motionless. What was he doing? Why would he not join his men and leave me be?

My brain pawed at the problem like a trained farrat, turning it over and over. Slowly, everything outside me stilled as I turned inward, into that peculiar half-dream state of complete attention, where one's faculties may suddenly cease thrashing, step aside as if following a pavane, and suddenly know every step of the dance.

If you may learn to use the Seal properly, you could do something, for good or for ill.

I straightened, taking in a sharp breath. Then, just as quickly, I slumped again, lest anyone had seen my sudden movement and guessed at the cast of my thoughts. I had already used the Aryx to protect the Guard. Could I do so again, to protect them further? Damp woolen material resisted my fingers as I pulled, twisting it tighter.

To have those doors open inside my head again, to feel that force pushing through me in its scalding tide, blind to the world, would be…gods.

It would be like…what? Ceasing to exist.

Like *dying*. I had not suffered death yet, but I imagined losing oneself in that swelling tide was very close. I shivered.

The Guard finished their meal. Some of them undid their sleeping rolls. The tingle of Court sorcery washed over my skin again—dry ground, the rain shunted aside from where they would rest. A toast was called out to me, for they would be sleeping in the rain if not for the Aryx's protection from tracking-sorcery. I smiled wanly and nodded, seeking to appear pleased, then went back to hugging myself, desperately weighing the chance of being swallowed whole by the Great Seal against the pressure of their faith in me.

Tristan's faith in me, however misplaced.

I sighed, rubbing at my forehead. I had only wished to change my clothes before waiting on Lisele. How on earth had I ended up pursued in the Shirlstrienne with a half-dozen noblemen and a head full of doors for the Aryx to open whenever it slipped the chain of my refusal?

The Captain brought a sleeping roll and laid it beside me. "You should sleep, *d'mselle*." His tone was chill.

Then mine should be, too. "I suppose I should." I did not dare look to his face, only his shoulder. "Captain?"

"For the sake of every god, Vianne, do not address me thus." His jaw set, his shoulders stiffened.

Well, if you wish me to address you otherwise, sieur, *I shall.* "Very well. *Sieur* d'Arcenne, I wish to ask you something," I persisted.

His shoulders stiffened, his jaw firming. Why? He smoothed a blanket over the sleeping roll, flicked his fingers. A breath of heat brushed my cheek—he was warming the blanket. Court sorcery tingled along my fingers, a familiar feeling.

"Ask what you will." He settled back on his heels. His boots creaked.

Perhaps I can make you see reason. I marshaled my arguments, made my tone soft and conciliatory. "If I drew pursuit away—perhaps to the east—would you be able to reach Arcenne safely?"

I watched his hand tense against his knee, I barely dared to breath. *See reason. Please, do not force this madness further.*

"And how would you draw pursuit away, Vianne?" Yet he sounded oddly relieved. Had he merely been waiting for me to broach the subject again?

I had my list of requirements ready. "I would need a horse. I am fairly sure I could create a commotion, or use enough Court sorcery to be tracked."

A shake of his dark head, tossing a thought aside. "If d'Orlaans—"

"I wish to give you the Aryx." *If I can tear it from my skin. If I can rip it free, dear gods, I will.* I did not let myself pause. "If you have the Seal, you do not need me. I can serve a better purpose distracting the bellhounds. You said yourself di Narborre has likely received word of our course."

He shifted slightly, turning to me, and before I knew it his hand cupped my chin. He forced my head up until I had no choice but to look at him. His mouth was drawn tight, into a straight line. "You will not leave my care until we are in the Palais d'Arquitaine again and d'Orlaans is dead. If I must tie you to the saddle, *Your Majesty*, I will. Is that in *any* way unclear to you?"

I swallowed. My heart leapt into my throat, began to dance a maying there. His eyes burned, pale d'Arcenne blue, fixing my gaze as a serpent would trap a bird. "Cap—ah, Tristan…I would not—"

"At the moment, we shall make no decision until we reach

Arcenne. Cease this, Vianne. You will not leave my side until we are in the Palais again and d'Orlaans is *dead*. Tis final."

I searched for an argument, found one. "If you think me a Queen, why order me about?" But the heat of him, and his blue gaze, did strange things to my well-ordered wits and my carefully arranged plans.

"Even a Queen needs counselors," he returned, callused fingers gentle against my cheek. "I was Left Hand once, and it seems you would need one more than Henri ever did. You are not ruthless enough, Vianne. Not ruthless enough by half."

Thunder rattled overhead. The trees moved uneasily. "So you *were* the Left Hand." It was different, hearing him say it so casually. Did his arm shake slightly? It seemed so.

He shrugged. "Did you ever doubt it?" He stroked my jaw with his thumb, the touch spilling a different heat down my throat. "I shall have your word you will not leave my side, *m'chri.*"

"Why do you—"

"Your word. I want your promise." Something dark passed over his face, graving lines upon it, the firelight leaping oddly across the plane of his cheek. Seen in this light, he was even more handsome than at Court—but different.

More dangerous.

My heart quivered like a rabbit's shudder in the snare. "Tristan—"

"Your word, Vianne," he repeated, inflexible.

I could not look away. "I promise," I heard myself say. "I give you my word."

"Good." He did not press the point, but neither did he look away. We stayed thus—his hand cupping my chin, me perched on a pad of blankets under the giant tam tree—until another vast wallow of thunder filled the air. "Sleep if you can, *m'chri*," he said, as soon as the cannonade died away. Someone laughed on the other side of the fire, but twas a hushed, sleepy sound. Someone else—it sounded like Jai di Montfort—was humming a song popular in the Citté about a noble, penniless damsel and her heart-true *chivalier*.

It was a pretty tune, but oh it made me think of Lisele.

My heart twisted savagely, and water rose behind my eyes. I denied the tears with every ounce of strength I possessed, swallowed the rock in my throat. He released me, and I huddled deeper into the shelter of the cloak. Tristan rose fluidly and stalked away.

It is hopeless. For good or ill, you are bound to his course.

Was it craven to feel relieved? Perhaps.

I stared at the fire, beginning to burn blue now as the rain found its way past the Shirlstrienne's canopy and sorcery forced the wood to stay alight. My eyes half-lidded, heavy and full of sand. The men spoke quietly over di Montfort's singing.

He was on the fourth verse now. Telling of how the *chivalier* gave up his pride and his place in the Guard for the love of the fair noble *d'mselle*, who sacrificed herself in an act of sorcery to keep the *chivalier* safe from the blade of a jealous rival. The song had been much sung at Court last season, a backdrop to the affair of the duel between Miche di Varonne and Alois di Cheremorce.

Di Varonne's mother had been rumored to be a royal by-blow, and he had died on di Cheremorce's rapier. I never had discovered what their duel concerned, since whatever intrigue it was did not touch my Princesse. I thought I would farrat out the cause later, for no knowledge is ever wasted. Yet I had never discovered another twist to that tale.

The King had been wroth, his face full of thunder at several suppers. I thought long on this, staring into the fire and hearing the storm walk the sky above, prowling through the vaults of the Blessed's heaven.

THE BANDIT

Chapter Fifteen

We passed deeper into the Shirlstrienne, days without sunlight because the rain kept washing over us. It was awful weather even for the season of late-spring storming, and I was soon an aching mass of misery from riding a-horseback in the dankness, our cloth damp no matter how many charms we used. At night, thunder walked among the clouds, and we saw lightning-charred trees as we rode.

It sometimes seemed to me that the world had shifted, that we had ridden into the Forests of Night that haunted Damarsene tales, those stories of blood and sorcery under the shade of huge black trees. In Damarsene legends the woods are hungry. There is no sunlight, and their hedgewitches feast on the blood of young children who blaspheme their bull-headed, jealous god. It is enough to make one shudder.

The nights were the worst. Each dusk I repeated the trick of hiding us from pursuit, struggling to keep the Aryx from shoving me through another temptingly-open door. It told on my strength to do so, but twas the only useful thing I seemed capable of. D'Arcenne sought to help, but the tide of sorcery took me so swiftly he could not do much but force me to drink sweetened chai afterward, his mouth drawn tight as the heat of the drink and the sound of his voice brought me back to myself.

Yet that was not the worst of it. Each night I dreamed of Lisele, in many ugly, broken, bloody guises, and I woke in the darkness hoping I had not screamed. I was grateful to discover none of the Guard said aught of it.

Perhaps some few of them had their own nightmares.

Tristan did not speak much. Nor did I, but oft I would feel the tingling in my fingers and toes as he repeated one charm or another to draw some warmth into me. It was a small bit of Court sorcery, and he gave without comment as I accepted without question. It helped me to stay awake, to push back the swirling double weakness of fever and the Aryx's persistent throbbing against my skin.

Ten days into the forest I felt even stranger, as if we rode under a weight of clear heavy water. The forest shifted and blurred like ink on wet paper. When we stopped for our nooning the tenth day beside a small stream swollen with the recent rain, I had barely enough strength to fall into Tristan's hands from the horse's back.

He felt at my damp forehead, his dark hair plastered to his forehead with rain. He had put his hat aside for some reason. "You are fevered again."

"I am not." My immediate refusal did not seem to convince him. I could not afford him to think me weak. "Only weary."

The Captain was haggard, bladed cheekbones standing out over hollows, dark circles under his blue eyes. For all that, it still made my chest tighten when he stroked my cheek with callused fingers and pushed a stray curl of my dark hair back, tucking it behind my ear.

I must look a sight. This was what worried me, there in the Shirlstrienne. "I have not combed my hair, though."

Perhaps I was not quite my usual self.

"Nor have I." A brief smile lighted his entire face. "Come. We shall halt here."

"No, I can go on—," I protested. But his hand closed around my arm, and he all but dragged me to the center of a loose circle of the Guard, clustered under the shelter of a pinon tree in full leaf. It kept the rain off, though silvery beads gilded its drooping needles.

"We shall halt here," he repeated, and there was no argument. Adersahl brought me his waterflask, freshly filled from the stream, and I took a grateful drink, though twas icy enough to sent a bolt of silver pain through my skull. My entire body itched miserably.

I handed Adersahl's flask back to him and watched as they built a fire. Pilippe di Garfour stretched forth his hand and made a quick gesture, flicking his fingers, and the wood ignited, flames billowing. The wood, being wet, smoked dreadfully.

I leaned against the pinon's massive trunk, resting my head against rough bark, watching. The presence of living wood helped, sinking into me as the tree recognized a hedgewitch and drew me into its embrace. It also helped quiet the persistent beat of the Aryx, a spot of molten heat under my shirt.

Jierre studied a waxed-parchment map near the edge of the tree's branches, holding it to the light. Luc di Chatillon and Robierre d'Atyaint-Sierre stood with him, their heads bent together. Robierre had a head for woodscraft; he was often consulted about whither and yon in the forest's trackless shadows. Tristan joined them, looking over Jierre's shoulder.

"*D'mselle?*" Tinan di Rocham handed me the same battered

metal travel cup, with steaming-hot chai in it. "Here. Drink, an it please you."

"Thank you, *chivalier*." I gave him a weary smile. After so many days, we were easier with each other, though I could not cease noting each man's particulars in case I should be called upon to use them later.

I cursed myself for it, though I knew it was my only protection. A woman cannot afford to let her guard relax.

Tinan blushed to the roots of his dark hair and mumbled. I was glad we were not at Court, for all that. I would have been teased endlessly about the young, blushing *chivalier*. As it was, I took care to treat him kindly. Of all the Guard, he was the most careful of me—and the most potentially useful.

I sought to make use of him a little, now. "Why is everyone so grim? Besides the rain, I mean."

He hesitated, but I had judged my quarry well. "We are being tracked," Tinan said, in a low tone. "By who, we cannot tell, but tis sorcery, Robierre says. The Captain agrees."

This caused a cascade of unpleasant thoughts, and I spoke unguarded, for once. "But why did not the Captain—"

"You have worries enough." Tristan spoke from close enough to cause me to start. I had not even noticed him approaching; he was catfooted even in heavy boots when it suited him. Tinan nodded to me and retreated. "I did not wish your worrying on account of a pack of peasant trash."

"Peasants with sorcery? More likely the Duc's men." I took a sip of chai. Twas oversweetened—they added stevya to it with abandon, endlessly seeking to bolster my strength. "Bandits seem hardly capable of noble sorcery."

"There, you see? You are worrying, exactly what I wished to avoid." He touched my shoulder, ran his fingers over my sleeve.

The chai burned me less than his fingers did. "Tracking does not mean *catching*, Vianne. Once we leave the Shirlstrienne we are but a few days away from the borders of Arcenne, especially if we brave the Alpeis."

"The Alpeis is full of—" I stopped. It was a childish tale, and one I blushed to repeat in the company of hardened *chivalieri*.

"*Demieri di sorce*. So they say. At least the tales may have kept the bandits away. Who can tell? But you have some of the finest swordsmen and sorcerers in Arquitaine, since entrance into my Guard requires proficiency in Court sorcery. If *demieri di sorce* haunt the Shirlstrienne, steel or sorcery will keep you safe."

I took another sip of chai, leaning against the tree. My knees had once again grown suspiciously weak. "Does nothing frighten you, *sieur*?"

"Some things."

Ah, there's an admission. "When have you ever been frightened?" I challenged. He seemed more at ease now, certainly easier than he had ever been at Court. I could see traces of the beating he had received, but not many. They would quickly be gone forever.

He cast his gaze over the camp, noting, cataloging, ever the Captain. "I lay in a cell and wondered if you had been caught. The thought of you frightened and alone, possibly taken by the Duc, without knowing what game you had been caught in—that frightened me." He smoothed his fingers down my shoulder. He did not look at me; he gazed at the fire, his clean profile presented as a sculpture. "Certainly, seeing you taken with fever, so ill you did not even recognize us—that frightened me. You have a talent for striking fear into my heart, Vianne."

I sighed, took another sip of chai. "You should sup, Captain.

You look ill-used." *What a magnificent thing to say. Why does he bring forth the idiot in me?*

He smiled, an open boyish grin. "Well, at least you notice me now. That is something to be grateful for, no?"

My breath caught. I could find absolutely nothing to say.

He waited, his smile broadening. He looked like a boy caught stealing apples, yet supremely confident the punishment would be slight. "Where is that sharp tongue of yours? Nevermind. Do not trouble yourself, *d'mselle*. All is well."

I gathered my courage, held my cup, and reached with my free hand to touch his elbow. My fingers brushed against his cloak's damp roughness. "I do not worry for my safety. I worry for yours."

He shrugged, turning his head aside to gaze at the fire as if it held a secret. "I treasure that, *m'chri*, I truly do."

My gaze fell. *Twas not just a King's jest. Or does he think to treat me lightly? No, he is not the kind for dalliance, or else I would have heard of it, would I not? Though there was so much I did not hear.*

It was no use. There was a question I burned to ask, and it escaped me before I could bolt my mouth shut. "Why did you watch me, Captain?"

"I had to, for your safety." He checked, drawing back whatever he had intended to say next as a falconer will pull a lure. "You look pale."

"I feel a trifle pale." *It is the fever speaking. He does not favour you, he favours his revenge.* My hand fell to my side, and I sought not to feel the needleprick to my heart. I took refuge in formality. "I beg your pardon, *chivalier*. You would already be in Arcenne but for me."

"Not without riding the horses to death." Thoughtful now,

still considering the fire. "I thank the gods you saw me in the passage, though I do not cherish the thought of you witnessing Simieri's death. Had I not been watching—had you not met me by *chance*—I would be beheaded in the Bastillion and you perhaps dead or wedded to the Duc."

Later, I would think of this conversation as if I held it suspended in crystal, like the classic *Illusionne Iluminatrixe*. I would think of it as the moment Tristan d'Arcenne spoke to me without reserve for the first time. I would think of it, as well, as the moment some tiny internal weight shifted—the first small stones falling in advance of an avalanche, the first thin drops that herald a storm, the uneasy waves that mark the sea's furious rising.

The first time I realized what I felt for him.

It is ever so—those moments pass unremarked, and it is only later, in the wreckage, that one realizes where the fatal seed was planted. But at that moment, under the pinon tree in the vastness of the Shirlstrienne, I merely shivered. "I do not cherish *that* thought. Tristan…"

I meant ask him if he truly favoured me, and swallowed the question just in time. It was not a question a well-bred woman should ask. Another query rose to my lips: if Simieri had been in the passage to catch me, bring me to the Duc as the conspiracy boiled to its climax, why did Tristan say it was by chance? Had he followed the Minister, or had he been watching me?

By chance, he said. A good chance, I should think, for it saved me from di Narborre's tender attentions, not to mention the Duc's.

I did not care to think on it too closely. I could always ask him later, when my head was not so muzzy.

"Vianne." He still looked away, but the set of his shoulders warned me something was afoot. Luc di Chatillon was stirring something—stew; one of the Guard had brought down a brace of woodsfowl. The rain was slackening, finally, its endless rushing retreating to spatters falling from soaked leaves. Tristan d'Arcenne gathered himself afresh and bolted forward, much as a duelist would. "If we were still at Court and I left a token for you, what would you do?"

For a few heartbeats, I thought I had not heard him aright. Then I knew I had.

He does favour me. If he had declared his intent to take an oath of celibacy and spend his life in the service of Kimyan, I could not have been more surprised.

As it was, I almost choked on my chai. But everything lightened within me, as if the Aryx held me in that hall of golden light and unlocked doors. Only this was a different gold; the vastness of a meadow inside me. "I suppose I would send you a token in return," I finally managed, around the beating of my heart high in my throat. "And ask you to meet me by the stairs from the herb garden." I paused, judiciously, but not too long. "Perhaps," I added, for to seem too forward was not what a noblewoman should do.

His breathing had quickened, and two spots of color burned on his hollow cheeks. "What token would you send me, then?"

I leaned against the tree, sighing internally. Why now? Of all the…*If only we were at Court, and safe. Though it seems Court was more perilous than even I thought.* "Tis not polite to ask. But I would not have refused yours, *chivalier.*" *Would I? Mayhap. But not for long. And if I did not suspect you of any interest in doing my Princesse harm. Perhaps we would have had some small luck, you and I.*

His mouth quirked into another, gentler smile, one I found

I liked almost as much as the boyish, proud grin. "I certainly hope not. I would be terribly embarassed if you did."

I strove for a light, laughing tone, failed miserably. We were at Court no longer, and coquetry was out of place here. Still, the habit steadied me. "I am certain you would have been able to overcome the embarrassment." I took another sip of my over-sweetened chai. Though it was not the chai that gave me fresh strength, the warmth of it was welcome.

"Not likely. You could strike me to the heart, did you realize it." His eyebrows drew together. "Are you certain you are hale? You are pale, and your hands shake. Do not think I do not notice."

I closed my eyes. "I wish we were somewhere safe. Anywhere but here." Twas ungrateful of me, perhaps.

"So do I. For now, however..." Amazingly, he stepped close and slid his arm around me, so I leaned against him rather than the tree. None of the Guard seemed to notice. In fact, none of them looked at us at all, which was odd. "Rest."

I laid my head on his shoulder, hearing the fire hiss. The rain slacked even more, thunder dying in the distance. "The storm is passing."

"We can only hope." His tone did not admit of much hope, and I silently agreed.

Why was Tristan in the passage? Why was Simieri truly there? I sighed, the thoughts disappearing under a weight of weariness.

His was a welcome heat in the eternal, damnable, dragging damp. It was a day for strange things, for he bent his head down and kissed my wet, disheveled hair. I felt a tingle of Court sorcery along my nerves.

New warmth stole through me. Slowly, a little life crept back into my numb fingers and toes. It was merely a simple charm, but it felt wonderful. I finished my chai, slowly, luxuriating in dry warmth. "I never knew you were such a Court sorcerer."

"I was born with some talent, and I've studied. Lean on me, Vianne."

And, may the Blessed forgive me, all questions fled me. I did.

208

Chapter Sixteen

The rain finally stopped, but I noticed little. I was busy swallowing spoonfuls of the hedgewitch's diminishing tisane and seeking to stay conscious. A great exhaustion settled on me, so large and deep every day took on the quality of a dream except for the Aryx's sluggish pulse.

Now that I know what was stalking us, I curse myself for not recognizing it in time.

I remember the Sun briefly smiling upon us the thirteenth day as we rode through a meadow, the nodding wet heads of dandille flowers smiling up at the cloudy sky. We pulled our horses to a halt—at least, *they* did; I was too busy hanging to the pommel. The sudden sunlight made our cloaks steam, and Tinan di Rocham laughed and sang a few lines of a hymn of praise to Jiserah.

I did not think him a religious man, being so young. But I took note, though it cost me some effort to do so. I knew them all by now, and some part of me was ashamed at how I hoarded my knowledge, added to it, all in service of someday, perhaps, saving them from themselves.

The Sun helped clear my head, and I straightened my spine, the Aryx sparking under my shirt. *Why do I feel so odd? This is not fever.*

Something teased at the corner of my memory, something—

—but the Sun hid himself behind a cloud, and I sank back against Tristan, who stroked my hand before we continued on. The sense of something badly amiss returned, but I was too draggled to try to discover the source of the feeling. When I had the energy to think, I realized this should intrigue me.

Then a cloud would descend upon me. Why bother? All was amiss since the moment I had climbed to the servants' passage and discovered violence and conspiracy. My nerves were simply threadbare, as any gently-born woman's would be.

One night I woke to a great blundering in the forest, branches snapping as something crashed close to our camp. I clawed my way out of sleep, bolting to my feet as steel sang loose from sheaths around me, the Guard all rising. Those on watch had arrows nocked, I know, because Tristan arrived at my side and pushed me back down to the bedroll, then stood poised with a bow in his hands, an arrow to the string. The shield of magic over our small camp held firm, its edges blending seamlessly with the night. Yet my heart knocked fearfully against my ribs, and I smelled something foul that fair threatened to swoon me back into my blankets. Twas merely a breath, and I choked on it before it vanished and I pushed myself painfully up to my knees, staring into utter darkness lit only by an edge of banked firelight.

The crashing and snapping faded.

"Demieri di sorce," someone whispered. Whoever it was, in

the dark they sounded very young, but twas not Tinan di Rocham.

"More likely a treecat," someone else replied. "Or an *ursine*."

"Enough." Tristan's tone sliced through the mutters. "We stand fast, and double watch."

He did not mention sorcery, and none of the others did either. I was not sure what I had sensed in the darkness, being possessed of no woodscraft at all. Yet I wondered, when I could find the strength to wonder.

On the twentieth day of our entrapment in that dismal forest, something else happened.

The rain had briefly ceased but clouds still filled the sky's eye, and the dark of the Shirlstrienne seemed more than the shade of trees and clouds. We rode single-file, following Robierre and Pilippe, who conversed in low voices. They seemed to disagree over our course, for the first time.

Prickles of unease roiled over my skin. I raised my head from the languor trapping me, weighting my body. "Tristan?" My voice was foggy, slurred as if I had been at mead during a wedding celebration.

"What is it?" Worried, far more worried than I had ever heard him before. It was not right—the Captain, my Captain, should not sound so.

My unease crested, sparking through the dragging weight. When had I become so heavy, so inert? "Something is wrong," I managed, my lips not quite meeting.

"Halt!" Tristan called. Between one step and the next, the hair rose on my nape.

A shrill whistle split the air. A crossbow quarrel buried itself in the leafy mould before Robierre's horse, and I let out a short, sharp cry. The Aryx sprang to life, thundering against my chest, a wall of force expanding outward. The doors inside my head revolved, flinging themselves open, and I gasped, struggling to retreat, seeking to close myself away from the riptide of sorcerous force.

Several of the Guard cursed in surprise. The milky shimmer of a globe-shield blurred in the air. I gasped, my heart laboring, and Tristan's arm slid around my waist. "Let it go, Vianne." Quietly, but with great force and utter command. "*Let it go.* Tis not worth your life."

If he had taken any other tone but quiet authority, I would not have heard. As it was, the Aryx's force glided through me, rumbled in the spaces between my veins…

…and the globe shimmered, folding down into the earth, draining away.

Most of the Guard had their bows out, and Jierre di Yspres held up a hand, the red glimmer of a firebolt limning his fingers. Twas a showy way to strike an enemy, but a bolt of Court sorcery would unerringly find its target—once Jierre caught a glimpse of whatever that target should be.

"Bandits," Tristan said crisply. "Let them show themselves, if they dare." Then, more quietly, in my ear, "Do not use the Aryx again, *m'chri*, not even to guard us. The fever will return if you do."

"Tristan—" My head fell back against his chest. Something had just become clear to me, some idea just on the very tip of my tongue. It fled, and I could have cursed with frustration had I not needed my breath. The Seal muttered, disconsolate, its pulse as tardy as my own.

"A fine morn to you, *sieurs*," someone called from the woods, a weird directionless voice. I recognized the hint of greenbreath sorcery—it was a hedgewitch charm to distort the sound of one's voice, and I felt a weary satisfaction at finally remembering a charm on my own, without my books. "Welcome to the Shirl-strienne."

"A fine welcome, served on a crossbow bolt," Jierre di Yspres returned clearly.

"Nobody was hit," the voice answered, cheeky as a Citté urchin. "So you have naught to complain of, *sieurs*. We have yet to discuss your toll for passage."

"A tollmaster should show his face," Jierre barked. "Not hide behind a peasant charm. Coward."

"I like the word *cautious*. Not that it matters—Adrien Jirlisse does not care. Now, *sieurs*, your purses, and be quick. You may leave them on the road, and we shall let you pass un-hindered." The voice, directionless, filtered through the dark woods.

I heard an odd trilling whistle.

I suddenly understood the Guard were spreading out, ready to commence a battle with sorcery or steel.

Just like men. Why must this all be so difficult? A solution sug-gested itself, and I lunged for some certainty in the soup my brain had become.

"Wait!" Silence descended on the forest. I was half surprised I'd been able to voice so clear a cry.

"A *d'mselle*. Well. This is a surprise." And indeed, the direc-tionless voice sounded surprised.

Careful, Vianne. You are playing for the safety of others, be quick and cunning. "Are you the same Adrien Jirlisse they sing of?" My tone was pitched to carry, and the Aryx rang under my words. Its pulse had hurried, shaking off deadly languor.

"What are you doing?" Tristan hissed in my ear.

Do not trouble me at the moment, Captain. I am otherwise

engaged. I ignored him. "The one they call the Scourge of Shirlstrienne?" My entire body was leaden, but my wits suddenly returned. *If there are more hidden in the trees, we may fight free but at a cost. If I can feed this man's pride he may well let us pass; tis not worth a bandit's time to fight a pitched battle against nobles on warhorses, even though we are few.*

Let us hope I am right.

"I might be." Now he sounded pleased. "Tis good to see a woman who knows quality."

Ah. So we may bargain, my fine friend. I struggled to force my tongue to work. "I am no merchant's wife, to test the cut of a word. Tis sung you are passing fond of riddles, *sieur.*"

Murmurs among the Guard. I prayed they would not do anything silly. Other murmurs, too—if my ears did not fail me, there were bandits in every direction.

Dear gods, let this pique his interest. We may yet avoid bloodshed.

"Twenty of them." Tristan murmured. "Vianne—"

"I might be," the directionless voice repeated. Yet there was an edge to the words that had not been there before. "And you are?"

I took a deep breath. *The hook has been swallowed. Give the line a tug, Vianne.* "If you are so fond of riddles, I shall play you a game of riddlesharp. If you win, we shall give up our coin with good grace. If I win, you shall let us pass unmolested."

The pause that followed was so long I felt sweat prickle under my arms. *Please, gods. Please. Let us have no more blood spilled.*

"We have you at arrowpoint, *d'mselle.* Why should I play riddlesharp at all?"

I sighed, loudly, theatrically, as if I were at Court and all eyes were on me. The very situation I hated and avoided, and yet I acquitted myself with some skill when twas necessary. I hoped my skill was still with me. "Then you are not the noble bandit the songs make you." I sought for the quarter-mocking tone of Lady Arioste di Wintrefelle, who had near every man at Court for a swain. Arioste could make even a priest of Danshar forget his vows, and she knew exactly the right edge of scorn mixed with faith that would tempt a man into performing some ridiculous feat for her momentary amusement. "And I should be gravely disappointed not to hear such a riddlemaster's skill."

There was a rustling in the bushes.

I had to admire the flair with which he vaulted from a low-hanging branch of a giant tam tree. Dressed all in brown and green, a bow slung at his back and a rapier at his side, a lean man with weather-brown skin and sharp glittering eyes regarded us from the faint track leading into the trees. "Well enough. Never let it be said Adrien Jirlisse disappointed a *d'mselle*, especially one so fair." He bowed, sweeping his hand back. It was an approximation of a Court bow, and I dearly hoped none of the Guard would laugh at him. If he had shown himself, he did not wish a pitched battle, and if they had been truly hungry for coin, one quarrel from a crossbow would not have sufficed for an opening thrust.

"What are you doing?" Tristan, in my ear again.

My head cleared slightly. *This game is mine to play, Captain. And it will require no bloodshed.* "Let me down," I whispered back. "Please, Captain. Trust me, I beg of you."

"What if he—"

"Tristan, *please*." I did not raise my voice. But he stilled as if I had shouted. "They do not wish a battle any more than we do. If I overmatch this man in wits, there's no shame in losing to a

215

d'mselle in the woods. Twill be out of a tale, and we shall go our way."

A long pause, during which the bright-eyed bandit folded his arms and regarded us. I could not be certain, but I thought I sensed a smile on his weather-darkened face.

Stiffly, Tristan dismounted. I half-fell from the saddle into his hands, but he lifted me down so lightly it looked as if I had planned it. He set me on my feet, yet his touch lingered at my waist. "As you like, Vianne," he said softly.

That was strange enough, but he set me free. I half-turned, and made my way through the screen of horses and my Guard. My legs shook with effort. The Aryx rang quietly, a bell-tone I suspected they would not hear. My eyes threatened to fall closed, I forced them wide and set myself the task of walking straight.

"Captain—" Jierre did not like this turn of events.

"Ware now," Tristan said over his shoulder. "If he makes a single move toward her, kill him."

The sense of wrongness returned, a giant sharptooth fish sliding through dark water, stalking. The forest floor was no floor for dancing, but I made my passage as gracefully as I could and stopped ten paces from the man.

I lifted my gaze slowly. This was the moment we would first truly match wits, the bandit and I, and much depended on it.

Jierre swore. But softly, and I did not flinch.

The bandit regarded me. His eyes were the color of the sea during a storm, thickly lashed with charcoal. Wide cheekbones, a generous mouth even now curving into a half smile. There was a shade of familiarity to his features, one I could not quite place. "Well," he said. "I spoke half in jest, thinking you a boy. Yet you are fair, *d'mselle*."

I blinked. His speech was now accented like mine—the half-singing sharp consonants of the Court. I straightened, wishing I'd half a chance to comb my hair, or a decent dress to be seen in. "I am Duchesse Vianne di Rocancheil et Vintmorecy." My shoulders went back, my chin lifted. My head pounded, and blackness clouded the edges of my vision. *Oh, no, do not, please. Let me not be useless this once. They are depending on me.* "You are?"

Did I imagine a swift darkening of his face? "Adrien di Cinfiliet, at your service." His pale eyes flicked up past my shoulder. I set my jaw, determined not to sway on suddenly numb feet. "And honored to have your acquaintance."

So Adrien Jirlisse is a use-name. What is a nobleman doing here? "And I, yours." My voice came from very far away. "What is a nobleman about stealing purses in a wood, *sieur*? May I ask?"

He shrugged, his pale eyes searching as they sought to read my countenance. "Hiding. Is it not obvious?"

"Hiding from what?" *I have you now, my fine bandit. No man can resist a woman's wide-eyed interest. Even if I do look a maying jest, dressed as I am.*

"If I were to tell a stranger, even one so fair, I would have poor skill at hiding, would I not? You owe me a game of riddle-sharp, *d'mselle*."

And I begin to suspect you will be more than my match. "I do." I swayed, cursing my unruly body. Tristan inhaled sharply. "And I—"

Whatever I wished to say was lost in rising darkness. The world shrank to a pinprick, a rushing black wind descending on me, plucking at my hair and twisting hot lead into my marrow. The stink of it filled my throat, branches snapping as hot wind pressed down like a giant's hand.

"Vianne!" Tristan, shouting. I fell sideways, his hands no longer gentle, catching me bruising-hard.

Confusion. Jierre di Yspres bellowing.

The Aryx woke in a blinding flash, a convex mirror of power, twisting fire poured into a shield of glass. Another door thrown wide, knowledge tipped into me as if I were a wineskin, over-flowing, stretching, *pushing* through me.

The reek was shoved aside, and I heard a snap as of a ship's cable breaking. The hunting-spell, cheated, turned back on itself, and I felt a moment of fierce satisfaction that it would recoil on its maker. Twas a piece of Court sorcery akin to a kill-spell, but requiring much more care and skill, and if I had not the Aryx standing guard under the surface of my skin I would not have known.

Down, I thought incoherently. *Down! I will not be used, no matter what god gave you to the Angoulême—*

The tide of flame retreated, folding down into itself. The Great Seal of Arquitaine released me.

It *obeyed.*

Men's voices. Tristan, very near. "If you've killed her—"

I heard my own voice. "Tristan—the Duc—"

"What?" Jierre di Yspres. "Shall I kill him, Captain?"

"Back—get *back*—," I gasped. It took so much, to ride the Aryx's shifting supple flare of power that was even now fighting the insidious spells that had been dragging us down for days, kept from us only by the Seal's sleepy defense. We had not even realized, so blind to the subtle sense of wrongness, the growing exhaustion.

"Carry her," someone said, all pretense of levity fled. "We shall take her to the village. Risaine will know what to do."

"I swear to you, if you do aught to harm her—" Tristan's tone was soft, conversational, but furious all the same.

"You think I would harm a helpless woman? Ho there, Timarche, lead them to the village. We shall follow with the *d'mselle*. Tis safe enough; they're no Orlaans dragoon."

Darkness, again, and I knew no more.

Chapter Seventeen

My auntie was at Court once too." The voice was familiar, but not one of the Guard. "Left under a cloud, as I am sure you well know."

"It matters little." Tristan, tense and exhausted. Someone held my hand, ran a callused thumb over my knuckles. "I care not a whit."

"I can see what you *do* care for. Look, she wakes, and pretty as a maiden in a tale." Shifting cloth. Smoke, and meat stew, and baking bread. I lay on something soft. I groaned, sought to make my eyes open. They did not obey, foolish things. Or perhaps they had seen enough, and would brook no more.

Am I blind? Sometimes, after the half-head, I felt this weak, and my vision would not work properly. The irrational fear of blindness would rise, and I would be too frail to combat it.

"Vianne?" Tristan, soft and hopeful. I had never heard that tone from him before. "Do not seek to speak, simply rest. You are safe enough."

"Aye to that, *d'mselle*." I thought I recognized this, too—the man in brown. The bandit.

Or was he? A bandit who spoke as a courtier hiding in the Shirlstrienne? And the Seal had chosen that moment to push aside the spells weighing us down, making it impossible to move.

How long had we been feeling the effects? *Why did I not know? I sought to keep them safe. Inexcusable inattention, Vianne. You must do better. You must do* more.

And the other spell, the circling blackness and crushing, fetid wave of power, had sought to strike at us as well. If not for the Seal, we would be dead or wandering witless in the woods.

I should have noticed. I endangered them. Inexcusable, Vianne. Try harder. Try again. "Tristan." My lips were cracked.

"I told you not to use the Seal. You've forced a return of fever." Stroking my forehead now, callused fingertips. Infinitely gentle, so gentle I thought perhaps I dreamed it. "Di Cinfiliet has graciously offered the services of his village for a few days."

"How could I not?" The bandit's laughter held an edge. "'Tis not every day a Duchesse falls into my arms. You have quite a talent for making an entrance, *d'mselle.*"

I tried not to use the Aryx, Tristan. You might as well scold it for using me. My eyes opened slowly, dim firelight pouring into my head. At least I was not blind. Twas a small mercy from the Blessed, that.

The first question, the most witless one, was all I could think to ask. "Where…?"

"The Shirlstrienne," Tristan answered patiently. "You must rest, Vianne. I cannot answer for my temper if you do not. And you frightened young di Rocham. He's been praying to the Blessed and wandering around sighing." Haggard despite his light tone, his cheeks hollow but freshly shaved, dark hair falling into his darkened eyes. Blue shadows ringed his eyes, and his mouth pulled against itself, a tight line.

I blinked. "What...?" I had no luck shaping more than the single word. My mouth simply would not obey me.

"You swooned. Our friend di Cinfiliet caught you, and there was some confusion, but nobody died. A few of the bandits have some bumps and bruises, and there is some scorching in the clearing where the Aryx woke—and Jierre swears he saw something in the trees." Tristan stopped, stroked my cheek. "Why did you not tell me you were so ill?"

There was something in the trees. Something foul. "We must...reach Arcenne," I croaked. *There is no time to waste. I am not strong enough for a repeat of that performance.*

"Not at the cost of your life." His fingertips still rested against my cheek. "Please, Vianne. Promise me."

I sighed. The room was low, exposed ceiling-beams with bundles of hanging herbs, and the green smell of hedgewitchery filled it from wall to wall. Firelight ran over every surface, and misty sunlight spilled in from a door I could not see. Sounds came, too—horses stamping, metal clashing, catcalls, murmurs.

Tristan perched on the bed beside me, holding my hand in his, touching my cheek with his free hand. He glanced at Adrien di Cinfiliet, whose storm-colored eyes were busy with a spot on the far wall. "Ask her what you will," the Captain said harshly, "but be quick. She has little time for foolishness."

"Who is the fool, *sieur*?" the bandit replied, comfortably enough. "Me for bringing you here, or you for allowing me to? Or her, for trusting *you* with her life? It seems you've done a fair job of placing her in danger." He had one hand to rapier-hilt, and I did not blame him. Tristan did not look away from my face, but the temperature of the air changed around us, and I was suddenly very glad he was not angry with me.

Dear gods. A pair of prickly men hissing at each other like prodded cats. "Cease this." I surprised myself. "Both of you." I had to take a deep breath, the swimming weakness was so awful. "*Sieur* Cinfiliet. My…thanks for your hospitality. Ask me…your riddles, I am ready."

Silence. The fire crackled.

Then Adrien di Cinfiliet threw back his head and laughed fit to die. "She near dies of fever and magical attack, and as she lies abed she wishes to play riddlesharp!" He found this extraordinarily funny, and I cannot say I missed the humor myself, now that he mentioned it. Still, it seemed improper to chuckle, even if I could have found the strength to do so. I contented myself with a sleepy, thin smile.

A shadow passed through the low door—a woman, her white hair cut into a cap of flyaway curls, ducked into the room and straightened, her hands on her hips. She wore a simple gray shift-dress belted with silver; her eyes were pale as the bandit's, and just as thickly fringed. "Cease that noise," she said sharply, and Adrien di Cinfiliet subsided, his eyes merry. He bit his lip, looking as unrepentant as any well-loved child. "'Tis not enough you bring a sick noblewoman here, and now you bawl at her like a fishwife? Out with you, Dri, go do something useful for a change."

"Like rob another caravan, or steal you more herb cutlings? Ease yourself, R'si Thornlet. She just awakened, and demanded to play the game of riddlesharp I promised her. Do you know they sing songs of me at Court?" Now a swift snarl passed over his tanned face, and I shivered.

Perhaps that gambit had not been the best one to use.

The white-haired woman was less than impressed. "You brought her here, now leave her to my care unless you wish her dead. Stop baiting the *chivalier*, too; tis bad manners." With that, she stamped across the packed-earth floor to the fireplace, and stirred briskly at a hanging cauldron. The richness of stew filled the air, and my stomach reminded me I was near starved.

"I do not bait him, *m'dama* Tante." The bandit folded his arms. "Besides, he takes no offense from a backwoods thief."

Tristan stroked my cheek, touched my lips. He ignored the rest, very pointedly. "Rest, Vianne. Everything else can wait."

My heart sank and swelled two sizes at the same moment. *We cannot delay, Captain. A Court sorcerer is seeking us, and I think his strength might overmatch mine even with the Aryx.* "If I continue resting, we shall…never reach Arcenne."

"I would rather never reach Arcenne than see you kill yourself for trying." Sharply, as if I were one of his men who had committed a silly error. But his touch was gentle, tracing along my jawline. "Shhh, *m'chri.* There's a fine hedgewitch here, and she has the tending of you."

"The sorcery—the *spell*—" My lips moved against his fingers, and he smiled.

"Di Narborre will not find us here. There is a defense of hedgewitchery around this camp, woven by *m'dama* here." The smile he wore filled his eyes, erased some of the gaunt lines scored around his mouth. "And you have given d'Orlaans more than a slapped wrist to nurse. The Seal is no trifle; the breaking of his tracking sorcery will most likely be unpleasant for him." He broke off, stroked my chin. "We are in little danger here, except from the bandits. Who have rather a high opinion of you at the moment."

"Tis the stuff songs are made of." The hedgewitch pushed her white curls back from her face. "Ease your mind, *d'mselle.* We have survived here by avoiding notice, and I laid the defenses for this place myself. I said to get *out*, Dri."

The bandit shrugged. His mood had shifted to almost-sullenness. "I have no pressing business."

A mercurial man. I stored this tidbit in my memory, watching him as best I could without seeming to. This altered my plans, perhaps.

"You do. Elsewhere." The woman turned a fierce glare upon him. "Give these two some peace and lee to speak. He has not left her side since he carried her here; you *get out*."

The bandit raised his hands. "As you like, *Tante*. Do not sharpen your tongue on me!" But he did not leave. Instead, he bent over the bed, peering over Tristan's shoulder at me. "Rest yourself, *d'mselle* di Rocancheil." His eyes were kind, for all the mockery of his tone. "I swear to you, no harm will come to you or your Guard while you rest here. You are under the protection of Adrien di Cinfiliet."

"My thanks, *sieur*," I managed to whisper. *You have a prickly pride, and sometimes such men are easily led if one is careful. Well enough.*

He left, whistling a tune I seemed to faintly remember. Where was it from? But I was interrupted from pursuing this line of thought.

As soon as the bandit was out of earshot, Tristan claimed my attention. "What songs do they sing of him, Vianne? How did you know?"

I closed my eyes. If I spoke slowly, I could string the words together in a necklace, and grant myself time to think as well. "I knew nothing, Captain. There are no songs. All bandits like to hear about themselves."

Tristan was still for a long moment. Then he leaned down, kissed my cheek, and I smelled leather, steel, and healthy maleness. A disbelieving laugh brushed my face. "You were wasted at Court, *m'chri*."

"Step aside, *sieur*, an it please you," the hedgewitch told him. "I've to tend my patient now."

He nodded, straightening and stepping aside—but not very far. "As you like, Marquisse."

Marquisse? Well, she speaks like a noble. I am unsurprised.

She did not react, simply bent over me, testing my pulse with dry, gentle fingers. This close, I could see the network of fine lines on her face, crow's-feet fanning at the corners of her eyes, laugh lines around her mouth. Her beauty ran bone-deep, her face simply settling on the framework instead of collapsing with age. The Angoulême's Companions had gifted us with such beauty, and even diluted it was a wonder to see. "So you guess, do you? And I guess what you are, and what she is. News reaches me even here, in the backwoods of Arquitaine among peasants and bandits; the Blessed know I've worked hard enough to stay informed. Greedy d'Orlaans has reached the summit of his dreams and still wants more, of course." She peered at the whites of my eyes, felt my forehead. "And you. What is the summit of your dreams, d'Arcenne?"

I held my peace. The conversation had taken an *extraordinarily* interesting turn, and I near held my breath as well, for fear that a sound from me would cause them to cease. Did they know each other? But the Captain had given no sign.

And what *was* the summit of Tristan d'Arcenne's dreams?

"Duty is a high enough summit for me, *m'dama*." His shoulders were stiff. "If I thought you meant her harm I would not hesitate."

"Any fool could see as much." The hedgewitch flattened her hand against my belly under the rough homespun blankets.

"Now let me concentrate. I would hate to botch a charm for such an august personage." Irony dripped acid from every word, and I almost winced.

This was most interesting, but I would have to wait before I could decipher it. The gray-clad hedgewitch closed her eyes, and a wonderful coolness laved me, washing away the shaky jittering of fever. It was a hedgewitch charm, true—but one of such power and elegant simplicity I longed to learn it.

When she finished and took her hand away, I felt much better. Still heavy and weary, but free of fever for the first time in weeks. I had almost forgotten what it was like to be warm, dry, and able to rest in a bed.

I gathered my voice. "A magnificent charm. Would you teach me, *m'dama*?"

Her fingers stiffened slightly as she checked my pulse again. "You would seek to learn peasant magic? Of course, you're a hedgewitch too. Some talent, but not enough practice, I wager. Too busy dancing pavanes."

Her tone needled me. And yet, she had the right of it. "It made me laughable, at Court. Yet it does seem to be useful."

Her mouth twitched upward into a smile. "A hedgewitch Queen. What a marvelous jest for the Blessed to foist upon us."

"I am simply holding the Aryx. In trust." I struggled to sit up. She pushed me back down, gently but with surprising strength from one so birdlike-thin.

"The first lesson in sorcery is *know thyself*. You cannot disregard that simple truth. You hold the Aryx, the Aryx is awake; therefore, you are the Queen."

I sighed. Why must I have this conversation with every noble I encountered? Why would they not leave me be? "I did not seek this."

"I would rather serve a liege who did not want the Aryx than a liege who killed to possess it," the hedgewitch Marquisse said briskly. "Now, I'll be dosing you with fevrebit and dantarais. You will no doubt hate it, but twill make you stronger."

I made a face. "No doubt." I sank back into the pillows. "My thanks for your care, *m'dama*."

"My nephew admires your bravery, Your Majesty."

"'Tis enough," Tristan interrupted. "She is wearied to death. Is there a point to this, *m'dama* Marquisse?"

"Do not bark at me, d'Arcenne. The point is, Your Majesty, you must accept what you are, or all of Arquitaine will suffer."

"Cease." There was a touch of a growl to the word, and Tristan took a half-step to the side, as if he wished to advance on her. His hands tensed, flexing, surprising me. I did not think he would ever strike a woman. "Later."

The white-haired hedgewitch shrugged. "Your wishing it otherwise does not alter truth, *chivalier*." She stood and shuffled to the fireplace, dismissing us with an ease that was almost royal.

"What—," I began, but Tristan shook his head. Dark hair fell over his shadowed eyes.

"Rest for now, an it please you." He settled himself on the bed, taking my hand again, running his fingertips over my knuckles. The touch made a strange warmth, very much like the hedgewitch charm, start at my hand and flood the rest of me. "A few days abed under the Marquisse's care, and you shall be strong enough to start for Arcenne."

There were more questions to ask. "The Guard. When may I see them?" *I wish to know they are hale—and there is a plan to set in motion, as soon as I know the map of this province, so to speak.*

"Tomorrow, perhaps." He settled himself as if he intended

to stay a long while. I could not say I minded. "When did you notice the spells laid to trap us?"

"Not until the Aryx moved to push them aside. I should have noticed…I ask your pardon. Twas foolish of me, and you all suffered for it."

He laid his finger against my lips. "No. I did not notice either, and I should have. Tis an old trick, to slow an enemy."

"Why slow us, unless they are following? And there was another spell, a darker one. It almost found us that night—when we heard the crashing in the woods, do you recall?"

He went utterly still, thoughtful. "Another spell? Twould not surprise me in the slightest. D'Orlaans has had much time to practice." His blue eyes fixed unseeing on my face. He stood abruptly, tall enough he had to duck slightly under a bunch of herbfiet hung up to dry. "I shall return."

I obediently closed my eyes and waited for him to leave. He did, and they flew open again. I stared at bunches of drying herbs, moving gently as the breeze from the open door touched them.

Something is amiss here. I must think, and plan, and—

But the hedgewitch came with a dollop of tisaine as foul as she had promised, and my worry fled before my fatigue.

Chapter Eighteen

The fever resurged over the next three days, fighting for me, but Risaine di Cinfiliet—her name sounded familiar, though I could not think of why—was a skilled healer, and by the third day when the fever broke for the last time in a gush of sweat, I was well on my way to mending. Risaine was marvelously patient, saving her sharp tongue for her nephew and Tristan, whom she disliked intensely—or pretended she did.

She treated me as an old *m'dama* auntie might cosset a beloved niece, cajoling me into eating, her voice soft but inflexible. Blotting my forehead, soothing me when I woke from nightmares—for terrible dreams there were, every time the fever crested, and Lisele bled in each of them.

Tristan visited, but he said little. He was unfailingly calm and polite, but he did not look at my face overmuch. Instead, he gazed at my hands, or at my knees under the blanket, or at the fire.

I must have looked dreadful.

By the fifth day, I could sit, shakily, in bed. I was sipping at a cup of broth into which Risaine had crumbled dried pungent fevrebit, grimacing a little at the sharp taste, when Adersahl and Jierre ducked into the low room. Jierre's forehead was clouded with worry, and Adersahl's mustache drooped a little, which alarmed me almost more than Tristan's new policy of distant kindness.

"Only a moment, mind," Risaine said sharply, following them into the sudden crowding. This house had only one room and a privy, and I had taken Risaine's bed. She slept in a wooden rocking chair by the fire with a quilt wrapped around her more often than not, and chided me briskly when I begged her to let me sleep upon the floor. *Fine physicker I would be if you caught chill after fever from sleeping on a Shirlstrienne floor. Do not be ridiculous, child.* And I meekly bowed my head.

Jierre ignored her, came straight to the bedside. He gripped his hat in his hands as if afraid it would fly away did he loosen his fingers. "*D'mselle.* You're well? Truly?"

"Not well," I admitted, offering him my hand. "But much better nonetheless, *chivalier.* My thanks for your concern. What ails you?"

"Grim news, *d'mselle.*" Adersahl spoke as Jierre took my hand and bent over it perfunctorily. "There is word from—"

"No," Risaine said sharply, from her position by the fireplace. She was preparing a tisane for woundrot, jars and jars of it. I did not dare ask why. "Let her rest for a little while longer, *sieurs,* an it please you."

The lieutenant shot her a look that could have cut stone. "*M'dama* Marquisse. I am under my Captain's orders, not yours."

"D'Arcenne is a fool if he worries her now. Look at her, *chivalier,* this noblewoman you've sworn to. Look at how thin she is, and the circles under her eyes, and the way her hand shakes."

Risaine let out a sharp chuff of annoyance, pushing back a white curl. "You will kill her, do you continue in this manner. Then where will you be?"

The urge to conciliate all but overpowered me. "I am not as bad as all that." I took my hand back from Jierre with a wan smile. "What has gone wrong? Tristan has been grim for days." I looked from Jierre to Adersahl, my wits taking on their accustomed sharpness. I found I could guess where the problem lay.

"Oh, no." My heart thumped, sickly, and settled into a high hard gallop. "They have found us. Or are about to."

"Not through my spells," Risaine muttered. "My nephew is merely rash. Excitable. Bloody stubborn."

Adersahl shrugged. He was broader in the shoulder than whip-lean Jierre, and his bulk granted some comfort. He slapped his hat idly against his stocky thigh. "The bandit wishes to fight them. This is their village, and we may be tracked here."

"Not through my weavings." Risaine turned to the fire. "Dri is young, but he still listens to my counsel. He merely speaks of it to needle your Captain. Which is far too easy to do."

Jierre brushed that aside with a dismissive wave of his hat, his other hand dropping to his rapier's hilt. "Tell her everything. Tell her about the plague."

Oh, sweet Blessed, no. Tis not even summer. Plague will spread far and wide without winter to contain it. And there has not been a plague since before the King's time. My gaze met Adersahl's. "There is plague? Where? And how badly?"

"What is this merry gathering, and I uninvited?" Tristan said from the door. I took a deep breath. The sight of him: blue d'Arcenne eyes, his clothes clean now—they had the means to take baths here, and I sorely wanted one once I could escape the bed—made my heart commence knocking against my ribs. He had found someone to trim his hair, too; slightly shorter than a *chivalier's* current fashion, but it made him even more handsome. "Lieutenant?"

I took another drink of broth, using the time to compose my thoughts. *Well. We are about to change the playing field, d'Arcenne. I hope you are unprepared.* "What is this I hear of danger and plague, Captain? Is there aught you wish to tell me?"

"I did not wish your worry." Tristan shot a sharp glance at Jierre, who shrugged, his lean face shuttering itself with an almost audible snap. "We shall speak of this later, di Yspres."

"You shall *not*," I disagreed immediately, but mildly enough. "You will speak of it now, and cease whipping di Yspres for my curiosity. I asked him, Captain, surely I have a right to ask for news?"

I do not know who was more shocked—Tristan; Risaine, who gave me an approving smile; Jierre, whose jaw frankly dropped; or myself. I sounded…

Well, I sounded like the King, amused and casually confident Tristan would obey my orders.

Let us pray he agrees, at least at this moment. I may likely pay for any show of independence later. But here, where there were more people, was a fine time for me to start working my own will, instead of being carried along by his. I had a possible ally in Risaine, and something told me she and her nephew were far from the worst friends I could have in the Shirlstrienne.

"You do." The Captain nodded slightly, as if to say, *proceed*. He did not look angered by my sudden authority. Instead, he seemed relieved. "Plague has struck Arquitaine, and struck hard. Citté D'Arquitaine has fallen victim. The plague starts with fever and ends with blood pouring from the nose and mouth until death. Few of those touched by it have recovered.

D'Orlaans is seeking the Aryx, though he dares not let anyone know the Great Seal is gone and he carries a false copy. Instead, every garrison and Guard in Arquitaine is looking for you. The tale is that I have kidnapped you and am holding you for ransom to buy my own safety." A muscle in Tristan's jaw twitched. "You have been proxy-wed to d'Orlaans in the Chepelle Ste-Mairie."

I stared *through* him, thinking furiously. *Perhaps I am not helpless.* It was a welcome thought. "Plague and a proxy marriage. Dear gods."

"The Blessed have expressed their displeasure with Arquitaine." Jierre's eyebrows were drawn together, and under his coloring he was pale. "You carry the true Seal, *d'mselle*, so we are safe from the plague, at least."

"We do not know that," Risaine interrupted. "She may have just recovered from the sickness. I have not seen this fever before, *sieurs*, and among this collection of ragtails that is rare indeed."

"None of us have fallen victim," Tristan pointed out. His blue gaze bored into me.

That is little comfort. And if I were surprised at Jierre di Yspres's sudden piety, I needed look no farther than the metal at my own throat to find a good reason for it. If the Seal had slumbered and was now awake...but *why*? Why wake now, and why plague *now*?

I could do nothing about the plague for the moment. There were other things I must know. "He proxy-wed me?" *He should be seeking to kill me, not still wed me. He has to know I am aware of his conspiracy.* "It makes little sense."

"It means nothing," Risaine said fiercely. "You hold the Aryx; you cannot be proxy-wed. It will not hold."

Tristan rested his hand on his rapier's hilt. "He has a copy of the Aryx and enough Court sorcery to make it *seem* to live. Especially since the Aryx…well. Court sorcery has become much easier in the past weeks. We have all noticed it."

"Fools," Risaine snorted. "All of you, *fools*."

No doubt. But I wonder why you say so, m'dama. I looked down into my cup. *Court sorcery stronger? I had not noticed, but then, I am not a Court sorcerer. At least, I was not before this.*

I must think. But first… "Could I be carrying plague?"

"If you were, one of us would be ill by now. Yet except for di Rocham's broken heart and Tristan's scowl, we all seem hale." Adersahl leaned against the table, examining the herbs piled in neat bundles, the jars standing ready to be scalded. "There is an easy enough solution to all our problems, *d'mselle*."

It is not the problems which worry me, it is the cause, which has acquired another tangle. "Which is?" I contemplated the bits of dried fevrebit floating in the broth.

"Is it not obvious? Contract a liaison, and make it public knowledge you have the Aryx." Adersahl picked up a sprig of rosemaire and crushed it between his broad, deft fingers, inhaled the scent. "Still, the nearest problem is di Narborre. We have discovered he was in Tierrce d'Estrienne some days ago."

My fingers clenched around the cup. Memory choked me.

"Make certain none still live." A crunch, and a wet stabbing sound—

I swallowed bile. *If I were a man, there would be an accounting for that.* Dull anger sparked red in my chest, through layers of numbness. *There is much I would repay di Narborre and his master.*

"Vianne?" Tristan crossed the room, shouldered Jierre aside, and rescued the cup from my trembling hands. "You are pale."

I was not short of breath, but I nodded, tendrils of dark hair falling in my face. "When do we leave?" My voice was a thin thread. It was not fear that made me so quiet. Twas instead a great hot-crimson anger, one I pushed aside. A lady must not ever betray such rage.

His hands were warm, and I near forgot every other person in the room as he steadied me. "We are at the edge of the Alpeis, in a hidden bandit's village. Do not fret, Vianne. This is why I kept the news from you a short while, I wish you to regain your strength before we flee to Arcenne."

I inhaled sharply. *Calm, Vianne. You must be cold as if you are hunting an intrigue meant to catch your Princesse. They caught her, and now you must serve them to their own folly, as quickly and neatly as you may. It will be difficult, but this you must do.* "Yet—" I meant to protest that I was fit to ride, that we *must* be on our way.

"Yet nothing." Risaine screwed a jar lid on with a practiced, savage twist of her wrist. "Your task is to mend your health. If you die, the Seal might not have a choice but to land in d'Orlaans's royal-bloody hands, and that would be a tragedy."

Tristan watched me, his mouth a straight line, his cheeks—was he blushing? And what was that glimmer in his eyes? Fear? The world had indeed gone mad. I searched for something appropriate to say, found nothing.

"An it please you," Tristan said finally, "I would speak with you privately, Vianne."

What now? Do you wish to take me to task, Captain? Why do it in seclusion? Your hand is strengthened by two of your Guard here, one of whom has no doubt told you of my idea of escaping you. I nodded, struck speechless, my wits racing to catch up. Recollected myself with an almost physical effort. "Jierre—my thanks for the news. I think I should speak with the Captain, indeed."

"That you should." Jierre left with a hurried bow, and Adersahl followed him, turning once to glance back at me. It was a meaningful look, but what it meant I could not say.

Risaine chuffed out a sigh, setting the jar down with a click. Today she wore an overdress of blue, and it suited her pale hair. "I suppose you wish to throw me out of my own house."

"Stay and hear a private conversation, as you like." Tristan did not look away. His eyes were so infinitely blue, I wondered for a mad moment if everything he saw was tinted with skyshade.

Risaine replied with a cheerful curse she might have heard from a Guard and left, shaking her head. She pulled the door to, and I heard her speaking outside, a low fierce tone—probably scolding Jierre.

My mouth was dry as sand. "Is this true? And what else, by the Blessed? What *now*?"

"'Tis as true as I can tell." He sighed and settled himself gingerly on the bed at my side, setting the cup away. "Di Narborre comes, and the fool of a bandit thinks the woods and a hedgewitch's muttering will hold him back."

I am a hedgewitch too, Captain, and I kept us safe for a short while. Still, that is not the most pressing matter here. "'Tis not what angers you. It angers you that the Duc thought to proxy-marry me. You did not anticipate that."

Amazingly, he dropped his head. I caught a flash of anger on his face, wondered why I could suddenly decipher his feelings so easily. "True. I should have thought—should have *planned*—for such an occasion."

"Is it true, that if I contract a liaison and make it public, that a proxy marriage will not hold?" I wished suddenly I had spent some time studying Arquitaine law instead of Tiberian verbs.

Of course, our legal code is built on the foundation of Tiberia. It took Graeca to make art, and Tiberia to make law, as the proverb went.

I held myself in readiness, watching d'Arcenne. Waiting for him to indicate what dance he intended to lead us into, since he had gone to such trouble to clear the floor.

Tristan shoved one hand back through his hair. It rumpled him most fetchingly. "Vianne—"

Answer me, Captain. Why is this so difficult? "Is it?"

His words spilled out in a rush. "'Tis true. You hold the Aryx, you must be wed in person. The law dates from the Angoulême's time."

Relief so intense it curdled my stomach made me sag against the pillow. I chose my next words carefully. "Good. I think tis time I made some decisions. Jierre said twas time for me to use my sharp wits to keep us all alive, and perhaps he is right." *Come, Captain, perhaps I should do the leading in this pavane. You are not as graceful as is your wont today.*

"Jierre is a fool." Tristan dropped his head forward into his hands. "Vianne, I…"

It frightened me, seeing him thus, his shoulders bowed, holding his head as if he was mazed with grief. Did he not wish to take me to task, then? What game was he playing?

Perhaps there is no game. I hardly dared credit it. Hesitant, I touched his shoulder, and he leaned into my hand. The bed creaked slightly.

He is accepting comfort, at least. My throat was still sand-dry. "He's a sharp-witted fool, to have chosen you for his Captain."

"Mistake after mistake, I have been so *blind*." His voice was muffled, choked. Was he weeping?

If he was, dear gods, how could I stand it? "Oh, no." I pulled at his shirt, a tiny tug as if to make the fabric hang aright. "Tristan? Please."

He tore away from my touch, bolting to his feet. Stood, shoulders hunched, staring at the fire, his broad back to me. The Aryx rang under my skin, distress and an electric pain spilling from warm metal into my bones.

Or perhaps mine was the pain, and I shared it with the Seal.

I watched, pulling my knees up under the blankets, a lump blocking my dry throat, all thoughts of intrigue fled. "Captain," I whispered. *How do I make this right? I do not know, and yet I must.* "I need your strength. If you cease now, I do not…I do not know what I shall do. *Please*, Tristan."

"How can you trust me?" The shout took us both by surprise. He rounded on me, his bootheel grinding sharply into the sweet-fairthwell Risaine scattered on her floor. His cheeks were wet, his blue eyes blazing. "I sent you to the Princesse, and almost caused your death. I was caught and you—*you*—had to come down into the donjons and fetch me like an errant child. And I have done nothing but make mistake after mistake. I almost cost you your life. That is not the worst. I am a *traitor*, Vianne!"

You hold yourself to such a fierce standard, Captain. It will break you, unless I hold you back somehow, like a horse that will run itself to death. I do not know how to rein you.

Yet rein him I must. For as little as I liked the idea of his casting me aside the instant I did not serve his revenge, I found I liked the sight of his grief and shame even less.

My hands turned to fists, and my heart gave a painful shiver inside me. "You saved my life," I pointed out calmly enough. "If you had not sent me to Lisele, d'Orlaans would have the Aryx at this very moment. If you had not given me the keys, I could not have hidden in the North Tower…and if not for you, your lieutenant would have left me behind on the Mont. You have kept me safe so far, and I—" Tears rose to choke me. *Oh, Vianne, calm him. He is fearfully upset, and likely to do some damage to everything.* "*Please*, Tristan!"

I did not say what I wished to say. *I am frightened,* I longed to shout. *I am frightened, and I do not know what I have become. You are the only safe thing in this madness, even though you are more dangerous to me than you can possibly know.*

He tipped his head back, his jaw working, his cheeks powder-white.

Come, Vianne. Tell him. Give him some hope, and stop being such a dimwitted frippet.

When I could speak over the tears seeking to force their way out, I found I knew what to say. There was only one possible avenue to take. "You are the Captain of my Guard. And my Left Hand—and future Consort. I need you."

That managed to get his attention, at least. His chin came down, his jaw dropped slack, and he stared at me gape-mouthed, like a Festival fool.

"How do you not *know*?" I tried again. "If there is one man in Arquitaine I can trust, Tristan d'Arcenne, tis you." I held his gaze, willing him to *understand*. My heart twisted afresh. *Give him strength. If he feels aught for you at all, use it to help him!* "I need you," I whispered. "Please, do not leave me adrift."

Tristan laughed bitterly. "What makes you think I would leave you, Vianne? Leave the only woman I have ever—" Maddeningly, he shut his mouth so quickly I was amazed his teeth did not take a piece of his tongue. But his cheeks were no longer so pale, and he was no longer shoulder-slumped and desperate. Instead, his fists clenched at his sides and his gaze blazing, he looked far more like the man I knew.

Or thought I knew, enough to save him from himself. At least, for the moment.

I smoothed the blanket over my knees, as if it were a silken skirt. *I do not think you are the kind to give an empty promise.* My heart throbbed painfully. *Do not let me embarrass myself, gods, please.* "Is it that you do not wish to be my Consort?"

It seemed to be exactly the right thing *and* the wrong thing to say. It broke him free of his silence—but it also drove him to a fury.

"You—you—" His fists shook, but I felt a curious comfort. He would not harm me just now. Of that much, I was certain. "How can you trust me?"

If he was this angry, at least he was not sunk in dangerous apathy. A furious Tristan d'Arcenne was a formidable ally, while an apathetic one was no use to anyone, least of all himself.

And this conversation, however it ended, would strengthen my hand in the coming time, when I set myself to doing what I must.

Now for the soothing—but not until you rough his waters a tiny bit more. "I can understand," I continued softly, smoothing the blanket. "I am only the di Rocancheil oddling. Tis miraculous that the Aryx has not fried me for insolence. You perhaps do not prefer a Court dame more suited to peasant magics and dry books?"

"Will you shut up?" he snarled. "You are the most infuriating woman I have *ever known!*"

Well, that, at least, is something. "Do you wish to be my Left Hand and Consort, or not?" The Aryx rang softly under my words.

"I would give everything I own and sell my soul in the bargain to do so," he said through gritted teeth. "I *cannot*, Vianne. The game of politics would require you to appear free. And I am—"

"I care *nothing* for the game of politics," I cried, dropping my pretense of calm. "If the Aryx wishes me to be Queen of Arquitaine, very well. If you wish to be my Consort, very well. If you do not—very well. But I *will not be forced any further*, Tristan!"

While I had almost certainly uttered words I would regret—for if I held the Seal I must care for the game of politics deeply enough that I was not hoodwinked—the last part was, at least, unvarnished truth. I was free of fever and on the mend, my wits had returned, and I was prepared to do my wretched duty once again. Another baton was ruling the musicians and the dance had changed, but I was required to follow the steps as prettily as possible, and not blunder.

But I would dance in my own fashion, and I would do all I could to take charge of the tune. My first step was wresting the lead from the Captain of the Guard, and his reaction was such I could hardly believe my good luck.

He did care for me. Perhaps it was only that we had traveled together, and that I represented his revenge. But he *did* care, and he did not think clearly at the moment.

He stared at me for a long moment, jaw working, eyes blazing. Then he gifted me with a single nod. "I would be honored to do aught you asked, Vianne." Clenched teeth, clenched jaw, clenched hands. "You are the Queen, and I shall redeem myself in your service."

Let us hope those are not empty words. "Then *I* shall decide how to dispose of myself." My pulse hammered thinly in my throat and wrists. "So we must find a temple, and contract you as my Consort as soon as possible. We must also leave this place. They have been kind to us; we cannot bring di Narborre upon them." *I trust Risaine's skill more than I would trust mine, but 'tis a chance I do not wish to hazard.*

My decisiveness calmed him. His shoulders relaxed fractionally, and his tone became more businesslike. "You are not hale enough for the kind of hard riding we must do to reach Arcenne quickly. It would kill you, Vianne."

I have no intention of dying just yet. Before, I might have, just to spite the Duc. But now…I cannot die. I have accounts to settle. I let out a short, sharp breath, the same sound I would make before a grand entrance at Lisele's side, echoed by hers. The small sigh was our private signal, a Court lady's battle call. "I will see what Risaine and I can do together, with the Aryx."

As I suspected, he had an immediate objection. "Court sorcery runs too much risk, especially with di Narborre in Tierrce d'Estrienne."

Court sorcery is not the only magic in the world. "Then we shall try hedgewitchery. I will be fit to ride, Tristan. I promise."

"Soon enough." He approached me cautiously, as he would a wary animal. Lowered himself down on the bed again, sitting on the edge. He looked away, across the room, his back to me. His head dropped again. "I will not betray you, Vianne."

"Of course not." *What a curious choice of words.* Yet we were faced with so much black betrayal, I did not wonder he felt the need to swear it aloud. And, truth be told, I was more than a little unsettled, as if I had prepared myself for battle and met instead with a fête.

I had thought the Consort offer would be refused with some pretty words about duty; I had anticipated the conversation to take a completely different cast. This was…unexpected.

To say the least.

We sat in silence, listening to the crackling of the fire and voices outside.

I waited until I could stand it no longer. I touched his shoulder for the second time, cupping my hand over the curve under his shirt. Muscle stood out under the cloth; tension vibrated through him, infecting my own flesh.

He caught my wrist with a swift movement, and pulled my hand to his mouth. Pressed a rough kiss into my palm, his teeth pressing through soft lips. I did not flinch. "Vianne," he murmured against my skin.

Then he kissed the inside of my wrist where the pulse beat. The Aryx rang, a thrill sharp as fire.

I had to swallow twice before I could speak with anything approaching a normal tone. "The King said you favoured me."

"Of course." His lips moved against my wrist. "Are you blind, *m'chri?*"

"I thought you hated me, after…" *After you ordered the peasants to be killed. And I do not understand your anger, Tristan. I do not understand your moods at all, for all I think I am making headway.*

"Of course not. I have never hated you. That was my downfall." He held my wrist to his mouth, his eyes closed, inhaling as if smelling my skin. For a few moments we stayed like that. It was as far from a courtsong as I had ever seen, but I felt light and happy, and for that moment it was enough.

Chapter Nineteen

Two days later I was allowed—with Risaine at my elbow, to bolster me—to see the bandit village.

I knew then why Tristan had argued so hard against it. For what I found in that village scored me deeply.

"See that?" Risaine said, ruffling a child's hair. The girl played solemnly with a threadbare doll, her hollow-cheeked face devoured by her eyes. "Just barely escaped the plague, arrived a week ago with four other children led by a boy not past his twelfth year. Their village was ransacked by armed thugs looking to eke more of the harvest from the peasantry. Oh, and that man? His family, killed by d'Orlaans's bullies half a year ago. That woman? Cannot stand to have a man touch her." Risaine clicked her tongue sharply. "Not after the Guard at Rouenne finished with her six months ago. A wonder she's alive."

I absorbed this as I leaned on the older woman's arm. Most of the "bandits" were thin, desperate-looking men with fierce faces and peasants' weapons. The women seemed hard, but their gazes were nervous as hungry birds. In the lee of a rude hut one woman—wide-hipped and red-faced, with cornsilk hair braided about her head as the peasants of Sainte-Ecy did—sobbed as another held her, murmuring soothing non-sense words.

"What of her?" I asked quietly.

"Her daughter was killed by tax farmers last week, and she still cannot believe it. The tax men are the law." Risaine drew me away. "Do you see this, Vianne? This is what the King brought us to."

The King bears the blame for this? "How so?" I found myself gazing upon a collection of ragged children taking a lesson from a rail-thin woman dressed in a dark priestess's cloak, her hair cropped close to mark her as one of Kimyan's elect. She was training them in arithmetic, counting on her fingers, a teaching-rhyme I remembered from my own nursery-school days. One bloat-bellied boy had a bandage wrapped about his left hand; he cradled it as his dark eyes followed the priestess's chanting. "Gods." My stomach churned. "Tell me."

"You did not know, of course." Risaine stopped at a fire in front of a low-thatched shelter. I gratefully lowered myself to the rude bench she indicated. Broken sunlight came through the branches far above, dappling the entire village. At the very periphery, a thin blur swirled through the air—protections and camouflage, laid with skill and care. "I did not know either, when I came here. We live noble lives indeed, secure in our knowledge of Court sorcery, secure in our right to take what we see fit, whenever the mood strikes us. The very gods gifted us with Arquitaine, and tis only right we do as we see fit."

I almost drew breath to protest, thought better of it when I saw her expression shift. Her mouth turned down, her sharp face softening. The breeze fingered white curls, lovingly. "Then I was blown here by an ill wind." She lowered herself next to me with a sigh. "These people fed us, clothed and sheltered us. And we learned. The King's payments for the wonders of his Cité and his Palais; his payments to foreign powers—where did you think they came from? And what do you think happens to those who cannot pay for his pleasures? A choice between starving to death or being beaten to death by a tax farmer; all the peasantry living in dire fear of d'Orlaans's Guard."

And the Aryx slept through this. I watched the village. A mongrel dog trotted past, head held high but its tail crooked as if broken. The huts huddled close to ancient trees, bandits fading in and out between light and dappled shade, dressed in their green and brown.

I gathered my thoughts, arranged them logically. "D'Orlaans was responsible for collecting taxes," I summed up, "and the King was not overcaring of how he did it."

Risaine nodded. "So it was."

"It seems nothing is true now," I said. "I saw…" What had I seen? The Duc had committed bloody fratricide, to be sure. But had the King been any better? For this place to hold such misery could not have merely taken a month.

"You saw a bloody coup." Risaine's back was straight as a priest's staff. She rubbed her fingers against her blue overdress as if there were something foul on them. "Tis a wonder it did not happen sooner. There were stories, of course, of the Court and the fêtes and festivals, merrily singing while the rest of Arquitaine groaned. Tis whispered the King was more a boylover than interested in his Damarsene wife, and the empty-headed daughter counted proof of it."

Protest rose in me. Lisele had not been empty-headed. But she had been spoiled, I could admit as much. And, much as I loved her, Lisele had not been overgifted with wits. Twas why I so often set myself to flushing out little intrigues meant to take advantage of her.

What if Lisele had lived, and not I? Another woman of gentle birth confined to her rank might not have survived the successive shocks I had already endured. To think of my Princesse forced to face such things pained me.

Would she have been strong enough to bear them?

Risaine's sharp eyes were on me. This hedgewitch's gaze missed next to nothing, and asked for—or granted—precious little quarter. "You hold the Seal. The fate of every soul in this village weighs on you now. Yet you could take the throne from d'Orlaans and continue on your merry way, taxing the poorfolk to pay for your pleasures. The Blessed, it seems, would not care enough to stop you."

I closed my eyes against the hideous thought. In the darkness behind my lids, I heard a child's laughter. The teaching-rhyme marked out its even cadence, the priestess's voice helping along a stumbler. Someone called out, and a woman's voice lifted in a light lilting peasant song about Baron di Wintrefelle and the Citrine War, in the time of Archimvault the Tall.

Truth is never pleasingly spiced. I swallowed bitterness, felt the Aryx's hum against my chest. Even though it was a gift of the Blessed, the Seal might not care for the agony of peasants.

It was merely a tool, for all its power. A tool that could slumber. And the Blessed? Perhaps they had larger concerns. At least the harvests did not fail under their care—but a single glance at this small village made me painfully aware that even that was no guarantee for common folk.

Yet Arquitaine was a rich land—what need was there for *this*?

"You must have wanted to show me this very much," I said

finally, when I could bear to speak.

"I never thought to have a chance to avenge myself on Henri di Tirecian-Trimestin and his foul brother. The Blessed have heard my prayers." She did not say it piously.

"What did he do to you?" I thought of the King's carefully curled hair and his silk and velvet, the endless banquets and Court protocol. Tristan had been rumored as the King's catamite, early in his Court career, but I saw no evidence of that. Still, there were others—though the King was also rumored not to mind a woman's bed when the mood struck him, either.

There were precious few of either sex who would refuse a King.

"Oh, not much. Sired a bastard and banished me from Court when the swelling began to show, so I would not damage the negotiations for his cow of a Damarsene bride. I believed a King's promise of love, and paid for it like any fool. I was no more than another silly little Court chit to him. And my son..." She laughed, shook her head as if freeing an unpleasant thought from its confines. "No matter. I have my nephew, strong in my old age. He should have been hunting and hawking with the nobles, at the King's table. Instead, he is a bandit and I am a hedgewitch bandit-woman, binding broken bones and salving wounded peasant hearts." I heard a rustle of cloth and opened my eyes to find her standing before me, her hands folded. She looked thoughtful, her sharp gray eyes staring across the village's quiet bustle. "My best revenge is this—I have shown you Henri was too self-centered to be a proper sovereign. He allowed d'Orlaans far too much power and asked no questions. He sired a princess unfit for the throne on his foreign wife, threw away a good Arquitaine heir because freeing us from the chains of paying tribute would require he bestir himself to war or diplomacy."

I had never heard the dead Queen referred to as a "cow of a Damarsene." It would have been highly impolitic to say that in Lisele's part of the Court, since her mother had died in child-birth, and my Princesse often felt the lack. "My thanks for the truth, *m'dama*." My voice was barely audible above the village's tapestry of sound.

She turned to me, her fingers clenched tight against each other. Now I could see the echo of old-fashioned manners in her gestures, and I knew why she stood thus. "Truth is the best revenge, child, and I have had much time to think on the wrongs done, not merely to me, but to others. I shall tell you this further; whatever crimes Henri di Tirecian-Trimestin committed in the name of kingship, his Left Hand committed more. Take care who you keep close to you, Vianne. Tis more important than you think."

That pricked me. "You mean d'Arcenne." I almost said *Tristan*, caught myself just in time.

"Sharp tools are necessary for a sovereign. I simply warn you that you do not cut yourself." But the spasm of distaste before she smoothed her features spoke much louder than the prettily-phrased warning.

Does she hate him because he reminds her of the King, or does she hate him for his part of the King's injustice? Tristan would not have lent himself to this misery, would he? And he is too young to be part of her *misery.* I nodded slowly. Twould not be useful to argue thus with her. "My thanks."

"Of course." Risaine dropped her hands to her sides, loosen-ing them with a shake. "I have other patients to physick. I think you are well enough to sit for a bit."

I agreed, and she left me under the shifting shade of branches. I sat, listening to the song of movement all about me, and thought long and hard. The motion and noise, subtle as it was, reminded me of the bustle of Court. There was always movement in the Palais, the sense of other breathing lives. I thought best with that quiet music enfolding me.

Where was her son now? Had the conspiracy reached even into the Shirlstrienne—or was there a darker reason for her to hate the King?

I found my hand at the Aryx, one thumb stroking the curve of a metal serpent through thin fabric. I ceased with an effort. The Seal purred, a subtle vibration against my skin.

It troubled me.

I watched the small village from my perch. Every thin, haunted face accused me. I could not help but wonder how many of the Court banquets I had been excruciatingly bored through, or had eaten at with good grace, had been bought with a peasant's blood.

Chapter Twenty

After another few days of Risaine's constant fussing and dosing with herbal tisanes, I found myself able to bathe in a tub I helped her laboriously fill in front of the fire. It was so delicious to be clean that I stayed until the water grew cool. Afterward, she clucked and fussed over me as she chafed my hair mostly dry and braided it. She hummed as she did so, and I shut my eyes, remembering Lisele performing the same task. A high honor, but we never saw it thus. It was simply what we did—I dressed Lisele's hair, and she dressed mine, as we had since childhood.

The memory sent a flintstrike of pain through me, yet I swallowed it. The time had come to make myself sterner. I could not hope to keep anyone safe if I did not temper what little steel I possessed.

After the bath, Risaine left me to my own devices. Every day brought more and more wounded souls to this small place, and I heard whispers of other villages hidden in the forest's vastness. A whole province of the fled and dispossessed, taking shelter in the Shirlstrienne as children will hide behind a nurse's skirts.

Here at the edge of the darker Alpeis forest, they did not fear the *demieri di sorce*. Instead, they feared d'Orlaans.

I had set myself to tidying her table of jars and herbs, and when a shadow filled the door I looked up, expecting to see Tristan. Instead, Adrien di Cinfiliet leaned against the door, his half-smile more mocking than ever. "And a good morn to you, my lady Riddlesharp." His sharp light eyes passed through the room once, the same glance I saw Tristan use so often. Gauging the ground, or searching for enemies.

"Good morn, *sieur* bandit." I set down the jar of woundrot, lining it up with the next. "*M'dama* Risaine went to—"

"—minister to her patients, I know. I thought you might chafe at this small cage, and came to offer my services as jester. Would you care to walk with me?" He delivered the invitation in such a light tone I was hard-pressed not to laugh.

It was, I admit, a pleasure to hear a cheerful voice. Tristan visited me daily, but he did not speak overmuch. Jierre looked in on me briefly every few mornings, and Tinan di Rocham was sober and constrained when he managed to knock on Risaine's door. I knew not what they did the rest of the time, but I did not imagine it to be pleasant.

"I should be glad of it." I straightened, smoothing down Tinan's leather vest. I must have been a sight in boy's clothes, with my long rope of hair and my fever-thinned face—for I could feel, when I touched my cheeks, the hollows left behind by illness. "If you take care to walk slow, *sieur*, for I am not in fit condition to dance."

"I shall seek to avoid dancing." He stepped out of the door as I approached, and offered his arm as soon as I moved into the open air. "Besides, I have no skill for it."

I doubt that. "You carry a rapier, do you not?" I took his arm, glad of the support. My legs sometimes decided to tremble like a newborn colt's.

"Tis not meant for dancing, lady Riddlesharp." We began to amble, and I sensed he had summat to say. But his tone remained light, though his uneasiness called forth an uneasiness of my own.

For all that, it was pleasant to walk with him and for a moment pretend I was in the formal gardens, perhaps strolling with a *chivalier* whose witticisms required attention and politeness. "Swordplay is a cousin to dancing, *sieur*. I do not think you heavy on your feet."

"Cats must land lightly. I would think dancing a *cousin* to something else, though."

The entendre caught me unawares, and I coughed slightly, a hot flush rising to my cheeks. *Highly improper. Yet he is a bandit, after all.* I gathered my wits, preparing to do battle, and suddenly felt at home. *This* was a situation I was not at sea upon.

"Of course, it could merely be fear," I remarked sweetly. "Some men do blanch more at a woman than a drawn blade."

He acknowledged the cut with a short, barking laugh. "You have a facile tongue, Duchesse."

"Tis a hazard of Court life, *chivalier*. What troubles you?" *You did not come here to trade petty jests with me, more's the pity.* I could have used the relaxation of a few more moments pretending I was nothing more than a lady-in-waiting again.

Old leaves crunched underfoot, and hard-packed dirt settled under the soft leather-soled clothshoes Risaine had loaned me. Di Cinfiliet was silent until we reached the edge of the village, the swirl of Risaine's spells hanging shimmering to our right. "I beg your pardon, *d'mselle*. I do not mean to offend. At least, not you, and not now."

Interesting qualifications. "No offense taken. You seem uneasy."

He indicated a fallen log with a nod. "Rest awhile, an it please you. Tis best to be uneasy, so close to the Alpeis. Only a fool goes blithely here."

And how much of a fool am I, to be so blithe as to walk unaccompanied with you? I settled gratefully on the log, and he sank down next to me with a creak of boot leather and a sigh. The woods smelled of verdant life, the earth fresh from nightly rain.

There had not been a storm since we'd arrived here. *That* was an uneasy thought. Another followed hard on its heels.

Was it chance that we happened upon a nobleman and his aunt hiding here? Was it chance I saw Tristan in that passage, or chance that I escaped notice in the Palais? It strains the mind to think of so much luck, ill or good. Was the Aryx taking a hand in matters, leading us here unawares?

That was discouraging. Even more discouraging was the thought that gods might be stirring themselves to take an active interest in Arquitaine, as they did in the time of the Angoulême's children. I do not grudge the Blessed their control of our land—though any good daughter of Arquitaine might wish that they would secure our borders without ado—but I was uncomfortable with the idea of being a pawn in such control. Any sane person would be, no matter how fashionably irreligious and Court-bred.

I had very little reason to doubt the Blessed at the moment. Rather than being a comfort, the thought was becoming a deadly discontent.

I glanced at di Cinfiliet's profile. He looked much like Risaine, especially at rest, with his long nose and narrow mouth. I dropped all pretense of levity. "Speak, an it please you."

He pushed a small bit of leaf mould aside with his boot-toe. "What are your plans, *d'mselle*? Summer is coming, and di Narborre haunts these woods. Our scouts report him moving hither and yon, seeking you. The pathways to Arcenne may be watched."

My mouth dried and I settled my hands in my lap, as if I wore a skirt. "I had not thought so far ahead," I admitted. "I have been occupied with becoming fit to ride, so we may not endanger you for longer than absolutely necessary."

"Well enough." He did not sound disdainful. "I have a thought, and I pause to lay it before you. You may take offense."

"What, again? If I did not take offense at your light speech before, why should I now?" I studied the weather-tanned skin and the bright slashes of his eyes. His hair was trimmed haphazardly, and his hands were rough from use. Grime tainted his fingernails.

Still, he had an honest face, and I had no reason to mistrust him yet. He had sheltered us for days now, and if his levity had an edge, I suppose he had reason. My own levity is too sharp for common consumption many a time, and as a woman I am rarely given lee to produce it outside the safe confines of my own thoughts.

He shrugged, pursing his thin lips as if finishing a long conversation with himself. "Then I shall be blunt. I have a cadre of good men and horses. If we go swiftly, there is the thin southron pass to Navarrin. Tis little-used and dangerous, and I would lay my last copper tis not watched as the passage to Arcenne may be. If you have reason to distrust your...current position, remember you have an alternative."

If he had bothered to look at me he would have found my jaw ajar like a stuck fish's. *Well. That is surprising, my fine bandit.*

And most welcome, though you cannot know why. I snapped my mouth shut and glanced down, smoothing the fabric of my breeches over my knees. The Aryx lay warm and quiescent under my shirt. "What does your aunt say of this?"

"Am I still in knee-breeches, to ask her? Yet I did seek her counsel. She is unhappy with the thought, yet will not forbid me. I never have taken well to forbidding, in any case. I am a nobleman, though I may not look it, or at least enough of one to help a *d'mselle* in difficulty. My duty is to see you safe."

Charming of you, and very chivalrous. Still… "And the Captain?"

"The more to guard you, the better." But his tone turned cool. They were ill-paired, Tristan and this man, by temperament. And, it seemed, by much more. I wondered at that. "Other men, peasants and petty nobles, have gone through the mountains. Tis a hard journey, but better than what lies behind. The Shirlstrienne holds more than just this village, and some bandits are not so fine as we. There are wolves who would as like to slit your throat as steal your purse, merely for the joy of it. Yet even they fear di Narborre and his hounds. I do not think it safe for you to remain here much longer. Rumor of a band of noblemen with a treasure is already seeping through the trees. Hedgewitch charms are all very well, but I saw the spell was unleashed on you at our first meeting. I like not the thought of witnessing it among these houses, poor as they are."

In other words, the sooner we leave here, the better. "I will speak to Tristan. I may be able to convince him." *If logic will not work, I shall find some other road.*

"The sooner the better, *d'mselle*. Should you find yourself in a position where your Captain's will is not yours, remember I place myself at your disposal."

A pretty choice. What reason have I to trust you overmuch? I did not like the thought, for he *had* sheltered us. Still, new caution crept into me. Could I but convince Tristan to take this far-southron route, I could perhaps overcome his determination to rout the Duc on the field of battle.

My stomach turned to a hard knot. "Why would you do such a thing, di Cinfiliet? You have no cause to wish me well or ill. We can only be a burden to you."

He rose, a swift motion I took care not to flinch at. "Perhaps I tire of skulking in the Shirlstrienne like an animal. What better way to regain a place of honor for myself? And my…my Tante R'si grows old, and I yearn for a softer bed for her to spend her age in." Di Cinfiliet turned to me, offering his hand. "Come, I had best take you back. She will scold my ears off if I overtire you."

I let him draw me to my feet, his hand warm and hard against mine. He smelled of the woods and smoke, and a faint healthy tinge of maleness. He rested his left hand on his swordhilt as he regarded me, our fingers tangled together briefly.

I recovered my hand and dropped my gaze. "I thank you for your honesty, *chivalier*."

He offered his arm again. "You are not an empty-headed woman, Vianne. If I may be so bold?"

It warmed me abruptly, and I slid my own arm through his. "You may, *sieur* Adrien. I shall speak to the Captain. Between us, we may make an impression on his stubbornness."

"I do not hope for much. Though if anything can make an impression on that harsh clay, I suspect twill be your speaking and not mine."

A vote of confidence, perhaps. We returned silently the way we had come, and when we came in sight of Risaine's house under its huge, spreading willum tree, I breathed a silent sigh of relief.

"I shall leave you here." Di Cinfiliet reclaimed his arm. "Should you have need of me, *d'mselle* Vianne, simply say the word." He gave me a bow, considerably more polished than his first—he must have been watching the others—and, turning on his heel, stalked away with his long loping stride.

I watched him. Sunlight fell through the leaves, and he blended into the forest's green and brown as if he had been born to it.

My cheeks, for some reason, were flaming-hot.

That afternoon I wore a fresh set of Tinan di Rocham's clothes as I stepped out of Risaine's low door, carrying a bundle that was the shift I had worn while bathing and some other bits of cloth Risaine wished taken to the brook to be washed.

I threaded my way slowly through the bandit village and had almost reached its fringes before Adersahl di Parmecy fell into step beside me. "And a good afternoon to you, *d'mselle*," he greeted, smoothing his mustache. "Where are you bound?"

I held up the bundle of linen. "Some of the women are doing washing down by the brook. *M'dama* Risaine's due along any moment." I tossed my damp braid over my shoulder. "I would speak to the Captain, though. Where is he?"

"Went with our bandit lordling to view di Narborre's tracks." Adersahl grimaced. "Also to lay traps along the approaches to the village. Di Cinfiliet is all but daring di Narborre to come and duel."

I absorbed this. Adersahl shortened his long strides to match my slow pace. "I do not think it wise. But di Cinfiliet is the leader of this village, I suppose he does what he feels best." *And perhaps he will broach the subject to Tristan himself, and I can add my own thoughts later. Though such a turn of events is likely to make my Captain even more stubborn.*

Adersahl nodded. The feather in his hat bobbed. "The Captain did ask me to watch over you today."

My heart lightened, turned soft inside me. "I thought so."

One of the many lean dirt-colored dogs trotted past, nose to the ground. I smelled woodsmoke, cooking food, heard a jumping-rhyme. "There are so many children here," I said. "They do not seem so dangerous."

"For the most part." Adersahl took my elbow as I almost tripped over a fallen branch. "Some are criminals, escaping the King's justice. We have kept careful watch."

I do not think I have much to fear from them. "I've spoken to none but di Cinfiliet and his aunt. They seem to think I am best kept a mystery." My fingers lifted almost of their own accord to touch the hard lump of the Seal under my shirt.

He smoothed his mustache again. Was he *nervous*? It did not seem possible, he was so phlegmatic. "I would agree. The less anyone knows of who you truly are, the better."

"Adersahl." For a moment I could not find the words I wanted. It was not ladylike to ask, but here I was in breeches, strolling about unescorted with men. Propriety could not be my sole worry. "I would ask you summat of the Captain."

What does he think of di Cinfiliet, and his aunt? What happened to Risaine's son? Was the King truly unconcerned with d'Orlaans and the tax farmers? How soon will we leave here, and what place is safe? Even Arcenne might not hold or hide us well.

I could not decide what to ask first, and I had to prepare my ground in other directions as well. While I framed my first sally, he neatly took me by surprise by slanting me a dark glance, his eyes twinkling merrily. "Certainly, *d'mselle*. Tis high time you did. Twas often a joke among the Guard that the Captain could not draw his lady's attention away from old books and peasant magic. He has haunted your steps a long while."

Tis not what I meant. My heart gave a thundering leap. "He did not ever seem to care before."

"Well, he was discreet. He has enemies, *d'mselle*, as do you. Someone might have known enough to strike at you to harm him, for there are few surer ways." Adersahl let go of my elbow. There was a small path worn down a hill toward the brook, and I chose my steps with care. "I think he has fancied you since he came to Court, but tis only the opinion of a lowly Guard."

"He came to Court when I was thirteen." Fascinating as this line of inquiry was, I had other business. "Who exactly is di Cinfiliet?"

"I suspect Tristan knows, and Jierre. But I do not. Not *exactly*."

You, sieur, *are a very unpracticed liar.* "Risaine bore a child to the King. She implies her son is dead, and yet she has a nephew of a certain age. I have not heard the Cinfiliet name before, and it would ease my mind to know a little more." I did not dare voice my darker imaginings.

Adersahl's gaze met mine. I paused on the path, looking up at him.

"You are the Queen." The stocky Guard did not smooth his mustache this time, but I sensed he wished to. As it was, he rested one hand on his rapier-hilt, and flushed like Tinan di Rocham.

I nodded, my chin set high. "Queen perhaps, but of what? A bare half-dozen of the Guard. I am not convinced of the wisdom of staying in Arquitaine for the Duc to catch us."

He mulled this over, and I let him. Some *chivalieri* can be led to the water's edge, and they will drink if you keep them there long enough. But all is lost if you try to force their muzzles down, no matter how thirsty they may be.

Adersahl was silent for a considerable while as we faced each other. When he finally spoke, twas in a level, serious tone I had not heard from him before. "Plague is spreading through Arquitaine. If the Seal is removed from the borders of the land of the Blessed, who can tell what will happen?"

I do not know the Aryx will allow *itself to be so removed. Yet that is a problem I will solve when the time comes.* "Tis the peasants who will suffer most," I said quietly. "I find I believe they have suffered enough. What must I do, Adersahl? Whatever move I make, someone grieves, and there is pain aplenty."

He cocked his head, and I saw strands of gray amid the dark curls. He was no longer young. "I do not envy you that. Yet I must say, if we are in your hands, I am content."

I sighed, frustrated. *Come, chivalier, I am inviting you to drink.* "Adersahl, I am not fit for this." *I do not know half of what I wish to, and I cannot see my way through this tangle.*

"Yet d'Orlaans thinks he's fit to be a King. Can you guess why I would rather you ruled Arquitaine, *d'mselle*?"

For the love of the Blessed, stop being dense. I was about to reply, but the Aryx warmed against my chest. I stilled, my attention turned inward, seeking.

I heard the thunder of hooves, and men shouting. For a moment my heart leapt, thinking Tristan had returned; then a scream pierced the air. The copper of fear started to my tongue, and my hands turned hot and wet.

His face changed. Adersahl cocked his head, listening. "What is it, *d'mselle*?"

"I hear horses. And shouting." I turned to retrace our steps, but Adersahl's fingers sank into my arm, the sword-roughened hand of a Guard neither gentle nor overly harsh.

He shook his head. "Not the village. They will expect you there. Come, this way."

I followed him, still stupidly clutching the bundle of washing. My emerald ear-drops were safe in a pocket. They were the only thing of any value I possessed, except the Seal, and the Aryx was not mine. Even if it was what they wanted of me, the Aryx is held only in trust.

Adersahl led me a good distance from the path. I heard steel clashing, and cries. Hooves resounded against the earth as fingers against a drumhead. It seemed a wonder he could not hear it; my skull rang as if the half-head was about to strike me in protest of the cacophony.

The elder Guard laced his fingers together, I stepped into them, and he lifted me into the branches of a tam tree, as if we were children in an orchard. He handed the washing up, and I clutched it to my chest.

"Climb, an it please you. I shall return with news. Here." He lifted up a dagger that glittered briefly in the afternoon sunlight.

I leaned down, clinging to the rough bark, my damp braid spilling forward over my shoulder. "Surely 'tis not di Narborre?" My heart lodged in my throat. I felt like a fool the instant the words left me, for what else could it be?

He shook his head. "I cannot give you a comforting lie, *d'mselle*. Climb as high as you may, do not make a sound."

I nodded. *Tristan. Dear gods, let him be safe.* "Be careful, *chivalier*."

He made a brief noise of assent, then turned and ran back toward the village, with the step of a much younger man.

I clung to the branches, working only a little higher before my courage failed me and I decided to wait. It was a warm, bright afternoon, sunshine filtering through the treetops, a slight breeze carrying the faroff sound of something terrible. I heard one piercing scream and shut my eyes, clinging to the branches.

Risaine. Was she caught in the village? What of the shimmer of spells that kept this place hidden?

And Tristan. Where was he? Out searching for di Narborre's tracks with di Cinfiliet. What of the rest of the Guard?

The noise grew greater, screaming and clashing steel. I clung to the tree, perched on a branch as thick as my leg, grateful the thick leaves hid me from view. But the foliage also obscured my view of everything but the tree. I could not look for danger or discover what transpired, even had I wanted to.

I rested my sweating forehead against the rough bark of the trunk, clutching at the bundle of cloth and the knife. *Please let it be something else, not the Duc's men. Please, let it be some other thing, some ordinary thing.*

What ordinary thing could this be? We had tarried too long. We? No.

I had tarried here too long, and others were paying the price.

The Sun had dropped in the sky, the light taking on a rich golden cast, when the noise finally ceased. Silence folded thick around me. I shifted uncomfortably. My body ached again—the aftermath of fever, hard riding, and now clinging in a tree. *What a queenly picture I present.* I had to bite back a laugh perilously close to panic.

What if night falls and I am still perched here? I listened as hard as I could. Heard only the wind through the trees and the sough of blood in my ears.

I had never noticed before what manner of silence falls with

no human beings present. Since I was young, I had been surrounded by the clamor of the Court, barely a moment left to
oneself, solitude grasped only in quick moments on back stair-
wells or a fraction of an hour hiding behind thick curtains.
Even in my bedroom there had been a servant at the door, and
Arioste and Lisele to listen for. Then with the Guard, I barely
had enough time to find a moment for the privy—and during
the day I was in the saddle with Tristan. Even in the village there
were the constant sounds of human presence.

How many times had I wished for solitude, as well as the en-
viable freedom of men's clothing? Now another of my wishes
was granted in a way I would rather not have had.

I bit back another laugh.

The awful, ringing silence lasted through the afternoon, as
I shifted every so often in the branches, aware of the deathly
hush whenever the sound of trees moving broke it. Birdsong
threaded through the hush, low and timid. Dusk came, purple
and glorious. I saw a slender doe balanced on graceful legs wander by underfoot. I held my breath, my heart hammering, and
she passed without remarking me—or perhaps being too mannerly to remark upon me.

Before the last of the light failed, I thought I heard more
horses. I strained my ears, but the trick of hearing had deserted
me. I could perceive nothing but the soughing of wind.

*What will you do if anyone finds you, Vianne? You are a cow-
ard; you cannot spill an enemy's blood. What will you do?*

I set my jaw and peered down. I had climbed up too far
to comfortably drop to the ground. *I cannot tarry here forever.
Night approaches, what will I do?*

I was already moving, stiff and sore, dropping the bundle of
wash. I flung the knife down too, judging its landing-point as

best I could. I did not wish to land upon it and cause myself an injury.

I moved slowly, climbing as low as I dared. Slid my legs off the lowest branch large enough to comfortably hold my weight, clinging. The most terrifying moment was when I hung from the shelter of the tree, my hands slipping on bark, and finally fell. A moment of weightlessness, and I landed on the washing. My knee buckled, but I soon enough found myself unharmed and sprawled upon the ground, glad of Tinan di Rocham's breeches.

I picked myself up, dusted bark and dirt from my hands, and spent a moment searching for the knife. My fingers finally closed on the hilt, and I took a deep breath. Adersahl had told me to stay, but how could I? He would have returned by now, if…

I shied away from the thought.

It took a little doing to find the trail to the brook. Once I found it, I stood, irresolute, in the shelter of a pinon tree, sweet, pungent sap dyeing the air with scent. I needed the privy, and if any of the women had been doing washing, perhaps some of them had survived?

I thought this, and then turned miserably toward the village. I had to know.

I relieved myself behind another tam tree and picked my way back to the path just as dusk deepened and cool evening wind began to sing among the trees. The path was a little more difficult to traverse this way, for I had to force my way up a slight hill and remain poised to dive into the scant undergrowth at any moment.

It seemed to take forever, and burning choked the air the closer I drew to the buildings. Thick acrid smoke drifted between the trees, full of a sick roasted sweetness.

I found myself on the outskirts of the village, hearing crackling and snapping sounds.

I forgot soon enough to shrink back into the undergrowth. There was nothing left to hide from. Risaine's shimmering curtain of hedgewitchery, drawn close to the village and encompassing the washing-stream, had evaporated.

Mounds of char that had once been houses now lay in smoking ruins. I did not vomit when I found the first body—it was a child, a *child*, so small—but twas only because breakfast had been so long ago.

It seemed a lifetime.

Hot bitterness rose in my throat. The sickly smell was roasting human flesh. I retched once, twice, and wandered from place to place, one hand across my rebelling stomach and the other clutching Adersahl's dagger. I had not smelled the smoke because the wind had blown it away from my hiding place.

I found nothing living. Even the dogs had been slaughtered, most with arrows buried in their flesh. I saw faces that were half-familiar from my stay, each one a fresh scar upon my heart. The smallest, sodden bodies were the worst.

I found Risaine's house, simply a smoking skeleton by now. There was no sign of Risaine's body, though I circled the fuming wreck to be sure.

Night fell while I wandered, dazed, from flaming house to broken house. The trees had not caught fire, still wet from the spring rains. At least I would not have to worry about the entire forest burning down about me.

I realized I had seen none of the Guard among the dead. Nor had I seen Adrien di Cinfiliet and most of the quiet, thin bandit men who followed him about. The dead were women, children, dogs. The few elderly peasants who stayed in the village.

None of Tristan's Guard. No sign of Adersahl. None of the bandits hale enough to fight.

What this meant, I could not fathom. I sank down before Risaine's burning cottage under the spreading willum tree, the crackling of flames echoing in my head. The tree's questing fingers that had made a veil over Risaine's roof were scorched now, curling back singed from the heat.

Dead, all dead. Death followed me like a swain from a court-song, dogging my steps. Inviting me to dance, then turning away to strike elsewhere.

I wept until full dark descended and the only light was a venomous glow from the smoldering ruins. Then I crept to the rear of Risaine's house and sat with my back against the willum tree, my knees drawn up and the knife clenched in my nerveless fist. If di Narborre came back, I would strike however I could. I would not let them take me.

What will you do tomorrow? I asked myself. *Tis imperative you think, Vianne, you witless worm.*

Bury the dead as best I can, then strike south for Arcenne, even if that route is watched. I must keep the Aryx from the Duc. Such a thing as this must not happen again.

My free hand rose, touched the Aryx under my shirt. "Tristan," I whispered. The Aryx's pulse under mine was strong and steady.

Women, children, even animals, murdered. My presence had brought the attentions of di Narborre upon these people, whose only crime was to shelter me.

I wiped slick wetness from my cheeks with one soot-blackened hand. I do not know how long I hunched there, sobbing, watching the smoke and flames through blurring eyes. My neck ached, my knees throbbed, my shoulders tight as ship's cables. I finally fell into a troubled doze, clutching the dagger, waking every time I thought I heard a footfall.

Each time I woke, I repeated to myself, *No more. I will not allow this.*

Never again.

THE TRAVELER

THE TRAVELER

Chapter Twenty-One

When dawn broke I wandered from house to house, wondering how I would bury them all. The ground was full of tree roots, and I searched, and I searched, but I could not find aught even resembling a shovel. By midmorn I was hungry, and far more terrified than I thought possible. I had not realized how much I depended on Tristan to tell me *go here*, or *do thus*. Even at Court, I was at the mercy of Lisele's schedule and the stifling etiquette, the propriety, the iron strictures of what could and could not be done.

Think, I scolded myself. *Think, you brainless ninny! Think!*

I stood at Risaine's shattered house—I always seemed to return to her door—and hugged myself, cupping my elbows in my hands. There was not a single thing living in the bandit village. Deep hoofprints scored the earth, but I had no skill at reading or tracking such things.

Where is Adersahl? I had not seen him among the dead.

I shivered. Di Narborre's orders were to capture, not kill me—or were they? What could have spurred him to level this hidden village? Or was it someone else, some other enemy?

Faint hope of that, Vianne. This is your doing, as surely as if you had ridden and slain with your own hands. The blood is on you, it will not wash away.

It will never wash away.

I took the dagger Adersahl had left me, and a square of smoke-darkened cloth pulled from a drying line and trampled into the ground. I wrapped the dagger in the cloth and tied it to my belt, then paused, staring at the wreck of the village.

"Forgive me," I pleaded, my voice thin in the morning bird-song and the soughing of wind brushing treetops with a velvet glove. "I would bury you decently, as you deserve, but I can find no shovel, and I must reach Arcenne. I cannot brave the path to Navarrin, and must take my chances."

I waited, but of course no answer came. I judged which way south stood by the moss on the trees and the slant of sun-light—being a hedgewitch was good for something; my heart twisted to think of Risaine—and struck out for the southron edge of the village. This took me through a haze of smoke, and before I realized it I was running, tripping over scattered, broken things and dodging through arrows stuck in the earth. I did not stop my flight until I plunged into the trees, hot salt water streaking my face again, though I had thought I had no more tears left.

I walked steadily through the day, aiming south as best I could, occasionally coming across a berry bush not yet in season. There were wild herbs one could eat, and I had a handful of cressten from a stream and two *pom d'tirre* I ate raw after washing them. I wished for a fire, or a cup of chai, or a bath. I had no skin to carry water—nothing but the knife, and the Aryx.

There was some small hedgewitchery I could use for survival.

Court sorcery would make me the quarry in a hunt I did not have the skill to escape, and I shuddered to think of the doors of the Aryx opening inside my head, swallowing me whole.

And no Tristan to call me back from that golden flood.

I did not have a horse—nor would I have known what to do with one. My horses had always been saddled for me at Court, and riding with Tristan had not taught me to do such things. Yet one more thing I should have learned and had not.

My list of such regrets grew long by the time afternoon sent golden spears through the treetops.

I found another small brook and drank, washed some of the soot from my stinging face and blackened hands. I scrubbed with a handful of soapweed plucked from the bank, and felt much better even if my clothes still stank of fire and carnage. Still, I spent a long time laving my hands, seeking to wash the feel of slippery hot crimson from my fingers.

It did not leave me, but my hands grew too raw to continue.

As night fell I was well and truly lost, simply striking south for as long as the light lasted and stopping by the shelter of a tam tree. I built a small circle of stones and gathered what deadfall I could, deciding it was better to have a fire than to risk freezing to death—or being struck with fever in the middle of the Shirlstrienne.

The hedgewitch charm to light a fire produced a small flame I coaxed into life with handfuls of pinon needles. I soon had a small but respectable blaze crackling merrily away, and the smell of it—clean, without the reek of burning human flesh—was enough to bring fresh tears to my eyes.

I could not find a comfortable space to lie on, and it was cold and damp, yet I did manage to catch broken snatches of sleep, waking to put more of my small supply of wood on the fire.

I have spent many sleepless nights since, but that was one of the worst. I started nervously, bolt-upright, when an owl's soft cry echoed in the darkness. Every slight sound I heard made me think of stalking men with bright swords, coming to *make certain*.

After the owl, I huddled with my knees drawn up, staring into the fire and thinking on Tristan. I would have given the Aryx to d'Orlaans without demur and wished him joy of it, if he could have produced my Captain from the darkness.

When false dawn began to paint the trees with cold gray, I doused the fire and was on my way, nerve-racked, stiff, and chilled clear through. The chill faded slightly as I walked south, again judging by the moss on the trees. There were hedgewitch charms for marking a path in the forest, but I could recall little of them.

And I did not wish my trail marked.

About midmorning, I began to see how silence and solitude could be, as Diodiorin of Scythandra stated, a balm for a troubled soul—or, as Euphorin of Thebim argued, could drive a person mad. I did not have to worry about assuming a pleasing expression or keeping my thoughts from showing, or about the length of my dress and the cut of my bodice, as I would have at Court. I did not have to worry for the Aryx or the safety of a few men mad enough to swear service to me. I had nothing to worry for but my bare survival, which was chancy enough.

Yet solitude also means nothing to distract the mind from chewing at problems as a dog will at a bone.

Where was Tristan? Who had razed the village? How did I think I could reach Arcenne without a horse or even a waterskin? Had the Guard been slain in a pitched battle and di Narborre's troops come to level the place daring to shelter them? That seemed most likely. But then, where was Risaine—and Adersahl? I had not seen either of them among the…

Say it, Vianne. The dead. You did not see them among the dead.

I was bone-weary and stumbling by afternoon, impelled forward more by will than by any real desire to continue. I stopped under a pinon tree and slid down to sit between two great roots, leaning against the rough trunk. I closed my eyes for what felt a mere moment, and when I opened them again the purple of dusk filtered through the trees, and I was thirsty.

There was no water nearby, but—thank the gods—there was a hollisa bush. A handful of the tart, not-quite-ripe berries cut the edge of my thirsty hunger, and I cast about for deadwood to use as fuel.

I found very little, but I dragged what I could to the pinon tree and spent a few moments making a fire. Thanks to Risiane's tender care I did not feel fevered, though my eyes watered fiercely and my strength ran away like water.

The Aryx pulsed against my chest, and of a sudden, as I was feeding fallen wood to the small hedge-charmed blaze, I was startled into thin, unhealthy laughter.

The Great Seal of Arquitaine, awake and active, the source of all Court sorcery by the grace of the Blessed—and I dared not use it. Oh yes, a fine Queen, standing idly by while a whole village of children, women, and old men were assassinated. I was even powerless to give them a decent burial.

All the royalty in the world is worth naught in the face of catastrophe.

My merriment sounded strange as it rose sharp and mocking,

echoing through the trees. I laughed until I feared the sound of it, clutching the trunk of the pinon tree, my eyes streaming, my braid torn free and mussed, covered in soot.

You are mad, Vianne. Mad.

Mad I might be, alive I was still. But for how long?

Chapter Twenty-Two

The next day I found such luck I could hardly credit it. Just past the brightest part of afternoon, I found a meadow and six goats.

It may not seem much of an event, but it froze me in place, stock-still and blinking, wary of leaving the shelter of the trees. The meadow lay dappled with sunshine, spring flowers carpeting its knee-high grass, and I heard the tinkle of a bell before the flock came into sight, driven by a dark-eyed boy in rough homespun with a long hazel switch he used to prod the wiry-haired creatures into motion.

I stared as if seeing a Court spectacular, then hastily made certain the Aryx was pushed below Tinan di Rocham's shirt. *He would not like the condition tis in now.*

I stared at the small peasant boy with his mop of gingery-dark hair and coppery skin.

Where there was a young boy and a flock of goats, there had to be a steading nearby—or another bandit village? Perhaps. I had little choice.

I waited for the boy to notice me, but he did not. He merely prodded the goats about and then, satisfied, flung himself down on a small rise in the high grass. One of the goats wore a collar with a tiny bell, the source of a merry tinkling.

I had just relieved myself behind a tam tree, so I was relatively comfortable, if still hungry. I watched as the boy appeared to fall into a deep slumber in the sunlight. I stayed in the shade, watching as the flock browsed its well-mannered way through the meadow. The boy seemed supremely unconcerned.

Now I was to solve the problem of how to approach him.

I cleared my throat with a small mannerly noise, moving out from the shelter of the darker trees. The boy did not stir. I forged ahead, fighting the urge to plunge back into the forest. *Who would have thought the Shirlstrienne so full of people? Or am I in the Alpeis now?*

I reached what I judged was a safe distance from the boy and cleared my throat again.

Nothing. He appeared asleep.

I tried it again, and then managed to speak. "*Sieur?*"

The boy's dark eyes drifted open.

For a moment we remained so, one battered noblewoman in men's clothing and one small dark-skinned goatherd boy.

"Cor," the boy said finally, "you doan look li' no *demieri di sorce.*"

A wild braying laugh nearly choked me. If he thought me mad he might hesitate to render aid. "That is because I am not one. Please, can you tell me, is there a steading or a town nearby?"

I do not know whether to call it chance or luck that I met Avier in that meadow. I do know he took a great risk in bringing me to his family's wagons.

Avier's people were R'mini, traveling tinkers and hedge-witches famed for their red-brown hair and their skill in mend-ing, be it pots and pans or wheels and cogs. The R'mini have traveled through Etharial, from Far Rus to Arquitaine to Tiberia, and mayhap even as far as Tifrimat, since anyone can remember. With their bright-painted wagons and large, patient horses or sleek oxen, they were a welcome sight in the depth of winter when amusement was hard to come by—though there are those who accuse them of bringing disease and ill-luck in their train wherever they roam.

I do not know why d'Arquitaines fear a wandering people so much. Mayhap because the Angoulême and his Companions had wandered before finding a home, and we fear to travel again. Who can guess?

I was brought to their headman, Avier's uncle, after the women had finished poking and prodding at me. Adersahl's dagger I surrendered to them with no demur. After all, I thought it unlikely they were loyal to d'Orlaans. And I could hardly blame them—I would have taken away my dagger, too.

Avier's uncle Tozmil sat on a small, decorated wooden stool by the fire. His wife, a lean dark woman dressed in the bright reds and golds R'mini women favoured, gilt coins dripping from her cap of bright meshwork, leaned against him. His daughters whispered and pointed from behind their mother, and the rest of the R'mini pressed close.

"Who are you?" Tozmil asked, after making a number of odd gestures. I did not know whether to laugh or weep. I found later his armwaving and finger-jabbing was meant to make me vanish in a puff of smoke if I was *demieri di sorce*.

The R'mini are cautious of such things.

"My name is Vianne." I had decided prudence was best. "I

have become separated from my traveling companions. I must reach Arcenne, in the mountains, good *sieur*, and I—"

"You stink of smoke," he interrupted briskly. "Are you *banditti*?"

I did not have to feign the start that gave me. "No, of course not." I sounded indignant. I wished suddenly for Tristan, or Risaine, or anyone. At least with my Captain I had some chance at guessing what he would do with me. "If you cannot help me, I will go on my way. I will not be the cause of trouble to you or your wagons, *sieur* Tozmil."

Tozmil's dark eyes sparkled. I did not know it then, but twas exactly the right thing to say. R'mini are often shunned and driven out of towns, and they sometimes feel a kinship with others similarly hounded. Yet for all that, they have a fierce pride, and those who come to them humbly are not oft well-received. "And how will you reach Arzjhen alone, V'na?" His accent mangled both my name and the name of the town. "You have no water, no wagon, no horse. Bad luck."

If you only knew how much luck I have had, both good and ill. I dug in my pocket while his eyes narrowed, and fished out my emerald ear-drops. "I have means to pay for passage." I opened my hand to show the glitter of gems. "These are all I have left of my life, *sieur* Tozmil. If you will help me reach Arcenne I will gift you these, and there may well be other reward as well."

He examined my face, and his wife leaned down to whisper in his ear. He nodded, slowly. Then his gaze left me and traveled in a slow arc over the rest of his troupe—perhaps thirty people, young and old. There were several children.

I tried not to think on it.

The silence stretched. I sought to keep my hand from trembling.

"Very well," Tozmil said. "Keep your gauds, we don' steal from th' poor. But you travel with us, you travel as R'mini, and you wear a woman's skirts. We'll have no *g'ji g'jai* in our wagons."

I nodded wearily, feeling filthy and very, very tired. "I could not agree more, *sieur*. If I could have been wearing skirts this past month, I would have much preferred it."

He stared at me for another long moment, then his wife laughed, tossing her head back. It was the high-pitched giggle that R'mini women use among themselves, a sign of cameraderie, though I did not yet know it.

At the sound of the women's laughter, it was as if I had passed some manner of test, for Tozmil clapped his hands and his daughters came forward, laughing and tossing liquid streams of their strange language back and forth, drawing me away. I tried to press my ear-drops on them, but they refused, shaking their heads. They exclaimed over my hair and my strange skin, so different from theirs, and I was at that moment made a lowly member of R'mini Tosh Tozmil'hai Jan.

Chapter Twenty-Three

They thought me slow and stupid until they found I was simply unused to the work of going from place to place in their wagons. I did all they asked of me with good grace, whether it was scrubbing dishes and pots with soapsand or learning to wash clothes in streams. I was grateful for the chance to sleep among people, and further grateful that they asked no questions once Tozmil accepted me as a traveling member.

Very soon they found I was a hedgewitch, so I was set to helping Tozmil's wife, Jaryana, the physicker of the troupe. The R'mini have their own form of hedgewitchery, and set I myself to learning as we traveled through the Shirlstrienne and the Alpeis, following a path I doubt I would ever be able to find again. The R'mini have their own secret highways and signs, even in the dark tangle of the haunted Alpeis, and the *g'ji*—as they call us—are hard-pressed to travel them without R'mini guides.

I have studied hedgewitchery most of my life, but I daresay I learned more in two months of travel with Jaryana than I had from all my books and even Drumiera's careful tutelage. Jaryana was a fierce teacher, given to sting-slapping my hand if I looked about to add the wrong herb to a tisane or paste, but she was kind in her own way. It had been her voice tipping the balance toward allowing to me travel with them, and her eagle eye was the reason I did not fall prey to a forced wedding with one of the R'mini men. They have a custom among them—does an unmarried man want a girl past menarche, if he can force or persuade her to stay a night in his wagon he can claim her as a bride. I slept in Tozmil's wagon or by his fire, and more than once Jaryana's sharp tongue drove a R'mini man away from where I worked.

I did my best not to notice.

Avier was often away with his goats, but he seemed fascinated by my strangeness and would follow me about after he brought the herd back from their grazing. More than once someone mocked him for it, but he made proud answer, as if he had found an exotic pet in the forest and could not stay away.

They did not ask me about the Aryx, though they all must have caught glimpses of it. Indeed, I wondered what I could have said. The longer we traveled, the closer to towns we drew, and the more nervous I became. They guessed, in their quick way, that I was likely hunted, and a danger to them.

The R'mini wandered through the Alpeis for the last of the spring and the beginning of summer, the men hunting, the women gathering herbs, spring roots, and other things. I had no say in our route, and they saw no reason to hurry me to Arcenne. Many herbs and other valuable things are found by the R'mini in the forests and wild places, and their wandering is often along a route that would fair drive anyone direct-minded to distraction. I do not know if they sought to shake pursuit, or if they simply disdained to hurry, since anyone looking for one lone woman could certainly not be bothered to spend so long on our twisting trail. More than once I tried to tell Jaryana there might be some danger in harboring me, but she gave the notion short shrift.

The guest is sacred, she sniffed, each time. *We hold to the Law.*

Their Law is strict in some ways, lax in others. A woman's virtue is guarded with a vengeance, since their inheritance passes through the male line instead of through the mother as Arquitaine deems right and proper. For all that, R'mini women have sharp tongues and a fierce spirit. No few of them carry short curving daggers, and hedgewitchery runs deep in them. Their Law does not give a woman lee to speak to strangers, but if she kills during a bloodfeud or to avenge her honor she is not seen as criminal. She may divorce a man by locking a wagon's doors, but then she will have to bargain for horses or oxen to pull said wagon—for the man is entitled to take those. Unless other women judge her sloughing of a Consort as warranted, and grant the use of other beasts, she may be abandoned, or forced to make her way with another *jan,* as their traveling family-groups are called.

They exercise their peculiar sorcery constantly, even the youngest of them, and it shows. They are skilled with horses and metal, and they carry news and goods from town to town. They are dour with strangers, though they chatter constantly among themselves and have a song for every event, it seems. Some travel into Damar, past Polia and Pruzia, as far as Rus, even. I have heard tell some tread roads that lead them to Torkai or Tifrimat, past the dragons that guard the edge of the world. Some even take ship and brave the Girdle off Arquitaine's north coast, seeking a way past the howling storms and into the fabled Westron Isles.

But that I have not seen for myself, yet.

We finally slipped free of the Alpeis and emerged on the south-and-eastron edge of the Shirlstrienne, looking down at the Siguerre Road from a high bluff. It was strange to feel the wagon wheels rolling on paving stones, and even stranger to be perched in the back of a R'mini wagon drawing step by slow step closer to Arcenne through civilized country.

If I had not had so much work to do, I might have fretted myself into impatient exhaustion. As it was, I was kept busy from morn to nightfall, and oft ate my supper silently among the laughing, catcalling R'mini. After eating, they would often sing and drink their fiery rhuma liquor, and sometimes the unmarried girls would dance. There were courtship dances too, and dances that told stories. It reminded me of Court—there were rules of behavior, and one had to keep one's eyes and ears open. I merely watched from the shadows, wrapped in one of Jaryana's old black shawls, my hair braided in two loops over my ears and a third braid down my back as the R'mini women do. I wore none of their thin, fluted gold jewelry, and felt like a gosling among the swanlike grace of the R'mini girls. Their skirts reached only their ankles, but since they are generally taller than I, mine draggled. I wore my garden-boots instead of supple R'mini sandals, a loose much-embroidered blouse, and a tight red sash wound several times around my waist.

It was obvious I was none of theirs, but I took pains not to remind them.

Jaryana often sat close as I watched the women dance, and asked me a question or two. I found myself telling her more than I intended, sometimes by my silences and sometimes by the way I chose to answer a seemingly-innocent query. She knew I was a *g'ji* noblewoman, and she knew as well that I thought often of a man.

She also knew of my nightmares.

The R'mini never remarked on the fact that I often woke sweating and terrified, shaking and unsure if I had cried out. I dreamed of Lisele, and of Tristan lying broken and bloody on the Shirlstrienne floor. I dreamed of the bandit village, of wandering from burning house to burning house, the bodies crumpled on the ground. I dreamed of blood on my hands, of sickish, rotting stench, of the clash of metal and the armored slippery backs of eels. Jaryana oft mixed me a sleeping-draught, but even the strongest potions of R'mini hedgewitchery were no match for my dreams.

The first night on the Siguerre Road, the R'mini camped in a sloping meadow on the other side of the wall of the Shirlstrienne, and I was eating my supper quietly and alone. I usually sat on the tail-step of Tozmil's wagon, watching the rest as they gathered about their communal fire.

Jaryana stood. At first I thought she was merely fetching herself a dipperful of water, but I soon realized she approached me.

She came to a stop before me and held out her hand. I set my bowl down beside me and stood, brushing off my skirts, waiting for her to tell me what was required.

"Come," she said, not unkindly. "You eat with us, V'na."

I obeyed without demur, wondering at this. Nobody spoke as I settled down between Jaryana and her oldest daughter, Mauryana. Vrejmil, Tozmil's brother, handed me a piece of bread. "Aye," he said. "Na' mun bad for a *g'ji*, V'na."

Faint praise. Yet it warmed me. "My thanks," I answered, with good grace and no little relief. It does hearten one, to be counted worthy of one's fellows.

That eased them, and they went back to chattering among themselves. I listened, having spent enough time to pick up most of their conversation, though I could only speak R'mini in a broken, halting child's way.

Sometimes tis the Palais that seems a dream, and this my real life. Would that it were.

Here I was useful, if strange. I was accustomed to being taunted and teased, though the R'mini taunted merely for amusement and not for cruelty. There was a peacefulness to the moving wagons and the communal dinners, a sense of something I had never known but sorely missed.

I finished my stew and my bread, and took a long draught of water, letting the sound of their voices wash over me. A manner of peace held here, and I welcomed it.

Jaryana touched my elbow. "A few days to Arzjhen. And towns, past here. You hide in wagon until we pass the city gate. Where in Arzjhen do you go?"

I had not even considered the question. The Aryx was quiescent and warm under my R'mini garb. I cast back through memory, found Tristan's voice in my ear during my fever. That gave me the clue I needed.

"I suppose simply to the Citadel. I think Tri—" I stopped myself just in time. "My…ah, a father of a friend," I continued lamely, "he lives there, and will give me shelter. I hope."

Her face did not change. "To the *g'ji* lord's house, then." She took a bite of their sour, dense flatbread and chewed with an air of deep reflection. "If he doesna take you in, you're a fair hand with *dromonde*. I would have y'travel with us, ah?"

My jaw threatened to drop. *I could not place you in more danger.* "Oh." My gaze darted away across the fire and found Avier between his uncle and his mother, chattering brightly in R'mini and petted like the cherished child he was. "My thanks, *m'dama*. My thanks. I…if he does not take me in, I would be honored." *It would be a poor way to repay you for your kindness, to bring you such trouble as hunts me.*

An entirely new thought struck me. If I managed to somehow give up the Aryx to Tristan's father, would I possibly, perhaps…be free?

Indeed it was a harsh life, traveling in wagons, backsore and moving from town to town. I was certain the R'mini were not welcome everywhere. Yet they had taken in a starving stranger, sheltered me, and now were offering me a place among them. Kindness once again extended to me, and I hoped I would not repay them with the vileness that dogged my steps.

If I could somehow loose myself of the Aryx, twould be a fine place for a noblewoman to hide. Who would believe a Court lady scrubbing pots in the wilds?

My heart fell inside my chest as Avier ducked his tousled head away from his mother's petting fingers. Tozmil laughed heartily, and one of the women crooned to the baby at her breast. There was more talk, more laughter, and I could not stay with them any longer than I absolutely had to.

Even though I would have wished it, with all that remained of me now.

"Think on it," Jaryana said. "Y' be a fair student."

It was worth more than all the Aryxs in the world, that one grudging admission. For though Jaryana was a harsh teacher, she would not give her approval unless twere true.

"My thanks," I repeated, and no more was said of the matter. My heart had turned to lead.

That night, after helping to scrub the dishes, I sat for a long while watching the unmarried women dance. One of them,

Azyara, tossed her braid back and pulled her sweetheart from the watching men to the accompaniment of many loud calls and clicking tongues. They danced to the music—Zisiyara singing, Tozmil and Vrajmil playing viols, Cesarmil drumming, Aliyara playing a gittern, and Mauryana shaking a tambour. The music was far from the well-mannered waltzing of the Court, even the fast-paced maying dances. I liked its melodies, its quickness, and its bright, supple shiftings. I smiled, watching Azyara dance with the R'mini boy. It was lively tune, played with a happiness Court musicians often lack.

"Thinking on your man?" Jaryana asked from my side.

I gave a guilty start, because Tristan's face rarely left my mind. I had no time to miss him, yet it seemed missing him was all I did. "How did you know?"

"You have th' look. Sadness, and listening."

I found myself smiling, through the bitterness. "He would enjoy this, I think." *I could perhaps even persuade him to dance. That would be a sight.*

She nodded. Her braids swung forward. "Lucky man. For a *g'ji.*"

The weight inside me lightened. When I made my bed that night inside Tozmil and Jaryana's wagon, I thought of Tristan before I settled, pillowing my head on my arm.

For once, I had no nightmares.

Chapter Twenty-Four

They never asked me why I had been wandering the Shirlstri-enne, and they never asked what I was hiding. Yet for the five days it took us to reach Arcenne on the Siguerre Road, I found myself in the wagon instead of walking outside, given bits of make-work to do when we stopped for the night, and kept in the camp. Normally R'mini settle on the outskirts of towns, but the R'mini Tosh Tozmil'hai Jan stopped their wagons a fair distance away. I noticed also they did not welcome strangers or the curious to their fires, but closed around me, keeping me from unfriendly eyes.

Golden late-afternoon glow spilled through slim, carved wagon windows as we approached the walls of Arcenne, and the troupe ground to a halt at the city's Gate. I heard the sound of a deep male voice, questioning in Arquitaine. I had been among the R'mini long enough that the sound of my native tongue was strange.

Tozmil answered, a high, jolly tone. He would speak for all of us, and among the *jan* his decisions were final. He was, however, elected every three years. If the *jan* did not like his methods, another would take his place at the next Gathering.

That was something to think of seeing—the *jans* coming together, the young courting and the great dances where every R'mini from every corner of Etharial who could make it to their secret fastness participated... yes, I would give much to see that. But I was *g'ji*.

I heard something about plague. My heart flipped inside my chest. I was alone in the wagon—the rest of the women walked outside.

A long, nerve-racking pause made my heart thunder. I wrapped Jaryana's old shawl about my head, hoping it would hide my paleness, and the fact that I was not R'mini.

One of the women—I thought it was Mauryana—sang quietly, a R'mini ballad of the open road. There was a breath of magic to the song, the R'mini's particular hedgewitchery. Twas dangerous, for if they were caught magicking the guards there would be dire consequence.

I closed my eyes. The Seal pulsed quietly against my breastbone. *Please,* I prayed. *Let me in. This is where Lisele wished me to go.*

Is Tristan here? I cannot hope. A hot flush scalded me. I found myself unbreathing, frozen, trembling in the wagon like a small animal in its burrow.

The Arquitaine man said something that must have been an affirmative, for the wagon jerked forward. I did not breathe until I was sure we were inside Arcenne's high girdling walls. The sounds of a city pressed around me. Horses, bellowing oxen, wheels grinding, people singing, laughing, speaking. The Aryx turned to muted song against my chest.

Tis awake and *stronger. What does that mean?*

So I entered Arcenne in the back of a R'mini wagon like a

thief, with the Aryx singing no less loudly than my heart.

Close to nightfall I found myself in the walled portion of the city housing the Citadel of Arcenne, at a fire with the R'mini. They were allowed to camp in an abandoned district, their wagons between a few boarded-up houses, the ground littered with refuse. For all that, they were cheerful as they went about setting their wagons in a circle and kindling their fires, just as if we were still in the Alpeis's green cavernous depths. It was a comforting sameness.

My throat closed as I contemplated the stew in my bowl, staring as if I could see the future there.

Jaryana patted my arm and told me to eat. "Take you to the *g'ji* lord's house. After."

I nodded, my heart knocking anew at my ribs. What I would do when I reached the Citadel, I had no idea. I knew little of Tristan's father, only that Lisele had judged Arcenne loyal. "Jaryana?" I held my bowl in both hands.

She raised her eyebrows slightly, her coppery face splitting into a very white smile.

"Thank you." I smiled back. Twas impossible not to.

"Is he tha? Your man?"

I shrugged. "I do not know. He might be dead." I was surprised I could speak the words so steadily.

"I think not." She handed me another piece of the flat, sour bread the R'mini favour. "Here. Hav'more."

There was but one gate into the Citadel, and it was closed and barred with iron. However, there was a smaller postern around the corner, with a man standing guard. He wore the uniform of Arcenne, a crimson doublet over white shirt and black trousers, the doublet blazoned with the black Arcenne mountain-pard clawing at the left shoulder over two broken arrows. The guard paced in front of the postern and retreated to an alcove, melting into shadow. He had repeated this operation twice so far.

The R'mini women gathered about me, whispering. There was some argument over who would accompany me.

I pressed the emerald ear-drops into Jaryana's palm. "I shall proceed alone. Do not be caught here; go back to the camp."

She gave me an arch look. "Your *dress* R'mini. Na' worry. We can vanish. Here." She pressed something cool into my hand as well. "Take this. Show to R'mini, we help you." She leaned forward, her hand brushing my hip, kissed my cheek, then pushed me gently by my shoulders. "Go find him, V'na."

I do not wish to find anyone. I merely wish to loose myself of the weight of duty. Oh, how I wish I could. "Thank you," I said in my halting R'mini. "Gods smile upon you." For their gods are not ours, and they do not speak of them to *g'ji*. "Thank you so much." I could not stop repeating my gratitude.

They whispered together—someone protesting I should not be left to go to the *g'ji* alone, another hissing to keep their voices *"down, idiots!"* I drew in a deep breath and stepped out into the street. They went quiet and still, sinking back into shadow.

Good. *Gods grant they do not suffer for helping me.*

I was praying more and more, despite my Court upbringing. I hoped the Blessed were listening and well disposed. Though I could not make up my mind which was worse—that the Blessed might be taking an active interest in events, so to speak, or that they were ignoring all of us, including the King and his brother who had brought us to this pass.

My worn bootheels clicked across the paving. I slipped whatever Jaryana had given me into my skirt-pocket, a chill touching my spine as I thought of Lisele gifting me as she died. The guard at the postern had surely noticed me, a lone woman out past dark. I forded the street, deserted except for shadows. A few torches burned on the walls, their flames hissing with blue-sparking Court sorcery against the wind.

The Citadel was a massive chunk of rock, five castellated towers with arrow-slits, an outer wall with the buildings of the city squeezing up to it. Here in Arcenne there were none of the Citté's graceful fictions—no, here the Citadel was a fortress, the lord's castle, meant to withstand attack if the other walls were breached.

The Baron d'Arcenne's seat of power, too, the ancestral hold of Arcenne. Had Tristan grown up in this stone block? Had he looked up at these towers before he left for Court?

I did not know, and the lack of knowledge obliquely pained me.

I was across the street before I knew it, Jaryana's old shawl slipping down my shoulders, my run-down boots clicking on the white stone Arcenne was famous for.

"Halt!" The guard sounded very young. I caught a glint—perhaps an arrowhead throwing back a stray gleam of torchlight, or a sword's point, aching to cleave unprotected flesh.

I stopped, my head held high. The Aryx sang below my heartbeat, power sparkling in my blood. "*Sieur*," I said, calmly enough. "Is this Arcenne?" I meant to inquire if Arcenne was still loyal, stopped myself just in time.

"Well…yes." He sounded far too young, and far too nervous. I prayed he would not grow so nervous he arrowed me on the step.

"I must see the Baron d'Arcenne. Tis passing urgent."

There was a hurried whisper. I could not see with whom he conversed, the shadows were too deep and the torches too few. Was there more than one guard? "The Baron has retired for the evening," the young voice said.

"Wake him. Tis dire, and I am passing desperate."

"Give me a name to take to the Lieutenant of the Guard, and he shall judge," another voice came, older and steely. "Who are you, to disturb the Baron thus?"

Well, what do I have to lose? I had to swallow a laugh. "I am Duchesse Vianne di Rocancheil et Vintmorecy, and I bear a message from the murdered Princesse Lisele di Tirecian-Trimesten to your lord, the Baron d'Arcenne."

Chapter Twenty-Five

It took nearly an hour before I was brought to the Baron, and my nerves were worn past fraying. I had been up since before dawn and ridden in the wagon all day—and been fretting myself dry to boot. They searched me for weaponry and found nothing, since Adersahl's dagger was still with the R'mini. Yet the men were kind, even if silent, and I could understand. If Arcenne was loyal, they had to be cautious—and if they were not, they would want to find if I truly was who I claimed, and could not have me bolting at a chance word.

The book-lined study was quite warm because of a roaring fire newly kindled. Leather ease-chairs crouched before the fireplace, a massive desk under a drift of paper and parchment, a tasseled Eastron sling hung on the end of one bookcase, red velvet drapes and a threadbare but priceless crimson Torkaic rug. Glowrock lamps in metal cages shed their soft silvery light, warring with the ruddy fire.

I chose to stand near the open window. Below, the lights of Arcenne glittered; torch, candle, and lamp. I wondered if the R'mini would suffer for helping me. Was Arcenne still loyal?

And would the Baron listen to my tale? I could be judged as something other than I was, mayhap, even despite the Aryx—

The door opened, and I whirled, my skirt belling.

It could not possibly be anyone other than Tristan's father. He had Tristan's build, his faint sardonic smile, and the likeness was fair to take my breath away. My heart squeezed inside my chest. I swept a Court courtesy, momentarily forgetting that I was dressed as a R'mini.

He was tall and had blue d'Arcenne eyes, his face sharply handsome even if graven. There were crow's-feet at the corners of his eyes, and his thick dark hair was salted liberally with gray. He carried himself straight, albeit a bit stiffly, and he wore boots and breeches and a white shirt that had been left untucked.

He also carried an unsheathed sword, its bright metal glittering. I tasted bright copper fear, took care to keep my face a mask.

"Who are you?" he demanded, with no preamble or courtesy.

"Duchesse Vianne di Rocancheil et Vintmorecy." I thought grimly that I could have introduced myself as V'na di R'mini Tosh Tozmil'hai Jan and perhaps gained a warmer reception. "I bring a message from Princesse Lisele di Tirecian-Trimestin, lately slain by treachery. I have traveled far to escape the treacherous regicide Duc d'Orlaans, and if you are loyal to him than I am in dire straits indeed, Baron." I paused, more to breathe than for effect. "I come also to ask for news of your son, for I sorely miss his face."

The Baron stared, as if I had just announced I was going to turn myself into a fish.

I reached up slowly, keeping my gaze locked with his, and drew the Aryx out from my R'mini blouse. "Princesse Lisele pressed this into my hand as she lay dying from a traitor's sword. She told me with her last breath to come to Arcenne. *They are loyal in the mountains,* she said. *Sieur*, I await your answer."

With that, I stoppered my mouth, holding the Aryx up. The serpents stirred uneasily against my fingers, their scales rasping.

The Baron sheathed his sword. His expression did not change.

"Gods above and below. You are a fool." He stalked across the room, and it took a great deal of my waning courage to stay still, my chin lifted, holding the Aryx as a shield.

He could push me out the window. I shivered. *Or I could fling myself hence and dash out my brains, did he seek to imprison me for d'Orlaans.*

Whether or not the Seal would seek to dissuade me, or even if it would fuse itself to my flesh again did I try to remove it from my neck, were two more hideous possibilities I did not like to contemplate.

He skirted the rug and reached me, and I noticed his hair was mussed and his belt-buckle askew. He must have been hastily wakened.

The Baron examined my face for a long while, and I suffered it. Then he dropped his gaze to the Aryx. He reached up, cautiously, and extended a finger, as if he would touch it.

I wished him much luck of the attempt.

A spark snapped. His hand flung back, and he nodded, shaking his fingers out. "Well," he said finally. Nothing more.

I could never remember the Aryx responding in such a manner before, but none had sought to *touch* it before, either. I gathered my courage with both hands. "*Sieur*, is there any news you can give me of your son Tristan?"

He returned to a thorough examination of my face. I heard

boots in the passage outside, low voices. *Is Arcenne disloyal? If he is the Duc's man I shall throw myself from this window-couvre rather than be taken captive, Seal or no.*

The old Vianne would hardly have thought such a thing—and would not have been determined to *do* it, either.

His face changed. I could not call the transformation an easing, but neither could I call it cruelty. "How did you come to be here, child, dressed as tinkerfolk? Sit down, have a glass of wine, and tell me. Are you hungry? Perhaps you are." He stalked for the door, opened it, and exchanged a few words with whoever stood outside. I sagged in relief. Possibly premature—who knew where his loyalties lay?—but I could do nothing more. I was in the hands of the Blessed, just as much as I had been among the R'mini.

In short order I was esconced in one of the leather easechairs by the fireplace, sinking into warmth and softness. Wine was brought, and flatbread, cheese, and fruit. The Baron settled himself in the other chair, his blue eyes steady. "Now tell me your tale. Leave nothing aside."

I began with the passage, Tristan and the Minister Primus, the King asking my silence, then the conspiracy's frantic unleashing. I told of Lisele's death, and my hiding in the North Tower. I told of finding Tristan in the donjons and setting him free, and of our flight to the Shirlstrienne, the assassin in the inn, and finally Adrien di Cinfiliet's bandits. I told of the attack on the village, how I found myself alone among the corpses, and of striking out into the woods and the great luck of finding a R'mini goatherd boy. More boots echoed in the hall outside, and I glanced toward the door, nervous, and continued my tale, with a brief account of traveling among the R'mini.

I spared myself nothing. I freely admitted how stupid I had

been at all stages, how useless I had been to the Guard, how dangerous to the bandit village, and how weak I had been not to bury the dead bodies.

It bothered me, to have left them for carrion.

"And so, the R'mini brought me here," I finished lamely. "As you see."

He nodded, his fingers steepled in front of his face. I was hungry—the smell of the bread taunted me—yet I made no move to take any crumb. I sat bolt upright in the chair as if at a Court *lévee*, forgetting my clothes and how I must have reeked of horse, woodsmoke, and tinker.

The Baron opened his mouth to reply, but there was a thundering at the door. I started, my eyes round. The Baron gained his feet with more speed than I would have thought possible for an old, stiff man. He looked so like Tristan, his sword drawn and his eyes full of fire.

My heart gave a shattering leap.

The door flung itself open. I stayed frozen to the chair, craning my neck to see what new shock lay in wait. The Baron let out a curse I had heard the Guards use, one unfit for a lady's ears, and my entire body was ice.

Tristan d'Arcenne shoved a Citadel Guard aside and stalked into the room, in breeches, bare feet, and an untucked shirt. He spared not a glance for his father's drawn sword, but strode squarely across the Torkaic rug, skirted the table of untouched food, and descended upon me. He grabbed my shoulders, hauled me out of the chair, shook me twice, then crushed me to his chest, his swordhilt digging into my side. "Gods damn me for a fool," he said. And, "Vianne, Vianne...gods..." Interspersed with this were most improper oaths in a ragged voice that did not sound like Tristan at all.

Tristan's father sheathed his sword, watching this with no discernable expression. "I see you've forgotten your manners, *m'fils*."

Tristan glanced at his father. "When did she arrive? *How* did she arrive?"

"Ask her. She has a very pretty tale, Tristan, and seems truthful enough. Even if she is a fool to come here and tell me half of it." The Baron folded his arms and examined his son. "She could not have known if I was still loyal."

I would have given a guilty start if Tristan had not been holding me too tightly to permit any movement. I breathed him in, staring witlessly.

I was beginning to believe he was alive.

"T-t-t—" My teeth chattered over his name.

Tristan let loose of me for only long enough to shake me again, print a bruising kiss on my forehead, and hug me even more fiercely. "I thought you dead and the Aryx lost. I thought you *dead*, Vianne, curse me for a fool—"

"Well," the Baron said. "I shall leave you two to greet each other. Your Majesty, we shall speak at greater length tomorrow, an it please you. Arcenne is yours to do with as you will." He bowed stiffly, and I thought I saw a glimmer of amusement in his sharp blue eyes.

I managed to stammer out something courteous, difficult to do with Tristan still crushing me. The Baron quit the room, shutting the door quietly, and his son held me at arm's length, examining every inch of my dishevelment. He looked haggard, unshaven, and I saw the beginnings of lines around his eyes. I saw a streak of gray over his right temple that had not been there before.

"You look awful." Twas hardly the thing to say, but it escaped me before I could measure the words for their fitness.

He grinned, his eyes lighting, and there was the Tristan I knew. "And you are lovely, Vianne. Even in this costume. How did this come to be? How did you survive? Tell me all, tell me *everything*."

I swayed on my feet, his grasp the only thing keeping me standing. Something occurred to me. "Adersahl!" I cursed myself for not asking sooner. "Where is he? Tell me he is hale."

Tristan nodded. "Hale enough. Sunk in his cups most nights, cursing himself for losing you. Twill be a relief to have him cease."

I nodded. Good. If he was alive, some part of this tangle could be mended. "And di Cinfiliet? Is he well?"

"He is well enough." Tristan's expression changed, harshness settling into his features. Twas not sadness, but I was so relieved to have him before me I did not care to examine precisely *what* it was. "We found no survivors."

"I did not see Risaine's…" I could not stop watching his face, touching it with my eyes. I freed one hand and tested his cheek with my fingertips, to prove to myself he was in front of me and *real*. "Gods." I shuddered. "I did not see her, among the…" I could not bring myself to say it again.

"Some of the women were taken, killed as soon as di Narborre found they were not you." He pressed his cheek into my touch. "Not now, tomorrow's soon enough. Tell me, where were you, what did you do?"

My knees very nearly gave out on me, and my hand fell back to my side. "I long to tell you. I also wish most heartily for a bath and a real bed. I've been traveling a-wagon for two months."

"We can find you a chamber," he started, but I shook my

head. Took my courage in both hands, so to speak, and tossed my dice.

"No. I want…I wish to stay with you."

My courage abruptly failed, and I dropped my gaze. It was not what a lady should say. One could hint, certainly, or delicately insinuate, but not baldly state. Still, I had asked him to be my Consort, and he had accepted, nevermind there were no proper proclamations published or copper marriage rings exchanged. I found I cared less for propriety than for the knowledge that he was safe and breathing.

Silence. Tristan let loose of my shoulders. I swayed again. His hand cupped my chin, forced my gaze to meet his.

He looked thoughtful, a slight smile tilting the corners of his mouth. The fire popped and crackled, shadows easing the worst of the ravages of care marking him.

"Of course," he said softly. "I…yes. Come with me, *m'chri*."

He half-turned, holding my elbow, meaning to lead me to the door, but I stopped him by catching at his shirt with my free hand. "Tristan?"

I did not even know what I wished to say, but he looked down at me with a mixture of amusement and concentration I had not seen in him before. "If you ask me news of any other man, Vianne, I might take it ill." Yet his tone was light enough.

I shook my head, biting my lip. The world seemed very dim, and very far away. "No. I simply wished to…" *What? What do I wish? I want you to speak to me, to take away this fear, and prove to me that you are real and I am not dreaming.*

Though I was fairly certain I was not sleeping. There was no blood on my hands, and I did not feel a nightmare stalking me. I feared to close my eyes lest he vanish, and all thought of intrigue had fled me. Even the thought of saving him from himself had disappeared in the great sharp swell of relief.

He shook his head, as if shaking away an unpleasant thought. "Time enough later. Come with me."

Once again I was towed in his wake, letting him do as he wished. No more decision was required of me, and for that I was secretly, shamefully, completely grateful.

Chapter Twenty-Six

Tristan led me through the stone halls of the Citadel, some-times passing guards who saluted him and eyed me curiously. The corridors were narrow: glowstone lamps hung from iron holders at even intervals, tapestries of past battles and the Arcenne family crest hung neatly to make the stone a little less harsh. I stumbled with fatigue by the time he pushed open a door and led me into a suite of dark blue and green: a sitting room with ancient weapons hung on the walls, a ta-pestry of yet another battle hung behind a long low padded bench. Elsewhere a rack of practice weapons, a stand holding a suit of armor, and two bookcases filled the room. He did not pause to let me look at this, and truth be told, I did not care. A great swimming relief had come over me, so deep I could barely put one foot in front of the other. This was a pleasant dream I would wake from to find myself still in the burning village—or in the wagons of the R'mini. I only wished for it to last as long as possible before I was forced to endure more unpleasantness.

He led me into the bedroom off the sitting room, also done in blue and green, a banked fire warming the air deliciously. "The bed is in a sorry state, I am afraid. I have not slept well these past weeks." He paused, looking down at me.

Nor have I. "Do you have…" I blushed, my cheeks hot as the fire. "Do you have a shirt, perhaps, or a shift I may sleep in?"

He left me standing on the rug in front of the fireplace. There was a large clothespress on one wall; he opened it and extracted a neatly folded sleeping shirt. "Here." He pressed it into my hands and pushed me gently toward the watercloset. "Go. I will wait."

I found myself in the watercloset, the door locked, a real privy and—oh, luxury of luxuries—a sunken bathtub. The tiles were clean, fresh drycloths sat folded on a rack. A glowing mirror showed me a dark-haired Arquitaine woman, utterly ridiculous in her R'mini braids. But my cheeks were flushed and my eyes glowed despite the circles under them. *Tomorrow I shall take a bath.* Relief burst hot and sharp inside my chest. *Tristan's alive, and tomorrow I shall take a bath.*

There seemed nothing more to want in the world.

When I finally emerged, in a sleeping shirt that reached below my knees, my hair free of its braids, I made it only halfway to the bed, carrying a neat stack of my R'mini clothes. Tristan appeared from the sitting room and took the pile of cloth from me. "I suppose even the hedgewitch tinkers were charmed by you, Vianne." He set the clothes aside on a chair, and it hurt me to see their threadbare state.

I looked longingly at the bed. Then I set myself to reassure him, if I could. "They were kind enough. They did not have to take me through the Shirlstrienne. They could have left me to starve."

"Then I owe them a great favour." He took my elbow and led me to the bed. A *real bed*, with crisp white linens and actual pillows, though twas thrashed a bit. I sank down gratefully. He pulled the covers over me and drew another chair I had not noticed to the bedside. "I shall keep watch. Sleep."

"I did not mean to push you out of your own bed." *Or was I thinking I should sleep on a stone floor? Though I am tired enough not to mind. Too tired to care about gossip. He is alive, and here with me.*

He shook his head, stripping his dark hair back. My eyes snagged on the patch of paleness at his temple. Had he worried himself into gray hair?

"Go to sleep, *m'chri*. I wish to watch over your dreaming."

"Did I wake you?" My eyes drifted closed. *He is alive. I am not imagining him.* "Where were you? Where did you go?"

"Tomorrow, *m'chri*." He said it gently, then leaned forward, took my hand in both of his. He touched my palm, held my wrist gently as a spun-glass figurine. My hand was lost in his. "I thought you dead, Vianne. Every day that passed killed me afresh." His voice broke.

Where was the stern Captain, the one I feared? Somewhere in the Alpeis, perhaps, I had lost him. And gained instead this man, who called me "beloved" and worried for me. "'Tis all well," I said dreamily. "You are alive. Everything is better now."

He kissed my knuckles, stubble rasping against my skin. "I feared you dead or taken. Everything, all for naught. I thought…"

"I feared for you as well," I whispered in return. "I did not know if you still lived. It frightened me."

"I will not leave you again." His lips moved against my knuckles. Instead of heat, the touch filled me with quiet comfort. "I swear it, Vianne."

For that moment, it was enough. He said no more, and nor did I. And again, there were no nightmares.

Chapter Twenty-Seven

I woke slowly, in unaccustomed comfort. Curled on my side, hugging a pillow, I blinked at the fall of afternoon sunlight. Had I slept through the morn's work? The wagons were not moving, and the world eerily hushed. Was there something amiss? Had an axle broken, or someone fallen so ill we could not travel?

I sat, of a sudden, clutching the blankets to my chest, and let out pent breath as I realized where I was. My heart, spurred into terrified pounding, eased slightly. I pushed my hair back from my face and sighed.

I was in Arcenne. I had done what I had set myself to do.

The Seal rumbled uneasily against my chest. I saw with no real surprise the serpents twisting against each other, straining, the copper serpent on top, now the silver. "Quiet." I reached up with a trembling hand to stroke the medallion. It stilled, though still thrumming nervously, soothed like a restive horse.

Tristan was not in the bedroom. The chair was still by the bed, but pushed back, as if he had leapt to his feet.

I stretched, felt the sharp familiar bite of hunger under my ribs. Braced myself on my hands, luxuriating in the clean warmth of the bed, and tasted morning in my mouth, grimacing. My heart fair threatened to burst with joy.

I had reached Arcenne. I had accomplished what Lisele had asked of me. And Tristan was alive.

I slid free of the bed and padded barefoot to the window, stretching afresh with rare contentment. For at least this moment, I could rest.

From the casement I could look down into the middle of the Citadel: a white stone practice-ground to one side, a garden unrolling its lovely green to the other. I tugged on the lock and finally managed to open the window, breathing in mountain air still crisp with morning coolness—summer never truly overwhelmed Arcenne, I later learned. The heat and dust and close stifling air of the Palais and Citté did not reach here to the mountains.

"By the Blessed," I said wonderingly. "I survived."

I spent some time at the window, enjoying the view and free of any pressing need to set my hands to work, before I felt the temperature of the room change slightly. I half-turned to see Tristan, fully dressed and armed but hatless, in the door. He wore a plain dark doublet instead of the uniform of a Citadel Guard, but the tilt of his chin and the signet ring glittering on his left hand made it plain he was a nobleman, accustomed to command. His hair was still shorter than was fashionable for a *chivalier*'s. He had a fall of some dark mellifluous material over one arm, and he stared at me, his mouth a thin line and his eyes burning.

Have I done something wrong? I stepped hurriedly from the window. "Tris—ah, Captain. Good morn. I beg your pardon—I slept so late."

He shook his head, abruptly, as if shaking away unpleasantness. I was suddenly acutely aware I wore only a sleeping shirt, and nothing else. I blushed from my toes to the crown of my scalp, a wave of heat rising through me.

"You were exhausted, Vianne. I expected you to sleep later, in fact." He still stared outright, in a most improper way.

I shifted from foot to foot. "I suppose I should bathe." Then I realized I had no clothes, save for the ones the R'mini had gifted me.

Idiot, Vianne. Have the shocks robbed you of all sense?

However, that seemed to bring him back to earth. "Oh." He held up his arms. "We...ah, well. This is for you. *Père* remarked you seem much my mother's size, and she sent this dress and has called for her dressmaker to appear tomorrow. She's looking forward to meeting you, especially since you're a scholar of Tiberia."

"Oh, gods," I groaned. "Tristan, no. Not Tiberian verbs." *I doubt I could remember any past the first declension by now.*

"Ease yourself, *m'chri*." The corners of his eyes crinkled. "A few moments, nothing more, since you're weary from your journey and no doubt a bit stunned. Mère is very easy, you shall see. And my father would speak to you at length. We have plans to make."

My shoulders slumped. I glanced back at the window, wondering if the R'mini had escaped the town and were already on the open road. I devoutly hoped so. I approached the pile of threadbare, brightly colored cloth he'd left on a chair. "Did the R'mini leave this morning?" *They will not suffer, will they?*

"Not a single one to be found in the city. Tis passing odd."

Not so odd. Merely another thing to be grateful for. Perhaps they would escape the ill luck that dogged me.

I dug in the pile of clothing, finding my pocket and pulling out Jaryana's gift.

Twas a small, flat medallion, gilt paint scored with a few peculiar angular signs. I examined it and the threadbare velvet ribbon it was tied to, and then felt at the pocket again.

Two hard lumps. My emerald ear-drops. Jaryana's quick fingers must have slipped them back into my pocket. "Oh." My eyes filled with tears.

"Vianne?" Tristan approached, cautiously. How he could move so quietly in such heavy boots was a mystery.

I wiped at my eyes with the flat of one hand, but tears still wet my cheeks. "Oh." It seemed all I could say. If I had kept my vow to Lisele, I had broken one to myself—the vow never to weep again. It seemed I was made of water.

"Vianne?" he repeated. It was almost a shock, to hear him so uncertain.

I turned, held them up. Emeralds glittered in the fresh mountain-bright sunlight. "I offered these in payment for passage and they...they would not take them." *We do not steal from the poor,* Tozmil had said, and I was poor indeed. I had nothing in the world to call my own anymore. Nothing except these baubles.

And your wits, Vianne. Though those are threadbare enough you may still consider yourself a peasant.

Tristan touched my shoulder. "Was it very bad?" And there was an awkwardness, new indeed in the Captain of the Guard. "I would not have had this happen, not to you. Not for anything."

"Oh, I know. Yet if we were still at Court, Tristan, what then?"

He shrugged. "I supose I would still be gathering the courage to ask you to wed me," he answered, matter-of-factly. "I shall order breakfast for you, *m'chri*. I suppose you cannot wait for a bath."

"No." I curled the medallion and my ear-drops in my fist. "No, I cannot."

He smoothed the shirt over my shoulder, gently. Silence stretched between us, thin and glittering in the golden air.

His face was far less drawn than it had been last night, and I wondered still at the brief patch of gray at his temple. But the lines on his face had eased. His mouth now relaxed, a brief smile all the more precious because twas fleeting.

"I have never known you to lack courage," I offered, tentatively.

"I find myself a coward when it comes to you, *d'mselle*."

Oddly enough, a smile broke through my tears. I sobered almost instantly as well. "I thought you dead. I wondered what direness had befallen you."

His arms slid around me and I leaned in to him, grateful for his solidity. For the first time, I embraced him as hard as I could. He kissed the top of my head, stroked my back, and rocked me slightly, as a nurse will soothe a child. I wept into his shirt, a dam broken and a storm unleashed, as if Lisele had just died. The numbing tension I had been wandering in snapped, leaving me breathless.

He held me until I quieted and produced a kerchief I used mercilessly, sopping at my streaming cheeks and blowing my nose. "L-l-look at this," I stammered. "What a m-m-mess. I b-beg your p-par—"

"Oh, hush." Gently, taking my chin and tilting it up. He looked relieved, the lines easing on his now-familiar face. "Tis no sin to weep, Vianne, when you've managed to survive conspiracy, armed attack, and the Shirlstrienne. I would be rather surprised if you did not shed a tear. Or many. That soft heart of yours."

It eased me, as no doubt he meant to, but shame still curdled in my throat. I searched for anything respectable to say. "I suppose I should take a bath."

"I suppose you should."

"I smell of the R'mini." Woodsmoke, the spices in their food, horse and oxen and the comforting breath of Jaryana and Tozmil's wagon. When I washed it from my skin, I would be adrift again.

Yet there was Tristan.

"Did they harm you?" A mere whisper, his blue eyes intent and focused. "Tell me."

"Of course not." I sounded horrified at the very thought. "They are not so bad, Tristan. Fair enough, if a bit harsh. They asked that I work, and Jaryana taught me of their hedgewitchery. Tis passing interesting—"

"Trust you to find something to learn from even the R'mini." He was definitely smiling now.

"*Learn what you can, where you can.*" I felt better, now that I had eased *him*. "Tis a Tiberian proverb; Catorus the Elder mentions it often. I survived at Court because I learned how to make myself agreeable. Even, it seems, to hedgewitch tinkers."

"Not just agreeable, *m'chri*. But truly, did they hurt you? Were you offered any insult, any at all?"

Why? Would you seek to avenge it? I do not cherish that thought, d'Arcenne, much as I... "No. I am merely fatigued, and very happy to see you again. I missed you terribly."

Between one moment and the next, the smile drained away. He looked down at me, his blue eyes shadowed, his mouth a thin line, as a hungry man contemplating a feast. That shadow was strange, and a thread of uneasiness worked its way through me.

"You missed me?" His seriousness might have frightened me, did I not know him.

Do I? I nodded, biting my lower lip.

"Missed me terribly?" he persisted, examining my face.

I nodded again, breathless, my heart racing. "I had awful nightmares."

He brushed my cheekbone with callused fingertips. Why did he not look happier at the thought of my longing for him? He seemed pained.

How on earth did I come to be standing here in Arcenne, with Tristan d'Arcenne's arms about me? "You look grim, *chivalier*." Why did I always say the stupidest things to him?

"Not grim. Thoughtful." He was bending down, slowly, his hand cupping my chin.

"Thoughtful—" I was about to say something silly once more, but his mouth met mine, and I forgot the very idea of speaking.

My hands crept up about his neck, one still clutching his sodden kerchief. I forgot the taste of morning in my mouth and the fact that I wore only a sleeping shirt. He flattened both hands against my back and pulled me against him, the Aryx giving forth a rippling thunderous melody. I had never kissed thus before, but it seemed I knew how, the knowledge springing fullborn into my body, perhaps from his.

I had heard enough courtsongs to know what he wanted, and to know I wanted the same. I did not care if it was proper, or if manners were served, or if twas my duty to do summat or aught, as Drumiera would have said.

I knew only the man in my arms and the Sun through the window, and the blessed relief of a moment in which I did not need to plan, or think, or *do*. I merely *existed*, melting into him, with no barrier of duty to remind me of what I should instead of what I wanted.

Tristan broke away, kissed my cheek, my forehead, my other cheek. His lips traced my jawline and I tipped my head back, allowing all.

"Vianne," he whispered against my skin. I could find no breath to answer him. "Gods above, you're enough to make me forget my duty again, *m'chri*."

"Duty?" I managed, blankly. *To the seven hells with duty. What now?*

"Breakfast for my lady Queen." He smoothed my hair with one hand, pressing another kiss on my forehead. "Then to bring you to your Guard, so they can see for themselves you are well. And my father, and my mother. We must plan."

"Plan?" I finally found my normal voice. "Oh, yes. That. We do need a plan."

And suddenly there was business at hand. "Do you still require a Consort, Vianne? There is a Temple here. I do not ask for—"

A sharp pang lanced the region of my heart. "There is no one in the world I would rather have for my Consort. And my Left Hand."

He nodded. But his expression was still serious, too serious. "You do not mistrust me?"

How could I? I touched the lock of gray at his temple. "And where did this come from, *chivalier*?"

He grimaced, an expression so unguarded it warmed me. He would not twist his face so where others could see.

"You noticed? I am not a gentle man."

Do you think I do not know? There is a brace of peasants in the Shirlstrienne who know, as well. I shook my head, dismissing the objection. "These are not days for gentleness, Captain. I need you, as long as the Aryx persists in…this. If the Seal chooses someone else, I shall free you." *Though I do not like the idea. At all.*

"If you contract me as your Consort, Vianne, it will be permanent. Even if the Aryx chooses another, I've sworn my oath to you, *d'mselle*. Do you think me faithless?"

"Very well." I was helpless to stop a foolish smile from rising. "You really do wish to?"

"Vianne, you idiot, I want nothing else."

I laid my head on his shoulder and sighed. He held me, stroking my tangled hair. At that moment, there was nowhere else in Arquitaine I would rather have been.

Chapter Twenty-Eight

The dress was dark blue silk, simply but exquisitely sewn, the neckline modest and the sleeves falling away from undersleeves of white silk. Twas fashionable, too, or at least, what had been fashionable at Court three months ago. It was too close in the chest and too long at the sleeves, and a trifle too long otherwise, but all in all it felt familiar. I had no desire to ever wear breeches again. The relief of being dressed decently was well-nigh overpowering.

Of such small things is happiness made, I suppose.

I had lost flesh; my hipbones and ribs stood out starkly, my cheekbones stretching from under the skin. The mirror was unkind—it showed me how gaunt I had become. I looked ill-used, all things considered, and far too pale. It was a wonder I had escaped more fever, despite all Risaine's and Jaryana's tisanes.

I had considered wearing my garden-boots, or battering my bare feet on the stone floors of Arcenne, but Tristan brought me a pair of soft slippers to wear inside the Citadel.

Twas odd to feel so much softness again.

After a short, luxuriously hot bath and lacing the overdress with Tristan's help—I had to laugh at how serious he was, and how his fingers fumbled with the laces—I combed my hair out and chose a simple braid, tying it off with a piece of ribbon. Tristan watched , and shook his head when I pushed the Aryx under my neckline.

"Leave it out, Vianne, an it please you," he said quietly. "Tis better for us to see it."

I nodded. "Did you speak of breakfast?" Now that I was clean, my teeth charmed, and my head a little less cluttered with fear, I found myself relieved and hungry in equal measure.

He nodded, and led me into the sitting room. There was hot chocolat, and chai, delicate pastries, fruit, cheese—the kind of provender I had not seen in ages. I set to with a will, my manners thankfully not rusty from so long without. Tristan joined me, pouring a cup of chocolat. I thought of Lisele while I drank, surprised tears did not rise to the surface. Instead, a hot dry-eyed grief rose, threatening to choke me.

It was tinted with anger, and the depth of my own calculating fury frightened me.

"Eat, Vianne." Tristan's tone brooked no disobedience.

After I could swallow no more, he gave me a few moments to gather myself, and led me out into the hall. A pair of Citadel Guard by the door eyed me cautiously. "*Chivalieri*," Tristan said, my hand firmly tucked in his elbow, "this is Her Majesty Vianne di Tirecian-Trimestin di Rocancheil et Vintmorecy, Queen of Arquitaine."

I was hard-pressed not to blush.

They both bowed, a stocky older man and a slender youth I recognized from last night. The black mountain-pards on their doublets eyed me no less dubiously. I would have swept them a courtesy, but Tristan had my arm, so I merely nodded. Their gazes snagged on the Aryx, and remained there.

"A pleasure to meet you, *sieurs*." I used the same tone I had been wont to address solicitors in, hoping it was not overly cool.

The older one gave me a glance I could only classify as astonished. "Likewise, *d'mselle*. Tis a pleasure to be in your service."

My service? I glanced up at Tristan, whose blue eyes were level and intent.

I see. There have been events at work while I slept. I sought a grave, though welcoming, tone. "I thank you for your pains, *chivalier*."

Tristan drew me away. I waited until we reached the end of the hall and turned into another corridor. "My service?" My eyebrows lifted. He had shortened his stride, since I was now gratefully encumbered by skirts—and a full stomach.

"Arcenne is yours, Vianne. My father swore so last night, and he is not one to make a promise lightly. You must have impressed him." Tristan's mouth curled, a trifle. This morning, freshly shaven and dressed plainly, he looked more the Captain I remembered from Court.

"I do not think so. I've been a silly goose ever since I s-saw you in the p-passage—" Words deserted me. *Just a moment. Just give me a short while to catch my breath.*

I did not, you see, quite believe I had reached Arcenne. The spring inside me had wound itself so tightly, and its release left me shaking with conflict.

Tristan stopped short and enclosed me in his arms, rested his chin atop my head. This hall was thankfully deserted, stands of armor and marble busts on pedestals tucked in small alcoves, a tapestry of yet another battle to my right. "Tis behind you now, Vianne." A warm spot in my hair, his breath as familiar to me as my own. "I swear, I will not leave your side again. Ever."

I nodded against his chest, my pulse thundering in my ears. Sinking into his strength was a novel sensation, and a welcome one. "'Tis hard to believe," I said into his doublet. He smelled familiar—leather, and steel, and the smell of him, male and clean. "I lived to reach Arcenne, and now that I am here I cannot tell what to *do*. What next?"

"Next?" He laughed, kissing my hair. Though he was gentle, the laugh was not. "Now that you have gifted us with hope again? We knew not if you were dead, or alive and in di Narborre's hands. Every day we have waited for news. D'Orlaans struggles to consolidate his power—several of the border provinces are jostling for position, nobody quite sure whether to revolt or not. Rumor racks Arquitaine no less than the plague—though Arcenne has escaped the plague; we are not certain how, but grateful nonetheless. Since d'Orlaans has not found you he is frantic, and since we had not found you we doubted our very lives. For two months, night and day, everything has hung in the balance, and we have been laying in provisions and preparing for war. Now we know you are safe, we may stop fretting and begin *doing*." He sighed.

I found I had little desire to ask after his plans just yet, and cast about for a safer subject. "What befell *you*? I had neither the time nor the strength to ask last night. How did you come to be here?"

He stiffened slightly. "We were hunting di Narborre. I cursed myself for that, for listening to di Cinfiliet when I should have stayed with you. Yet we had to track d'Orlaans's dog; we had to know. We found his trail an hour before nightfall, I wished to return to the village, but…there was no time. We tracked him until dark fell, then made camp. I thought of you, before I went to sleep." Now his tone dropped, became fierce, as his embrace tightened considerably. "The next morn we found his tracks, and they led directly for the village. We found Adersahl wounded, following our trail, hoping to bring us as reinforcements. I sent di Chatillon and Jierre to collect you, Adersahl swore you were hidden near the village, and the rest of us set to following di Narborre again. For Adersahl told us he had taken some of the women, no doubt thinking you might be among them. When I found how narrowly you had escaped…

"Luc and Jierre returned, saying they could not find you. But by that time, we had discovered the women. It seems di Narborre had found none of them were you. Their end was not kind, Vianne. I…I thanked the Blessed you were not among them, and cursed the idiocy that had led me from your side. We returned to the village and searched, but the rain had started, and we could not find you. Adersahl cursed himself; he had thought you safer hidden than traversing the forest with only one Guard for protection. We buried the bodies we could find and searched the Shirlstrienne—as much as we dared. It took three weeks for Jierre to convince me to flee to Arcenne. He threatened to tie me to the saddle, and di Cinfiliet had some fool's fancy of broaching the thinnest pass to Navarrin. We could not believe you could survive in the Shirlstrienne without even a waterskin."

I am glad to see you, Tristan, but I wished you had listened to di Cinfiliet. It would do my heart good to know you safe in Navarrin, where the Duc could not touch you. "I do not know what might have befallen me, if not for the R'mini."

His arms tightened. "I owe the tinkers my life, then."

I leaned against him. "I did not know if you were alive or if di Narborre had fought a pitched battle with you, then razed the village. When I could not find Adersahl, it seemed I had to reach Arcenne myself, or die trying. For my Lisele."

He paused, as if searching for words. "I would have had you wait for me, but you could not have known. I am simply glad the gods have seen fit to give me another chance at honor." He had turned steel-hard, and I wondered at it. It seemed impossible he could be so worried; I could not imagine a dishonorable Tristan.

I did not wish to move, and there seemed no answer I could make. So I simply rested against him, content, breathing him in.

A few moments later, he reluctantly loosened his arms. "Come. We are late."

"Late?"

"They are eager to see you again, *m'chri*, no less than I was."

"They?"

"Your Guard, Your Majesty. Your Guard."

Chapter Twenty-Nine

The Guard was housed in a long barracks hall, and when we stepped inside Jierre let out a whoop and leapt from his chair. Cots ranged along either side of the hall for a distance. There was a space of long tables and benches, a fireplace with chairs and benches set before it, a large cauldron of something familiar-smelling bubbling over the fire.

I had missed the smell of their stew, without knowing it.

I found myself surrounded. Luc di Chatillon embraced me, Jierre kissed me on both cheeks, Tinan di Rocham, blushing fiercely, clapped me on the shoulder hard enough to hurt. The hall became a hubbub of shouted questions, congratulations, and oaths cheerfully yelled.

Though I have been greeted in many ways, I believe this is the welcome I cherish the memory of most.

I was hugged, kissed, buffeted from one place to another before Tristan gave a sharp bark of an order and the fuss died. I looked around the wall of leather doublets and swordhilts. I did not see Adersahl. Tristan offered me his arm, but I peered around Jierre, whose lean dark face held two tear tracks none commented on.

Adersahl sprawled in a low chair tucked almost behind the chimney, a deeply shadowed corner.

I looked up at Tristan. "A moment, please?" I had fallen into sharply accented Court Arquitaine again. The R'mini drawl so quickly fled my tongue, for all I still carried Jaryana's medallion in my skirt-pocket.

An expectant hush fell over the Guard, broken only when Luc di Chatillon let out a sharp breath. "He is drinking himself to death, *d'mselle.*"

Jierre's hand closed over di Chatillon's shoulder. "Let her." He nodded to me. Jespre di Vidancourt folded his arms over his lean chest, his blond eyebrows arched.

I approached Adersahl quietly, my skirts brushing the clean wooden floor. A scabbarded rapier lay across his knees. You could scarce see Adersahl's face, but his shoulders slumped and he seemed frailer now.

Older.

I was less than six feet from him when Adersahl lifted his head. He'd lost his fine mustache. His chin and cheeks were marred with stubble, hollows lay under his eyes, and his gray-salted hair stuck up in wild tufts.

"Oh." I could not help myself; I sighed. "Adersahl."

He had a crock of something that smelled stronger than rhuma tucked into the crook of his elbow. "As you see," he croaked, lifting the large jar slightly. I did not allow my nose to wrinkle, though the smell of unwashed man soaked in alcohol and stale sweat was enough to make even a seasoned courtier sniff. "Come to mock me?"

This may not end well. I searched for something useful to say.

"I must beg your pardon. For I lost your dagger, *chivalier*, and you entrusted it to my care."

He snorted rudely. I had seen no few men in their cups, at feasts or fêtes, but this was some other type of drunkenness, bleak instead of gluttonous. "Lost'er. Slip of a girl. Too brave by half. Stupid, stupid, *stupid*."

His slurred speech was no surprise; he smelled as if he had drank a sea's worth. It must have been *valadka*, that clear liquor that can make a man blind if overindulged. I strove for a gentle tone, no laughter or pity. "I should thank you. If I had not the dagger, I would not have survived."

There was a fierce whisper behind me. I paid no attention, kneeling down, my hands taking care of arranging my skirts as they had not for months. The silk pooled about me, and I touched his knee with two fingers.

Adersahl's weary, baleful glare sharpened. He was bleary enough to serve as a caution to younglings. "*D'mselle*? Duchesse?"

"As you see." I found myself smiling. "You did well, *chivalier*. If not for your advice, di Narborre would have caught me. I barely escaped him, and would I have stayed where you set me, I would not have been lost." The Aryx tilled against my skin, as a softly stroked bell. "Next time, I swear I will listen to you more closely."

He blinked at me. "*D'mselle*?" As if he could not quite credit it. "Lost. You were *lost*."

"Lost no more." I peered up into his face. *Give him a task, he requires summat to focus on.* "I require your assistance, *chivalier*."

He grunted, unimpressed, settling further into the chair with a creak. I could not judge his expression with any surety; the firelight was simply not enough to penetrate this corner.

I tried again. "I shall need every member of my Guard." I leaned earnestly forward. "For the border provinces are preparing for war, and d'Orlaans will learn soon enough that I live." I sighed, as if saddened. "And if my Guard is less than it was, I am sorely afraid I shall be in peril."

Twas not very elegant, but Adersahl mulled over my words, some life stealing back into his shadowed face. He burped, and I was hard-put to stifle a gasp. *Valadka* slopped against the side of the crock as he leaned forward.

I took the earthenware jar from him. He made a grab for it, but I was quicker, having spent two months working among the R'mini, who prize dexterity. They had not taught me the secrets of R'mini thievery—I was, after all, still *g'ji*—but I had learned enough to keep liquor away from a drunken man.

Adersahl's hand curled around his swordhilt. Tristan said something I did not hear, but his tone was fierce and cold.

"*Not fit!*" Adersahl half-shouted, harshly. "Slip of a girl! Dead in the woods."

A chill spread through me. *Very nearly, my friend. If not for a goatherd, you would be right.*

"*Chivalier* di Parmecy et Villeroche," I said crisply, "your Queen requires your service. Are you, or are you not, a member of my Guard? You swore your oath to me, and I call upon you now."

Silence crackled in the barracks. Then Adersahl slid forward off his chair, going to his knees. He was near as thin as I was, a far cry from the solid, stocky man I had known. He still wore the crimson sash of the Guard, but twas soiled and dull. His cloth was sorely the worse for wear.

He presented his swordhilt to me. "Not fit t'be a Guard."

"Nonsense. No more *valadka*, Adersahl. Are you a member of my Guard, or not?"

He stared blearily, blinking, and burped again. "'F y'want me. Pretty Vianne, pretty pretty Vianne. Slip of a girl."

That, at least, is a hopeful sign. I shall overlook the flattery this once. I nodded. "Very well, then. No more drinking."

"No more drinkin." He blinked and then made a quick motion. I felt the tensing of the Guard behind me to a man, but Adersahl merely presented me with his swordhilt again. "Owe you m'service, *d'mselle*. Accept m'oath."

I touched his swordhilt with two fingers, keeping the crock well away from him. For I have learned well that a drunken man may be cunning when it comes to soaking himself afresh. "Accepted, Adersahl di Parmecy et Villeroche. Now, on your feet. Take my hand."

He grabbed at my fingers, clutching his sword loosely in his other sotted fist. I found myself struggling to my feet, praying I would not take yet another blow to any grace I might have. If I fell to the floor now I would look very silly indeed.

We hauled each other up, absurdly, like overtired Harvest Festival celebrants. Adersahl steadied me and nearly fell over, so I steadied him in turn. "There." I brushed his shoulders. It did little good, but he seemed to have a fresh lease on life. At least, he was upright now. "You look a trifle more proper. Perhaps Tinan and Jierre can help clean you up and put you to bed, and when you recover we shall have a long talk. Well enough?"

He would have bowed to me, but I kept his hand, so he could not finish and topple himself. "Well 'nough," he mumbled, and twas a good thing Tristan was at my shoulder now, for Adersahl promptly lost consciousness and would have tumbled us both to the floor if Tristan had not caught him. Tinan and Jierre were next, taking Adersahl's weight.

"Well." I shook at my skirts with one hand, seeking to adjust their hanging. "I made a right proper mess of *that*. Will he be well, do you think?"

It fell to Jierre di Yspres to answer me. "At least he'll not be drinking tomorrow. Tis a wonder to have you back, *d'mselle*, for he would not listen to any of us."

"I am not sure I have not made it worse." I looked down at the crock. It smelled awful—I have never been one for drink. Tristan deftly removed it from my hand. "Tis awful stuff, that." *I hope he did not swallow enough to damage his eyesight.*

"Very." Tristan touched my arm. "I must take you to my father now. We are late as it is."

"Well enough," I said. Jierre and Tinan carried Adersahl between them. The rest of the Guard stood, hats in hand, some of them grinning like fools. "Tis good to see you. All of you."

"Good to see you too, *d'mselle*," Luc di Chatillon said in the silence that followed. "We were fair worried."

So was I, chivalier. *But I may not admit to it as you can.* The Aryx cooled to the temperature of my skin, no longer singing its muted melody. Yet I could still hear the music below the surface of my mind, like the song of earth and wind that made up hedgewitchery's background. I was still thinking on this when Tristan led me out of the barracks.

"Well." He closed the door, offering his arm again. "Miracles, again. You are more a *demiange* than ever. I cannot wait to see what sorcery you work on my father."

I rather think him unimpressed with me. But we shall see. "Will Adersahl be well? He's so...thin."

Tristan's face paled slightly, his jaw set. "He took it hard when we found the bodies."

"The bodies." My stomach flipped. Tristan guided me up a flight of stairs, going slowly. He kept his hand over mine, tucked in the crook of his elbow, and I found myself worrying whether someone would see.

As if we were still at Court, and I had to be careful of propriety.

"The women, of a certain age, from the village. When it was clear none of them were you, di Narborre ordered them killed." Flat and cool, the same tone he had used when speaking of the dead peasants. "Twas not a gentle end. But it was none your fault," he added hastily. "I would not have you thinking it was."

"Gods." My breath left me in a great swoop. I hurried to keep pace with him, and the sound of my skirts was a balm. I felt myself again with heavy material swaying, the brushing of fabric against my legs a familiar reassurance. "And... Adrien?" I meant to ask if Risaine had been found, but my mouth shaped di Cinfiliet's name instead.

He shortened his strides, granting me a single indecipherable glance. "He and his bandits are on patrol, riding the borders of Arcenne. Vianne, Risaine sought to fight di Narborre and his men." Tristan steered me down another long hall. "She killed two of them."

Blood drained from my face. "Gods," I said again. *Blessed, grant her peace.*

"Twas not your doing, Vianne." Tristan did not slow further, but his tone gentled. "The fault lies with di Narborre and his master."

"You are certain twas not another who—"

"There was no doubt it was the Marquisse." Tristan stopped short, surprising me, and righted me as I swayed. This hall was bare and plain, racks of weapons along either wall, lit by glowrocks and pierced with shafts of Sun-arrows from high, narrow windows. "Look at me, *m'chri.*"

Tristan's face was grimly serious, his blue gaze winter-chill and sharp. The streak of gray at his temple glowed in the directionless light, and it was obvious how the stone of this place was in his very bones. "There was *nothing* you could have done. If you had been taken, their deaths would *be* for nothing. D'Orlaans would be King in truth as well as in name, and I would most probably have killed myself seeking to free you from him." He clasped my shoulders, not hard enough to bruise but firmly enough to hold me upright. "I would not lie to you. There was nothing you could have done."

I nodded. But something deep-buried in me did not believe him. "Tristan—"

"Strength, Vianne. If you have none left, use mine." He kissed my forehead, stroking my shoulders with his thumbs. Silk crushed under his touch. "Do you understand? *Use mine.*"

I nodded. *I have been using your strength as my northneedle since this ordeal began.* "I do not feel very well." Twas laughable understatement, to say the least.

He paused, and I knew he was on the verge of suggesting I go back to bed. My chin lifted, my shoulders coming up under the familiar weight of duty. Twas a heavier duty than the one weighting me at Court, but I was robbed of choice. I could not swoon like an empty-headed Court dame now, taking refuge in weakness. After what I had endured, I wondered how much more I could bear.

If I am wearing the Aryx, I must be as strong as I can.

"Yet I am to meet your father." I made the words as decisive as possible. "I owe your mother a polite greeting as well. Lead the way."

Chapter Thirty

The sitting room was a surprise, dressed in light colors and decorated with silk pillows and pretty floral hangings. A needlework frame stood in one corner, a large harp in the other. The windows were wide and airy, since this room faced the gardens inside the walls.

Tristan closed the door and I found myself enveloped, two soft arms around me and a woman's greeting-kiss on my cheeks in turn. "Oh, you poor child." Soft and clear, a cultured voice. She had me whisked away from the door and into a seat by the fireplace, tucking a blanket around me. "Tris has dragged you all through the Citadel, has he not? Of course. Regrettable, that boy, just like his father. Not a thought for us lesser mortals. Oh, child, you're pale."

Tristan's mother, her long black hair piled atop her head and threaded with pearls, twitched her pale green skirts back and sank onto a footstool. Her wide hazel eyes were full of merriment.

Her perfume was apple blossom and silk, a scent that reminded me of Lisele just as the harp did. "Baroness—," I began, a pretty speech summoned from the recesses of my brain, but she held up one pale, elegant hand.

"Hellsfire," she swore cheerfully, hazel eyes sparkling. I could see Tristan in the softness around her mouth—his infrequent look of happiness seemed to have come direct from her. "Call me Sílvie. Well, let us have a look at you." Her gaze moved over my face. "Hmmm. Tristan told me you were lovely, but he never mentioned how beautiful you truly are."

My cheeks grew hot, savage embarrassment rising. Did I seem to need the flattery? "Oh, I am sure he…he…"

"Stuff and nonsense. You're exquisite. My dressmaker will be pleased—she is an artist, and loves to have a canvas. Now, Tris, fetch her a cup of chai, very sweet. And Talya will be along with a very light lunch soon—I thought sweetrolls and soup, and some of the apples from the orchard. I love the apples here, they remind me of Vintmorecy. You did not know I was of Vintmorecy, did you? Though your father's family is liege, and mine merely a *chivalier*'s holding."

Slightly stunned, I stammered out something polite.

"*Mére*, do not fuss at her." Tristan crossed to the window, glancing out. "There should be a guard here."

"I sent them to sup," she said. "Poor men. You're too hard on them. Just like your father. And you are looking finer than I've seen in months, Tris. Did you know, young *d'mselle*, that our son—"

"*Mére*," Tristan said firmly. "She is weary, and she has just endured a—"

"A series of nasty shocks." The Baroness fixed her son with a mother's level, serious gaze. "The best thing for her is a bit of normalcy. Let me fuss over the ill, Tris, tis my duty. You've probably frightened the poor girl half to death with your serious face and your *always* this and *never* that and *danger* the other." She tossed her black curls and laughed, and I saw another echo of Tristan in her face. I found myself smiling.

"*Père* will wish to speak with her soon." Tristan laughed, spreading his hands to indicate defeat. "Do not give me the sharp edge of your tongue, *Mère*. I cannot stand it. Vianne, tell her not to scold me."

I was so enchanted by the spectacle of him truly laughing, I barely comprehended what he said.

The Baroness patted my arm comfortingly. "I was not certain the dress would fit well, but Perseval said we are of a size, you and I. Though I am a trifle taller, I think. And my long arms fill me with dismay. So tell me, child, what do you think of my Tristan? He quite fancies you—do *not* give me that look, Tris, I am your mother, I can say so—and he wrote about you in his letters. Said he danced with you."

I stole a glance at Tristan. He leaned at ease next to one of the windows, out of the sunshine, and there was a definite crimson stain in his cheeks.

Tristan d'Arcenne was blushing. In front of his mother. He wished to be my Consort, and he was *blushing*.

The Baroness watched me with a faint line between her charcoal eyebrows. *She is not as carefree as she seems. She is seeking to set me at my ease.*

I rallied, and took a deep breath. "He danced with me twice. He forgot it quickly, too, for he asked me if it was at the Fête of Flowers, when it was the Festival of Skyreturn."

The Baroness's mouth twitched, then she chuckled. It was a happy, musical sound. "Just like a man!" She rested her hands on my knees, just as I would sometimes do with Lisele. It sent a pang through me. "Forgetting a dance. I thought I raised him better, my dear. My apologies." That startled me into a laugh, and we were on familiar territory. "Tris *m'fils*, why are you in that dark corner? You see, dear, he and his father are of a pair, nothing in their heads but Guard rosters and politics. Boring, dry, dreadful stuff. If not for me, everyone in the castle would be eating hardtack and sausage, doing endless weapon-drill." She smiled at me, her ear-drops glittering. They held pale peridot stones, and a matching necklace clasped her slender throat.

"You might someday thank me for being dreadful and boring, Sílvie," Tristan's father said from the door.

I sank back down in the chair. The Baroness did not seem to notice that I had jolted upright upon hearing a new voice. Tristan's gaze rested on me from the shadow near the window, and I knew he had noticed.

It was absurdly comforting.

Baron Perseval d'Arcenne moved precisely two steps into the room and closed the door. He wore the uniform of an Arcenne guard, though his doublet was finer than a plain *chivalier's* and his sword probably an heirloom, with a ruby in the hilt. His dark hair was thickly peppered with gray but less mussed than last night, and in the unforgiving daylight I could see the lines on his face more clearly. Time had visited the elder Baron, whispered her secret in his ear, and he looked as if he had only nodded and pressed on.

I was about to rise, wishing to be on my feet to meet this new challenge, but the Baroness caught my hand. "Do not, child," she said quietly. "It is not meet."

She was correct—a lady does not rise; tis a nobleman's duty to gain his feet when *she* enters. And there was the Aryx, as well.

"There you are, bossing everyone about," Tristan's father said drily. "I trust you have rested, Your Majesty."

I suppressed a guilty start at hearing the title applied to me. "Well enough, *sieur*. Rest has been hard to gather of late, and I suspect that state of affairs shall continue."

The Baron examined me for a long moment. "Well."

"That's *Pére*'s way of saying you look weak and pale, Vianne," Tristan said from his shadowed place. Why on earth did he stand *there*? "*Pére, m'Mére* sent the guards away again."

"So I see." When the Baron gazed at his wife, his face changed. The austere lines relaxed into an infinitely tender expression, his blue eyes softening. "Sílvie, you must think of your safety."

"I am in the middle of Arcenne, Perseval, what could possibly happen? Especially with the city closed, the Citadel closed too, and *your* son stalking the corridors daring anyone to step out of line."

"Well, if you will not think of your safety, think of hers." The Baron lowered himself into a chair opposite me. "Your pardon, *d'mselle*, but my bones ache. It has been a busy day."

"Please. Do not trouble yourself for me." I found my gaze could not stay away from Tristan, still watching out the window. His shoulders were stiff. "I have been traveling with the R'mini for months. Tis a treat to sit on a chair not in a moving wagon."

"I can imagine." The Baron settled, steepling his fingers before his long nose. "I must know, *d'mselle*, what your intentions are."

That must be a habitual pose with him, he thinks and hides his mouth at the same moment. "My intentions?" *Is he asking if I mean to wed his son? Blessed, they* are *direct in the mountains.*

"Hellsfire," the Baroness broke in, "give the lady some time to rest, at least, before you start questioning her!" She tapped my knee, a sharp deft gesture. "Do not answer him. Let us speak of something easy first. Look at how pale she is, Perseval!"

"I am well enough," I said, as gently as I could. "Truly, Baroness. I simply wish to finish whatever duty I have now so I may go back to sleep. I must confess I am extremely weary." I brought myself up to sit straight, instead of sinking into the chair. "Now, *sieur* Baron, what do you mean when you speak of my intentions?"

"I must know if you intend to field an army before or after the winter." His eyes half-lidded, an inward-turning expression. "We must also turn our attention to a provisional Council for you, and the best way to publicize your survival—and your possession of the Aryx."

My fingers leapt to touch the medallion. It thrummed under my fingers. The serpents shifted slightly, and the Baroness gasped, her curls shaking. Soft and wondering, her hazel gaze was a burden. "The Seal. Blessed, I never thought to see it." Her hand lifted, as if she would seek to touch it.

Oh, how I wished her luck.

"Careful, Sílvie." The Baron's sudden tension did not go unremarked, for Tristan stepped forward, just to the edge of the bar of sunshine. "It sparked last night."

She stopped. There was a sapphire-and-silver signet on her left hand, and a copper marriage band too. "Oh."

Tristan's gaze met mine. As if he had thrown me a rope that stretched taut between us, a wave of strength came down that rope and cleared my head. I had made my way through the Shirlstrienne and to Arcenne with my own wits as a guide; surely my wits would not fail me now. And with my Captain with me, what could I not do?

"I know little of Councils, *sieur*, so you will have to guide me." I thought for a moment, decided to ask the most pressing question first. "Is there no way to avoid war?"

A slight smile touched the Baron's lined face. "Wiser than I credited."

A well-mannered knock at the door jolted me again. Tristan crossed the room, opened it, exchanged some words in a low tone.

"Always thinking of food, *Mère*," he said, as three serving maids bustled in, their starched white caps glimmering in the sunshine and their gray skirts brushing. "I think we can eat and strategize at the same time, can we not?"

The Baron did not move. "Well enough. At least this child-Queen has the sense to ask for help when she is out of her depth."

"If your tongue were any sharper, you would cut your own teeth out," the Baroness replied. "No more, Perseval. We have waited long enough to have these questions answered. An hour or so over a small meal will do no harm."

I sank back into the chair as the Baroness rose, and Perseval d'Arcenne hurriedly rose with her. He took her arm and said something in a low tone.

She laughed, tossing her raven hair, and the light was kind to her. Another thing Tristan had inherited; hers was a face that would not collapse with age, the bones a fine structure that would hold to loveliness as long as she breathed. "You are too serious by half. No wonder the poor child is frightened out of her wits!"

"She is the Queen of Arquitaine, and a bloody usurper squats upon the throne, murdering all in his way. We should bend our minds toward keeping our country from full-scale civil war." He brushed a loose curl from her face. "We have no time for the gentler things, Sílvie, sorely as I miss them."

Tristan touched my shoulder. I had not even noticed him beside me. "They shall bicker through the soup and finally settle to business after chai," he said softly. "My father is harsh, but he has a fine mind, and he's loyal to the Aryx."

I nodded. "I can tell as much. All is well, Captain. Though I would dearly love more sleep, for all that I had a surfeit this morning." I sought to ease him—after all, I had traveled with the R'mini and simply endured, and before that I had dealt with stronger shocks than a sitting-room conversation over soup.

"After an engagement, some soldiers love to sleep. I think you are no less battle-weary, Vianne." His hand did not move from my shoulder, and something in the pressure of it was *very* improper, though his fingers did not move. "My father has made arrangements for us to visit the Temple this evening. If you have not changed your mind."

I took his hand, our fingers lacing together. "I would think you would be wary of how much trouble I seem to attract."

His mouth quirked. "You seem to be constantly escaping trouble, tis certain."

"How dire is it?" For I needed to know.

He shrugged. Now that he had moved into the light, blue highlights in his dark hair showed, and the lines of worry about his mouth and eyes were clearly visible. "Dire enough that my father would press you to act quickly. Di Narborre is making himself troublesome, and there has been little news other than d'Orlaans seeking to keep control of the nobles. The plague is ravaging, and—" He saw my expression and ceased, closing his mouth firmly.

Plague and restive nobles. "I am well enough. I must hear it all."

"You've gone pale. And you're swaying, Vianne."

"I think tis relief." It was a lie, but merely one to ease him. "I am heartened, Tristan. As long as you are alive, all will be well."

Why did he look so troubled at that? The Blessed knew the news was terrible enough. But was this sadness for something I had done, something I had said? I had certainly caused him enough worry.

His face did ease, so perhaps I had not been entirely useless in that regard. "Thank you, *m'chri*. I will strive to be worthy of your faith."

"You could strive to bring her some soup and a sweetroll," his mother said laughingly. She was supervising the laying of the table. The Baron inspected both of us, his arms folded as the servants set out the china. I suffered a brief flash of unreality—less than two days ago I had been scrubbing pots in a R'mini camp. Now I watched the serving maids, one middle-aged matron and two fresh-faced girls, and I wondered who they were. Did they possess Consorts, sweethearts, fathers, brothers—men who could die if I made the wrong decisions? And what of the suffering that attended war? I had read more than enough Tiberian histories to know what misfortunes followed in an army's wake.

Tis not merely Tristan and the Guard, or a few lone peasants. Every person I see could come to harm because I have the Aryx, and d'Orlaans will kill to keep Arquitaine. He must be mad, to murder his brother and niece. Mad. And di Narborre—how did he find us in the Shirlstrienne? Was he the author of that terrible spell, or was it the Duc? What hope have I of fighting a Court sorcerer that powerful without losing myself to the Aryx? "Captain?"

"What thought has struck you now, *m'chri*?" Lightly, but with an edge.

"How did di Narborre track us?"

He seemed almost relieved by the question. "Di Palanton,

almost certainly. It gave him enough for the tracking spell. The Duc is a fair Court sorcerer, Vianne, perhaps the strongest in Arquitaine. Yet you have the Aryx." His voice dropped to a murmur.

I nodded, resting my head against the back of the chair. If it came to fighting d'Orlaans as a sorcerer, would I be able to endure the Aryx's swallowing of my soul?

If I must, I must. And Tristan will bring me back to myself, will he not? "Tell me what I must do, Left Hand."

"I would suggest partaking of luncheon, as you certainly need it. Tonight we shall visit the Temple. Tomorrow there will be dispatches, and plenty of work. For today, my father will ask questions, and we shall answer as best we can."

"*You* eat, and answer. I might merely sit and think." *Since I can see very few avenues that do not end with death and blood.*

Very few? No. I cannot see a single one.

"You worry me." His mouth curled into a smile. "We shall have to stuff you like a partridge, to regain your lost health."

That won a weary laugh from me. "What can I say? This would tax any constitution, even a di Rocancheil's. I am glad you are here."

"Tris, *m'fils*, as you love the lady, bring her to the table," the Baroness interrupted. "She is so thin it makes me hungry to look at her. Come, child, have a cup of chai and some sweetrolls. Cook is a genius, and she is quite pleased to have a royal to cosset."

A stray memory of Head Cook Amys pierced me. I wondered how she fared—and if she was preparing eels for d'Orlaans.

If she is, may he choke on them.

I let the Baroness bully me into eating, though I barely tasted

Cook's cosseting. I was too busy pondering what Baron d'Arcenne would ask of me.

Now I must plan for Arquitaine. I have come this far, but there is more yet to do. Much, much more. My eyes strayed to Tristan, who had folded his snowy napkin into a flower and presented it to his mother with a mischievous smile. She laughed, and I could see how her husband and son prized her.

I wish my mother… What could I wish for, that would not be ungrateful? I looked down into my chai-cup, the specks of leaf in the swirling liquid making a pattern for a bare moment before twas whisked away.

I have no time for regret. I must think of Arquitaine. Everything is different now, and I must be different, too.

Chapter Thirty-One

The Temple of Arcenne stood above the town, blocks of white stone on the mountainside. Inside, incense-scented quiet enfolded me. I had rarely been in a temple since my Coming-of-Age, and Lisele's Coming-of-Age ceremony a year after.

I breathed in, looking about. *Thirty-six provinces, three each for the Blessed both old and new. The six that were, and the six who came, all watch over our land.*

It was a teaching-rhyme, and an old one. The Angoulême and his armies had brought their gods, and the arms of Arquitaine had opened to both. The Old Blessed—the old gods of hedgewitchery and harvest—had greeted the New Blessed, of war and conquest, hearth and hunt, trade and sorcery. The Aryx was a relic of that time, granted by the gods themselves at the Field d'Or, when the invading army and the defending had gone to their knees on the battlefield, a great light breaking over both.

Or so twas said, and I had never disbelieved it. Or truly believed it, for that matter. Teaching-rhymes were all very well, but I preferred Tiberian histories, dry tomes of hedgewitch charms and plant lore, and the comfort of dusty pages, where scratches of ink did not require such decisions of me.

The rest of the Guard gathered outside in the falling dusk. Jierre and di Chatillon stayed behind with Adersahl, but a contingent of Citadel Guard accompanied us up the hill, Tristan on his horse and I on a docile white palfrey from the Arcenne stables. It was strange to ride sidesaddle again, let alone in the midst of a procession.

A round, smiling priest of Danshar, Jiserah's husband, took our names, not remarking on the Aryx against my dress. He wrote out the contract, we signed three copies, and he sealed two to be kept—one in the Temple, one sent to the Great Archive in Avignienne by carrier pigeon. Though d'Orlaans might well be watching the Archive, yet it did not matter.

Even the Duc could not gainsay me in this matter.

The third copy he gave to Tristan's parents, to be archived in the Citadel library. With that done, the Baron and Baroness took their leave to wait outside—and Tristan accompanied me into the empty main hall of the Temple.

Tristan's arm settled over my shoulders. Candles burned before the statues of the gods, the New Blessed and those brought out of the fabled Old Country by Edouard Angoulême and our ancestors—Danshar the Warrior-King, patron of Arquitaine; Jiserah the Gentle, his Consort; Kimyan the Huntress; Alisaar the goddess of love; Cayrian the god of thieves and trade. There were foreign gods too: Taidee the Eastron Mother-Goddess; the round-bellied Hoteei, god of luck from those parts beyond Torkai.

I considered making an offering to him, I was luckier than any woman had a right to be. My fingers touched the Aryx. "Or unluckier," I murmured.

"Vianne?" Tristan was suddenly attentive.

"Merely a thought spoken aloud." I straightened my shoulders, gathered my skirts. There was no time for a betrothal dress, not that I minded the lack. The more quickly we could accomplish this, the better. "Where is our priestess?"

"Here," a clear female voice drifted between the clouds of incense and the slender *fleurs-di-lisse* pillars. "One moment."

We waited at the end of the hall, my eyes drawn up to the benevolent faces of the stone statues. Hoteei was to our left, squatting over an altar heaped with food offerings—it seemed Arcenne had been lucky lately.

Or the peasantry were seeking to avert the plague. Gentle Jiserah and Havarik the Physicker, Alisaar's Consort, also had many offerings before them. Danshar glowered, since his altar was bare. None wished the Warrior King to come a-riding.

Why has the plague not struck Arcenne? I had asked aloud, earlier.

The Baron's grim reply made my stomach turn on itself, knotting terribly. *The sickness has not struck a province that has refused d'Orlaans.*

The priestess came down the central walk, between the statues and the columns. She wore a dark robe, belted with silver, and her shaven head told me she was of Kimyan's elect. My heart leapt, hammering in wrists and ears and throat like a bird struggling in a trap.

She stopped before us, a woman with the sharp face of Arcenne, her eyes a clear, light gray, disturbing in her hawklike face. I could see why this woman was one of the Huntress's—she certainly *looked* like Kimyan's statues. The Huntress took maids, or those sworn to celibacy, and with her twin-Consort Torvar they ruled the harvest and the hunt. Yet many women cried to

Kimyan in childbirth, and she and her adoptive brother were said to watch over fools and drunkards as well.

"Greetings." The priestess placed her hands together, bowing. Her gaze moved over me with no surprise at all, and if the Aryx gave her a start she concealed it well. "You are here to contract a Consort before the gaze of the gods."

Tristan's arm tightened on my shoulders.

Courage, Vianne. This is not so difficult as slipping unremarked through the Palais or scrubbing pots, now, is it? The answer was mine to give, so I gathered myself and gave it. "I—yes." My voice fell flat in the fragrant smoke of incense.

The priestess nodded. "Follow me to Jiserah's altar, then, and may the gods smile upon you."

"My thanks," I managed around the lump in my throat.

"So there *is* something that frightens you," Tristan leaned down to whisper in my ear. A mad snicker rose up inside me, was choked by propriety, and died away. Yet it left relief in its wake. As long as he was with me, this would be easy.

Or if not easy, then at least conquerable.

We walked, Tristan's arm over my shoulders, and childhood training rose inside me. My mother had been religious, or so I had been told, a devotee of Jiserah. Her tiny, gem-encrusted statuette of the Gentle One remained at Court, in my rooms—or perhaps it had been taken for some reason. The thought of my mother's statue in d'Orlaans's limp white hands hurt me somehow, though I had seldom looked at its calm face since my arrival at Court lo those many years ago.

As things stood, I could perhaps see becoming *slightly* less irreligious.

Kimyan's priestess halted before Jiserah's altar. The Gentle's statue was white marble, polished to a creamy shine, threads of gold inlaid in her robes. Her eyes were closed, her face unlined and serene; yet the jewel set in her forehead sparked with its own light, peering into the hearts of men and women alike.

The priestess turned to face us, producing a long cord of white silk. I glanced up at Tristan, who studied the other woman intently. "Left hands," she said, kindly enough. "Your names, an it please you."

Tristan did not let loose of my shoulders. I lifted my left hand. "Vianne Athenaisse di Rocancheil et Vintmorecy, in the sight of the gods."

The Aryx spoke, a rill of muted melody. The priestess smiled. "Peace be with you, Vianne."

"And also with you." My throat was dry and my heart knocked afresh against my ribs.

Tristan's right arm was over my shoulder, but he reached across his body to take my left hand in his. "Tristan Dijian d'Arcenne, in the sight of the gods."

"Peace be with you, Tristan."

"And also with you." He sounded so calm, while my knees shook. *What if he changes his mind? Oh, gods, I am not brave enough for this.*

I remember little of the actual vows, except that they were—it gave me a shock to hear—the old pledges, longer and more archaic in their phrasing, as well as more violent in their content. No yearlong liaison, but a permanent Consort contract.

This meant I could divorce myself of him with traditional ease simply by returning the marriage band, but he was not free to do the same unless I repudiated him in a Temple and he took a year-vow of seclusion.

Such things are not done nowadays. At least, not often.

Tristan had produced the copper marriage bands while we signed the papers. They glittered in the temple's smoky light. He spoke his "So I will" in a clear firm voice, and I as well, though my hand shook and my heart did its best to free itself of my chest and go merrily running toward the woods.

The priestess, her fingers quick and deft, wrapped the cord around my wrist, around his, tied the complex knot. "Bound in the sight of the gods, let nothing separate your hearts now. One in thought, one in word, one in deed; be honorable, honor each other and the gods will smile upon you." Her clear gray gaze searched first my face, then Tristan's. The Aryx glittered, power sparking from the serpent curves, its gemmed eyes winking as the metal writhed, tiny scales rasping cat-tongue at my dress. "By my hand and my vows, I pronounce you wed from this moment. Go forth happily, and may peace be with you."

"And also with you," I answered, Tristan's voice matching mine. It was strange to hear us speak in unison.

The priestess's fingers flicked again, freeing us. She took the cord to Jiserah's altar, up three steps. A copper brazier fumed there; she tossed the cord onto the coals. There was a brief burst of perfumed smoke, and Tristan d'Arcenne was my Consort, in the eyes of the gods and the law.

My knees threatened to give. Tristan steadied me. "There," he said quietly. "Was that so horrible?"

I bit back another shaky, relieved laugh. "I seem to be a coward." My fingers tightened in his. "Tristan, she spoke the old vows. I—"

"I wished it so. There are those who would say that I forced you into a contract to secure a hold on power. There are those who would—"

"I would not believe them," I interrupted.

He seemed almost to wince. "Then I am content. Gods grant me the strength to honor your trust from this moment." He glanced up, his forehead furrowed. "Where did she go?"

"I should beg your pardon," a woman's voice came from behind us, echoing down the columned hall. "I am late, I know, but there was a fevered sister, and I had to wait until someone could relieve me."

We turned to find a priestess of Jiserah hurrying down the central aisle, her green and white robes glimmering in the dim light. "I am Danae," she said, her round cheeks scarlet as she puffed. "*D'mselle, chivalier,* pardon me, and if you will just give me a moment, we shall have the ceremony."

"We already did. The priestess of Kimyan—" Then I realized the priestess had not given us her name. "The gray-eyed one. She was at the altar but a moment ago."

Danae stopped short, her robes shushing. She had a round, pleasant face, with laugh lines around her mouth and eyes. "Your pardon, *d'mselle.* But we have no priestesses of Kimyan here. We have not for two years. There are two priests for the Huntress—Shoyo and Dijirich—but they do not perform weddings. We have none of Torvar's Elect either."

"Then who—" I turned to gaze at the statue of Jiserah.

As I did, the Aryx sparked again, the serpents moving. The priestess gasped and fell to her knees, her face open and transported. Blazing, shocking in the dark torchlit gloom, the statue of Jiserah pulsed with light.

I did not kneel—my knees were now locked. The Aryx filled me, a rushing tide of melody prickling at my skin, as if I were a fruit bursting at the point of ripeness, light and song and power straining at the borders of my consciousness. The doors inside my head trembled on the verge of opening, I sought to look away, to deny the power rising in me.

No. Not now. Leave me in peace.

Tristan's arm fell from my shoulders. He sank to one knee, his face upturned. I knew this even though I dared not look, the light filling my vision. The statue glowed, scorched, sizzled, white marble running with life. Iron bands seized my skill, the brightness threatening me with the half-head—strong light is dangerous, it can trigger the pain swiftly.

As quickly as it had happened, though, it was gone. Welcome dimness returned to my dazzled vision, and the Aryx's melody quickly faded, draining away. I sighed and sagged, reached blindly for my Captain's shoulder. *What was that?*

"Tristan?" My voice was a pale shadow.

He rose slowly, his face tilted up to the statue of Jiserah, now mute and dark, only torchglow running over the marble. "Vianne." Hoarse and pale, drawn and sweating, he seemed awakened from a dream. Or a nightmare. "Do you doubt yourself, even now?"

I found I did not know how to answer.

"I…I am sorry. Your Majesty." The priestess rose behind us, I could hear her robes moving, cloth against cloth. "I think…" But she did not say *what* she thought, and I did not care to guess. "I did not know. Forgive me. I did not know you were—"

Oh, gods. This is the last straw the cart-horse can bear. "Not a word of this. I shall have your silence, *m'dama* priestess." I forced myself to turn away from the statue, chills roughening my skin into gooseflesh. "An it please you."

She was pale, her apple-cheeks now flour-white. And the way she gazed upon me was uncomfortable, for it was the same face I suspected she turned on the statue of her goddess during prayers. "But—but the goddess—that is a blessing, and you are the holder of—"

"No. Not a word. Your oath, *m'dama*." My tone took on an unwontedly hard edge. "Swear by your goddess, not a word of this."

She swore, finally, in a trembling voice, her gaze fixed on the Aryx, still shifting lazily against my chest. Tristan said nothing until she was finished.

"Do we ask for another wedding, then?" He took my hand. But his own fingers shook. However irreligious one may be in the whirl and glitter of Court, when the Blessed speak, 'tis wise to listen.

I did not know what this sudden light and strangeness meant. Later I would speak privately with this priestess, and discover what I could. For now, I simply wished to escape, backing away from the sense that a stricture had been laid on me, or that the gods had bent their gaze to earth and suddenly noticed the Seal they had gifted to Arquitaine was alive and in new hands.

Which brought me to the question of whether the gods had been paying attention to the King, his brother, and the tax farmers. And the bandit villages in the Shirlstrienne. And—

But my attention was called in a different direction. I rallied. "I suppose so. Though I might faint, if 'tis anything like the first." *Might? No. If that happens again, if the Aryx seeks to take charge of me again...but Tristan is here. Nothing can harm me if he is here.*

Such faith I had in him.

"Twice-vowed, bound all the more surely." Very quietly. "To be certain, Vianne."

I eyed the priestess of Jiserah, who was still chalk-pale. "*You do not intend to disappear as soon as the ceremony is over, do* you?" I sought for levity. After the fantastical, laughter serves to smooth the fabric of life.

She shook her head, gravely. Her hood fell back, her gray-threaded hair lying sleek-braided. "No, Your Majesty. I am merely a priestess, and an uncertain one at that. The gods have pronounced their will; I can only follow."

"Wise of you." Tristan mercifully did not sound as sarcastic as I suspected he wished to. "Let us continue, then, before I lose my courage."

The second ceremony was a little easier than the first. The priestess stumbled over some of the words, her eyes round as she watched the Aryx's slow shifting. When she tossed the silk cord onto the brazier, the same puff of perfumed smoke burst free. I waited, nervous, but the priestess came down the steps, turning back to the statue of Jiserah to genuflect quietly, murmuring an old prayer and pulling her hood up to cover her hair.

It was a relief when it was finally over. We thanked her, and Tristan let out a long, jagged breath. "Shall we leave, *m'chri?*"

"Before aught else happens? Absolutely." My voice was high and nervous now. I could not seem to take my accustomed tone. "There is a reason why I never went to Temple. Gods have a way of disarranging one." It was something Comtesse Rochburre might have said. "I have no desire to tarry."

I half-expected one of the statues to take me to task, but we escaped the Temple without mishap. Standing on the white stone steps, night gathering close, yet another shock awaited me. For when I raised my hand to greet the assembled people, I heard a cheer that fair threatened to shake the Temple off the mountainside.

The townspeople of Arcenne had gathered, drawn perhaps by the procession of armed nobles. Torches flared. The Aryx responded, shaking the air with a welter of melody. I waved, thinking of Lisele's Coming-of-Age and the crowds in the Citté d'Arquitaine, and the way their cries had blown the snapping silken banners away from the wind.

I had never thought to hear such a baying for me.

I have tied myself to this course even more securely. I glanced up at Tristan. He nodded, his blue eyes dark and thoughtful, spared me a smile that warmed me all the way down to my chilled bones. But he looked strained, and worried. *Nothing will ever be right again. Lisele is truly dead, and I am Queen of Arquitaine. Queen without a throne, with a murderous half-uncle nipping at my heels.*

I smiled, waving, and arranged my face so the sudden fear would not show. I had practice, after all—I merely wore my accustomed Court mask, and even though I had not had cause to do so for months, it still felt familiar. Not natural, but not strange either.

Tristan helped me to mount the white palfrey, who stood obediently flicking her tail. I lifted a hand as I had often seen the King do. The cheering was immense, I was newly wed, the Aryx was singing—but the weight of responsibility settled on me, grinding into my shoulders more heavily than duty had ever weighed. I did not have time to stop to wonder if the light from a god's statue was a blessing, a warning, or merely a symptom of the Aryx's wakefulness.

If I had wondered, I might have felt even more afraid.

THE QUEEN

THE QUEEN

Chapter Thirty-Two

I was glad to escape the usual wedding festivities; the ribald jests during supper, the escorting of the Consort to the lady's chamber, the shouting of highly improper jokes, the showing of the linens. Instead, there was a small, quiet sup with Tristan's parents in the Baron's study, papers to be looked over—dispatches from several provinces, information and declarations, my head hurt to think of it all. The Baron and Baroness drafting a proclamation—*whereas the Duc d'Orlaans in violation of all holy and common law murdered his brother, etc., the Aryx has chosen a new bearer, etc., Queen Vianne di Tirician-Trimestin di Rocancheil et Vintmorecy, formerly Duchesse Vianne di Rochacheil et Vintmorecy, escaped the Duc by the grace of the gods, so on, so forth, dear gods, has taken Tristan d'Arcenne as legal Consort, loyalty, all subjects loyal to the Crown freed from the burden of taxes to d'Orlaans's administration, so on, so forth, all aid and succor denied to d'Orlaans or his lieutenant, Garonne di Narborre.*

I would much rather have been composing Tiberian quatrains until a half-head struck me. And given the agony of the half-head, that rather says something.

I ate slowly, without much appetite, and drank enough straw-yellow wine to make the world spin slightly when Tristan finally rose to his feet and offered me his hand. "Vianne?"

I nodded; he steadied me as I gained my feet. I wore the slippers he had brought me, and Tristan himself had taken off his boots before supper. His own slippers were leather-soled, impervious to the stone.

"Do not worry," the Baroness said, patting my other hand. "Tomorrow will be easier, dear. I promise."

"I certainly pray so," I answered, my tongue strangely dull in my mouth. "I doubt I could stand another day like today."

"Wedded life is a trial, child." The Baroness's eyes all but sparkled. "Gods know how I have survived it."

The Baron made a slight sound, clicking his tongue against his teeth. "Do not frighten her, Sílvie. Tomorrow is soon enough for everything else. And may I say, Your Majesty, that I feared the worst before meeting you. I am far more sanguine about the future of Arquitaine than I have been since news of King Henri's untimely passing reached me."

I felt only weary surprise, and a great longing to settle my face against a pillow. "My thanks for the compliment, *sieur*." I was too weary to even think of making a courtesy, though I was sore tempted to give him a subtly cut-rate one. "If I manage to live up to your standards, I shall be none the worse for it."

That earned me a very startled, very blue glance from the Baron, who set his pen back in his inkwell. The Baroness laid her hand on his shoulder. She wore dark green velvet, her fair skin contrasting with the rich material in the mellow lamplight. Together, they were a beautiful painting—and the way her lips pursed told me she could barely contain merriment at my ill-tempered sally.

Tristan drew me out into the hall. "Well." He nodded to the guards, who both saluted him. "Tis the first time I have ever seen my father struck speechless."

"I do not wi—," I began, but he waved it away.

"No need, *m'chri*. He has ever been hard to please. When not well-nigh impossible." Tristan walked slowly enough that I was not breathlessly trotting beside him, and we threaded through corridors that did not feel familiar.

I shrugged, searching for something to say. My heart had taken to pounding again. I found a subject not likely to lead us into war or treachery, with a sigh of relief. "Among the R'mini, there would be music, and dancing, and drinking rhuma—but none for the Consort, he stays sober. Sometime during the dancing, the wedded pair would slip away, and pass their honey-night in a wagon, or under the stars."

Oh, dear. Perhaps this is not such a safe subject after all. My nerves were most definitely not steady enough for this.

Tristan's smile took me unawares. "You sound different when you speak of them, Vianne." He glanced down at my hand caught in his. I could not remember how we came to be walking, our fingers linked as if we courted. "Almost, dare I say it, happy."

An unfamiliar smile teased at my own mouth. "They were kind enough, and brave to a fault. If the Aryx were to go elsewhere, I think I might travel with them, would they have me."

"Why?" We reached the door of his chamber while I was still mulling the question. I halted, seeing no guards, and Tristan stopped too.

Could I explain? I thought on the question. "Because they did not want me to be other than I was. To them, I was V'na di R'mini Tosh Tozmil'hai Jan. That was enough. A poor R'mini hedgewitch…and yet twas better than Court, where every smile was a lie and every glance a danger." *Intrigue under every skirt, every glance a potential trap, and my Princesse to keep safe at all costs. Poor Lisele, she did try…but she could not see the venom under a honeyed word. The sweetness would blind her.*

He cupped my face in his callused hands. He seemed to be…trembling? Tristan d'Arcenne, the Captain of the Guard, shaking?

Twas a day for miracles at every turn.

He gazed down at me for a long moment, his jaw tight and his expression odd. "I would free you, Vianne. Or follow, wherever you led."

I bit my lip. *Would you? Or is this merely another way to serve the King, and a softer service than others you have been called upon for?* "Why?"

The question took him aback. He examined my face, his fingers warm against my cheeks. The trembling would not cease, it seemed. He stroked my jawline with his thumb. "Do you not know, even now? I am an utter fool for you, Your Majesty. I would give up my honor for you, and count the cost small."

I must tell him. My breath would not come smoothly. It seemed I could not fill my lungs. "I have never done this before, Tristan." I tried to speak firmly, but what came out was a frightened whisper.

Did that ease him? Or had his shaking infected me, so I could not feel his? "I know," he answered softly. "Or at least, I guessed. Else I might have had to fight a duel or two more, at Court. You noticed none of your admirers, *m'chri*, saving them from untimely doom. Wise of you, no?" He spoke lightly, but with a serious face. It won a shaky laugh from me. If he had taken any other tone, it might have made me weep. But instead, he kissed my forehead gently. "Come. A few more steps, tis all."

It was kind of him, to speak of other admirers. Still, there had been none—or none I could risk granting a glance to, since the danger of them seeking to compromise me for some dark reason involving Lisele's position had been too great for me to indulge myself.

I have a duty too, Tristan. Perhaps we are locked into a pair of duties, like two cart wheels, and we shall never truly touch. I let him lead me into his chambers. He locked the door behind us. I stood just inside the door, my arms crossed, cupping my elbows in my palms. My nervousness demanded I speak further. "Truly. I have never done this before. I never found a man I would share myself with before, or a man who would not seek to use me."

He flinched, and I wondered at that. But his voice was steady and calm. "I would not hurt you, Vianne. Or frighten you."

The only light was from the fire and two candles, a low glow that was kind to his sharp face. "I am not frightened." *I merely do not wish to fail at this. I can turn aside a man's interest with a pretty word and play the game of courtsongs, but this is something different.*

This is something more, for all I suspect you of serving a dead King with it.

He approached me cautiously, folded me in his arms, rested his chin atop my head. "Shhh, *m'chri*," he whispered, soothing. "I would not touch you until you are ready. I do not wish your fear of me."

"Fear you?" Sudden laughter seized me. I swallowed it. "No, of course not. I am simply new to this. Be gentle."

"As gentle as I can, as always, for you."

I stepped away, freeing myself from his embrace. He stood, hands fallen to his sides, watching me intently.

This may be battlechess, and you are required to sacrifice. Think of it that way.

Yet I did not wish to.

I took his hand and led him to the bed. I stood for a long moment, undecided, before I turned and looked down at his swordbelt.

It took a little tugging, but my clumsy fingers finally undid the belt. He took his sword, leaned it against the night table, and I started to unlace the throat of his shirt, my fingers gradually stopping their shaking. As long as I focused on the problem of laces, I could ignore what loomed afterward.

He, in his turn, simply stood still, frozen. I glanced up at him. "Are you…?" I could not ask if he were *well*. Was this disagreeable to him?

He was pale. His forehead was damp. "If you knew," he said softly, "how many times I…wished for this, you would laugh at me."

The knot inside my chest eased all at once. "Hm." I concentrated on the unlacing, slowly. "I do not think I would laugh, *m'cher*." The endearment felt natural. "This might go a trifle easier if you kissed me, Tristan."

The moment I said it, I could not believe something so forward had left my mouth.

"It might." His blue gaze fixed on my face, as if I were the north star and him a traveler setting his course. "But then you would close your eyes, Vianne, and I might miss seeing them."

"You have developed a courtsinging tongue." I freed the laces of his shirt, finally, and he stripped it off over his head. Muscle moved under his skin, and scars striped along his ribs—battle scars, dueling scars. There were two fresh-reddened ones, and I flattened my hand along them, carefully, marveling at the feel of his skin, so different from mine. He leaned in to my touch. I bit my lip, thinking of the wounds. "Where did you gain these, *chivalier*?"

"I cannot remember," he said hoarsely. "Vianne."

"Well." I looked up at him, my fingers still on his skin. He seemed vulnerable without his sword and his shirt, and of a sudden I was no longer so uncertain. "Help me unlace my dress, then."

He did, and when the dress was half unlaced, falling from my shoulders, he slid the ribbon from my braid and ran his fingers through my hair until it fell over my shoulders. "Gods—," he said, and I let the dress fall.

I am a coward. Please, gods, please. Do not let me fail at this.

His mouth met mine, his hands working to free himself from his breeches, and I laughed. I could not help myself, we were both shaking, and he kissed me blindly, desperately. The sound I made, laughing while he kissed me, made it even more nervously amusing, until his hands closed around my bare shoulders. I gasped, taking a mouthful of air flavored with his breath. Then, just as with the kiss, it seemed the knowledge of what would happen sprang into my body. I had heard ribald songs and seen lovers before, but it seemed so different—perhaps because I was now one-half of a whole, perhaps because Tristan kept breathlessly repeating my name, perhaps because I cried out when I lost the title of maid. Or perhaps it only seemed different because I finally understood why lovers chose dark corners, and why they were blind to all else during their love.

He was not as gentle as he could have been, but I did not

complain, for he shook with need. Little broken phrases came out of him, endearments, while I simply closed my eyes and gave myself up to him. When he finally shuddered to a stop in my arms, I held him and whispered soothing nonsense in his ear until he slid away to the side and took me in his arms, printing kisses over my face.

Well, so that is what they mean. A great weariness settled on me.

"Vianne," he whispered against my cheeks, my throat, my breasts. The Aryx pulsed under his touch, its silent song taking on a new depth.

I let out a long breath. Twas irrevocable. Tristan d'Arcenne was my Consort. *Gods grant it does not kill him.*

He finally lay still, my leg over his, my head on his shoulder, his arm under my head, his other hand stroking my shoulder, my hair tangled over the pillow. I sighed, and his fingers paused, continued.

"Are you well?" he finally asked, and I wondered if he was as uncertain now as I had been before.

"I am well," I assured him, tracing my finger up his ribs. He took in a sharp breath, tensing. "My thanks, *chivalier.*"

"Surely we are past formality." He caught my wrist, bringing my palm to his mouth, pressing a kiss against my skin. I would be sore tomorrow, and my thighs were sticky. I wanted a bath—but not just yet. Not while he held me so closely. "I am sorry, Vianne. I was not gentle enough."

I shrugged, moving my cheek against his shoulder. "I expected little else." I wondered why Alisaar was so worshipped, if this was all love was.

"The second time is better, I've heard," he said against my palm, causing a shiver through my entire body.

"Is it?" I asked curiously, and he laughed.

"Much. Speak to me, Vianne. Tell me what is in that marvelously sharp brain of yours."

I sighed again. "I am thinking that I am lucky, and this is a dream. And any moment I will wake at Court, in my own bed—or in a R'mini wagon, bumping through the wilderness."

"No dream." He kissed my palm yet again.

"'Tis merely a feeling." I touched his lips with my fingertips, marveling afresh at the feel of his skin. In the dark, it was easier to speak to him. "I was lost without you, Tristan."

"I will never leave your side again." His voice shook.

Were his cheeks damp? I brushed them, wondering if this was part of the event. "'Tis well. For I must confess I had not an idea of what to do once I lost your guidance. I wish I could give you the Aryx." My eyes closed, heavy as lead.

He shuddered as if stung. "I would make a terrible King, Vianne. I know this."

Whatever reply I would have made was lost, for I fell into slumber in his arms.

In the darkest region of the night, I woke, screaming, struggling against Tristan's hands. "No! *No!* Lisele! *Do not!*"

"Vianne!" He caught my wrists, held me, kissed my temple, I collapsed against him. "Hush, Vianne. I am here. Gods above, how did you bear it?"

It seemed I would never reach the end of weeping, not even as he kissed me, my forehead, my cheek, and finally my mouth. He kept repeating, over and over, that he was sorry, that he was here, and that I had nothing to fear. He took his time, gently, until the terror of the dream faded, replaced by the reality of Tristan d'Arcenne. His skin against mine, his hands sliding up my arms, cupping my face, his thumbs wiping away my tears.

It was the only defense against my despair, and I took it, grateful he was there to give. In his arms I could forget, however fleetingly.

And he was right—it was far better the second time.

Chapter Thirty-Three

Adrien di Cinfiliet returned a fortnight after my wedding, bringing dispatches from the road and the news that all was quiet. His small band of dusty, weary men had harried di Narborre forth from Arcenne, but I knew better than to hope the Duc's dog gone for good.

Jierre di Yspres brought the news of Adrien's return while I was at chai with the Baroness, and I hurriedly excused myself. Adersahl, who had accompanied me to chai in Tristan's stead—since the Baron had wished his son's attendance at a drilling of the Citadel Guard—paced at my side as I found my way down to the stables, a seething mass of activity.

I saw Adrien, his head bent together with a slim dark man—one of his bandits, I surmised, for he looked passing familiar and had the gaunt fierceness of all di Cinfiliet's *chivalieri.* Tristan had told me some of the Arcenne nobles asked to ride with Adrien on his border patrols, and there was even a song in the lower quarters of the city, extolling his almost-suicidal bravery against di Narborre and the men hoping to bear the Duc's authority as King into the province. It seemed a brutal business, cat-and-mouse ambush, but at least di Narborre had not wanted to stay in Arcenne.

It was a long way from the Citté, and di Narborre's numbers were too few.

"Adrien!" His name bolted free, and the high note of a woman's voice cut through the confusion of men's cries. Di Cinfiliet straightened, pushing his ragged hair back from his silvery eyes, and a hot bolt of shame lanced me.

"My lady Riddlesharp," he said as I reached him, giving the man at his side a nod. The bandit bowed his head and disappeared, and Adrien's dusty horse whickered. "I hear you braved the Alpeis without me."

His tone—informal, easy, yet not mocking—brought me to a halt just outside his horse's stall. A stable boy pushed past me with a murmured apology, tugging his forelock. The heat-haze reek of horses rose thick to my nose.

"I did indeed, though I would rather not have. Tis good to see you, I thought—" My throat did not seem to be working properly. "You look weary," I finished lamely. "I will not trouble you further until you have had lee to rest and break your fast. Do they treat you well here? What news? Are you well?" *Risaine*, I wanted to say. *I beg your pardon, noble bandit, and I fear you will not give it.*

His face changed, his lips thinning. Dust clung in his hair, and instead of the brown and green of the Shirlstrienne he wore plain, serviceable cloth, doublet and shirt and breeches, good boots that had seen hard use. Still, his hair was indifferently trimmed, and the weather had darkened his skin still further. "They treat me well enough; I am out riding the country more often than not. Arcenne holds its breath before the plunge." His eyes flicked past my shoulder, perhaps at Adersahl, who had flattened himself against one stall door, staying out of the way. He had regained some little of his bulk, had di Parmecy, though the former glory of his mustache was missing. "I sent the dispatches up to the Baron. Tis a wonder any of the northern ones came through, the land is thick with d'Orlaans's spies and dragoons."

There was a fey gleam to his light eyes I did not know if I liked. Had I not been so quick at reading glances at Court, I might have missed the flash of sullen anger crossing his countenance.

"I am passing glad to see you." *Vianne, you idiot, he needs a bath and a good meal. He is thin as a Seivillia rapier.* "I shall leave you to it, and speak with you anon."

He caught my arm as I turned. "I would have audience with you, Vianne. But privately. There is summat I would say to you not meant for prying ears."

My heart leapt to my throat. *Risaine.* "Of course. Have them bring you to my study in the West Tower when you are ready. I..." The words rose in my throat, were denied, and fell away. "I crave your pardon, *sieur* Adrien di Cinfiliet, and I would beg for it without prying ears as well."

He released me, a faint gleam of surprise entering his gaze, and I turned away. Adersahl caught my elbow to maneuver me through the now-orderly confusion of horses being unsaddled and cared for. They had all seen hard use, it was evident, and were coated with road dust.

We left the stables, turning to the right, and Adersahl stopped as I did when we rounded the corner. The main bailey was full of echoes, and I leaned against warm white stone, turning my face up to sunlight reflecting from the pale wall towering opposite.

"*D'mselle*?" Adersahl sounded uncertain.

"A moment, an it please you." My voice was thick. "I merely need a moment to recollect myself."

He stood silently aside, as the noise inside the stables died down and Adrien's men trooped off to the barracks set aside for their use. I closed my eyes, feeling my pulse in my throat and wrists. The Aryx sang, rippling under the Sun's welcome gaze.

My shoulders came up, I opened my eyes, and I stepped back into the wagon traces of my duty. Adersahl said nothing as we wended our way back, for which I was grateful indeed.

The afternoon kept me occupied with plenty of work, the dispatches to be read—news was still not complete enough for my taste, and the country was in a roil. At least *some* news was reaching us, mostly from Tristan's network of informers left over from his days as the King's Left Hand. A cadre of sturdy Arcenne peasants had dispersed through the border provinces to spread our own news, and sent back by hook or crook such things as might be useful. In some of the provinces—Siguerre directly to the west, and Markui to the south, as well as Dienjuste with its fertile fields—the lords had declared themselves openly against d'Orlaans, and all manner of correspondence flooded in from them. The post service was also so far uninterrupted, which was all to the good. Whoever the Duc had appointed as Minister for that department had not tightened his grip sufficiently to cease deliveries to restive provinces.

Twas enough to make one's head spin. That afternoon also saw the arrival of the cranky old Conte Siguerre, who looked me over and snorted something a trifle impolitic at seeing the Aryx against my chest on its chain. Yet the Baron recommended him, and once I had exchanged words with the hatchet-nosed man I could see why. He was disagreeable, true, but under that crust lay a mind both fine and loyal. As the beginning of my Queen's Council, with Perseval d'Arcenne, he would do very well indeed.

I collapsed into a chair after he and the Baron had trundled off to dinner, rubbing at my temples. "*Lock* the door. As you love me, Tris, if I must listen to one more—"

Tristan shot the bolt on the study door, but he smiled. "My mother will wish to see you for dinner. And you gave a good accounting of yourself, *m'chri*. I have rarely seen Siguerre's temper so sweetened."

"Dear gods, you mean he had put his best boot forward?" I rubbed harder at my temples, seeking to dispel the headache. Twas not a half-head, but painful nevertheless. "I never dreamed this would be so *disagreeable*. Dispatches, proclamations, drafts, plans—I swear I shall throw the next set of papers out the window. Where does one *find* all this paper? Tis a wonder the forests are still standing!"

He crossed the comfortable, cluttered study, his blue eyes alight, and leaned over the chair to kiss me. Miraculously, the headache had abated by the time his mouth pulled away from mine. "At least there is an antidote," he murmured. "Think of the maying bonfire we could build of all this."

"Hm." My hand crept up to slide behind his nape, his shorn hair growing out fast. "Give me the antidote again, *m'cher*, and we shall see. The maying is a whole winter away."

"Always so bound by propriety—"

But I had pulled his mouth back down to mine, and the world once again stopped its course.

Until there was a knock at the door.

I groaned, and Tristan sighed. "Probably someone sent to

fetch you to dinner. *Mère* says she hardly sees you." He kissed my forehead, stroked my cheek, and strode to the door as I pulled myself upright, smoothing back a strand of hair that had come loose from my braids. Twas such a relief to be able to dress my hair properly again; the braids in the style of di Rocacheil suited me.

Tristan pulled the door open.

Alerted by the sudden silence, I took two steps forward, enough to see Adrien di Cinfiliet enter as Tristan stood aside. He had bathed, and his rough-trimmed hair was not quite so shaggy. His gaze swept the room and lighted on me, and again my throat sought to close.

"Adrien." I sounded breathless. "Yes. I beg your pardon for the door; we just finished a very disagreeable meeting."

His sudden smile did wonders for his lean face, and I saw another resemblance there. It gave me pause, my brain suddenly making a connection it had been struggling with for months.

He did not merely look of Risaine's family. He looked so much like her it took the breath away, especially when his entire face shone with that smile. He also looked very much like a certain hawknosed, gray-ringleted, now-dead man—though *that* man would not have suffered the weather to darken his skin so.

Well, of course. And I am a silly little fool not to have seen it sooner, though I did suspect. Relief and fresh shame rose in my chest, and I smoothed my skirts with my hands. "Tristan, an it please you, attend your mother. Convey my regrets for my lateness. Tell her I shall be along to dine with her as soon as I may, but not to wait on my account."

Tristan paused, his eyes darkening, and his gaze snapped to Adrien. Who calmly returned his glance, with no trace of the smile he had worn just a moment ago.

I opened my mouth to explain—*I owe this man an apology, and I would give it privately*—but Tristan nodded curtly, one hand on his swordhilt. "As you will it, Vianne." The faint emphasis on my name sounded so intimate I could have blushed, were I not so suddenly puzzled. "*I* shall wait for you. *Sieur.*" He gave di Cinfiliet a short nod and was gone, sweeping the door to with a leashed, precise little click.

What was that? Did I not know better, I would think him jealous. The notion was driven out of my head by Adrien's sigh as he dropped into a chair. "Your pardon, my lady Riddlesharp, but I am weary to the bone." His tone was light enough, but the glint in his eye gave me pause.

"It is no matter." I gathered my courage, my hands clasping before me. "*Sieur…*" It sounded bloodless, so I began again. "Adrien. I would beg your pardon. I am sorry for your loss."

Beyond the casements, the Sun sank red in the sky, painting half di Cinfiliet's face with the glow. "You mean Risaine." His gaze focused past me, sightless, to the shelves of books and the two swords hanging crossed over the mantel. "Yours was not the hand that performed that deed. Though I…I thank you, for your concern."

His throat sounded as full as mine. I looked at the scattered paper on the top of the long table we had used this afternoon. An empty winecup from the afternoon's meeting pointed its blind bowl at me. "Had we not sheltered so long with you, it might not have happened. I…I should have insisted we leave." *There, I have said it.*

Leather creaked as he moved, and he sighed. "You have enough to carry, *d'mselle*. Do not carry this. The fault is mine. I should have sent her south a half-year ago; there is an estate in

Navarrin that would have welcomed her. In truth, I did not because I could not bear to be without her. She is—*was*—all my family."

I felt his gaze on me, and lifted my own. One of his eyebrows had lifted slightly, and his mouth was a grimace of bitter pain. Oddly enough, the resemblance to King Henri was more marked when his features turned themselves graven, despite my never having seen the King bear such an expression.

I took my courage in both hands. "Not all your family. We share some blood, you and I."

"So you've guessed."

"I have." *And this is welcome news to me, in more ways than one. You cannot imagine how welcome.* "I am proud to claim you as kin, Adrien. It will not balance out the wrong done you, but—"

"I will balance those scales soon enough, and in my own way." He pushed himself to his feet, restlessly. "Di Narborre will feel my steel in his gullet before this matter reaches its end. Tis not what I meant to speak of, though."

He strode to the window as my heart eased its frantic thumping. "Oh." I sounded blank. "I must confess, I have thought of little else all day. Of the wrong done you and my part in it."

"You had no part in that wrong. Do not seek to take any." He made a slight dismissive movement, halting at the casement. With the bloody light behind him, his hair took on russet tones. "My offer still stands, *m'cousine*. If I may be so bold."

Tears sprang hot to my eyes, prickling. "You may." I cast about for a kerchief, found none, and wondered if I could clear my nose on a dispatch. It would certainly express my sentiment toward such things. "You may, *m'cousin*. I think together we shall deal extremely well."

"Perhaps. If we may trust each other. I am a backwoods bandit, and you a noble lady."

I rubbed my hands together briskly. "I think we may trust each other as far as kin, Adrien—and we are kin in a very particular way. D'Orlaans is no longer the only alternative for Arquitaine." The immensity of my own forthrightness almost shocked me. "You would hardly be half as intelligent as I suspect you to be, had you not already thought of this." *In other words, if you harbor an ambition, be plain with it. Gods willing, the Aryx may see you as far more fit than me.*

If it caught him off his guard, he did not show it. "That gaud at your neck does not concern me. If I wanted more, I would *have* it. I would have braved the Citté and done it as a nobleman. It suited me to stay in the Shirlstrienne, my lady Riddlesharp, and while we are kin—and I glad of it, I would add—I would not wish the burden of that *thing*." His lip curled, but only briefly. "Besides, as your Captain pointed out, if that bit of sorcery-soaked metal sought my company, twould have had it and to spare by now."

So, Tristan has discussed this with you. Interesting. What else have you said to each other, the Captain and the bandit? Silence filled the room, though the papers on the table stirred uneasily under a wind from nowhere. I found myself clutching the Aryx, digging my fingernails under it, but the obstinate thing refused to budge. Even with Adrien in the room, it would not loose its grip on me. It seemed fused to my dress instead of my flesh, and the uncomfortable idea that if I tore at the fabric the Seal would merely take advantage of it to sink into my skin was enough to make me queasy.

"You see?" Adrien sounded bitterly unsurprised. "Tis yours, and I am no di Narborre, to kill a woman. Do not insult me, *m'cousine.* I will brook it from you, but I would rather not."

I uncramped my fingers with an effort. My throat was dry. "I mean no insult."

He relaxed, much as a cat will suddenly sink into sleeping. "I know. Nor do I. I have not the pretty manners of your Guard."

"Manners may cover many faults, *sieur* bandit. You, at least, are honest. Or honest enough."

He caught my levity and grimaced good-naturedly. "Small compliment you pay me, *m'cousine.* Now that we are in accord, I would speak on other things." Another broad, wolfish smile, so genuinely amused I could not help returning it.

"As you like." I wished I could lean against the table or a chair, to bolster my knees. They were decidedly unsteady.

"I do not think it safe here for you, Vianne." Another mercurial change—his tone was deadly level, and his face had lost all trace of amusement. "D'Orlaans has been suspiciously quiet, and I hear fragments that make me uneasy. I hear of foreigners in general and Damarsene in particular. He may seek to bring their fine army to Arquitaine, and if that happens…"

If that happens the land will run with blood, Aryx or no. The strength ran out of my legs and I sat down, *hard*, in a happily convenient chair. My wits raced. "He would not risk it. No man who means to hold Arquitaine as a King would risk that. We cannot fight d'Orlaans and the Damarsene at the same time, no matter how the Baron rattles his sword. It would be madness. The entire country will tear itself apart." Breathless, I halted.

But you may not be dealing with an opponent who cares for the damage to what he sees as his possession, Vianne. Some men will mar a thing so no other may hold it, and count the cost small. I swallowed dryly, glanced longingly at the empty wineglass. A draught would certainly bolster me now.

Adrien shrugged, a supple movement. "Still. It does not strike me that d'Orlaans would balk at more blood, having already spilled his share and more. In any case, he may contract corps of mercenaries to fill his ranks, and think of paying for such an act much later, when his grasp on power is secure."

When I am dead or force-wedded to him, you mean. And I had not thought of it in *that* fashion. "Dear gods."

"I would not worry just yet. As you say, it is madness. Yet the mere thought makes me uneasy." He turned from the window to face me, his silvery eyes glowing as the Sun's dying bloodied the entire casement, gilding his hair and the buckle on the leather bowstrap crossing his chest. "Should the situation become dire, I stand ready—and every man who owes allegiance to me, few as they are, stands ready as well—to take you over the border into Navarrin. There, at least, you will not be in danger of losing your life in a fool's gambit."

It was good I was already in the chair, for I could not feel my legs. My hands also seemed numb. "I thank you for the offer, m'cousin. But Tristan…I do not think I could flee without him." *And taking the Aryx from the borders of Arquitaine…who can tell what may happen, if I perform such a feat?*

Would I even survive the experience? The Seal has never left the land since the Angoulême received it from the joined hands of Danshar and Jiserah. Or so the legends say.

Adrien shrugged. "Ah, well. He is welcome to come along. If he prizes you as he should, it will not give him much pause to place your safety above his own games." He folded his arms. "I leave as soon as dark truly falls. There is still work to be done outside the walls, and di Narborre to watch for."

"You will not tarry? I would speak more with you, Adrien." *And I would hear you speak more of Tristan. What ill will do you bear him?* "I like not the idea of losing a cousin so soon after finding him."

"'Tis safer for me among my men, especially if your Captain has guessed my blood. I do not put it past him to consider me a threat." His half-smile chilled me a little, and I could not find the words to protest. Still, I made a soft, inarticulate sound, and he shook his dark head. "Soft, lady Riddlesharp. I do not speak against his honor. I would not, to save you discomfort." He studied me as shadow deepened in the casement, and I heard the bell clang sharply in the South Tower as the changing of the Guard was announced.

He was much taller than I and spare of frame, but I hazarded that in a certain light I might bear a small resemblance to him. At least, I hoped so.

"I do not like it." My voice startled me, I spoke as if in a dream. "Each toss of the dice worsens this game."

"You are still alive." He left the window, his boots clicking on the stone floor. "I shall take my leave of you now. If you need aught, send for me. I shall keep scouts waiting for your word."

I nodded. "I will send for you, or await your next visit. Take care with yourself, Adrien." If I could have made my legs work, I would have forced myself to my feet to perhaps embrace him, as improper as that might be. Still, my heart ached.

"And you, with your sharp wits. Take care yourself." He gave me a Court bow, and I was startled into a thin little laugh.

"You do that as if you were born to it."

His smile surfaced, then just as quickly was lost as he glanced to the door. "I was, was I not? And so were you. Between us we shall find a way, Vianne. I have no doubt of it."

With that he left, without looking back. The door closed and I heard his footsteps, reached blindly up to feel the hot salt water on my cheeks. I smoothed the tears away, over and over again, wishing I had a kerchief in my skirt-pocket.

You cannot let him leave thus. The thought spurred me and I rose on numb feet, held to the table for a moment to brace myself. *You must say something else, Vianne. Something kind, perhaps. He is all the kin you have left, no matter how tenuous the connection. At the very least give him something.*

My fingers crept from my tear-wet cheek to my ear, where a familiar weight dangled.

My emerald ear-drops.

I ran for the door.

Chapter Thirty-Four

I ran on slippered feet, took a wrong turn at the end of the hall. No Guard stood outside my door, for Sílvie's sitting room was merely down a winding stair and along a pleasant garden path from the study. I doubled back, noiseless except for the swishing of my skirt, and took another set of stairs—those leading to a gallery that would take me to the bailey—in a rush. I heard voices ahead and ran down a torchlit hall, slowing as I approached the open arch to the gallery and stopping short, for the tones had turned harsh.

Court-bred instinct froze me on one side of the arch, and I peered around it to see the gallery, brightly lit with a reflected sunset, and three men in a tableau that made my breath catch.

Jierre di Yspres stood in quarter-profile to me, his hand resting on his swordhilt and his entire posture betraying tension. Yet that was not what made me draw back into shadow, sensing danger.

Tristan d'Arcenne faced Adrien di Cinfiliet in the gallery. I could not see his face, for it was shadowed, but the gleam of his eyes was soft and deadly. Soft and deadly too was his tone, the quiet perilous voice that turned my hands cold.

"You and I shall come to a disagreement someday, bandit."
He did not move, and the fading light fled even faster from the
chill in his voice.

"Is that so." Adrien's shoulders were tense, yet his tone was
calm, without its usual mocking edge. I breathed out softly in
relief, but caught myself anew when he continued. "Not today,
then?"

"I would not stain my honor by dueling a man who has
none." The words were clipped, the cut direct. My hands turned
to fists, rubbing against the velvet of my skirts. I had drawn
back, instinctively seeking the deepest shadow, the same instinct
warning me to stay unseen. It was as if I were in the passage
again, my skirts held back and the Minister Primus choking.

Adrien was silent for a long moment, and the sharp unsmell
of violence drifted in the gallery's warm air. The pops and crack-
les of a building settling itself for the night began to tick softly,
and I wondered if I should step through the arch, cough, or
make some noise to distract them, and avert the brewing storm.
I peered into deepening gloom, the Sun having fled, full dusk
settling in the sky. Glowlamps hung along the gallery began to
diffuse their light, but it would take an hour for them to reach
full strength.

"What honor do you have left, *Captain*? And if you challenge me to a duel, there is a dark-eyed lady who will not think
kindly of it." The suddenly-regained mockery in Adrien's voice
took my breath away. I leaned against the wall, my hot forehead
longing for the touch of cool stone.

Tristan's reply was not mocking. Instead, it was quiet, conciliatory, and utterly dangerous. "Go carefully, di Cinfiliet. If you
threaten her—or if it seems likely to me that you will—*I will not
hesitate*."

Adrien's laugh was a knife to the chest. "I am no threat to her, *vilhain*. You would do well to be cautious yourself. You are not such a secret to me as you are to our *d'mselle*." He laid particular stress on the *our*, and pushed past Tristan, their shoulders striking. "Besides," he said as he walked away, his bootheels clicking, "I look forward to the day all is revealed."

He vanished into the darkness at the other end of the gallery. There was a soft sound as the door to the bailey opened, his gaunt figure silhouetted for a moment against the purple dusk outside.

Jierre relaxed a trifle, his shoulders dropping. I drew back further, behind the arch, and prayed they would not notice me.

"It can be arranged," di Yspres said after a long silence. "Captain?"

What can be arranged? Are you asking what I think you are, Lieutenant? Another long pause. My heart was bitter in my throat. *Be logical, Vianne. They do not like each other at all. Yet there is somewhat else here. What am I to think of this? I am spying in a corner, and I do not know what occurred before I came along.*

It could not have been much; I had run to catch Adrien. What had I missed?

"He is useful enough." Tristan's tone had taken back some of its wonted warmth. He did not sound so furious now. "For now. Our concern is d'Orlaans, not a backwoods bandit."

"The Queen?" I heard faint sounds, their boots on stone. Were they coming toward me, or away?

"She has worries enough." Now Tristan sounded heavy, and weary. "I would not add one more."

Are they coming toward me, or going away? Please, gods. The Aryx cooled against my skin, its muted song threading through my head. I reached up, clutching at the Seal and the velvet of my bodice, one hard supple curve against my thumb.

"I do not think she will break," Jierre said.

Away. They were moving away. I slumped against the wall. Tristan's reply was almost too far away to be distinguished, but I strained my ears.

"She may not break, but I would shield her from all I can. Come, I am due at dinner."

I stood there trembling, the chill of stone seeping through my dress. Copper filled my mouth.

I must take care to keep them apart. For if the man I loved and my only remaining kin came to blows, what would I do? True, I had just discovered my kinship with Adrien, and I could not weigh him against my Consort.

Still, they had both sheltered me, in their fashion.

I would shield her from all I can. The words made my heart turn warm and soft inside my chest. Men flung harsh words at each other sometimes, and they were both weary and strained.

You are not such a mystery to me as you are to our d'mselle.

It meant little, for Tristan was not a mystery to me. Or if he was, he was the mystery of a man I wished to spend my life decoding. He was my *Consort.*

All the same, I wished the Aryx had chosen Adrien. If I let it take me, if I wandered through those doors of sorcery, could I find the one that would teach me how to shift this burden from my shoulders?

And onto his? You would wish this on anyone?

Perhaps not, but certainly he was better fit for it. Why the Seal persisted in this folly was beyond me.

I gathered myself as best I could and retraced my route to the turning that would take me to Sílvie's sitting room. I could not speak of this, and there would be no need to, as I suspected Tristan would not, either. I would merely resolve to keep him and Adrien separated. It should not be too hard.

An uncomfortable thought remained. Were I called to intervene, I suspected I would choose my Captain. I had lived without kin before.

I did not wish to live without my Consort.

I was right. Two weeks passed, and Tristan made no mention of Adrien. I was glad of it, and held my own peace.

Chapter Thirty-Five

The door flung itself open, banging against the wall with a violence that gave my heart an ugly shock. Jierre di Yspres strode into the room, a scroll clutched in his fist. "Your Majesty. News."

"Dear *gods*. What?" I gained my feet, paper shuffling on the tabletop. Tristan's hand eased itself from his swordhilt, and I noticed how he was suddenly between me and the door. How quickly had he moved to set himself there?

"A message." Jierre strode grimly through a square of sunlight from the open window. Tristan's father had offered me the use of Arcenne's library, a pleasant book-walled room that looked out onto the garden, once it became apparent the study was far too small. I was glad of it, for every day seemed filled with nothing but paper and unpleasantness—dispatches, reports, decisions to make, Councils to attend. It was small wonder the King had only rarely attended to his daughter—if he had been choked with this much paperwork I did not much blame him. "From the traitor himself, *d'mselle*, and addressed to you."

What now? At least tis a scroll and not an army. I took the offending article with numb fingers and looked at Tristan. "I think your father had better hear of this."

"Aye. Take word to my father, Jierre. Tell him to bring who he sees fit. Where is the one who brought this?" Tristan's eyes were hard and cold as late-winter frost.

"A Messenger. Held under Guard, awaiting the Queen's pleasure." Jierre's eyes were as cold as Tristan's.

"Offer him no violence. Be as courteous as you can; I shall wish to speak to him." I held di Yspres's gaze for a few moments, measuring him. "Feed him, stable his horse, and tell him he will spend the night at our hospitality. Not one hair of his head is to be harmed, di Yspres, but keep him under guard."

"Aye, Your Majesty." He assented with a small bow.

I looked at the scroll thrust into my hands while Jierre saluted and ran for the door again. It was tightly wound, sealed with red wax bearing the imprint of the Lesser Seal, two serpents twined in a dagger, with d'Orlaan's personal device below it—another serpent, crowned.

I broke the seal, cracking the red wax.

"Vianne?" Tristan's hand rested on his swordhilt. "It may hold some unpleasantness."

I would smell a killspell strong enough to anchor itself to parchment, my darling. I did not say it, contenting myself with misunderstanding him. "Tis said to be for me. I might as well read it." I unrolled it, the crackle of parchment oddly loud in the hush.

It was written in a fair, clear script, in archaic High Arquitaine.

To Our Best-Beloved Niece and Best-Beloved lady of the Realm of Arquitaine, Duchesse-Royale Vianne di Tirecian-

Trimestin di Rocancheil et Vintmorecy, Our greetings and most perfect love.

We have received an ill-considered proclamation, in which the lies of rebels have been spread, purporting to come from your mouth. We say unto you that We do not believe you would in truth flee the justice of the King of Arquitaine. The murderous regicide Tristan d'Arcenne hath kidnapped you and forced you to his will in an alliance most unwise. Therefore We say unto you, We demand your release from the treachery of Arcenne and your safe transport to Our Capital, where We shall welcome you as Best-Beloved Consort. The fury of Our anger will be unleashed upon the traitors of Arcenne unless your merciful intercession spares their lives. Your release is demanded immediately and your presence in the Citté d'Arquitaine is requested no later than the third day of the fourth month of the Year of the Stag.

By Our hand, bearing great love for you, signed and sealed, His Majesty Timrothe Alonsin di Tirecian-Trimestin, Duc d'Orlaans, Comte di Tavrothe, Marquis di—

I did not go through the list of pointless titles. "Well. He must think I am very stupid."

I handed the parchment to Tristan, whose eyes had not moved from my face the entire time. He scanned it, twice, then flung it down on the table with far more violence than necessary.

I did not flinch. I had thought perhaps this would displease him.

"He addresses you thus, knowing you have a Consort," he said through rage-gritted teeth. He was pale, and his eyes blazed.

I smoothed my skirts—pale green watered silk, cut to my measure by the Baroness's eagle-eyed dressmaker; it was a never-ending relief to be clothed properly—and took measure of my Consort.

I had never seen him this livid. His eyes flamed blue, his jaw seemed made of steel, and the air around him swirled with tension.

"He cannot afford to acknowledge that I took you as a Consort of my own free will," I pointed out. "And now he knows where the Aryx is, and how it came to me. I wonder if he truly thinks you hold me against my will."

Tristan paled. Two fever spots of color burned high on his whitened cheeks. "He has dared insult me for the last time, Vianne. I swear by the gods I will—"

"*Tristan!*" I am not ashamed to report that I yelled. He stopped short, staring at me, his eyes infernos of chill blue. "Tristan, *m'cher*, my darling, *please*. Halt your tongue before you utter an ill-considered oath."

I think it was the first time I dared to say anything of the sort to him.

Amazingly, he shut his mouth with a snap. Nodded, once. His fingers wrapped so tightly around his swordhilt I could almost feel the bloodless aching in my own hand.

I heard a slight cough outside the door—one of the Guard. From the open window came a breath of sound—shouting from the practice-ground, the clash and clatter of an afternoon weapons-drill. An idea struck me. "Does it occur to you, *m'cher*, that this missive is not necessarily sent to entice me back to the Citté, but to drive you into a rage? He must know that I saw the carnage in Lisele's rooms, though he may not know you were with me when the trap sprang, and therefore I have proof of your innocence."

Tristan started, almost as if struck, but I looked down at the table, lost in thought. "I think tis likely he considers me a pawn and you his real opponent." I studied the scroll, lying innocently on the table over a pile of dispatches from the Baron di Timchaine, Arcenne's neighbor shared with Siguerre. "If he ever guessed at Court you had any regard for me—"

Tristan drew in a deep breath. "It seems your open secret was royal blood, and mine was my regard for you. I thought I kept it well hidden, Vianne. I sought not to let it be used against either of us."

"Very well indeed, since I had no idea." I still contemplated the scroll. *Calm him, Vianne.* "Why on earth did you dance with me, Tristan? I have often wondered."

"I could not stay away." His hand eased from his swordhilt. "At Lisele's Coming-of-Age—you wore the red velvet. You looked..." Now he dropped his gaze to the floor as I glanced at him. "And the Festival, I tried to summon the courage to ask you for a favour. I failed miserably."

I smiled, unable to stop myself. The smile faded as I continued to gaze at the scroll.

"What are you thinking?" He sounded worried. "Vianne? You have that look again."

What look? But I suddenly glimpsed another turn to this labyrinth. I leapt to my feet. "Where would the Guard hold him, this Messenger?"

"Probably in the barracks under the West Tower." He fell into step beside me. "Vianne, what—"

Do you not see? "I have the Aryx," I said. "If I free the Messenger to return to d'Orlaans, he runs the risk of one more person who has seen the truth of the Aryx with his own eyes. He will kill the man, or has—"

"—already laid a killspell on him," Tristan finished, and swore. I ran for the door.

I am certain the Guards did not expect to see me bolt past them and down the hall, Tristan close behind me. He snapped an order over his shoulder and such was the accord between us that by the end of the hall he said, "To your left, up the stairs," and continued to guide me through the maze of Arcenne. I had explored no few of its corridors, but not yet all, and was glad of his guidance.

I was breathless and aching from a stitch in my side as we arrived at the barracks under the West Tower, and Tristan flung the door open. I skidded in, for once cursing my skirts, and several Arcenne guards rose hastily. Some were at table, others at a card game—and there, by the fire, sat a man in the blue surcoat of a King's Messenger, gold braid on his sleeves, a tall Arquitaine with thick dark curls long as a *chivalier's*.

I barely paused. Flung out my hand, tasting the beginnings of the peculiar sour flavor of Court sorcery meant to kill, triggered by the presence of its intended victim. I recognized it, as well—wet fur and sour apples, a poison killspell to match the one laid on the Minister Primus.

The Messenger straightened, his face blanching as he saw Tristan behind me, my Consort's eyes blazing, hand on his swordhilt.

The Aryx let loose a welter of sound, and a wall of hedgewitchery and Court sorcery smashed outward, catching the killspell as it struck, a flare of silver light jetting from my outstretched palm.

The noise was incredible, and a table between me and the Messenger exploded into matchsticks, smoke and wood whickering away to strike the walls and pepper the onlookers.

The killspell snapped, recoiling on itself like a gittern string stretched too far, splitting and shredding. Another door inside my head, flung open, showing me a far country of magic lying thrumming and obedient to my will.

The drowning sense of being swallowed alive was slightly less this time. I held fast to the only thought that could survive the riptide overpowering my senses.

Tristan. The killspell is meant for him. Protect him, just as he would protect you.

Screams, shouts, the thick reek of poison and fear, Tristan's voice raised to a battlefield shout. I came back to myself slowly, standing, holding the glowing ball of sorcery that was the killspell in my palm, draining the power from it. The Aryx sang a slow, sleepy, sated song. Tristan touched my shoulder. "Vianne?"

"Not merely a poison killspell," I said dreamily, "but a spell designed to kill someone with him when triggered." I blinked, returning to myself. "Twas set as a snare, Tristan. *You* were its target."

There was a murmur of sound. I looked, and found one of the Arcenne Guard had the Messenger at swordpoint. The others stared at me, men I recognized, now kneeling on the stone floor.

"Put that away, Stefan," Tristan barked, and the guard, slightly shamefaced, sheathed his sword.

The Messenger, fever-pale, stared at me with eyes as big as dinner plates. I leaned into Tristan, grateful for his strength.

Grateful, too, that the thought of him stayed with me even in the devouring maelstrom of the Aryx. "One crisis averted," I managed, through numb lips and a sand-dry throat. "Tristan."

"Your Majesty." Was that awe I heard in his voice as well?

Please, no. I cannot bear it. I pitched my voice loud enough to carry through the room. "Stand, *chivalieri*, an it please you. *Sieur* Messenger, would you be so kind as to accompany us? I think it best to speak to you sooner rather than later."

One by one, the Citadel Guard rose. I saw the open adoration on several faces, and wished it had not been necessary to use the Aryx. The Messenger stammered something, and two of the Guard stepped forth to accompany him.

Tristan gave a few quiet orders to bring lunch to the library, then ushered me out into the hall. He said nothing else as we retraced our steps, the Guards behind us with the Messenger. I would have dearly loved to speak to my Consort, but it was impossible with the others watching. "Are you hale?" he asked me, quietly, as we rounded a corner.

I had to use the Seal again. My head ached, and I hoped I would not fall prey to the half-head. "Hale enough. Tristan, that spell could have killed you, had you decided to question him alone."

"True. And you, *m'chri*?"

"If you were questioning the Messenger, it might have looked as if he had murdered you, with steel and magic. I would be unlikely to view such an event, being an empty-headed Court frippet." My tone was less calm than I would have liked. "What does he hope to gain? He must know the Aryx—"

"The Aryx was sleeping from the time of Queen Toriane's death. He has no way of knowing it has awakened. Despite the sudden strength of Court sorcery returning…" He sounded thoughtful, and I looked up at him, my hands moving automatically to gather my skirts.

I kept my tone low, conscious of the footsteps behind us. "But how can he not feel the Aryx is awake? He uses Court sorcery!"

"I do not know, and it will take some time to find out." Tristan now sounded calm, the furious killing calm of revenge.

I halted, and he stopped short as well. "I need your wit, not your anger, Tris." The footsteps behind us drew nearer, we had outpaced the Guards.

"Aye." His eyes were near incandescent, and if his jaw clenched any harder he might well injure his own teeth. "Give me a few moments to compose myself, *m'chri.*"

"I need your wit *now*," I said, inflexible. For I was badly shaken, and I steered myself by his northneedle. I understood that if I let him go much further into rage he might well swear an oath he would regret. And something about his fury perplexed me, obliquely frightened me.

Something was not right.

He slanted me one flaming-blue glance. "You sound like Henri," he murmured, and was the Tristan I knew again, his fury reined, his face smooth and interested.

I shall choose to view that as a compliment. I blew out between pursed lips. "Good." *You almost frighten me, beloved.*

The Guards and the Messenger rounded the bend in the corridor, and we had to hurry to stay a stride ahead. But Tristan walked more slowly, and by the time we reached the library he had regained control of his temper. Barely, but enough.

I pointed the Messenger to a chair. "Sit, an it please you." I motioned the Guards away. "You may leave him with us. I will be safe enough."

The Guards for once did not glance at Tristan, simply obeyed me. I picked up the parchment from d'Orlaans and smoothed it on the table. "Your name, *sieur*?"

"Divris." The Messenger's throat worked. "Divris di Tatancourt." His cheeks were pale, and from the way he sweated and glanced at Tristan, I guessed he was uncertain of his survival.

Still, he is alive. The killspell was meant for him, too. "Get him some wine, Tris, to bolster him."

"As you like." Tristan crossed the room to the sideboard, but kept the man in sight. His hand strayed near his rapier's hilt more than I liked, but he seemed in control of his temper, at least.

"Di Tatancourt." I mused over his name, threading it through my memory. "Your younger brother was in the King's Guard, on duty the day Princesse Lisele di Tirecian-Trimestin was murdered."

Di Tatancourt's gaze flicked toward Tristan, flinched away. "The tale is that the Captain of the King's Guard caused the Princesse and her ladies to be slaughtered in a rebellion against the King. After he slew the King himself."

I arched an eyebrow. "Tristan was with me that day, *chivalier*. I myself witnessed Garonne di Narborre and his men moving from body to body in the Princesse's quarters, making certain Lisele and her ladies were slain." The memory rose, taunting me. I closed it away with an effort. "You have seen me use the Great Seal of Arquitaine. Do you doubt me?"

He shook his head, running his fingers back through his thick dark hair. "No, Your Majesty." Quietly, but with great force. "I do not doubt you. I know a plot when I see one. And I have been asking inconvenient questions of the manner of my brother's death."

Hence, the killspell. Two birds netted in one snare. I swallowed bile. "I wish I could have saved him, *sieur*. I truly do. He was courting Lady Arioste." *And not having any luck with it, I might add, for she was after bigger prey. Or at least, prey with deeper pockets, for she had expensive tastes.*

Di Tatancourt's mouth twitched, amusement and bitter memory combining. "Aye. That he was."

Tristan handed him a cup of wine, his other hand resting a-swordhilt. "Here, *chivalier*. Drink, and be welcome."

The door banged open, and I whirled, my hip striking the table. Baron Perseval d'Arcenne strode into the room, and I found where my Consort had gained his cold fury from.

"A killspell!" the Baron raged. "Does Timrothe d'Orlaans never tire of seeking to murder my son?" His blue eyes flamed, and my mouth was dry.

Well, d'Orlaans killed the King, blamed Tristan for it, is still seeking to kill him and turn me against my Consort. It is enough to unsettle even Jiserah.

"Baron," I said, calmly enough, "I present to you to Messenger Divris di Tatancourt, sent to die because he was asking inconvenient questions about his brother's death. His brother was assigned to guard Princesse Lisele's door the day I left Court. Would you be so kind as to draft a reply to Timrothe d'Orlaan's recent missive?" My fingers found the parchment, held it up. "I wish to inform the Duc d'Orlaans that he is stripped of his titles and styles forthwith, and that he shall remand himself to my justice immediately. I wish a proclamation drafted, and diplomatic letters sent to Navarrin." It seemed someone else was speaking through me, someone with a voice as crisp and clean as new steel. "And I wish to know *exactly* where Garonne di Narborre is, or as near as we may," I added, as an afterthought.

The Baron's jaw set. "As you wish, my liege." He took the parchment from me. "I will have a proclamation and the letters drafted in a matter of hours."

"Good." I looked at Tristan. "Fetch me a scribe, as well. There are other letters to write."

"D'Orlaans will know his killspell failed." Tristan folded his arms, but his tone was not combative.

He will. "He will only know it did not kill anyone, not a whit else. It is the more imperative we move quickly. I will hold a Session this afternoon, Baron, of all members of my Council that are here. We may fill the vacancies later."

The Baron nodded. The crackling anger in his tone had smoothed. "I will send a scribe and gather the Council. Is there aught else, my liege?"

"Not at this moment. My thanks."

He turned on his heel, nodding to his son, and was gone just as swiftly as he'd entered.

Tristan took a long gulp of wine, perhaps to bolster himself.

I settled myself down in my chair, forcing calm. "Now, *Chivalier* di Tatancourt. Tell me of Court, and of d'Orlaans. You are a Messenger, so you will know what is of import."

He nodded, and took a swallow of wine. His cheeks were still flour-pale, and he trembled just the slightest bit. "My thanks, Your Majesty."

"No thanks necessary," my new, brittle voice told him. *Who am I? Who have I become?* I no longer knew. "Now, we shall start with the Court. Tell me, what is the latest gossip?"

Tristan opened the door, and I leaned on his arm, stepping inside his sitting room. "Gods above. Another day like that, and I may save everyone the trouble by retiring to a convent."

He laughed, then kicked the door shut and took me in his arms, resting his chin atop my head. I fell into the safety of his body, sliding my arms around him. He moved slightly, restless, and I felt his readiness, a hardness against my lower belly. He looked almost giddy with relief. "I seem to always be thanking you for saving my life, *demiange*."

That made me shiver. "Do not name me so—it might attract the attention of one."

"Which would not be a bad thing—you seem to need more protection than I can provide." He buried his face in my hair, inhaling deeply. "My darling Vianne. Do you have any idea how utterly magnificent you are?"

"I thought Lord Siguerre was going to pop when I told him to hold his tongue, and that I shall have no war before spring. He is a disagreeable old stoneshell turtle." I could have picked many another term for the man, but none were fit for a noblewoman's mouth.

"He is tactics-wise, and organized. And he holds the adjoining province. Enough of business." He kissed my forehead, my cheeks, then crushed me to him again. "I wish to hold you."

"You could comb my hair." I laughed, a weary chuckle, as his fingers fumbled with the pearls the Baroness had insisted I wear. He swore good-naturedly, and the pearls finally came free. He threaded his fingers in my hair, kissed me deeply. I turned to water against him. He picked me up and twirled me once, then twirled me again as if he could not help himself. Yet a thought struck me, and I had to voice it. "Tristan, why did your father say Navarrin is no true ally? I thought you always planned on seeking help from Navarrin."

He groaned. "Must you always speak of business, Vianne? I am beginning to think you torment me for sport."

"Oh, never that." I traced the line of his jaw with one fingertip. I knew of the first flush of love and hoped it would not fade too soon, and also hoped that we would be friends after the sweetness had passed. "I do not seek to torment you. I would never be so unkind."

"I know you would not." He changed between one moment and the next, his face gone serious, his mouth a thin line. He cupped my face in his hand, the pearls his mother had pressed upon me smooth and hard against my cheek. "What are you thinking, *m'chri*, my beloved? Your eyes are dark, and that is a sign of trouble."

I am merely curious and unsettled. Something does not seem aright to me. "I am thinking of Navarrin and how I wish my curiosity satisfied. And how do you know my eyes go dark when there is trouble?"

"I have watched you enough to tell, and I shall satisfy any curiosities you care to voice to me. What else?" His thumb stroked my cheek.

I blushed at the entendre. "I am only uneasy." I would have looked down, but he did not let me. "Truly, Tristan."

"What of, *m'chri*?"

Of everything. Of all this madness. "Merely…I thought when I reached Arcenne this would be over. I thought I could give the Aryx up to someone and—I do not know. Go about with…something. My life. I thought I would be free, d'Orlaans would fall, this would make everything right again." The truth rose to my lips and would not be denied. I could not produce more than a whisper. "I suppose I thought it would bring my Lisele back."

Tristan kissed my forehead again. He was silent.

"I do not wish this burden." As if telling him a terrible secret. "I thought Court was so awful, I hated it there. Yet I wish to go back. At least there, I…I do not know." *At least it was familiar. And I am still terrified of you wasting yourself for your duty to a dead King, Tristan. I cannot stand to lose you.*

But though I could admit to much, I could not say that to

a nobleman. A noble's honor would make him stubborn as a Scythandrian horse, and Tristan d'Arcenne had more than his share of prickly d'Arquitaine pride. To speak to him of danger would merely make him rash.

He rested his forehead against mine, closed his eyes. "I am sorry. I was too late."

"You did what you could." I tried to smile, but it felt unnatural. A mask. "I do not mean to hurt you."

His mouth tilted up, a charmingly lopsided grin as his eyes came out, surprising me again with their blueness. "Come." His arms tightened, he picked me up and half-dragged me over the stone floor. I let out a blurt of surprise, and he tossed me carefully on the bed, following me with a sigh. A moment's worth of rearranging ended with my head on his shoulder, my hair beginning a tangle on the velvet coverlet. Lying down only made me more acutely aware of how weary I was.

"There." Tristan scooped up my free hand, lacing his fingers with mine. "Better? Speak to me of what you will, *m'chri*. I do not even begrudge your perpetual obsession with dispatches."

"I know you would prefer—," I began.

"I do not think you do. Speak to me, Vianne. Weave me a tale."

"But you must—" I bit my lip. It was not a thing a lady should say.

"You think I am dragged about by my breechclout, my liege? I am *occasionally* capable of chastity, am I not? You have no idea what it was like, sharing a saddle with you through half of Arquitaine. I thought I would die of frustration."

Indeed? "Really?"

"Do you know how lovely you are, dear one?" He raised my knuckles to his lips. "You could make Danshar himself forget his sword and think of bedplay. But tis your quick mind, I think, that makes you so alluring."

"I do not recognize this picture you paint," I laughed, and breathed into his shoulder, smelling leather and male and the indescribable that made *him*. "I rather wonder that you think to court me now."

"Making up lost time. Now listen, Navarrin is a greedy marketwife, but she does not demand tribute payment from Arquitaine. Partly because the Santciago House of Navarrin is related to Tirecian-Trimestin by both blood and marriage, and also because the Passes Cirithe, not to mention the Thread Pass, are both too narrow to supply an army through without holding the mountain provinces. Besides, Arquitaine menaces Rus and Torkai to the east, acts as a buffer against Damarsene, Pruzia, and Polis, balances against Tiberia for trade interests. And more. So. Were Navarrin to come to our aid, their lines of supply would be stretched thin, and tis no inducement for them unless a weak Arquitaine will no longer hold back Rus and the Damarsene. The tribute payments to the Rus'Zar are bad enough, but Rus knows Arquitaine can field an army at need and come to the aid of any of the client-states, or the Principalities if necessary, and be richly rewarded. But north-and-eastward, closer to our borders than the Rus…that is what troubles me. There was news in that quarter having to do with the conspiracy, but I had not ferreted it all out yet, being too busy seeking the killer of the King's line before he struck you down." His tone was careful, almost overly so. I wondered why he chose his words with such delicacy.

"Hm." I thought of old maps, straining my brain to think of dangers from the east. "Pruzia. And the Sea-Countries, and Haviroen in their mountains. But the Havi are traditionally neutral. Anyway, Pruzia. Oh, and the Damarsene." A cool finger of dread touched my nape, remembering Adrien's suspicions. That the two of them would worry over the same country for different reasons was thought-provoking, to say the least.

"Yes, Damar. Where most of the tribute goes, since the King's Consort died so mysteriously." Tristan's lips touched my knuckles again. "Only now that the Aryx is awake, perhaps tribute will become a thing of the past."

Enough of this. I sighed, settling myself further at ease into his shoulder. "I am glad to have you, Tristan. I pray the Seal will choose someone else eventually."

"I do not think it will. For good or for ill, you are the Queen." His tone changed. Was he sad?

"I do not wish to be."

"I know." He stroked my shoulder. "My poor hedgewitch darling."

"Tristan, do you think…" I touched his jaw, felt the roughness of stubble. "After you no longer find me so attractive, will we still be friends?"

"Is that what this is about?" He kissed my knuckles again. "Hmmm."

Now I had offended him. I trailed my fingers over the plane of his cheek "Well?"

"I adore you, Vianne." His tone had grown serious, but he sounded relieved. "You think me faithless?"

It scored me to the quick, that he could think so. "Of course not." Who was loyal to me, if not him?

"Then do not trouble yourself with thinking I will suddenly lose my taste for you. Do you think a man who has watched over you for years, dragged you through half of Arquitaine on his saddle without touching you, and has gone grey worrying about the trouble you fling yourself into will tire of you after a few nights?" He laughed, stroking my hair, except his merriment was not pleasant. "You have such a low opinion of me after all."

I wondered where his bitterness came from. There was still so much I did not know of him. "Oh, cease. I have a very high opinion of my Consort, I shall have you know." *High enough that I do not ask you what lies between you and Adrien di Cinfiliet. High enough that I have given myself to you.*

He still stroked my hair, gently, lifting a few strands, playing with them. I shut my eyes.

"You still surprise me, *m'chri*. Every time I think I have your mind mapped, it takes another turn."

"Di Yspres said you have had a hard life," I found myself saying. Sleep threatened, now that I was abed and motionless, and I could not ask him of Adrien. "Is that true?"

"Jierre said that? No, I am fortunate. Twas hard to leave home and go to Court, but I had reached my Coming-of-Age and it was my duty to do what I could. Father needed someone to make certain the border provinces were heard at Court, and the Guard is a good way for a young man to make himself. And then…"

"Then what?" The sound of him telling a tale soothed me.

"Then I caught the King's eye and became the Captain, and four years later the Left Hand. It seemed there was nothing I could not do. Except court a King's half-niece. I tried, but you did not see me, and I doubted Henri would let…then the conspiracy was afoot. I suddenly had no time to worry, being very busy indeed with death in every corner of Arquitaine." He took a deep sharp breath. No doubt twas unpleasant to think on.

"When did you try to catch my notice?" I was suddenly very

curious about this, even more curious than I was about Navarrin and Damarsene and the thousand worries outside our chamber door.

He laughed again. This time it was not so bitter, and I was glad of it. "I haunted your steps like a *demieri di sorce*, Vianne. I finally acquired a habit of leaving you books instead of nosegays."

Oh? My sixteenth birthday, just before you became Captain. I remember this; it went on for months. "That was you? I thought someone had lost them, and I tried to return them to the Palais library."

"There was no end to the merriment among the Guard when you did so." Now he sounded wry. "I finally admitted defeat. It was not safe for either of us. My Guard was loyal, but a man in his cups can speak ill-advised words. I had to pretend not to care."

"When did you..." Again, not something a lady could ask.

He answered anyway. "I was seventeen, it was my first night at Court as a Guard. You and Lisele played riddlesharp, and after a few games you let her win. Then she wished to dance, so you did with good grace. It was the first time I ever saw you dance, I think I was lost that very moment. You wore green silk, and you looked one of Alisaar's maidens come to earth. I fell, and have never been free since."

I barely remembered that dress; I had only been thirteen. "I did let her win at riddlesharp, but I had to be careful not to let her think so." *She was prickly with her pride, my Princesse. She could not know I let her win, but if I looked amiss while doing so she would guess, and then it would be unpleasant.*

"Hm. That sharp mind of yours." His touch was soothing. My head was so heavy, and it ached. "Rest, Vianne."

Now I could ask; the idea was lain gently in my brain as if the gods themselves had whispered in my ear. "Tristan?"

"What, *m'chri*?" He stroked my cheek, touched my lips tenderly.

"Why do you dislike Adrien di Cinfiliet?" I sounded half asleep even to myself.

His hand tensed. "It does not matter."

I fell silent as he stroked my hair, but I did not sleep for a long while. He would not speak of it, and I could not ask. I lay thinking as his breathing deepened, and wondered why I felt so suddenly bereft.

Chaos. Crashing. Tristan's oath, deadly quiet, as steel chimed.

I sat up, clutching the covers to my chest. Ducked as something came flying, sensing more than seeing it in the blackness; I was lucky whatever it was did not strike me. My skirt slid against the sheets—I had fallen asleep in my clothes.

"Get *down*, Vianne!" Tristan yelled. The cry propelled me out of bed on the opposite side, almost hitting my head on the night table. Clashing chime of steel, a horrifying, bubbling gasp.

What is that? An injury; a lung-cut. Oh, dear Blessed, let it not be him—

Silence. The room was dark, the fire banked and a moonless night outside, not a candle lit. I wondered if I should use a witchlight.

"Come forth," Tristan said, softly. I flinched to hear that tone. "Come forth and face your death."

I stayed where I was, shivering, my skirt tangled around my knees.

Another clash of steel, and a solid sound of flesh being

carved. I shut my eyes, my heart in my throat. *Tristan?*

Light bloomed, ruddy through my eyelids. I peeked over the bed.

Tristan stood, his shirt bloody and his sword in hand, surveying the room. His blue eyes were cold as death. The lamp's wick, guttering into life, burned with the peculiar blue flame of a Court-sorcery lighting. "Tristan?" I could not speak louder than a whisper.

Three black-clad shapes lay twisted on the floor. Tristan crossed the room, checked the watercloset, came out and paced toward the window. "Stay down, Vianne."

"What is *happening*?" Although I could guess—murder, in the dark. But aimed at whom? And so soon after the killspell-laden Messenger, too.

If there were assassins here, twas more far more dangerous than I had ever imagined. It would mean d'Orlaans had begun a different game, and I would need to find the rules and the disposition of the board quickly, in order to outwit him.

"As you love life, Vianne, stay there." He checked the window from the side, to rob a projectile of its target, nodded to himself. Paced to the chair near the bed and was in his boots in a trice. I stared, almost-witless with surprise. "Whatever you see or hear, *stay there* until I come for you."

I cannot, do not ask me to wait, this might as well be a tree in the Shirlstrienne, with di Narborre coming to kill us all. "But—"

"Trust me, Vianne." He gained his feet in a rush, wrenched the door open, and was gone.

I do not like this. I hunched beside the bed, let out a shaky sigh. My hands would not cease moving, plucking at the coverlet's edge. Had they come for me? And now, long as I lived, I would have to worry. Knife in the dark, poison in a cup, treachery and deceit. I wanted no part of it; I had seen enough of treachery to fill me to the back teeth. Enough of blood, of death, of pain to fill the Maelstrom's sea itself.

I pushed myself up to stand, mindful of the danger even in silence. Three bodies. Each in a pool of blood, each masked with black. The stink of death rose. I gagged. *He told me to stay here.*

Gods, no, the rest of me wailed. *I cannot. Oh, please, gods, no.*

My hands fisted in my skirt. Pale green silk rustled. I heard the wet crunching sounds again—*Make certain. Make certain none still live.*

A small, helpless sound died at the back of my throat. I eased away from the bed, stole toward the door on bare feet against cold stone.

The hall outside was deserted. Where had Tristan gone? I heard raised voices and the clatter of booted feet.

Instinct took over. I darted across the hall, to a window-*couvre* wrapped in red velvet. A few moments' worth of work hid me between the wooden *couvre* and the floor-length drapes; I made certain my feet were hidden as I peered out through a tiny gap in the drapes. My heart pounded in my throat.

A shadow drifted along the other side of the wall, slipped into the bedroom. A man dressed in black, his face masked, a clubbed tail of dark hair along the back of his neck. A wicked curved dagger showed in his right hand, gleaming as he slid with oiled grace through the door.

The drumming of booted feet drew closer. Shouts. I closed my eyes, forced them open. I had to look. *Had* to see.

A deathly silence from our chamber. Who was the man in black? An assassin, definitely—but for whom? It did not seem likely that a d'Arquitaine would do such a thing—but then, a man had tried to kill Tristan by stealth in Tierrce d'Estrienne.

"Vianne!" Tristan's. The corridor echoed with the din of alarm and suddenly-awakened men.

I bolted from the *couvre* and ran down the hall toward the noise, my bare feet soundless. Snapped a glance over my shoulder just as I rounded the corner and ran headlong into the Guard, their unsheathed swords reflecting glowglobe and torchlight. Jierre caught at my shoulder, pushed me toward Tristan, and hurled himself past, vanishing around the corner.

"*Assassin!*" I gasped. "He has a knife *Jierre take care!*"

Tristan's fingers closed, ruthless-hard, around my upper arm. "I told you to stay!"

A howl of pain from down the corridor made the color drain from his face as the rest of the Guard surged past; I caught a glance of Luc di Chatillon with his rapier out and his young blond face suffused with anger, Jespre di Vidancourt with his hair wildly mussed and his lean face ashen.

Tristan kissed my forehead, bruisingly hard. Embraced me so hard the breath left my lungs in a rush. He was bloody and sweating, his shirt dappled with crimson and flapping as his ribs heaved. "Vianne," he said into my hair. I shook, a small cry of distress wrung out of me. Cursed myself for being so weak. "Vianne." He held me at arm's length, looked me over for damage.

I was very glad I had fallen asleep in my clothes. The idea of facing this chain of events in a shift—or, Blessed forbid, without a stitch to cover me—was, for a moment, more daunting than what had actually just occurred.

"I am unharmed. There is someone in the room, Tristan." My voice trembled to match the rest of me. "He had a curved dagger. And his hair was in a tail bound with black ribbon—"

"A Pruzian Knife." He still examined me, from my soles to

my crown and back again, his gaze roving over my dress, my face, my shoulders. "Three to attack me, three to attack my father. If you saw another one, there are two left in the Citadel. We shall find them. Come, let us bring you to safety."

"A P-P-Pruzian Knife?" I actually stammered. He drew me away, his boots clicking and my bare feet soundless. "But they're *myths*!"

"No, they are very real. And very deadly, not to mention very expensive."

Expensive? How does he know? I did not care at the moment. I had a more pressing concern. "How b-badly are you h-hurt?" *He has blood on his shirt, he's bleeding. Dear Blessed, he is wounded.*

"I am well enough," he said grimly. "Come quickly, Vianne."

Shouts, more clattering feet. Tristan pulled me aside into a shadowed hall, pressed me back against the wall. Several more of the Citadel Guard passed at a run, Tristan shook his head. Pressed another kiss onto my temple, through the fraying mat of my hair. He swore, in a low shaking voice. "Nine knives," he whispered. "*Nine*. This rather changes things."

I was about to ask again how badly he was hurt when he clapped his hand over my mouth. I looked past him, out into the running torchlight of the hall, and saw the two remaining assassins, each masked and dressed in black, their hair in tails clubbed and bound with ribbon. They drifted in the wake of the clattering Citadel Guards, deadly shadows. The Guard was making enough noise to warn even a deaf man of their passage.

Tristan moved away from me. His gaze met mine, a silent warning; words and breath died in my throat. *No. No, stay here with me, where it is safe.*

Yet I could not tell *what* was safe. If there were assassins boldly trailing after a pack of Guards, could more not be hiding in this passage?

Oh, gods…

His sword whispered free of its sheath, and the two Pruzians froze.

Tristan attacked.

If I live a centuriad I will never forget that sight, Tristan d'Arcenne dueling two Pruzian Knives in the hall of the Citadel. I understood then why he was Captain of the Guard.

He fought as if the blade was a part of his hand, forgotten until the hilt met his palm, the steel weaving in a complicated pattern that kept the Pruzians at bay. He backed them away from the mouth of the darkened hall, their longknives sorely unprepared for the reach his rapier gave.

One of them actually flung a knife, and I gasped. But Tristan ducked and lunged, his boot sliding along stone and his knee grating against the floor, and in the same movement had run one Pruzian through. Blood whipped free of his blade as he flung himself backward, somehow on his feet in one sharp movement, the rapier describing a complex movement I do not have the knowledge to name even now. The black-clad man dropped without a sound, and Tristan faced the last Pruzian as the sounds of the Guard returning grew louder.

I bit down on the soft fleshy part of my hand under my right thumb, unaware that I had covered my mouth. *Tristan, oh be careful, gods, please*—I could barely even pray. The fear threatened to smash me as the Aryx did, robbing me of myself.

The Pruzian's gaze, dark and narrow above his mask, flickered toward me, but Tristan lunged at him, both men moving back toward Tristan's room, out of my field of vision.

Thus it was I did not see the end of the duel: the Guard coming from Tristan's chambers with a bloody but unbowed Jierre at their head, the last flicker of the knife, Tristan moving in on the assassin and smashing the knife away with a contemptuous movement, his hilt-armored fist blurring in to crunch at the man's masked face. The Pruzian dropped, and Jierre told me later Tristan looked sorely tempted to run him through, but halted himself. "Strip him, bind him, and chain him. Then put him in an *oublietta* and wait further orders." His voice was quiet but harsh. "But before you place him in the pit, Jierre, teach him a lesson."

They dragged the Pruzian away past the darkened hall I cowered in, Jierre favoring his left shoulder. Blood soaked his shirt, and his eyes wore a fey glitter that warned me not to speak. I stood there stupid and useless, biting down on my hand. Four of the Guard remained; there was shouting in other parts of the Citadel. Every room and corridor would be searched now.

Tristan's voice. "Vianne? Are you hale?"

It took a fair bit of courage to step out. I bit down harder, afraid I would start screaming if I loosed the pressure of my teeth. I did not dare to look to see how badly Tristan was injured. Luc di Chatillon knelt by the fallen Pruzian and made certain he was dead by the expedient of sinking a dagger in his throat with a meaty crunching sound.

I swayed. *Make certain.* Shoved the thought away. I could not afford to keep it.

Tristan caught me, his fingers coming up to gently free my hand from my mouth. "Gods." His voice had lost its hurtful edge. "You need a physicker, *d'mselle.*"

I almost choked on the final crowning absurdity. He was bleeding, and Jierre too. And yet he said I needed a physicker for a hand bruised by my own teeth. I summoned every scrap of my wit that remained. "I have never seen you duel before." I sounded faraway and strange even to myself.

He shrugged. "Peasants armed with knives. You are pale, *m'chri.*"

"Should not I be?" It was a faint witticism, but he laughed. Took my right hand in both of his, gently.

"Come, to the hedgewitch with you, Your Majesty. The rest of you, take care of that…thing." Faint disdain colored his voice. How could he be so calm? I was only holding to my composure by a thread. "Burn it. I wish a report in less than a candlemark. I want every corner searched and every person in the Keep accounted for."

Chapter Thirty-Six

They came over the west wall," the Captain of the Citadel Guard—thin, intense di Vantmor—said. His fine waxed mustache was now sadly drooping, his curly hair ruffled. But his blue mountainfolk eyes were keen, and his sword had seen blooding this night, too. "One of yours was on the wall with the night-watch, *sieur*."

Tristan shut his eyes as Bryony, the Citadel's head hedge-witch physicker, probed at the slash on his ribs with gentle fingers. The small infirmary cubicle was stone-walled, with a faded red curtain drawn over the door. Tristan sat on a high bench while Bryony examined him. A cot was made up in the corner, but Tris had no need of it, for which I was profoundly grateful.

I stayed sitting up only by sheer force of will, in a hard chair next to the healer's table.

"The di Rocham boy. He is alive, but—" Di Vantmor's blue gaze flicked over to me. I sat numbly with my bandaged right hand lying quiescent, placed prettily on my silken lap.

"Tinan?" I gained my feet in a single convulsive rush. My

skirts made a low sweet sound. "Where is he?"

"They are bringing him now."

My Consort sighed. "Patch me up quickly, then. Jermain, would you have someone bring me a fresh shirt?"

"*Sieur.*" Di Vantmor bowed. I felt a slight twinge—I should have thought of that.

I was at the door of the small cubicle, all but on di Vantmor's heels, when Tristan spoke again. "Vianne? Wait a little, an it please you. I would accompany you."

I looked over my shoulder. My hair was a tangled mass against my back. "The infirmary is full-to-choking of armed men, Tris. I doubt I am in any danger."

His face changed, and I leaned against the wall by the door. It was no affected pose—I was simply too weak to stay upright on my own unless I was moving. Tristan did not look threatening, simply weary—but I knew that if I went through the door he would follow me, disregarding the physicker's care. My heart gave a huge throttled leap.

"This should just take a moment," the young peasant healer in his pale shirt and green trousers said. He had been wakened roughly, as had we all.

I smelled the peculiar green of hedgewitchery, dropped my eyes as Bryony's power became evident. He was a much better hedgewitch than I had ever been. I longed to have time to study with him, as I had with Risaine and Jaryana.

"There. Try not to fall on any knives anytime soon, Tris?" Bryony had been a child in the Keep with Tristan, and was easier with him than most of the Guard.

"If the Pruzians would stop sending assassins, I would. Is my Vianne well?"

"The *d'mselle* is well enough, a bit of rest and some food will ballast her nicely. I would offer her a drop of wine, but she has already said nay."

I felt the weight of Tristan's gaze on me. "Vianne, *m'chri*, would you bring me some wine? I feel a trifle pale."

I peeled myself away from the wall and managed to reach the wine jug, poured both Tristan and myself a healthy dollop—and tossed the contents of one cup back and poured another measure. Warmth exploded in my stomach. *Well. I've survived my first assassination attempt.*

If I did not count Lisele's murderers among assassins, that was. Had the Pruzians come to kill me, or Tristan, or Tristan's father? Or all of us? And so soon after the other attempt.

I needed to think on this, to tease out the implications. First, though, there were questions to be asked. "How is the Baron?" At least I sounded relatively calm.

"Well, and cursing at everyone in sight. The Baroness is doing her best." Bryony sounded amused. "Well, you're ready for more mischief, *sieur*. I am to take care of other poor souls."

I brought my Consort the winecup, awkward with my bandaged hand, and settled on the bench beside him. Bryony swept from the room with one last eloquent glance at me. If he meant to give a message, it was one I did not understand

Tristan took a swallow of wine, rolled it in his mouth. Grimaced as if it had turned, though it seemed perfectly fine to me, if strong. "You did not stay in the room," he said quietly. "'Tis a good thing, too; the other Knife would have found you. But in the future, Vianne—"

Gods grant there is never another episode such as this. "I shall tarry still and quiet, I swear. I simply could not stand the thought of…you were alone. And I could not stay there with the…the bodies." I wished to add, *Yes, I am a coward,* but I did not.

"My apologies." He smiled, a little ruefully, over the top of his goblet. "I did not wish to leave you, Vianne. I had to."

"I know." I poured down the rest of my second cup of wine in four long swallows. Blinked owlishly at him. "I believe I am handling this rather well."

"Good, for I am halfway to a nervous wreck." He took another swallow. "I adore you, *m'chri*. You are too brave for my comfort."

I leaned in to his shoulder, happy for his solid warmth. "Who would hire a Pruzian to kill you and your father? And why?"

"Besides d'Orlaans and whoever he is depending on to prop up his claim to the throne?" Tristan leaned against me, too, a subtle movement but one I cherished. "Have I told you how lovely you are, *m'chri*?"

"No." A silly smile spread over my face as a warm haze swirled through my middle. "You could, though. Before we visit di Rocham."

"Ever duty, hmm?"

"I am worried for him." I rested my head on his shoulder, the goblet loose-held in relaxing fingers, resting in my lap. "How pretty am I, Tristan?" *For I would like to hear this, even if tis vain to ask.*

"Beautiful enough to bring a man to his knees crying out in praise of Alisaar." He turned, kissed my forehead gently. "Are you hale enough to stand?"

"You should finish your wine."

"I have lost my taste for it. Here." He offered me the goblet.

Why, very sly of you, my Consort. Nevertheless, I drained it with good grace. "I know I am merely Lisele's plain little lapdog. I was told enough." *And it does me well to hear you gainsay it.*

And so he did, as a good Consort. "You were lovely when I came to Court, Vianne. Time's only made you more so. Here, lean on me; we shall see what misfortune befell Tinan."

The world tilted slightly under me. "Dear gods; the wine's at my head." *Or the fear.* Both were equally likely.

"'Tis unwatered, the strongest we have. Bryony believes in it as a tonic, I think. I also think you should have more."

For once I did not argue. "I think that is a most excellent idea." I rather suspected I would need it.

Di Rocham was feverish, and Bryony looked grave. I settled into the chair by the cot in another cubicle, watching Tinan's fair young face as he lay drug-quiescent, sweat sheening his brow. Bryony lifted the dressing over the wound on the boy's belly, and his sharp mountain face grew even graver.

"He will recover, will he not?" I felt childish for asking, my head muddled with wine.

A low knock sounded at the door. I looked up to see Jierre di Yspres. "The Knife has regained consciousness." A bandage glared white against his shoulder, under his shirt's open throat-laces. I could see a bead of drying blood on his collarbone. His lean face was chalky, and grim. "How is our *d'mselle*?"

I lifted my chin. "Hearty and hale." My mouth did not seem to work quite properly. *And well-tonic'd, though now I regret the last glass. 'Twill not do me well for long.*

Tristan shrugged. "Unwounded. Her nerves have taken a shock, tis all."

"And Tinan?" Di Yspres did not glance at the bed, but I sensed he wished to. We all turned our gazes to the physicker, and hope rose under my pounding heart.

Bryony opened his mouth, closed it, glanced at Tristan, at

me. "He will not last the night," he said heavily. "I can do nothing for him."

What? I could not contain myself. "But you are a hedgewitch!" *And a fine one, too!*

"There are other wounded." Gently enough, his jaw set, his hands curling into fists, relaxing. "This young one's gut-cut. I cannot sew his intestines up. I have not the charm nor the power for it. The most I can do is ease his passing—"

"Get away." I did not recognize the harsh, croaking voice as my own. "Now."

The peasant physicker paled swiftly. Twas gratifying to see he did not look to Tristan; he simply bowed and obeyed.

"Is he ready to speak?" Tristan asked, as Bryony retreated to the door. Tinan did not moan—Bryony had dosed him with poppy and caresfree—but his breathing was labored.

"Pruzian. And difficult." It was di Yspres's turn for a shrug.

"I care not how difficult he is," Tristan said. "*Make* him speak."

It occurred to me they were speaking of the assassin, the one who had survived. My Consort's gaze, extraordinarily blue, met mine.

I read his expression, and sick unsteady heat filled my stomach. "*No*, Tristan. As you are my Consort and I am the Queen, *no*. I will question him tomorrow, as soon as I know if Tinan lives or dies." The Aryx warmed against my chest. "I will have your obedience on this, *sieurs*, or I swear I shall prosecute *both* of you for treason."

"*D'mselle*—" Di Yspres, in a patently reasonable tone that threatened to ignite my temper.

Does he think this no more than an attack of women's vapors? "Your word, Jierre di Yspres. And yours, Tristan d'Arcenne. Your sworn oaths that you will not damage the Pruzian."

"This is not the time to be merciful," Tristan remarked. Bryony looked from him to me, as if expecting the next volley in a game of *laun*, his mouth slightly open and his color no better.

"Nevertheless, that is my command. You call yourself the Queen's Guard; in this you will do as I say. I do not wish him broken until I may question him myself."

Perhaps it was the wine speaking. But I dropped my gaze back to Tinan di Rocham's fair young face, the sweat standing out on his pale brow. "Now get out, hedgewitch. You too, di Yspres, and set a guard on our prisoner. If there is a mark on the Pruzian tomorrow, I shall hold you personally responsible. Send a message to the Baron that the Pruzian is mine, remanded to the Queen's justice. I care not if I have to threaten to turn myself over to d'Orlaans to make it so, but I *will* have obedience. Is that clear?"

Bryony left, with more haste than decorum.

Jierre swept me a fine Court bow, pausing long enough at the bottom of it to make it sarcastic, his hand aside as if he held his fine feathered hat. "If that is the Queen's will," he managed through gritted teeth, and slammed the door for good measure.

The silence inside the small stone room lay tense and aching until Tristan broke it. "That was ill done, Vianne. Jierre is not your enemy."

The wine had loosed my tongue. "Neither are you," I retorted sharply. "Yet you would torture an assassin to death to salve your wounded pride, and you would call it duty. I know your duty in this matter, Tristan d'Arcenne, and I *will* have obedience." *There is death lying on this cot; does not it make your heart break? If it does not, why? Why are you so willing to spread more of it?*

420

"Very well." He shrugged, winced slightly as if his side pained him. "I can always kill him later."

How can you say such things so calmly? Is that what a man is? "You may. But not until I say so."

"As my Queen commands." Was that a new coolness in his tone? I hoped not.

If it was…I would mourn the loss of warmth, but it would not alter my course.

I turned my attention to the boy on the cot. Bootless, sweating, the bandage at his belly staining with fresh bright red and darker, fouler matter, he seemed very small.

I have not served you well, chivalier. *Dear gods.*

I took Tinan di Rocham's hand in both of mine. "Tinan," I whispered, and the Aryx shifted against my chest. A fine thin vibration ran through my marrow.

I closed my eyes. The wine loosened my mind, dilated my heart, turning inside my chest like a giant gyre. *Show me,* I pleaded. *You have power, a great deal of it; you showed me once how to use it fully. Show me now, please. Let me save his life, and I will not fight you.*

The Aryx, wonder of wonders, answered, doors flung open inside my head again and the golden riptide of sorcery swallowed me. Yet I did not witness it. I did not gainsay the Seal, only gave myself up to it. When the gold faded there was only soft restful darkness, and a brushing like wings.

I woke the following morning, in Tristan's bed, with my Consort standing guard at the door.

He was silent as I dressed myself, not offering to help with the laces as he usually did. That was sometimes worth a half-hour of my laughter and his good-natured cursing before the dress was laced properly, and kisses as well. Today, however, it was indigo satin and quiet; I laid the Aryx atop the fabric and braided my hair with unsteady hands.

Tristan exited the watercloset and stalked to his clothespress, pulled on fresh breeches and a new shirt. He struggled into a leather doublet without my help. The silence between us grew brittle. I stood at the window, looking down over the practice-ground and garden, now familiar sights. I tied off the last braid with a bit of ribbon and sighed, leaning against the stone. Lisele would laugh to see the simplicity of my hair lately, but I was far too hurried during the day to stop and re-dress my braids. Besides, I had not a ladyservant to help; Tristan had been more than enough help with laces, and I had not felt I needed more. He was not so fine at braiding a woman's hair, not quick-fingered enough. It was the only clumsiness I saw in him.

Tristan approached me slowly. He stopped at my shoulder, looking past me out the window. Or at least, I felt his breath upon my cheek and thought that was where he gazed. The heat of him was a comfort and a grievance at the same time.

"Are you angry with me, *m'chri*?"

Of all the questions I expected, that was the last. "With you? Of course not." My own question rose hard on the heels of that denial. "I expect you are rather furious with me, though?"

"No." His hands stole around my waist. "You were right. I was not…calm, last night. I *am* furious, but at the thought of you in danger, *m'chri*. I wish him to suffer."

Again he surprised me. I was glad we were both gazing in the same direction and not at each other, for my jaw gaped in a most unladylike manner. And there are things that may be said while two people study a vista instead of each other. "Ah." I searched for aught else to add. "Tristan, I am sorry. I was unkind last night."

"You were right, Vianne. You often are." He drew me back against him. I could dimly hear the sound of clattering wood and effort from the practice-ground; they were at morning drill. Sunlight bleached the white stone of Arcenne. "Do you think me a murderer?"

I do not know what to think, but I doubt you would not murder, did you need to. "I do *not*—"

"Hush." He covered my mouth, but it was gentle, a reminder of the road from the Citté. "Do you suppose I have any honor left, after being Henri's Left Hand? After…what I have done in his name?"

Whatever crimes Henri di Tirecian-Trimestin committed in the name of kingship, his Left Hand committed more. Take care who you keep close to you…tis more important than you think. Risaine's words rose up to haunt me. Hard on their heels came the words of her son:

You are not such a secret to me as you are to our d'mselle…*Besides, I look forward to the day all is revealed.*

But Tristan was so gentle. He had done nothing but watch over me. Who did I have to thank for my escape from the conspiracy? What did he speak of?

And now that I knew more of lovers and having a Consort, the thought of the Duc's limp white hands touching me made me sick all through.

"Whatever you did for the King is finished." I tried to make my tone a balance of light and serious, to put paid to his uncertainty. "You are my *chivalier*, and my Consort. Well enough?"

"More than I deserve," he said into my hair, a long sigh. "On my honor, then, Vianne; I will never be so angry I cannot comfort you. Well enough?"

My heart swelled to its normal size, and melted at the same

moment. "Indeed. And on mine, likewise."

He paused, as if there was summat else he would add. I waited, but when he spoke next, it was to turn to business.

"Then I am content. I suppose you have some new variety of heartstopping excitement for us this morning?"

"Questioning the Pruzian. And di Rocham..." *Dare I ask?* Abruptly, I felt the bite of shame. That should have been my first question.

"He lived through the night, and likely will mend." Tristan paused. "The Aryx."

"Yes." I leaned in to his warmth. "I do not recognize myself anymore, Tris."

"I know you." He pressed a kiss onto my hair. But his hands trembled. "You are my Vianne, and the Queen of Arquitaine."

I did not protest. Instead, I let Tristan hold me until a maid knocked at the door, bringing breakfast. Twas a respite before the storm; and a welcome one. Had I known what was to be, I would have cherished it all the more.

Chapter Thirty-Seven

The Baron d'Arcenne was exceeding unhappy. "He sought to kill me, and my wife, and my son," he informed me, as if I did not already know. "I want him hanged. I want him *dead*, for the crows to peck at his—"

"He is remanded to my justice, Baron." It took work to keep my tone even. I stood at the fireplace, my hands clasped in front of me. The Baroness, her hazel eyes wide and unwontedly dark, sat on a divan, her embroidery in her lap. I wanted badly to ask her if she was hurt or frightened, but Tristan's father had given me little time. Instead, he had set upon me the moment I arrived, without even a *good morn* greeting.

I did not blame him, but still.

Tristan himself was outside the door, conferring with Jermain di Vantmor. I did not ask of what; I would learn of it later if necessary.

The Baron fixed me with an icy blue d'Arcenne glare. "Your justice? And just what is your justice, you silly little—"

"That is enough." The Aryx rilled softly under my words, a tone sharp enough to cut glass. He was silenced with gratifying speed. "You will not serve Arquitaine or your Queen with a head clouded by anger, Baron. Do me the good grace to trust my judgment, since you have declared me fit to rule. I will *occasionally* reserve the right to make some small requests of *my* subjects."

I matched him glare for glare, the air boiling between us.

"Perseval," Tristan's mother said, breathless. "Please."

He looked away. I would not have been surprised had the breaking of our gazes made a sound like cords snapping. I cut my own gaze to the fire, letting out a silent sigh. The Baron was furious enough to do me harm if I argued more with him, and that would go ill for all involved.

Give him some other bone to worry at. His home was attacked, and he prides himself on its safety. "Gather the Council." I was careful to keep my tone soft, but inflexible. "I wish Adrien di Cinfiliet recalled, I have a task to set him. I also wish a messenger found to take a proclamation and another missive to Navarrin. I will see Divris di Tatancourt after lunch, then I will see my Council." I gathered my skirts, the black pearl eardrops the Baroness had loaned me swinging against my cheeks. "I trust by the next time I see you, Minister Primus, you will be in better temper. Baroness, I would very much like to lunch with you, unless you are discomforted by the recent…unpleasantness."

I sound like the King. Faint steely amusement rose at the thought. *Good.*

The Baroness took my cue neatly, as if we were dancing a maying ganaire. "I would be honored to lunch with you, Your Majesty. And I hope you will forgive my Consort, he is extraordinarily upset."

"My sleep was interrupted last night, as well. I understand.

And please, Baroness, address me as Vianne." I gave a nod, and swept from the room with Perseval d'Arcenne's anger a hot weight against my back.

Tristan sent di Vantmor away with a curt gesture. "Vianne? My father—"

"He is merely angry, Tris. Leave him be; I gave him another fox to bay at. Come, where is the Pruzian? And how does Tinan?"

"Tinan is recovering. The Pruzian is in the *oublietta*."

Is that what mountainfolk call a donjon? "Good. Take me there. We will no doubt pass Guards on the way; we can send one for a scribe. Find me anyone in the Citadel who speaks Pruzian." My skirts snapped as I strode down the hall. "And we shall have a breakfast brought to the donjon, including watered wine. We shall need Bryony, too."

"What are you planning?"

I have an idea, m'cher. *Let us see how well I cast my dice.* "You shall see. Come along."

We made our way to the deepest parts of the Keep, far away from the Sun's eye. I held my skirts up as we descended a long flight of narrow damp-stone stairs, and the thought of the tunnel under Mont di Cienne rose in my memory, made my breathing short. Tristan led me down, and down, and down, past neat rows of stone cells. Finally, I saw more torch-light ahead—and Adersahl, whose mustache was resurrecting itself with a vengeance. He stood guard with thin, curly-headed Jai di Montfort. They both swept me Court-polished bows.

"Adersahl. Jai." I inclined my head, accepting the honor. "How does the Pruzian?"

They exchanged a look I read all too well. Anger rose up my

throat, I set my jaw and swallowed it. *I cannot find what I must know if this man has been ill-treated. Why did they not listen?* "Ah. I see. Di Montfort, would you be so kind as to fetch me di Yspres?"

Jai di Montfort bowed again, did not look to Tristan to reinforce the order. He merely brushed past us and his footsteps faded against stone.

I stepped forward.

Tristan's hand closed around my elbow. "Vianne—"

"No." I shook free, took another two steps. Looked past Adersahl and into the room.

Featureless stone, water plinking damply from a ceiling festooned with rusting chains. I did not see the Pruzian, but what I did see chilled me.

A rough hole in the middle of the floor. "Gods above," I breathed.

I pushed the rusted gate aside with a screeching and approached the hole cut in the floor, my skirts whispering sweetly. Peered into the darkness of the *oublietta*. A single glowglobe attached to a rusted hanging chain overhead struggling to pierce the gloom; I saw a shape that might have been a dark-haired man lying chained at the bottom, in a blackness like night-spilled wine.

A glitter of eyes, and the dampness on him was perhaps not all water.

I turned on my heel. "Bring Bryony *now*," I said tightly. "Tristan, go fetch him. Adersahl, come help me."

"Vianne." Tristan. "He is a Pruzian *Knife*."

"Do as I *bid* you, d'Arcenne!" I snapped. I did not glance at him, for if I did I was afraid my tongue and my temper would both perform feats they would regret.

Adersahl approached. I heard Tristan's footsteps recede, unwillingly.

But he obeyed.

"*D'mselle*—," the stocky Guard began.

Enough of this. You thought I would be biddable? No. The game has changed, and I am no longer content to let any of you do as you please when I have made a simple request. "Help me. How do we get him out?"

"'Tis an *oublietta*. You do not stroll forth from one alive—Vianne!"

I halted at the very edge. It looked a very long fall, though it was no more than two bodylengths. "Undo your belt."

"What?" He stared as if I had gone mad.

Tis a simple enough request, to match my first. "Undo your belt. Now, *chivalier*."

He slowly unbuckled his belt. "I do not think—"

"Be silent. I do not *care* what you think or do not." My skin crawled at the thought of what I was about to do. "You will have to lower me down."

"Tristan will—"

"I do not *care*." My voice bounced off the stone. "Either you will lower me, or I leap and break my leg like a foundered horse. Choose." I leaned forward, and Adersahl twitched.

He had gone pale, and the gray in his hair reflected the glowglobe's weak shimmer. "Why do you do this? *D'mselle*, why?"

Must you ask? I would have thought it obvious. "Because I will not be the Duc d'Orlaans. I will not be made a monster because we are faced with the problem of *defeating* one." My hands closed around the end of his belt. "You may tell them I leapt, Adersahl. I shall not blame you if you do."

"If you are determined to be insane, so am I. Hold fast, be careful now."

I wrapped the tough leather around my right hand and trusted Adersahl to lower me down. My slippers slid against the damp stone, my dress hanging, and for the first time in a very long while I wished to be wearing breeches again. This would *ruin* the fabric.

A horrible smell rose to greet me. *Oh, gods above.* The glimmer of a naked skull atop a jumble of ivory thrown against the wall leered at me, and I pushed down a swoon. *How long ago did the Baron last use this thing? Does he know there are bones? It is a donjon, yes... but think of dying here, alone, in the dark.*

It would not do to think on it for very long.

I dropped the last four feet or so, landing with an impact that jarred my teeth.

The Pruzian moaned. His eyes were almost swollen shut. He was naked, and his hands and feet were chained together. "Gods." I looked in vain for water, for food. Nothing. "Adersahl, a waterskin. A cambric—no, I have one. A waterskin, for the love of the Blessed."

"Be careful, Vianne."

"I do not think he is a danger. He is chained and beaten near to death." I knelt by the Pruzian, pinching my nose shut against the smell.

Last night he had been a figure of terror. Now he was merely broken.

The glimmer of a hedgewitch charm began on my free hand's fingers, the Aryx moving sleepily to obey me. I had spent so long fighting; it was no longer necessary. The Great Seal did as I asked with only token resistance, without trying to force the doors of magic open and propel me through them.

I was still in danger of drowning, but at least I was learning to swim.

Jaryana had taught me this charm, one to still a fever and bolster a sick man's strength. It took a new depth of power from the Aryx, and I had to take care lest the sudden flow of sorcery harm the life I sought to save. I wished suddenly that I had known what Jaryana and Risaine had taught me before. I might have been able to stave off death from Lisele, and save her from the Duc as well.

Wishes will not stop the tide, nor will they bring the dead back to life. Ware your work at hand, Vianne, not what you wish could have been.

The man's skin was fever-hot under my fingers. He moaned. I saw marks on him, terrible marks, and my heart compressed itself with a pang. He lay curled into a ball like a child, his long dark hair tangled and matted with blood.

I repeated the charm, the magic sliding through my fingers and into his flesh. The Aryx, muttering, sank back into quiescence and I was left with merely my own power to charm. Twas enough, now that I knew what I was about.

I could not hold my nose clamped shut forever, and the fresh green scent of hedgewitchery mixed uneasily with the reek of rot, stone, pain, blood, and foulness.

Above me, I heard returning footsteps.

"Where is—oh, no. *Vianne!*" A horrified cry bounced off stone. The Aryx muttered, spilling fresh force through me, and I had to throttle the flow lest it drown my patient.

I returned to myself slowly, the tide of sorcery retreating. "I am safe enough, Tristan," I called up. "But you shall have to find a way to bring us both out. He is sorely injured. Can you lower the waterskin, Adersahl?" I brought my square of cambric out.

"And are there keys for these cuffs?"

Tristan's face appeared at the top of the *oublietta*. His eyes were alive with blueness. "Vianne." His cool, soft dueling-tone; as if I were an enemy. "He is a *Pruzian Knife*. Get away from him."

Do not order me about. I bit the words back, chose summat else to say. "He is chained and beaten to a pulp. I suggest you turn your wits to finding a way to get us both out of this hole if you are so worried for me."

Chapter Thirty-Eight

"Have some chai." Sílvie poured; I rubbed my fingers against the green satin of my skirt. The indigo dress needed cleaning, twas fouled with donjon and other things. "Would you care to speak, or do you wish silence?"

"I cannot tell." I picked up a strawberry. Set it back down. "They might have killed him, Baroness."

"If you are Vianne, then I am Sílvie. There." A single nod, curls swinging free over her ears. The rest of her dark hair, caught back in a complicated knot, glowed in the bright warm light. "Yes, they might have killed him. You stopped them." She handed me the delicate porcelain cup, its saucer held correctly. I accepted, my smallest finger just *so*, a little Court mannerism.

"They are too angry. I had plans which required that man." I sounded plaintive. My shoulders slumped before I straightened, Comtesse Rocheburre's ghostly voice ringing in the mists of memory. *A noblewoman does not slouch, Duchesse. Keep your shoulders back, and sit straight.*

The Baroness's gaze was kind. "Tis well *you* hold the Aryx, then. Have a pastry, Vianne. You shall need it. You have a long dreary afternoon full of angry men before you."

Tristan was outside the door with Luc di Chatillon. I did not know what they would say to each other, and despite my determination I was still afraid of my Consort's anger. They had hauled us both out of the *oublietta*, and I had supervised the installing of the Pruzian in a freshly-swept infirmary cell, Bryony had examined him and added his own hedgewitch healing to mine. Tristan was tight-lipped and silent during the whole process. The Pruzian had not regained consciousness, so the scribe was sent back to his work in the Archives. Nobody in Arcenne spoke Pruzian, it seemed, so I had to hope the Knife spoke Arquitaine.

I had left Adersahl to guard the Pruzian and made it understood to others of the Guard that I needed information this man had, and he had to be whole to give it. Jierre still had not shown his face; Jai had not returned either.

I could only guess at why.

I had also made it understood that any Guard who lifted a hand to the Pruzian would be summarily dismissed from my service. Oddly enough, that made even Adersahl blanch. I was as certain as I could be that the assassin would be safe.

Until he awakened and was well enough to question, that is. Which presented an entirely new set of ugly plans to be made.

Sílvie's sitting room was a haven of peace, sunlight slanting through the windows. The needlework frame seemed dipped in gold glow, and the harp vibrated with its eagerness to make music.

Still, uneasiness had invaded the Keep along with killspell and Knives. I could almost *taste* the brittle copper of fear, hanging in the halls and creeping in the corners. "I fear Tristan is rather angry at me for denying him the pleasure of beating the

Pruzian to death." *Ware what you say. This is his mother.*

"Mh, *that* storm will pass. He cannot stay angry with you for long. Have a dainty, I implore you." Her eyes twinkled. Altogether she was too sunny-calm, and while I cherished her ease, I wished she would be serious with me.

I selected a biscuit. "Oh, he can stay angry at me. And I am rather afraid he will." It was a plea, and she must have recognized it. *Dearest Baroness, how do I handle your son?* "I should beg your pardon, for you were attacked as well."

"Oh, well. What can one do? I must confess I barely woke, even when Perseval cursed and dragged me out of bed. I cursed him back roundly for disturbing me, too." She laughed, her ruby ear-drops swinging. I had to admit that there was nothing Perseval d'Arcenne denied his Baroness, for all his harshness. "I think you have the right of it. If it were up to Perseval and Tristan we would all be endlessly doing our wretched duty without respite. Tis something in the d'Arcennes, I think. Bones from the Mountains and a sense of noble obligation to match."

"I am not practiced at this at all, Sílvie. I belong at Court with my books and nothing more pressing than which skirt to wear and which gossip not to repeat." *And Lisele to watch for.* "I shall get us all murdered and d'Orlaans will triumph…" I bent my head, dabbed at my eyes with a linen napkin. It was terrible manners to weep so, but I could not stop myself. "And I ruined the lovely dress you had made for me," I finished mournfully. The indigo would likely never be the same.

"The dress matters not a whit." She selected a biscuit of her own. "Of all those in the world, in Arquitaine, the Aryx chose you."

We were not truly speaking of the Aryx, were we? No, we were not. "What good is it if I have not wits enough to play these games? No. They are not games, they are deadly serious, and I—"

"Vianne, have another biscuit. You are merely frightening yourself." She pressed the biscuit on me, and more chai.

I managed half the crunchy, delicate pastry before my stomach closed. "I *am* frightened." It did not sound so terrible a secret when I let the air carry it. "I only leap from one crisis to the next. And what if Tristan decides…" Even my newfound hardiness could not carry me further.

"One moment." The Baroness rose, laying aside her cup and saucer. She crossed her sitting room, her skirts soughing sweetly, and opened the drawer on her small desk covered with letters and two inkstands, a rack of charmed quill pens bobbing their feathered fringes at her. She drew out a sheaf of papers, rolled and tied with a crimson velvet ribbon. "I would show you summat." She pulled out the dainty rosewood chair next to me and settled down with a sigh of silk. "Tristan wrote these." She shuffled through them, laying the ribbon aside. "Does that look familiar? It should; you dropped it at a fête. He sent it home and asked me to keep it for him."

"A hair ribbon?" It seemed so unlike the practical, level-headed Tristan I knew that I picked up the velvet, smoothed it in my fingers. If it was one of mine, I would have worn it with my red satin, the one cut so low I was always half afraid my breasts would spill out, though I was laced so tight they never did. "I would have worn this with the red satin. It was too tight, I thought I was going to expire halfway through the pavane."

"Suffering for fashion; and Perseval wonders why I do not wish to visit Court. Ah. Here we are." She finished ruffling the pages. "Listen. *I watched the* d'mselle *again today, Mami, and I have to ask: how does one approach a woman? Do not laugh. I leave flowers for her, follow her from one end of the Court to the other, and yet she never notices. I take it back, you will laugh at me, ma Mére, you warned me, did you not?"* Sílvie's smile was proud and tender in equal measure. "He did not know quite what to do. I wrote back to ask him what you liked, and he replied, books! So I told him to send you a package of books, and he replied that he could not without casting suspicion on himself." Her sudden laughter rang in the sunshine falling through the windows. "I promptly wrote back demanding if that was not ex-actly what he *wanted*, your suspicion."

I had to laugh as well. The thought of Tristan penning frantic missives to his mother about an oblivious woman was highly amusing. Curiosity overcame good manners. "What else did he write?"

Her mischievous grin shouted that pricking my curiosity had been her intent. "Well, here, see for yourself. As long as you eat, child. You have not gained a red copper since you came here. Have a bread-and-cress, and read this one. No, wait, this one's better."

I had forgotten what it was, to converse with another woman so. She made me laugh, and roundly scolded me into eating while I read some of Tristan's old letters, choice passages escap-ing aloud. It was deliciously wicked. For a moment I was back at Court, and she a little wickeder and certainly sharper than my Lisele, and good company to boot.

We were laughing heartily, our heads close together as we conferred like myrmyra birds, when there was a courteous tap at the door.

Sílvie dexterously swept the letters under the table and into her lap as I clapped my hand over my mouth, tears of merriment making my sight waver.

Tristan glanced over the room. "Vianne? You said to call for you when Divris di Tatancourt—good gods, are you well?" The soft edge of duel-hunger was gone from his tone; he sounded concerned.

I blinked away merry tears and nodded. "Well enough, indeed." My voice did not tremble, though I had difficulty keeping another spate of laughter caged. I rose slowly, another small chuckle escaping me as I saw his face wander into perplexity.

Sílvie patted my hand, the letters kept out of sight in her lap. "Tomorrow. Lunch again. We shall speak more on this."

"Oh, indeed we shall." My mouth wanted to twitch. The letters were amusing indeed; though I felt a bit guilty reading a son's private musings to his mother. It was a welcome shock to find just how closely Tristan had watched me at Court.

Yet the Baroness had just steadied the world under my feet. And I *had* eaten, my stomach calming and accepting lunch with good grace. "My thanks, Sílvie. Tomorrow cannot come soon enough."

She waved her fingers, unable to speak for suppressed laughter. It set me to grinning foolishly as well, my heart light as a maying breeze.

Tristan held the door with a slight bow as I swept past. Luc di Chatillon saluted me and I nodded in return.

"What mischief are you twain planning?" my Consort asked incuriously, as we set off down the hall. "Do you feel better, then?"

"Much." Yet I sobered. The holiday was past, now twas time for the disagreeable. My hands took care of my skirts so I could match his longer stride, but he tarried a little. "Where is di Yspres?"

"Possibly afraid to face you." He looked somber, his mouth a straight line. "Tinan woke for a short time; Bryony says there is no doubt he will recover."

"Thank the gods for that." Fervent relief threatened to weaken my knees. "Why is your lieutenant afraid to face me? I asked di Montfort to bring him."

Tristan shrugged. There was a shadow in his blue eyes. "They fear your displeasure, or being thrown from the Guard. Perhaps."

Oh, perhaps. I sighed. He did not move to take my hand as he usually did. This new distance between us was painful. "You are angry, again. At me."

Did he pale slightly? His left hand dropped to his rapier, touched the hilt. "The Pruzian could have killed you. You *must* take more care with yourself."

"He was chained and beaten, Tristan. Against my orders, I might add." Irritation made my tone much sharper than it needed to be. "I require information from him. I need to know precisely who hired him and *precisely* who their targets were."

"Why?"

How can you not know? Or do you think me empty-headed, caviling merely to be obstinate? "Because if the Duc has stooped to sending assassins after me as well as after you, it means he has reexamined his willingness to let me come back to Court so he can bed me as he pleases and get a filthy brat to carry on his line. It will mean the game has changed, and I must learn the new state of the draught-board so I may play with a clear head." I stopped in the hall, my own irritation bouncing off the stone and rustling against a tapestry with the Arcenne mountain-pard worked in scarlet against a black field. "If his target was merely you and your father, what dance was the third trio intended for? You see, it is a riddle, and I dislike this manner of riddle." *And I will not be responsible for more death if I can possibly help it. You do not seem to understand that, no matter how much I love you. And oh, gods help me, but I do love you more than you may ever know.*

The realization was sweet and bitter in equal portion.

"Ah." Tristan nodded. "That quick mind of yours. I beg your pardon, Vianne."

I nodded. My ear-drops swung against my cheeks. "I understand there are things you must do that are…unfit for a lady's sensibilities. But I cannot afford to be overly a lady if I am the Queen. I *do* understand, Tris. I simply wish you would trust me to know what is best once in a great while as well." I took a deep breath, my eyes moving over his face. "And your being Left Hand does not mean I should not know what you do in my name."

Did I imagine it, or did he start as if I had pinched him? He paled even more. "I do what I must for your safety, Vianne." Tight-spaced, the words were biting-bitter.

"I know," I soothed.

"That is all I ever seek. You must know as much. *All* I seek is your safety, and I will do as I must."

"I trust as much. I asked you to become my Consort, did I not?"

"You did." He dropped his gaze, examining the hem of my skirt with much fascination. Was this the same man who had written about me with such agonized care, pleading with his mother to give him advice to catch my eye?

I should have noticed him at Court. It was unacceptable that a lady whose duty had been to catch intrigues had not noticed the *chivalier* at her window. "Tristan? May I ask you something?"

He shrugged. "We are late for your meeting with di Tatan-court."

True enough. Rebuffed, I smoothed my skirts. "Then let us be on our way," I said, and swept down the hall. Now I knew the way from Sílvie's sitting room to the library, and I was not afraid to lead him, his step echoing mine. His silence was as thunderous as any I've ever heard.

At the door to my study, I paused. "Thank you, Consort." Twas easier—and harder—than I liked to keep my tone level and cool. "Now, if you will be so kind as to farrat out wherever Jierre and Jai are hiding, and shepherd them into my presence before my Council Session."

"Vianne—"

No. If we are to perform this dance, we shall perform it in measures that suit me. "Now, Tristan." I held my ground. "Divris is to be trusted, and Arcenne is well guarded. Go, and the quicker you return the safer I am."

He did not argue further, but his jaw set so hard I was surprised his teeth did not shatter. *Well, if I wished him to hate me, I am going about it the right way.*

I sighed.

Then I arranged my face, entered the study quietly, accepted the Messenger's bow, and set myself to question Divris yet again about the Duc's Court. He was a wondrous observant witness, and he knew far more than he thought he did—at least, when I questioned him, his answers illuminated much, even if he did not know quite what he had told me.

He did not need to know, I decided. I had not time to teach him, and twas not his place to hold such knowledge. I had much more to learn now, and the stakes were growing rapidly higher.

Chapter Thirty-Nine

The Council Session ran late and led to two shouting matches—both of which I won by simply waiting until the men finished rattling their rapiers and then informing them all coolly that it was bad form to shout in front of a lady, and that I was, I would remind them, *in case* they had forgotten, the Queen.

And if they doubted the wisdom of my commands, or would seek to choose only those commands that suited their purposes, they were no better than d'Orlaans. If they insisted, they could hie themselves hence and field an army against me—or go to join the Duc, being of his stripe.

That handily put an end to discussion, though I disliked using such arguments.

It was after dark when I finally arrived at the Pruzian's cell accompanied by Bryony to find Tristan, Jierre, and Jai di Montfort standing guard with Adersahl, who eyed them while he twirled his reborn mustache.

"D'mselle." Adersahl greeted me with a low, sweeping bow. The others followed suit. Even Tristan.

"Your Majesty..." Jai di Montfort's voice failed him as my glance rested on his lean dark face.

I must look forbidding. Well, if I do, I am grateful for it. I have had enough of men arguing, of late.

I stood with my hands clasped in my skirts, examining all three of them. "Bryony? Please attend the Pruzian. Adersahl, accompany him."

A murmur of assent. Even Bryony's frosty silence did not wound me. What did a peasant hedgewitch's tender feelings matter, if Tristan was past his first flush of care for me?

Now we would see if we could remain friends, my Consort and I. I let the disobedients simmer a trifle longer, until even di Yspres flushed like a guilty boy caught stealing apples.

"Well," I said finally. "*Sieurs* di Yspres and di Montfort. Tis pleasant to see you. I had expected you to obey my summons without needing to be fetched hence like schoolboy truants."

Jierre blushed deeper. Jai di Montfort dropped his gaze to my feet.

"Now," I continued. "I found the Pruzian damaged when I gave explicit orders he *not* be touched. This is *most* disappointing. Then to compound that error by refusing to obey my summons? Not fit behavior for the Queen's Guard, is it?"

No answer but their hung-head silence. Boys being taken to task by a headmaster, deserving more than a sharp crack against the knuckles.

But I must tread softly. If I pricked their pride *just* right, it would bolster their loyalty instead of deflating it. And I might well need them in the future. "Very well. I've decided your punishment."

"Your Majesty—" Di Montfort, unable to contain himself.

"Hold your tongue, *sieur*." Much to my gratified surprise, he did. "I am extremely disappointed, *chivalieri*. For the next two days, you will not wear the uniform of a Queen's Guard, and you will leave your rapiers in the dormitory. You will carry only daggers. After that, you are readmitted into the Guard and all is forgiven." I found a smile rising, banished it. Now was a time for severity. "The next time you disobey me and hide from me, I shall throw you out of the Guard with stripes. This is not a place for children; you are *chivalieri* sworn to the Queen of Arquitaine, and I expect you to behave as such." I inclined my head slightly. "You are dismissed. Go to the Guard dormitory and do as I bid you, to the very last inch."

"Yes, Your Majesty." Di Montfort was now pale. Di Yspres echoed the words. Did the lieutenant look relieved? They trooped past me, stopping only to sweep deep, respectful bows. I waved them away and faced Tristan.

Now for the next hurdle. Gods grant my strength holds.

"So." The sound of their footsteps faded. He pitched his tone low enough that it would not carry, a skill learned at Court.

I copied his tone, speaking softly without losing enunciation. "You did not return, either." I tried not to sound hurt, failed miserably.

"I feared your temper." A bald admission, his hand resting on his rapier-hilt and his expression so grave my heart compressed within me.

"Fear *my* temper?" I shook my head. "And I have been fearing yours."

"I would never harm you." His eyes burned, almost luminous in the torchlit gloom.

"I fear the loss of your affection, *chivalier*, perhaps more than any harm you could do me." The admission sent a frisson up my back, and I stepped nervously toward the cell's barred iron door.

"You think it possible to lose my affection?" Yet his face eased.

I learned mistrust too thoroughly at Court. And everything that has happened since has not helped. "I think it possible I might, Tristan. And it frightens me." I moved through the door before he could reply. It was childish of me, yes. But I did not wish to cross wits with him to this degree just yet.

I needed my wit for other things.

Adersahl di Parmecy stood in a corner, his arms folded. The Pruzian was awake, flat on his back on a cot against one side of the narrow cell. His eyes glittered under tangled dark hair as Bryony gingerly took his pulse, then flattened his hand against the assassin's chest and began to whisper his charm. I watched, the pleasant sensation of hedgewitch magic tingling over my skin. He had considerable skill, and I watched carefully to see if I could learn aught of what he did.

"He will live." The hedgewitch's grudging failed to wound me, though he looked as if he wished it did.

Still, my graciousness did not waver.

Well, perhaps it wavered slightly. "Thank you, Bryony."

"'Tis my duty." Bryony gathered up his physicker's implements, and left without so much as a good-bye. He had to press past Tristan, whose shoulders nearly filled the door.

"I need summat to perch upon—Adersahl?" I did not wish to loom over the wounded man.

The stocky Guard pointed out the low, three-legged stool near the door, which I fetched myself, overriding his protests. Then I set it by the cot and sank down, arranging my skirts. I am not so tall for a woman, so I was able to rest my hands on my knees properly, my back straight.

It was time. I met the man's glittering, fevered glance.

"*B'joure*," I said, as if meeting him at Court. "I am Vianne di Rocancheil et Vintmorecy. Do you speak Arquitaine?"

He blinked. His gaze flicked over Tristan and Adersahl. Back to me.

"Oh dear." I switched to Tiberian. "Tiberian? Do you speak Tiberian?"

He coughed. It was a low, thin sound. "Some," he rasped. "Arq'taine." His accent mangled the words—Pruzian is an unlovely tongue at best. It sounds like hacking with a heavy cold and chopping the words into little bits as you spit in the face of your conversational partner. "You. *D'mselle.*"

My eyebrows lifted. "You speak some Arquitane. That is very good." I made my words slow and distinct. "What is your name?"

He had a strong jaw, stubbled with charcoal hair; the swelling on his face had gone down. "Fridrich." His lips shaped the word oddly, and he smelled of illness and pain. "Fridrich van Harkke."

"'Tis a pleasure, *sieur.*" I offered him my hand, dropped it back in my lap when he made no move. "I am very sorry they mistreated you. It will not happen again." *Or I will be forsworn, and I will do much more than give the Guard a verbal spanking.* "I wish to ask you questions. Surely you understand?"

"Hired. Word is bond." He shook his head painfully, his hair rasping on the pillow. "No name of *aufsbar.*"

"*Aufsbar?*" It was my turn to mangle a word, my mouth would not shape the harsh sounds.

"Client," he supplied, his eyelids drooping still further.

"Surely you can tell me who your targets were? Please?" I reached up and gently pushed the tangled dark hair from his face. I tried not to touch his bruised skin. Sickness, like a fruit laid too long in a dark corner, an unhealthy reek. "If that is an affair of honor too, I am afraid we shall have to keep you in the donjon. It will not be comfortable, but you will not be mistreated."

His eyes glittered, glittered. Watching me as a wounded snake might watch a bird hopping just out of range.

I sighed, and laid my hand against his chest where Bryony had. Fever-heat blurred through the cloth doublet they had given him.

The charm rose, simple and undeniable in its rightness, the Aryx lending its strength to the healing with no demur. When I opened my eyes and took my hand away, the faint green glimmers of hedgewitchery still clung to my fingers. "As you like. But hear me. If you tell us who your targets were, I offer you your freedom, Fridrich van Harkke. You may leave Arcenne as soon as you are well enough, and we shall give you a horse and supplies too. You may go home, or whither you will."

That seemed to strike him as terribly amusing. He gave a dry whistling laugh. "Was not meant to kill. Bring back the pretty-bit—you. Kill blue-eyed Baron and his son. Was our job. You were not meant to be harmed, *fralein*. Only *brought*."

Well, that's comforting. At least the game has not changed to that high a degree. "Thank you, *sieur* van Harrke. You shall be visited every day by the physicker, and I shall visit as well. When you are hale enough, you shall be set free outside the town's walls."

He closed his eyes, blowing out a sigh. He obviously did not think much of my promises.

I did not blame him.

There was only one thing left to say. "Your friends." My voice was soft. "I am sorry for them." *I would not have more death, not even yours. I cannot prevent it, but I would not have it.*

"Know the risk. *Das miez'weizs*," he rasped. His breathing deepened into the steady harsh rhythm of sleep.

I made it to my feet a little less than gracefully, backed away from the cot for a few steps before turning to the door. Tristan offered me his hand. "Did you learn aught of interest?" His eyes rested on the assassin, and he made no attempt to disguise his loathing.

Far more than I thought possible. "I did." *I learned the Duc wishes me unharmed, that I was to be brought. Presumably there were plans to take me from Arcenne, which makes it even more imperative to know precisely where di Narborre is. I have also learned a little of this man, and I think he may be amenable to further usefulness.*

After all, returning to the Duc is not a choice he can make. Not comfortably, at least.

Adersahl followed us out, locked the door. I saw the shadows under his eyes. *I should set another Guard, but who can I trust?* "Adersahl? Who may I trust to watch him, and not slip a knife between his ribs?"

Adersahl considered this, glancing at Tristan, who manfully restrained from commenting. "Jespre di Vidancourt. Level-headed, not given to impulsiveness."

"I shall have him sent down. Thank you." He had been on guard for far too long, down here in this dank hole. "No—it strikes me, Tristan and I shall stay here. Go tell Jespre to hie himself here, and you take some rest."

He swept me a bow with alacrity. "Now there is a happy thought. My thanks, Your Majesty."

"Oh, do not flatter." I offered him my hand, which he kissed. "Thank you, Adersahl. I am glad of you."

He grinned, twirled his mustache, and left. Which left me alone with Tristan outside the Pruzian's cell. He leaned against the wall, his entire posture languid and easy. But his jaw was too tight, and his left hand clenched on his swordhilt.

I peered through the door. The Pruzian lay in torch-dappled shadow, and I wondered if I could see a gleam of eyes. I wondered also if he needed more than just a thin blanket against the chill damp. "You *are* angry." I stated the obvious once again.

"Why do you say that, *m'chri*?" But his fingers tapped his swordhilt.

"Because I would be a poor Consort indeed if I could not tell."

He sighed, deeply, an aggrieved sound. "I am not angered at you."

"Who else *would* you be angry at?" *Speak to me. Let us not allow silence between us, my darling.*

"The *vilhain* that sent Pruzian Knives to collect you, perhaps? The *vilhain* who killed my King? Or perhaps the *saufe-tet* that chased us through Arquitaine and nearly cost you your life?" He shook his dark head, the gray at his temple flashed. "But I could not ever be angry at *you*. Why do you not understand?"

I slanted him a glance that might have been ironically amused if I was not so unsettled. If he decided to stride into the room right this moment and kill the Pruzian, I would not be able to stop him. He had the rapier, and enough volcanic fury to do it. All I had was the Aryx, the thin protection of custom—and my own wits. What I saw in him frightened me, for his eyes all but glowed as he observed me, narrowly. His mouth was a thin line and his fingers tapped at his swordhilt, a meditative rhythm.

I lowered myself from my tiptoes and faced him. The torches hissed.

His hand fell away from the hilt. "Your eyes are dark again, *m'chri.*"

I shrugged, my shoulders moving under silk. *Oh, Tristan. I do not know what to do.*

He peeled himself away from the wall, approached me slowly. Cupped my face in his hands, his gaze moving slowly over my cheeks, my mouth, resting on my eyes. "I have done many things for the throne of Arquitaine," he murmured. "I have acted as Henri's Left Hand; I have done things you cannot imagine. For all your sharp mind and political acumen, you are still the same very sweet young girl who let a Princesse win at riddlesharp and could not believe a man would court her by leaving books. I have betrayed and lied where I had to, and done things no honorable man would stoop to."

You are still my only defense, m'cher. "I care little what you did for the King, Tristan. I care what you do *now.*"

Oddly enough, my reassurance seemed to wound him. His mouth pulled down sourly. "Very well, Vianne. Gods grant me strength to be worthy of you."

There seemed nothing I could say. Instead, I leaned forward, his hands slid down and pulled me in. I rested against him in the torchlit dimness of the donjons, breathing him in, and for a moment felt the heavy weight of what I had promised when I took the Aryx from Lisele's fingers slip from me for a moment. "I do not care what you did," I whispered into his shoulder.

Did I imagine his flinch? In any case, Jespre di Vidancourt soon arrived, and it was time to move to the next task. But that conversation made me uneasy, though I did not know quite why.

Chapter Forty

Four weeks later, the storm broke.

I was uneasy that morning; there were dispatches to be sorted through. Perseval d'Arcenne had observed a frosty courtesy toward me since the affair of the Pruzians that might have managed to hurt my feelings had I not been occupied with a greater mystery: that of missing dispatches. Normally I would have simply waited for the vagaries of man and horse to bring them to me a day or two late, but they were all from the road to Ivrielle, and that meant the road out of the province and to the Citté.

Adrien di Cinfiliet was late as well. I could not help imagining the worst, until something even worse than the worst occurred to me—whenever I had time to think. Hard on its heels would come another terrible thought, and I sometimes laughed at my own imaginings.

Then I would sober, as the cycle of imagining began afresh.

Mornlight came warm and clear; wind snapping the pennants from the towers that day. I had breakfast in the library while I dictated diplomatic responses to Navarrin and messages to Arquitaine cities and provinces. It seemed no few had declared for me, a fact heartening and terrifying at the same time. More lives to depend on my wit, and me frantically trying to think of a way to reach a resolution with d'Orlaans that did not require bloodshed.

None seemed possible, especially in light of two assassination attempts.

Something else bothered me, too. I understood d'Orlaans wished me alive if he was to legitimize his reign and get heirs upon a noblewoman whose House would not rise against him in revolt. My House was all but extinct unless I produced an Heir, for my mother was dead and there were no other branches of Rocancheil *or* the ruling of Vintmorecy.

If I met with some misfortune, the Aryx would be forced to choose another holder, and mayhap the Duc thought he had extinguished all but him and me? It was an indication that he did not know of Adrien's existence, which was heartening.

Still, the fact that assassins were sent to fetch me was not guaranteed to ease my heart. True, I was only to be *brought*, not dispatched immediately. But that could only mean the Duc wished the pleasure of strangling me himself. He had to suspect by now that I was not amenable to his plans.

Tristan's behavior made me uneasy, too. He seemed on edge, waiting for a fresh disaster, though he was unfailingly gentle with me; especially at night as we lay together in his bed. He held me as if he expected me to vanish did he not keep a tight enough grasp; and if he was desperate in his use of me I was just as desperate in my use of him. What I learned of love in those days has remained with me ever after as a lesson in anguish, how two people can sense an approaching disaster and use each other's bodies as a shield against questions growing more and more pointed.

The half-head visited me once that month; I lost half a day lying abed and weeping with agony as my skull sought to rive itself to pieces. Tristan did not leave my side, holding my hand so tightly both our fingers were bruised. He whispered a Court sorcery that plunged the room into blackness, for any stray gleam of light during the half-head is more agonizing than the worst battle-wound. *Gods,* he whispered after the pain had left and I lay limp and too exhausted to do aught but breathe. *If I could take the pain from you, Vianne, I would. I would suffer it twice for your sake.*

Thank you for the darkness, I had replied, before losing consciousness.

It was not until later that I wondered why he knew such a charm. At the time, I was simply grateful. And there were other more pressing concerns. For Navarrin was hanging back, waiting to see whether the Duc or I would finish the course. Haviroen and Badeau were pleasant but noncommittal; Tiberia was more than willing to open diplomatic relations *if* I agreed to trade concessions once I was firmly in power—the same concessions they were perhaps pressuring d'Orlaans for, banking their coin securely on either horse. Sirisse, girdled in their mountains, cared little, for their god sleeps but holds their tall sharp borders inviolate. Scythandra would be no help, and the Principalities of Damar-Hesse and Sea-Countries besides, both nervous of Damar on their borders, played for time.

From the Damarsene, only a chill silence. Truth be told, I did not send them a missive. If they demanded tribute from d'Orlaans and I as both styled rulers of Arquitaine, I was ill-prepared to pay, promise, or insult them in such a way that they would not hold me to account for it later.

Yet it was the missing dispatches that worried me most. So

when I heard the faroff shouts and clatter in the bailey, I thought little of it except to frown and go back to the paperwork awaiting me, thinking it only a rider come with late news, who would be ushered into my presence soon enough. Tristan had gone to confer with his father about guard rosters and some points of trade with Navarrin that I wished counsel on.

So I was alone in the study—except for two of the Citadel Guard at the door—when Adersahl burst in, flushed and breathless.

I leapt to my feet, paper falling in a drift to the floor. Adersahl skidded to a stop. His bootheels all but struck sparks. "Tis di Cinfiliet," he gasped. "Bloody and missing half his men. Come quickly!"

I wasted no time with silly questions but bolted for the door; he whirled on his heel and ran before me, trusting me to follow.

Through the corridors of Arcenne we ran, and a stitch clawed at my side under pale-blue silk. I had to pick up my skirts, cursing them for once. We took a staircase headlong, I almost tripped and had to clutch at Adersahl's shoulder when we reached the gallery. So it was I arrived in the bailey amid a confusion of horses and shouts, me clasping Adersahl's arm and ducking under stray hooves as a bay reared. Adersahl cursed, I swallowed a burst of language most unfit for a lady, and the stocky Guard pushed me back.

"Vianne!" A familiar voice, throat-cut hoarse with shouting. "Vianne!"

Twas di Cinfiliet, and right glad was I to see him. I shook free of Adersahl, ducked past another lathered horse, and caught the reins of Adrien's exhausted gray-dappled gelding. Foam flung, spattered my dress. "Adrien!" *Safe and here, thank the gods. What new disaster is this?*

He was bloody, sweating, his shirt was in rags and his eyes burning with the kind of rage I had grown uncomfortably familiar with seeing on men's faces lately. "Milady Riddlesharp," he greeted me, with Risaine's sharp accent. "You look a sight better."

"And you a sight worse." Sick dread thudded under my heartbeat, the Aryx rilling uncertainly. "I worried for you. Why did you not come when I sent for you?" *Though it looks as if you had good reason.*

"I have been busy playing hide-in-the-bushes, *d'mselle*. And worse games." He swung down as I dragged on the reins; the horse pranced. Then the gray gave up, his head hanging; I stroked him soothingly.

After the war-trained behemoths the Guard rode, this gelding was far less daunting. And after coaxing and feeding and harnessing the horses the R'mini used sometimes to draw their wagons in place of oxen, I had learned at least not to fear a horse, even if it was more sprightly than a placid saddle-trained mare. "Easy there, *k'vrim*," I crooned to the gray in R'mini. "Ah, big fellow, be easy in your skin and hooves, be easy in your mane, eh?" I could almost hear Jaryana as she soothed a nervous beast, clicking her tongue and half-singing.

The gray shuddered, hung his head. He had been ridden almost to death.

Adrien reeked of sweat and horse and blood. "Vianne." Hoarse and urgent, my name pronounced as a talisman. "Tis good to see your face."

"Likewise." Arquitaine was strange in my mouth now after murmuring in R'mini. "Adrien, I—"

He shook his ragged dark head. "Later. Listen to me. There is news, grim news, and right glad I am to see you first and alone." He sought to calm his breathing and slumped, running his hand along the horse's trembling, lathered neck. "An army approaches, milady. Arcenne will soon be besieged."

The bottom dropped out of my stomach. *You predicted this, did you not? And I did not listen.* "Siege? By whom?"

He spoke the words I dreaded hearing.

"Damarsene. Flying the Duc's colors, though." My cousin coughed rackingly. Blood coated his sharp, tanned face like paint. Iron-shod hooves rang against stone. The bailey ran with sound, echoed with it, spilled over with the shouts and shrills of horses.

"How many?" My knees threatened to buckle. Damarsene. *They do not leave once they have marched past a border, not without much bloodshed. Is d'Orlaans mad, or does he think them easily fobbed off once he has what he wishes?* The horse's heaving sides eased. He had run his course, and mine was just beginning.

"Enough to take this city, fair lady Riddlesharp. Some few thousands, with a siege train and engines." He caught my arm, fingers sinking in carelessly hard. "I have other tidings, cousin mine. Later, if I may speak to you? Alone?"

Had I realized how he would soon rob me of all peace, I might have refused. No, that is not correct. I could not refuse, even if I looked back on this moment as the last before my world crumbled yet again.

The Aryx rasped uneasily against my dress. "Of course. Adrien—"

His fingers dug in, merciless. "Listen to me. Trust no one. I have a tale for you, my fair one." His lips skinned back from his teeth, a wolf's grimace. In the distance, a battlefield yell cut through the noise.

"*Vianne!*" Tristan, searching for me.

Court instinct rose. I did not struggle and cause a scene. Adrien's fingers prisoned my flesh, a bruise already rising on my arm. I did not flinch, simply gazed into his bloody face. "Tell me a tale, cousin." *What could be worse than Damarsene approaching, and the Duc—*

"Vianne! Vianne!" Tristan's voice, ringing through the bailey.

"I know a little tale, of a man who killed a King." Di Cinfiliet's whisper dripped venom in my ear. "He was a part of a conspiracy, and was so close to the King none suspected, not even fat Henri himself. But he was crossed; expected to be sacrificed like a *chivalier* on a battlechess board. Only he twisted as a *chivalier* does in that game; he disappeared with the key to it all, a girl with long dark hair and pretty, pretty eyes. I have proof to give you, *m'cousine*, captured from di Narborre himself. Your Captain, *m'cousine*—" Adrien's fingers fell away, but his gaze held mine. I saw again how much he resembled Risaine, both in the shape of his face and the set of his mouth. There was another resemblance, under the dust and weather and blood.

The King surfaced from Adrien di Cinfiliet's features, as if rising from his tomb.

My heart pounded thinly. I tasted metal.

"Vianne!" Tristan arrived, and spun me to face him. "Are you well?"

It took every scrap of Court training I possessed to face him. "There is an army approaching, Captain. Your father—I must speak to your father. These men have ridden to warn us. We must stable the h-horses...How many? How many of yours have arrived, Adrien?" I was well to witless, but it could be supposed that the news of an approaching army would maze my humble brains.

I know a little tale, of a man who killed a King.

Bile scorched my throat.

No. Tristan was the King's Left Hand. Proof? What proof could Adrien have? It was the Duc's lie, that Tristan had killed the King.

And yet.

Whatever crimes Henri di Tirecian-Trimestin committed in the name of kingship, his Left Hand committed more. Take care who you keep close to you...tis more important than you think.

Or had she only mistrusted any man who could be the Left Hand to the King who had discarded her so ruthlessly?

He was my Consort, and had led me through the tunnel under Mont di Cienne.

Yet the Duc had ordered Tristan's tongue be taken so he could not speak. Tristan had been waiting in the passage for me, with Simieri—or had Simieri come along to take Tristan unawares?

Or had Tristan been the one to catch the Minister Primus at a different game?

I had not seen my Captain the *entire* time of the conspiracy's unwinding. He had left me in the passage when the alarums began. And something had bothered me for a long, long while, never quite articulated.

It simply did not make sense that the King had been poisoned, for I was not so untalented a hedgewitch as to miss poison in pettite-cakes no matter how exotic the toxin...and why, oh why, had Tristan been waiting for me in that passageway?

No. I could not mistrust him, could I?

"Fifteen." Adrien's voice cracked harshly. "Fifteen of my riders left, tis all. We slowed them, killed some sentries. Much

as we could do. They fear the countryside now. And the night."
He patted the horse's wet neck. His grimace was fey, an animal's
bared teeth. "We caused some damage."

"Good. How many? And who?" Tristan's tone was needlessly
harsh, but this was dire news for both of us. It was slim comfort
that he thought to ask the same questions I did.

"Some thousands," I said. "Damarsene. Flying the Duc's col-
ors. And with a siege train." This time my knees did buckle.
Tristan caught me, swore, and pushed a strand of my hair back.
His fingers were tender, but the thought would not leave me.

*Were you part of the conspiracy, Tristan? What proof could this
bandit have? "When all is revealed," Adrien taunted him once before. So, did he suspect, or...*

The noble bandit was my newfound kin, and he had little
reason to lie so grievously to me, unless he hated Tristan
d'Arcenne beyond reason.

Or unless there was truth to this tale, of a man who killed a
King.

There were too many unanswered questions. Too many mysteries conspiring to cloud my Consort, dogging his heels. If
Tristan had lied about poison in pettite-cakes, why?

And what other words of his should I mistrust?

"Inside. Come, di Cinfiliet, there's wine for you. And bandages. The physicker's been called." Tristan sounded just the
same. Just as he always had.

My heart turned to ice. I could not doubt him, my Consort,
my love.

And yet.

I had only his word for what had happened to the King.
Divris di Tatancourt could not tell me anything but rumor,
which painted Tristan as the blackest of murderers. At least, the

official tale spread by the Duc was that Tristan was the King's killer. Now I wondered just who Tristan truly was a traitor to.

Or was I the traitor for even entertaining the thought?

Proof captured from di Narborre. A poison well to draw from, to be sure. Or proof so damning it could not be denied.

Everything hinged on the remainder of Adrien di Cinfiliet's tale. I could only wait, and see.

He refused all help from the hedgewitch, took only unwatered wine, and told my Council of the approaching army as he was: bloody, battered, and swaying with exhaustion. I caught a glint in his steely eyes as he did so, which led me to think there were other reasons behind his choosing to appear weakened. Risaine should be proud of him; he was playing his part to perfection.

What other part is he playing, Vianne? Wait, watch. Practice your patience.

Twas agony to keep still and to watch. I sat in the chair at the head of the table, listening through the roaring in my ears, barely aware of what he repeated: an army, some thousands, with a siege train, answering other questions about horse and man, dispositions and colors. The Council took the news well, Perseval d'Arcenne questioning him closely as to exactly where, the manner of their siege engines, how many Adrien and his riders had killed, the speed of the interlopers. How many cavalry, how many infantry, if he had taken any prisoners.

Which, of course, Adrien had not. His hatred would not allow it, for the one who led the army was the Duc's dog, Garonne di Narborre. A murmur ran through the Council at that tidbit.

I closed my eyes, sank back into the chair. The Aryx shifted, carved scales rasping against silk fouled with horse-lather. I let out a soft sigh. Breath and my usual wit threatened to desert me.

So close to the King none suspected, not even fat Henri himself. But he was crossed; expected to be sacrificed like a chivalier on a battlechess board. Only he twisted as a chivalier does in that game; he disappeared with the key to it all, a girl with long dark hair and pretty, pretty eyes.

Adrien had little reason to lie so flagrantly, for my protection gave him and his men shelter against di Narborre, as well as a chance to avenge the wrongs done them.

Perhaps he had even suspected, before this. But how? Did any among the Guard know aught, or suspect? How many of the men I had trusted my life to had darker secrets?

He said he possessed proof. If he had killed one of di Narborre's men, would he have proof of a conspiracy even deeper than I had dreamed?

The argument roiled around me. Voices raised, Lord Siguerre's cranky whistle, Perseval d'Arcenne's baritone, Tristan speaking harshly for once. I rubbed at my temples. Marquis di Falterne making a few acerbic remarks, *Chivalier* d'Anton seeking as usual to smooth the ruffled feathers. He and the Conte di Rivieri I had chosen because they were naturally calm and unruffled, balanced with Conte di Dienjuste's fiery excitability and Irion di Markui's rumbling disapproval of everything. On such short notice, and from the border provinces, I seemed to have found a great deal of talent the Court and King Henri's Council had overlooked.

My skull twinged with pain. Twas not the half-head; yet bad enough. *Each time I think this cannot possibly become worse, it becomes so.*

From the beginning, Vianne. Adrien di Cinfiliet had little reason to lie to me.

That does not mean something has not been concocted to use his

461

honesty against me. But then again, what proof could he have from di Narborre that he would trust? As much as he may dislike Tristan, he is certain to hate di Narborre more, for di Narborre killed his mother.

My heart was a chunk of lead, senselessly pulsing, though I perhaps would rather have stopped it outright, to save myself the tearing that would result if my Consort had—

"—Your Majesty?" D'Anton, appealing to me.

Brought rudely back to the present moment, I did not answer, massaging my temples. I stank of horsefoam, and a vision of the charred bandit village rose in front of me. The stinksweet of roasted flesh, the charred homes, the small, helpless bodies of children. If I did not find some solution, would the same happen in the clean white stone halls of Arcenne, in the streets below where the people went about their lives, going to market, going to the Temple? And the R'mini, scattered throughout Arquitaine, would suffer as well once the Damarsene were finished with our rebellion and turned to bring the country under their heel once and for all, whither the Duc d'Orlaans willed it or no.

Each of those lives hung on me, both the lost and those needing to be preserved.

I pushed myself to my feet, the chair scraping against the floor. Silence fell.

I opened my eyes, paced to the window. Below, Arcenne lay packed behind its wall, the Keep lifting like a stone ship's prow. A haze of smoke drifted up from the town and the outlying settlements. Trees clothed in summer leaf swayed gently in the sunshine, mountain wind mouthing the wavery glass. "Dear gods," I whispered.

On the mountainside, the white blocks of the Temple glistened. I remembered the statue of Jiserah, glowing with a radiance far beyond starlight or moonlight. The mysterious priestess of Kimyan, with her piercing gray eyes; and the Aryx ringing as if it would burst, power running through its straining serpents.

The gods were watching, perhaps. But theirs was not help I could do aught but beg, and I was a beggar in so much else. I had nothing to trade save the Aryx, and it belonged to them in any event. No, there was no help from that quarter.

And Tristan…

I was alone, as surely as I had ever been at Court, even among the whirl and glitter. Loneliness in disaster is the fate of every man or woman, though, and it does little good to bemoan it.

"Your Highness?" Perseval d'Arcenne. "We await you."

And you will have to await me a few moments longer, Minister Primus. I touched the glass. Ran my fingertips over its rippling surface. *I cannot do this. I cannot. I do not know why the Aryx has chosen me, but tis wrong. I cannot order more death, I cannot be responsible for this.* A war on the other side of winter I thought I could avert, or at least it would give me enough time to find a solution. But a war here and now, and the Damarsene on Arquitaine soil?

Blessed preserve us all. How much more prayer would I indulge in before I ceased to think of myself as irreligious?

"*D'mselle?*" Baron d'Arcenne's voice held irritation, and the snap of command. "If you would be so good as to—"

"Enough, Perseval." My tone could have shattered the window. "When I wish for you to speak to me as if I am your lackey, I will inform you of the event. Until that time, be more careful of your manner. Tristan?"

"Aye, my liege?" Suitably hushed, carefully obedient.

"How long do we have?" My throat closed around the words, thick with tears. I wondered that I sounded so haughty.

"Three days, four at most. Enough time to get everyone inside the walls and—"

"I will spend tonight at the Temple. Send to Danae, priestess of Jiserah, to inform her I wish her services. Gather every hedge-witch and Court sorcerer you can find, prepare them for siege. Make certain Adrien's men are given aught they require, and wait for me in your chambers. Go."

The air crackled with his reluctance, and I am sure he exchanged a look with his father. The door soughed closed behind his bootsteps.

I rounded on my Council, my head held high. Adrien di Cinfiliet had dropped into a chair, and he watched me carefully from beneath the glare-white bandage. But he smiled, encouragingly, just a tiny curve of his thin lips.

It made no dent in the armor closing about me.

"*Chivalieri en sieurs.*" I let my gaze linger on Perseval d'Arcenne, who looked angry enough to spit like a Guard averting ill-luck. "I will decide tomorrow morn if I am to risk open war, or if I will surrender myself to the Duc and hope for peace. I am loath to risk even a single life."

They stared, jaws hanging. It was a moment that would have been comic if not for the tension crackling between each man and the next. I had only a short while before their shock turned to shouting matches as they sought to change my mind, and I had little patience for such an event.

"Until I decide, I leave the preparations for this city's defense to you. I have another duty now. *Sieur* di Cinfiliet, I ask for a few more moments of your time, tonight, in the Temple. Until then, rest, and look to your men and horses." My eyes moved slowly over the faces of my Council, and the howling loneliness settled more deeply over me. "And now, *chivalieri en sieurs*, I wish to be alone. Be so kind as to withdraw."

The Aryx rilled softly under my words. I did not sound like the King, but neither did I sound like a woman who could be disobeyed.

Of all of them, only d'Anton tried to speak. I lifted a hand, effectively silencing him. When they were gone, only the guards outside the door remaining, I dropped back into the chair and looked at the table, scattered with paper and candleholders. The wine decanter looked very tempting, but I required a clear head.

I let out a long breath. My head pounded. My entire body shook as if I had been struck with palsy. My right hand crept up, touched the Aryx's pulsing. Sunlight slanted through the windows, dust dancing in each bar of thick warm yellow. The Aryx moved, serpents straining against my fingers. One hard gemstone—a serpent's eye—drifted under my fingertip. "Gods." My voice shook. "What did I do to deserve this?"

There was no answer. Nothing but the Aryx thrumming, singing, almost conscious against my skin. My stomach flipped, revolving, as if I had slipped on a staircase and was now starting a long fall. "Tristan," I whispered.

I would wait until tonight, in the house of the Blessed, to speak to di Cinfiliet and hear his proof.

And what of it? What if Tristan d'Arcenne had killed the King? I had said I cared little what he had done beforehand, and I loved him. It seemed now that I had always loved him, even at Court, and only been blind to it. It hurt my heart to think of him as a traitor, but perhaps he was not. Perhaps it was another trick, a lie, something to make me mistrust him. After all, assassins had been sent to fetch me, not to kill…*if* I could trust what the Pruzian said.

What if I went to the Temple as suppliant and the gods were silent? What if I found no answer in the house of the Blessed? What if the city was besieged and there were yet more deaths to lay upon my conscience, people who followed me because of the Aryx, who trusted the judgment of a lady-in-waiting, a bastard royal? And what if I gave myself over to the Duc and had to endure his limp white hands on me while plague swept Arquitaine and Damarsene armies marched through her fields and orchards? What were Damarsene troops about under the Duc's standard?

I did not trust my wit when faced with this, and the strength I would have depended on had just been rudely struck from me. What if I could no longer trust Tristan d'Arcenne? What if he was just as guilty as the Duc who had killed my Princesse?

You have suspected, Vianne. You may never fully know. But the suspicion itself will work in your heart like the poison that was not in the King's pettite-cakes. You have known since Tierrce d'Estrienne something was amiss with Tristan's tale, and yet you closed your eyes to it, for you needed him.

My fingers left the Aryx. I cupped my face in my hands as the sunlight burned through the empty room.

And there, alone in the Keep among hundreds depending on my wit and strength, I wept.

Glossary

Ansinthe: A venomous green liquor distilled from wyrmrithe

Aufsbar: (Prz.) Client

Blessed, the: (Arq.) The Twelve Gods of Arquitaine, six Old (indigenous) and six New (brought by the conqueror Angoulême)

Demiange: (Arq.) Sorcerous or half-divine spirit; many of them wait upon the gods in the Westron Halls

Demieri di sorce: (Arq.) Sorcerous spirits of night and mischief

D'mselle: (Arq.) Honorific, for a young woman

Festival of Skyreturn: One of the great cross-quarter festivals

G'ji g'jai: (R'm.) Foreign (lit. *"Other"*), whore

Hedgewitch: (Arq.) One who practices peasant sorcery

M'chri, m'cher: (Arq.) Beloved, dear one

M'dama: (Arq.) Honorific, for an older woman

Piniel: An evergreen tree with a sharp distinctive scent, whose bristled cones bear small nuts inside."

Rhuma: A clear, fiery liquor distilled from sucre

Sieur: (Arq.) Honorific, for a man

Valadka: A clear, very potent liquor that may cause blindness if overly indulged in

Vilhain: (Arq.) Bastard

extras

orbit

meet the author

Daron Gildow

Lilith Saintcrow was born in New Mexico, bounced around the world as an Air Force brat, and fell in love with writing when she was ten years old. She currently lives in Vancouver, Washington. Find her on the web at www.lilithsaintcrow.com.

introducing

If you enjoyed THE HEDGEWITCH QUEEN,
look out for

THE BANDIT KING

A Romance of Arquitaine

by Lilith Saintcrow

An Excerpt from
The Bandit King

I struck to kill.

The flesh, fat-rich and fed on luxury, parted under my blade. And I rammed my sword—sworn to the service of Arquitaine's King—through the heart of that same king.

The alarums were still ringing, but a great silence had descended on me. Running feet and shouts resounded in the corridor. Henri gasped, the death-gurgle I have heard on many another's lips.

I had killed for him too many times to count. Did he feel surprise, that the tool he sharpened had thus turned in his hand?

My throat was dry as sand in the Navarrin wastes. My heart pounded, running like a hare before hounds. Up to this moment it had been a conspiracy, one I had played at catching out. Now, with one decisive lunge, I had committed my soul entire to the enterprise

I gave the blade one last twist, freeing it from the suction of muscle. The thrust had been true, years of daily practice on the drillfield honed and distilled into murder. Henri's elaborately-curled hair fell in disarray, and his lips shaped a question. He fell before he could give it voice, a bubble of bright blood bursting on his lips, so recently touching a dainty teacake.

He hit the floor in a sodden, shapeless lump of velvet and silk. I crouched easily, a duelist's move once the duel was done, to watch an enemy's last gasping moments. The sucking sound of a breath caught in a bloody throat, echoed by so many victims, now visited the man who had made me a weapon.

"You should have let me have her," I whispered. "You are responsible for this."

He made no reply, merely thrashed and choked his last. And as they burst into the room, d'Orlaans's Guard, I came up from my crouch and met the first few in a clash of steel and confusion. Everything now depended on secrecy, and speed, and how willing I was to kill.

I suffered no qualms. But they took me anyway—d'Orlaans, the king's brother, had suspected me, and sent his dogs to yap at my heels. He had not sent them unarmed, either. Pieces of the puzzle fell into place when they unleashed the first jolt of Court sorcery, a spell meant to wound and disable an opponent.

So the King's brother was a far better sorcerer than even I had guessed. It was hardly the first of my mistakes.

I could have screamed, the cheated howl of a wolf when the lamb is snatched from its teeth. Yet I did not, for the howl would have turned into her name, and that I could not allow.

I would not sully her name by speaking it here.

But I thought it. One word, encapsulating the bait for this trap, the lure I had taken unknowing, like any stupid caged falcon at the mercy of its instinct.

Vianne.

I fell into darkness, holding her name behind my lips. The beating they meted out to me was only kisses, after the tearing pain of *knowing I had failed, the prize snatched from my grasp at the very last moment.*

I was doomed.

Thief, liar, assassin, and whore. Tale-bearer, spy, extortionist, confidante, scandal-smoother. A knife in the dark, poison in a cup, a shield and a defense on the battlefield as well as in the glittering whirl of Court. Puppetmaster, spymaster, whoremaster, brutal thug, protocol handler, catspaw, pawn, troublemaker, cutthroat, fiend, pickpocket, swindler, brigand, pirate, kidnapper, alter ego, usurer, false witness…

This, then, is the Left Hand.

The Left Hand does what must be done to cement the hold of the monarch on the realm, to protect the king or queen we swear fealty to—even at the cost of our own lives. Even at the cost of our honor. There is only one word never applied to the Left Hand, only one thing a Left Hand has never been.

Traitor.

To be the Left Hand is to be the most trusted of a monarch's subjects, a position of high honor though none will know your face or name. Most of a Hand's work is done in shadow, and well it should be. The Hand does those things which are necessary, by blood or by leverage, the things a monarch cannot do. According to the secret archives in the Palais d'Arquitaine, the first of us was Anton di Halier, who created the office in the time of Jeliane de Courcy-Trimestin, the Widow Queen of Arquitaine who depended on Halier for her very life during the great wars, both internecine and domestic, of the Blood Years.

I find it amusing the first Left Hand spent his service under a Queen. Sometimes.

www.ingramcontent.com/pod-product-compliance
Lightning Source LLC
Chambersburg PA
CBHW010646100726
47901CB00009B/2452